THE *NEW YORK TIMES* BESTSELLING SERIALIZED NOVEL, COLLECTED IN ONE VOLUME FOR THE FIRST TIME

## JUST ONE NIGHT

### PRAISE FOR *PART 1: THE STRANGER*

"A quick, fun, and sensual read that left me wanting much more! Any fan of the erotic romance genre will enjoy a quick fix with *The Stranger*."

—*Romance Book Junkies*

"Tempting, seductive, and purely romantic, *The Stranger* is absolutely fantastic! From showy, skintight designer dress in Las Vegas to ultra-conservative business wear in Los Angeles, Kasie Fitzgerald is a hot and spicy contradiction."

—*Lovey Dovey Books*

"Exceptionally well written . . . intensely sensual."

—*Sinfully Sexy Book Reviews*

"Beautifully put together and written . . . It flows seamlessly from scene to scene and it hooks you instantly."

—*Reviewing Romance*

### PRAISE FOR *PART 2: EXPOSED*

"Sex, guilt, passion, betrayal, revenge, and orgasms—lots and lots of orgasms—fill every page [and] gives *Fifty Shades of Grey* a run for its money."

—*New York Journal of Book Reviews*

"If you enjoy ravishing, desperate, and breathtaking love scenes, then *Exposed* is for you. Just be aware that Robert Dade will steal your heart and take your breath away."

—*SinfulReads*

"An intense read! . . . passionate, sexy, emotional story."

—*Anna's Romantic Reads*

## PRAISE FOR *PART 3: BINDING AGREEMENT*

"An excellent erotic trilogy—a little darker and quite a little different from the rest."

*—Sinfully Sexy Book Reviews*

"I couldn't envision a better ending if I tried! These books are definitely different than anything else I have read in this genre."

*—Jessy's Book Club*

"Loved this one! . . . *fans self* It's a very steamy series, and its sure to get your heart beating double time."

*—Tyhada Reads*

# JUST ONE NIGHT

## KYRA DAVIS

GALLERY BOOKS

NEW YORK   LONDON   TORONTO   SYDNEY   NEW DELHI

Gallery Books
A Division of Simon & Schuster, Inc.
1230 Avenue of the Americas
New York, NY 10020

First Gallery Books trade paperback edition December 2013

GALLERY BOOKS and colophon are registered trademarks of Simon & Schuster, Inc.

For information about special discounts for bulk purchases, please contact Simon & Schuster Special Sales at 1-866-506-1949 or business@simonandschuster.com.

The Simon & Schuster Speakers Bureau can bring authors to your live event. For more information or to book an event, contact the Simon & Schuster Speakers Bureau at 1-866-248-3049 or visit our website at www.simonspeakers.com.

Manufactured in the United States of America

10  9  8  7  6  5  4  3  2  1

Library of Congress Cataloging-in-Publication Data

Davis, Kyra.
    Just one night / Kyra Davis.
        pages cm
    1. Romance fiction.  I. Title.
    PS3604.A972J87 2013
    813.'6—dc23
                                        2013020533

ISBN 978-1-4767-3060-8

To the love of my life

# CONTENTS

✸

# PART 1

---

*The Stranger*

---

# CHAPTER 1

❁

T HE RED HERVE LEGER bandage dress I'm wearing is not mine. It belongs to my friend Simone. Yesterday I would have laughed off the very suggestion that I wear anything this overtly provocative. Tomorrow I'll dismiss the idea out of hand. But tonight? Tonight is a night of exceptions.

I stand in the middle of the hotel room Simone and I are sharing at the Venetian and tug at the hem. Can I even sit down in this dress?

"You look so sexy," she coos as she slips up behind me and pulls my black, wavy hair behind my shoulders. The move feels a little too intimate and I feel a little too exposed.

I step away from her and twist myself into a pretzel as I try to see the back of the dress in the mirror. "Am I really going out in this?"

"Are you kidding?" Simone shakes her head, confused. "If I looked half as hot as you do in that dress, I'd wear it every day!"

I pull down on the hem again. I'm used to wearing suits. Not the kinds of suits women wear in the movies, but the kinds of suits women wear in real life when they work at a global consulting firm. The kinds of suits that make you almost forget you're a woman, let alone a sexual being. But this dress sings a melody I haven't sung before.

"I won't be able to eat so much as a carrot stick while wearing this," I complain as I stare down at the neckline. I'm not wearing a bra. The only thing I was able to fit under the dress was a delicate little thong. But the dress is designed to prop everything up . . .

which I have mixed feelings about. What surprises me is that my feelings *are* mixed. I'm slightly embarrassed; that's to be expected. I also feel a little sinful just putting on this thing and yet . . . Simone's right, I look *hot*.

I've never thought of myself in those terms. No one does. When people hear the name Kasie Fitzgerald, they think responsible, reliable, steady.

Steady, steady Kasie.

That's the reason Simone dragged me to Vegas for the weekend. She wanted me to be unsteady on my feet for just one night before I fully embrace a life of stability with the man I'm going to marry, Dave Beasley. Dave is going to propose . . . or maybe he already has. "I think next weekend we should go ring shopping," he had said as we finished up a quiet dinner at a Beverly Hills café. We've been dating for six years now and he has been talking about the possibility of marriage for five of them, examining the idea from every angle and putting our hypothetical marriage through hypothetical stress tests like a bank preparing for another financial crisis.

Dave is careful like that. It isn't sexy but it's comfortable. Once, after a few too many drinks, I told Simone that kissing Dave was like eating a baked potato. She gave me no end of grief for that. But what I meant was that a baked potato, while not the most exciting food in the world, was warm and soft and it was enough to stave off hunger. That was Dave. He was my comfort food, my baked potato.

*You should sleep with a stranger.*

That had been Simone's advice. One last hurrah before I get married and while I'm still in my twenties. I wouldn't do it, of course. I had bargained her down to flirting with a stranger and I was still trying to work up my nerve to do *that*.

*When you're old, do you really want to look back at your life and realize that you were never young?*

Those had been Simone's words, too. But she didn't understand. I didn't know how to be young. I hadn't even known how to be young when I was a child.

"She's so much more serious than her sister!" my parents' friends would say as I sat next to them, my head buried in a book. "Not a girly girl at all!"

Somehow it had been understood that femininity and studiousness were mutually exclusive states of being.

But here I was, a Harvard graduate working at one of the top global consulting firms in the country. And I looked *hot*.

"Blackjack," Simone says with confidence. "You sit down at the high-roller blackjack table wearing that dress and all the guys at the table will forget how to count to twenty-one."

I snort and then throw my hand over my mouth as Simone breaks out in giggles. Even this dress can't make a snort sexy.

WHEN WE GET to the casino, heads turn. I'm not used to this. Men are watching me move; their eyes are appraising, measuring up their chances, taking note of all the secrets my dress reveals . . . and it reveals plenty. The women are watching, too. Some of the looks are judgmental; others, envious. I blush as I realize that some of their stares are every bit as appraising as the men's.

Part of me wants to hurry through the room but the dress keeps my gait slow and careful. I've heard stories of models falling on the runway during Herve Leger shows and I can see how that could happen. With the shoes Simone insists need to be worn with this and the tightness of the dress itself, each step presents its own challenge.

A man walks by me and runs his eyes up and down my body without even making a thin attempt to hide his desire. My blush deepens and I turn away. The way he looked at me . . . does he think I'm a hooker? I'd have to be a pretty successful one to afford this outfit. I glance over my shoulder and realize that he's stopped to watch me as I move away from him. He looks slick and arrogant. I don't want him . . . but I like that he wants *me*, and even that small pleasure makes me feel a little shameful . . . and scandalous.

We stake out a blackjack table that has a $100 minimum. That doesn't exactly make it for high rollers but it's so much more than I would normally risk.

As I sit down, my hem inches up and I'm reminded of the thin thong, the only undergarment I'm wearing.

*What am I doing here?*

I swallow hard and focus on the table. I'm not exactly an expert at the game but Simone proves to be much worse than I am. She places huge bets and then keeps trying for the twenty-one even though her attempts lead her to bust more than once. Eventually she gives up and tells me she's going off to the craps table. I stay where I am. I can handle adding up cards but I have never mastered the art of rolling the dice.

"This looks like a good table."

I turn just as a man wearing dark jeans and a brown T-shirt sits beside me. His sculpted arms are an odd contrast to the salt-and-pepper hair . . . but I like it. He looks over at me just as I'm taking him in and I quickly look away. It was an obvious dodge and I inwardly cringe at my awkwardness.

A woman with a clipboard walks over and smiles at the man now by my side. "Mr. Dade, so good to see you."

"You, too, Gladys. I'm going to start with five thousand."

The woman nods and after he signs a slip of paper, a pile of black and purple chips are placed in front of him.

This is not the way people normally get their chips.

I put down a $200 bet and the dealer doles out a few cards. I start with a five and an ace. It's not a bad beginning. Mr. Dade isn't so lucky with his ten and six.

I tap my finger next to my cards and am given another. Mr. Dade does the same.

My card's a four. I smile to myself. I'm on a roll.

Or at least I thought I was until Mr. Dade is handed a five.

Twenty-one.

No one says the words but chips are pushed in his direction.

As the dealer adds a few chips to my pile, a smaller acknowleddgment of my win against the house, Mr. Dade leans toward me, ever so slightly. "Care to make it interesting?"

"I thought that's what we were doing." I contemplate my chips, not because I need to count them but because I'm a little too unnerved to look directly at him.

"More interesting," he clarifies. "If I have the better hand, we'll leave the table and you'll have a drink with me."

"And if I have the upper hand?" I ask, twisting the words to my liking.

"Then I'll have a drink with you."

I laugh. Between the excitement in the room and my new, albeit temporary, look, I'm already feeling a little light-headed. I can't imagine what a drink will do to me.

"If I win, we'll have a drink right here at the table and keep playing," I say. From an economic standpoint my plan is probably the more risky one but from every other perspective it's decidedly safer.

"A negotiator," Mr. Dade says. Although I'm still not looking at him, I can feel his smile. The energy he's exuding is sexy, but also a little mischievous.

I like it.

The dealer doles out a few more cards. I get a three and a six while Mr. Dade gets a king and a four. It's anyone's game. It all depends on what we're dealt next . . . a nice little metaphor for life.

But I keep that thought to myself and quietly tap my bloodred fingernails against the felt green table. Mr. Dade gestures to be hit as well.

This time he's the one who gets to twenty. I don't even get to eighteen.

He stands up, offers me his hand. "Shall we?"

I collect my chips and hesitate as I mentally plan out how to get up from the table without exposing more than I'd care to display.

Again, I can feel this man's smile. An old song pops into my head, "Devil Inside," and I mentally play it as a soundtrack while I carefully get to my feet. He doesn't rush me as he escorts me first to the cashier, where I can cash out my chips, then to the escalator. People are still looking, but now they're looking at us.

*But there is no us,* I remind myself. This is a fantasy. A fleeting and insubstantial encounter. We'll drink, we'll flirt, and then we'll vanish from each other's lives like smoke from a controlled flame.

"Here," he says as he moves us over to a bar with walls of glass.

People are being drawn into the fantasy of us.

He sidles up to the bar and waits as I struggle to get on the bar stool. I pull out my cell to text Simone my whereabouts but before I can even enter the first word, the bartender is here.

"I think the lady would like a glass of your finest champagne, Aaron," Mr. Dade begins.

"No," I say quickly, some deleterious impulse getting the better of me. "Whiskey."

I don't know why I upped the ante except that this isn't a champagne moment. It feels grittier, stronger; it calls for grains, not bubbles.

Mr. Dade smiles again and orders us each a whiskey, a brand I've never heard of. "So," he says as the bartender moves away, "blackjack's your game?"

"No." I lower my head as I send the text to Simone. "This is only my second time at the tables. I don't really have a game."

"You're playing one tonight."

I look up, asking the question with just the rise of my eyebrows.

"You don't normally dress like this," he continues as our drinks are placed in front of us. He slides the bartender some money. He's not asked if he would like to start a tab. Our server seems to sense that this is not the time to interrupt.

"How do you know how I normally dress?"

"You don't often wear heels like those. You don't know how to walk in them."

I laugh nervously. "No one outside of Cirque du Soleil knows how to walk in these."

"And if you dressed like that all the time, you'd be used to people looking at you. You're not." He leans forward and I can smell the faintest wisp of woodsy cologne. "You're self-conscious. You're not comfortable with the stares or how much you enjoy them."

I start to look away but he takes my chin in his hand and holds it so that I'm facing him directly. "Even now, you're blushing."

I don't know this man, this man who is touching me. He's a stranger. A blank slate. I should walk away. I shouldn't let the rough skin of his thumb move back and forth over my cheek like this.

*You should sleep with a stranger.*

Slowly, I move my hand to his and then move it away from my face. But I don't let go. I like the feel of it: strong and textured. These hands have built things and been exposed to the elements. I visualize them grasping the reins of a horse. I see them inside the engine of a sleek sports car that can drive fast and hard away from the constraints that hinder the rest of us. I imagine these hands touching me, his fingers inside of me. . . .

*What am I doing here?*

"My name's Kasie," I say. My voice comes out raspy and flustered.

"Do you want to know my name?" he asks. "My full name?"

I realize immediately that I don't. I don't want to know who he is. I don't even want to know who I was yesterday or who I will be tomorrow. I just want to know who I am now.

"I don't do this," I whisper. But even as I say it I know that I'm talking about yesterday, tomorrow. Tonight is . . . different.

This man, he's not like the man who raked my body with his eyes, all conceit and sleaze. This man isn't pushing his agenda on me. He's drawing out mine; reading my movements, my smiles, the quick path of my eyes. In his face I can see my own desire. He's no longer a blank slate. He's my fantasy and the chemistry . . . the intensity that exists between us . . . it's what I would have longed for if I had known what it was.

But I know what it is now.

I notice the button at the top of his jeans. It reads Dior Homme— $600 jeans—and yet the T-shirt could have been bought at Target.

Like his youthfully muscular arms and conservatively cut salt-and-pepper hair, it's his contradictions that seduce me.

"I'd like to make you a drink," he says.

It doesn't take me a moment to grasp his meaning. I know he's inviting me to his room. I glance around the bar. I've never had a one-night stand. I'm studious. I'm the girl everyone can count on for her rock-solid, solemn consistency.

Except tonight. Tonight I'm the girl who is going to sleep with a stranger.

# CHAPTER 2

❀

Like college kids, we stop at a store in the lobby to buy our own liquor. I almost laugh as the cashier hands Mr. Dade a brown paper bag containing the bottle, as if we're about to sneak off under some bleachers instead of up the tower of a luxury hotel, as if the plan's to get drunk on cheap wine coolers rather than sip $200 Scotch.

I've never been the girl under the bleachers, but I don't judge those who were. Even as I rejected the idea for myself I could see that there was a certain clumsy innocence to that particular American tradition. Nothing about what I was about to do with Mr. Dade was innocent.

We don't talk as he leads me to his room. It's a suite. I knew it would be. The floor of the parlor has enough square footage to hold a party. The untouched kitchen could accommodate a caterer. We don't need all this space but I find its excess darkly delightful.

I hear him close the door and my eyes dart to the French doors on my right. I don't have to ask to know what room they lead to.

I sense him walking up behind me now. I can feel the heat of him and I tense as I wait for his touch.

But it doesn't come.

Instead he brings his mouth close to my ear. "Make yourself comfortable," he says, his voice growling as his words entice. "Take something off."

I turn to face him. I can't speak. Thoughts of Dave push their way into my consciousness. This is a betrayal. Can I live with this? Can I compartmentalize this one night from the rest of my life?

"Your shoes," he says, his smile teasing. "Take off your shoes."

I exhale a breath I didn't know I was holding. But I'm not safe. Not from him, not from myself. Keeping my eyes on his, I ease down into a chair. He kneels before me and his fingers gently brush against my ankles as he unfastens the small, delicate buckles of my heels. My legs are pressed tightly together. I'm not ready to show him my world. Not yet.

But as the shoes come off, his hands slowly move up my calves, to my knees, to the outside of my thighs. Again the air I had just inhaled gets caught in my chest as I momentarily forget how to breathe. This skirt is so short, his hands keep getting higher and yet he hasn't reached the hem . . . until he does, and he pushes it higher still . . . and then stops.

I wait, expecting him to go farther but his hands fall away. "I'm going to pour you that Scotch now," he says.

And there it is again, that devious grin, that careful balance between urgency and patience.

He gets up and I close my eyes and try to find some balance. I hear the freezer open and close, then the clink of ice cubes falling into an empty glass. I don't move. I *can't* move. I was worried about something only moments ago; there was something I needed to think through. . . . What was it? I can't focus.

When I open my eyes, he's before me, a single drink in his hand, which he extends toward me.

"You're not joining me?" I ask. I'm whispering now. I'm afraid of breaking the moment . . . afraid of pulling myself out of this twilight reality. This is only a dream after all and if I keep it to myself, it will feel more like a dream with each day that passes. But right now I'm not ready to wake up.

Mr. Dade's smile widens as he places the glass in my hand. "Oh, I'll be joining you."

I sip the Scotch and then sip again. It's beautiful. Just like this room, with its warm gold hues and notes of luxury.

He takes back the glass. "My turn."

He extracts an ice cube, uses it to trace a path along the neckline of my dress. As the cool, wet surface touches my breasts, I feel my nipples harden as they reach out to him, begging him to go further. He responds by tasting the hints of Scotch on my skin—light kisses filled with heat, his hands now on my hips. I'm breathing again but each breath is shallow as I struggle to stay still.

He lifts the Scotch glass again and brings it to my lips, tipping it back just slightly so that the smoky taste only trickles over my tongue. And then his fingers slip into the glass again and this time the melting ice is moved up my thighs. My body and my mind are no longer connected. I feel my legs part, only slightly at first but as he pushes my dress higher and higher, I encourage him with increased access.

Again he lowers his mouth to the chilled Scotch trail on my skin and I watch as he follows it up my legs. With a sudden and decisive movement he pulls my dress up to my waist, which he now holds firmly in his hands as his mouth moves higher and higher. That flimsy little thong is the only thing that stands in his way. He removes one hand from my waist and strokes the silky fabric.

Through lowered lids I see him smile again. I know what he's thinking. The fabric is wet. It's another invitation that I have no control over.

But it's not enough for him.

"Ask," he says; his finger hooks around the waistband of my panties.

I feel my cheeks heat up once more. A voiced request means that I won't be able to say that I was just taken or that I wasn't thinking. I'm ready to expose my body to him but now he's asking me to share in this in a way that is so complete, it terrifies me.

"Ask," he says again.

"Please," I murmur.

"Not good enough." His voice is still soft but I can hear the edge of authority in his tone. "Ask."

"Take them off."

He raises himself up now so that he is leaning over me, his finger still hooked around the thin strap of my thong. "What exactly would you like me to take off?" The slight smile on his face doesn't do anything to lessen his intensity.

"Please?" I speak so quietly, I have to struggle to hear myself. "Please take off my panties."

"Louder, please."

Hesitantly, I raise my eyes to his. I can see the spark of mischief dancing there and it makes me smile. A surge of unexpected courage bursts through my soul and I reach forward and grab his T-shirt, bunching up the cheap cotton in my fist. "Please," I say, pulling him closer, disturbing his balance. "Please take off my panties, Mr. Dade."

And now his smile matches my own. The thong is ripped from my body and before I fully know what's going on, I feel the slight sting of Scotch against my clit immediately followed by the shocking warmth of a kiss there, a kiss delivered to my very core. His mouth tickles and teases. I moan and grasp at the seat beneath me. I feel his finger gently touch me as he continues to lick and taste, first softly, then there's a firmer pressure, a faster speed. His tongue dances over every nerve ending, his solicitations unrelenting. I whimper and throw back my head as the orgasm comes hard and fast.

But I have no time to get my bearings. He yanks me to my feet. He doesn't need to search for the hidden zipper on this dress; he just intuitively knows where it is. In an instant I'm wearing nothing.

Ah, the stares of those men in the casino were nothing, not even pale imitations of the look that Mr. Dade is giving me now. His eyes don't just move over me, they consume me. I stand there, wanting, throbbing as he slowly circles me like a wolf planning his attack, like a tiger stalking a mate. . . .

Like a lover, ready to worship.

I don't reach for him; his eyes hold me as still as any rope ever could. Once the circle is complete, he takes off his own shirt. His torso matches his arms, hard muscles under soft, vulnerable flesh.

He pulls me to him and I can feel what I've done to him. His erection presses against my stomach.

I gasp as I feel fingers push inside of me. First one, then two. He plays with me, stroking and probing as I shiver against him. I try to unbutton his jeans but my hands are shaking. I'm going to come again, right here, standing up, pressed against him.

And then he has me against the wall as he continues to caress. I wrap my arms around his neck and dig my fingernails in as I cry out. I explode and contract around his fingers. I breathe in and realize that traces of that woodsy cologne are now on my skin, too. Nothing separates us.

I feel courageous and vulnerable, one more delicious contradiction. I finally manage to unfasten his jeans. And as I strip him of his remaining clothes, it's my turn to stare.

He's beautiful and perfect and . . . impressive.

We might not make it to the bedroom.

With the tips of my fingers I explore every ridge of his cock until I make it up to the tip.

*Cock*: it's not a word I use but my head is spinning and euphemisms suddenly hold no interest for me. I don't want to see what's happening through a soft-focus lens. That's not my fantasy.

"Fuck me," I whisper.

"Yes," he breathes. And then I'm being lifted into the air. My legs wrap around his waist, my back still pressed against that hard wall, and again I cry out as he pushes inside of me, again and again.

I feel myself opening up for him. I feel myself getting wetter, a primal reaction to this welcome intrusion. I feel *everything*.

He's filling me with a hard, pulsing, and unyielding energy. He's crashing through the doors behind which I've locked away all my secret desires, and those desires are bursting through me with the savage force you would expect from any jailbreak. As he continues to hold me up, I bend my head and softly bite his shoulder; I suck on his neck. I want to devour him even as he consumes me.

And now we're on the floor. My hips never leave his. I'm still embracing him with my legs, pulling him to me. Every inch of him holds its place inside my walls as he lowers me onto my back. The thin carpet beneath me adds a touch of gentleness as I scratch up his skin. His hands are on my breasts, pinching my nipples before moving to the small of my back. We're moving to our own rhythm, one that is as rousing and radiant as anything ever heard within a Beethoven symphony. Each thrust brings me to a new level of ecstasy.

*I didn't know it could be like this.*

It's a cliché. A line every ingénue in every bad romantic comedy is forced to utter. The words are always spoken delicately as if our heroine has reached a new level of innocence.

This doesn't feel innocent. This feels fucking amazing. It feels like I'm coming alive.

*I didn't know it could be like this.*

It's the last intelligible thought I have before he brings me to the brink again. I feel his shoulders tense under my grasp and then he pins my arms over my head, physically constraining me when my ecstasy can't be held back at all. The combination makes me wild and I thrash my head from side to side and buck my hips forward, forcing him even deeper inside of me. He groans and pushes faster and harder, as our crescendo moves us closer to a dizzying climax.

I cry out one more time as we come together, right there on the floor of a suite at the Venetian.

*I didn't know it could be like this.*

# CHAPTER 3

✿

I DON'T BELIEVE IN an afterlife. I've always thought that when someone's gone, they're gone. Maybe that's how it is with moments, too. I have the memory of being with Mr. Dade, only two nights ago now, but with nothing tangible to connect me to that memory, that *moment* has simply . . . stopped breathing.

He held me afterward and stroked my hair. The tenderness had been out of place. I wasn't prepared for it. So I simply got dressed and walked away. He didn't try to stop me but there had been something in his expression as he watched me leave that made my pulse quicken. He wasn't looking at me the way a stranger would. He was looking at me like he knew me . . . maybe better than he had the right to.

Simone was back in our room when I got there. She pressed me for details but I gave her little. I placated her with stories of flirting with a mysterious man in a bar with glass walls while he plied me with spirits that cost a little too much and tasted like seduction.

She was disappointed. "You're a lost cause," she complained as I traded the Herve Leger for the innocuous white robe provided by the hotel. She zipped up the dress in a garment bag. As I watched it get swallowed into the black plastic, I was reminded of a coffin. It wasn't just the moment that was lost to me; I was also burying a version of myself . . . burying it inside a garment bag that wasn't even mine.

But as I sit in my Los Angeles office, with its light yellow walls and neatly organized files, I realize that's how it's supposed to be. It

was a dream, that's all, and like all dreams it has virtually no consequences. The lessons it teaches can be studied or dismissed. It was
just a few hours of time during which my subconscious was able
to take over and a little hidden part of me was allowed to dictate a
story in vivid colors. A story marked by its passion and excitement,
two things that can never be maintained for long in real life.

Just a dream.

I pull out a client file. My job is to tell other people how to do
theirs. Invest your time and money in this, not in that, and so on.
I came to think of corporations as people long before the Supreme
Court weighed in on the subject. They're multifaceted entities, just
like us. And, like people, the successful corporations know which
parts of themselves are worth developing and which parts must be
suppressed, hidden from the public eye. They know when to cut
their losses.

To me, the only part of the personhood of corporations that
people have gotten fundamentally wrong is the idea that money is
a company's form of speech. In truth, money is a corporation's very
soul.

And that makes me a spiritual advisor.

I smile at that idea as I review my file in anticipation of passing
the collection plate.

"Kasie Fitzgerald, we've struck gold!"

I look up to see my boss, Tom Love, standing in my doorway.
My assistant, Barbara, stands behind him, smiling apologetically.
Tom never gives anyone a chance to announce him before barging
in. His last name seems like an unfortunate joke since I have never
seen him give or inspire anything that resembles love.

"We have a new account!" Tom says as he steps inside and closes
the door behind him, apparently unaware that he has essentially
slammed the door in Barbara's face.

I close the file in my hands. I am not the person Tom runs to
when a new account comes his way. I'm still working my way up
here and my climb is made all the steeper by the fact that I used

Dave's family connections to get my foot in the door. An Ivy League education should have been enough . . . but then nothing is ever enough these days. You have to graduate at the head of your class, have internships under the direct supervision of the captains of industry. You have to have a solid golf game.

I have a job that many magna cum laude Rhodes scholars would kill for. I got it because I'm smart, capable, and have an Ivy League education . . . and because my boyfriend's godfather is one of the cofounders of the company.

I have something to prove.

"I take it I'll be part of the team handling this account?" I ask as I watch Tom claim the chair opposite me and idly look through the appointment calendar on my desk. I've learned to record my personal appointments exclusively on my phone and to keep my phone out of Tom's reach.

"No," he says as he thumbs through the weeks and months of my professional life. "You're *leading* the team."

There's a shift in the room's atmosphere. His eyes are still on the calendar but I can see he's not reading it. He's waiting for my reaction. I've wanted to lead a team since I got here but have long since accepted that I have a few more years to wait before the honor's granted. And yet here is Tom, handing me this gift . . . why?

"It's a small account?" I ask, trying to make sense of the nonsensical.

"No. It's Maned Wolf Security Systems."

Now the atmosphere isn't so much shifting as it is deconstructing into a swirl of confusion. Maned Wolf Security Systems. It provides security for the biggest corporations on the globe, produces the highest tech surveillance systems, firewall protections, and even has an armed guard division that operates in some of the more volatile parts of the world. It has government contracts and politicians who vie for its support.

I have no right to lead this team. There shouldn't even *be* a team. Maned Wolf is as insular as it is powerful. A billion-dollar operation that has yet to go public. It's Apple meets Blackwater meets Willy Wonka's Chocolate Factory. Secrets are kept; outsiders, unwelcome.

I haven't earned the right to break them out of their shell.

But I really want to.

"Why me?"

Tom raises his eyes from my calendar. "He asked for you."

And now the atmosphere has weight. I feel its pressure on my shoulders and against my chest. Tom looks at me with an expression laced with curiosity and suspicion.

"Who's *He*?" I ask.

"The CEO."

I should know his name, but I don't. I know their contracts, their marketing, their strength. Their people have never been of much interest to me.

And yet, as I wait for Tom to say more, I sense that the focus of my interest is about to be irrevocably altered.

"His name is Robert . . . Robert Dade. He says he met with you in Vegas."

People say there is nothing more wonderful than having your dreams come true. But some dreams were meant to stay dreams. Sometimes when our dream life sneaks into our waking world, it causes a chemical reaction.

And when that happens, everything explodes.

I'M GIVEN ONLY a few days to prepare for the meeting. I put together a team, but, per Mr. Dade's request, the first meeting will be private. Just the two of us.

When Tom had told me *that,* I once again saw the suspicion in his eyes. It was easy to attack Tom's mannerisms, even his management style, but not his intelligence. I made up a story as to how I had met Mr. Dade. How I had told him what I did for a living and boasted of professional successes as we stood in a painfully long airport security line. I said I had given Mr. Dade my card but had been separated from him before getting the name of his company.

Even as I utter my explanations and excuses, I can see their transparency. But I so want Tom to suspend disbelief. I want him to accept the ridiculous idea that I inadvertently and unknowingly gave a powerful CEO the pitch of a lifetime. I want him to put away that curious smile he's been sharing with me these days. I want him to stop looking at me like he suddenly realizes that I might be hiding something under my boxy blazers and wide-legged pantsuits. I want him to stop treating me like I'm as unscrupulously ambitious as he is.

Tom now stops to talk to me on a daily basis.

But right now I'm not in the office. It's Friday morning. I take extra care with my appearance. I pull my hair back into a severe twist. My navy blazer falls in a straight line to my hips without so much as a hint of femininity. I pair it with a matching straight skirt. There is no invitation whispered within the folds of this fabric. There's nothing here to entice.

As I stare at my reflection in my pale blue bathroom, I debate the problem of makeup. Without it I look softer, younger, more vulnerable.

I always wear makeup.

I drag a moist sponge across my skin, spreading foundation over my little imperfections; a small pimple along my hairline, the few freckles I earned while bicycling through those childhood days of summer . . . covering up all the tiny details that make me human. I darken my cheeks with bronzer and press a gray pencil against the tender flesh beneath my lower lashes.

This is the version of me that I'm allowed to show the world. This is not the woman Mr. Dade met in Vegas.

I buried that woman in a garment bag.

BECAUSE I ARRIVE at the offices of Maned Wolf Security Systems fifteen minutes early, I can pause to admire the building that houses them. It should have been cold with its darkly mirrored exterior but here, in Santa Monica, it reflects the sun and the palm trees that surround it, adding warmth to its power.

And he had been warm when I had touched him. The kisses against my neck had been gentle even as he had pinned me up against the wall. Then there had been his fingers . . . when he had stroked me with them, pushed them inside me, playing me just so as if he was a master pianist bringing forth the aching notes of Beethoven's Moonlight Sonata . . . warm, powerful . . .

My purse vibrates as my phone jerks me back to reality.

"Hello?"

"Miss Fitzgerald? I'm Sonya, Mr. Dade's executive assistant. There's been a slight change of plans. Mr. Dade would like you to meet him at the bar La Fête. It's located one block south of our office building."

"Any particular reason for the relocation?"

"Mr. Dade will, of course, cover the expense of anything you order and the valet."

That hadn't been my question, but it seems unlikely that this woman would have been able to give me a satisfactory answer.

I look back up at the building and then down at the briefcase in my hand. "I'll be there. . . . *My* firm will cover all additional expenses."

"May I ask how far away you are?"

"I'm here," I say, "at your building. One block away from Le Fête."

I hang up and walk past the building, with its darkly tinted windows and reflected palm trees, to Mr. Dade.


HE LOOKS THE SAME. I stand by the host station so I can discreetly observe him. He sits alone at a small bar table while he reads something on his iPad. He's wearing a light gray cotton shirt with black trousers. Still no tie, no blazer, nothing that demands deference from the world he controls.

Then again, Mr. Dade doesn't need clothes to announce his authority. That statement is made in the way he holds himself. It's in the intensity of his hazel eyes, the obvious strength of his body; it's in the confident smile he's directing at me.

Oh yes, he's spotted me all right, and under the intensity of his gaze I have to work harder to remember the little things: *keep your head up, walk with purpose, breathe, don't forget who you are.*

I walk through the maze of tables to his side. "Mr. Dade." I keep my voice cool and professional as I offer him my hand.

"Kasie." He gets to his feet and presses his palm against mine, demonstrating a firm grip and holding on for far too long. "I am so glad to see you again."

He's moving his thumb back and forth over my skin again. It's such a small thing, something I should be able to easily brush off. But instead goose bumps pop up all over my arm.

He notices and his smile gets a little wider. "Last time I saw you this fell out of your purse." He holds up my business card. "I found it on the floor of my suite."

I yank away my hand and take a seat.

"I always conduct my meetings in offices, Mr. Dade."

"Ah, but I'm afraid my office was ill-equipped for you today."

"Ill-equipped?"

He nods and out of nowhere a waitress appears with two glasses balanced on a tray.

"Iced tea." She puts the tall glass in front of Mr. Dade. "And Scotch on the rocks."

I feel myself heat up as she places the much shorter glass in front of me.

"I thought of ordering a glass for myself," he explains, "but then I remembered your willingness to share."

I stare down at the bobbing ice cubes in the light copper liquid.

I know what can be done with those ice cubes.

"I'm here for business, Mr. Dade."

He smiles and leans forward, propping his elbows on the slightly unsteady table. "You know my first name now. You're allowed to use it."

"I think it's better if we keep things professional." There's a slight quiver to my voice. Against my better judgment I reach for the drink.

"Very well. Continue to call me Mr. Dade and I'll continue to call you Kasie."

I take a long sip of the whiskey; the taste's too familiar, the memories are too animated. "I'm here to talk to you about my ideas for Maned Wolf Security Systems."

"For the sake of convenience, let's just call it Maned Wolf."

I nod. It's the first nonloaded thing he's said and I'm incredibly grateful for this small gift. "If you're seriously considering taking Maned Wolf public, and the documents your staff e-mailed me suggest that you are, you need to grow your personal Internet security business. Everyone knows the government relies on you to keep its files safe. The average customer will want to feel like they're buying in to that same level of protection."

"Why try to reach so many when I can reach a few who will pay me so much more?"

"Because the greatest growth and most impressive profits fall to those who value volume over exclusivity. A single high-volume Starbucks will always be more profitable than Le Cirque."

"I see." I watch as his mouth forms the words with exaggerated slowness. I like his mouth. Some would say it's a little too big for his face but it's sensual. "So you're not a fan of exclusivity," he continues. "You like to mix it up."

The innuendo is clear.

"Mr. Dade, are you familiar with the sexual harassment laws of California?"

"Kasie, are you telling me that you're ready to go public with our little escapade in order to charge me?"

I don't answer. My hand's clenched around the handle of my briefcase.

"Have another sip of your drink . . . your ice is melting."

"Did you ask me here because you want to hear my proposals?" I want the question to sound like a challenge, not a plea.

I'm not entirely successful with that.

"Yes," he says firmly. "I've done some checking. You're a rising star at your firm. I'm paying for your expertise, that's all."

I drink more of the Scotch and wait for it to give me the artifice of courage. "You don't need me."

"No, I don't. But I do want you."

Another sip of Scotch—it burns my throat and sharpens my edge. "My proposals." I carefully prop up my briefcase on the edge of the table and then manage to take out a folder filled with material without dropping anything on the floor. "Shall we go over them now? Or should we reschedule?"

I watch as his body shifts, changing its posture from one of provocation to one of welcome. He gestures to my file. "Please."

Even that simple word is a reminder.

And yet I manage to keep my focus. I tell him stories of growth, unfathomable prosperity, the kind even a company like Maned Wolf has yet to achieve. But they could. My team could get them there. *I* could get them there. Given the chance, I can find those little flaws that can quietly hold a giant back from achieving an ultimate conquest. Sometimes those imperfections can be cut out, removed entirely. Sometimes they just need to be covered up with a little foundation.

Mr. Dade listens. He's an active listener. He doesn't have to say a word. I can see he understands; sense when he approves, when he's impressed, and when he's not. I feed off this, changing my pitch ever so slightly with the changes of his expressions. I know when to give him more details about one thing, when to brush over another. We're in sync.

It's business. It shouldn't be sexy.

And yet . . .

Eventually he steeples his long fingers. He's the businessman, the pianist, the devil. "Of course you're speaking in generalities," he says. "In order to get specifics and introduce any idea that's implementable, you're going to have to look at our company a little more closely. Talk to the directors of the different divisions. You're going to have to get inside the walls of my world."

"But I'm going to do so much more than that," I quip. "I'm going to break those walls down. It's the only way you can reach your potential."

He laughs. I'm feeling relaxed now. I'm enjoying myself.

More than I should be.

He places a credit card on the table; it's the only hint our attentive server needs. It's all I need, too. I get to my feet but he stops me with a small gesture of his hand.

And again I find myself held by his gaze.

The waiter charges the card, returns it; Mr. Dade writes in a ridiculously large tip before escorting me out. "Where did you park?"

I jerk my chin in the direction of my car.

He starts walking with me. He doesn't ask if it's okay.

"I hate your suit."

"Good thing you don't have to wear it," I say. There's my car, parked parallel on the street, ready to spirit me to safety.

"Neither do you."

I stop in front of my car. My keys are in my purse. I need to get them out, right now. Why can't I move?

I feel his hands even though they're not touching my skin. They're on my lapel. He's unbuttoning my jacket, removing it from my shoulders, pulling it off me, right here in the middle of a busy sidewalk. I can't let people see him doing this to me. I can't let him do it period.

Sometimes I'm shocked by how weak the word *can't* can be.

"This is my suit," I whisper.

"It's a habit."

I look up at him, making a silent request for clarification.

"Like the habit of a nun," he says. "Clothes designed to hide every curve, every alluring detail, a respectable choice for a woman who has chosen a life of chastity. But . . ."

He pauses and brings his hand to the back of my neck. I shiver as his fingers slide up, then down, then up again to the base of my skull, into my hair. "We both know you're no nun."

"I'm dating someone. We're going to get married."

"Really?" The corners of his mouth twitch. "Well, habits come in all different forms, don't they? Some women hide their true selves under multiple layers. Sometimes those layers are made of fabric, some are made of misguided relationships."

"You don't know anything about my relationship. You don't know me."

"Perhaps not. But I know what you look like when you're completely stripped of all those layers."

My skirt hangs straight to my knees; my shirt reveals nothing. And yet I feel naked, standing here on the sidewalk, being quietly inspected by this man whose vision is aided by one intimate night I had recklessly given him.

People are watching. I don't have to look at the many pedestrians passing by to know it. I feel their gaze the way I felt it in Vegas.

But there is one important distinction: in Vegas audacity has a home. Displaying myself in that tight dress in front of a room full of stares: it fit with the expectations of the city. It's all detailed in the brochures. Vegas has a fantasy-based economy. It's just how it is.

But here, standing in front of a Santa Monica office building, miles away from the street performers who line the Promenade, Mr. Dade's attention is out of place.

People are looking at us. They can see the sparks, feel the tension. They want to know what's going to happen next.

I want to know what's going to happen next.

But I can't give in to that. I suck in a sharp breath, roll my shoulders back, try not to feel their stares, his stare.

"You've put me in a difficult position, Mr. Dade." Is that my voice, filled with convincing but false confidence and composure? Is that me staring into his eyes, as if daring him to push me? "My boss thinks I slept with you to get this account. You've compromised my professional reputation."

He tilts his head to one side as his eyes continue to slide up and down my body the way his fingers moved over my neck only a moment ago. "I don't throw business to every woman I sleep with. Only the ones with Harvard business degrees."

"Ah," I say. "Well then I guess it's a good thing I didn't go to Yale."

I gently pull away from him, turn, and get in my car. His warm laughter follows me as I make my exit.

I'm miles away before I realize he still has my blazer.

# CHAPTER 4

❁

I't's friday night. I cook dinner for Dave at my place on Friday nights. Always. It's a little ritual that erases some of the irksome uncertainty from our lives.

Now he sits at my dining room table eating rosemary chicken and steamed asparagus. A glass of white wine sits untouched by his plate.

"I've worked out a budget for the ring," he says.

"A budget?"

"I was thinking we should spend around twelve thousand," he suggests. "Twelve thousand buys quality, not flash. We want to keep it real, right?"

I turn my gaze to the glass door leading to my backyard. Dave is always suggesting we *keep things real,* but he doesn't seem to actually know what the term means or how to properly apply it.

Do *I*? When Mr. Dade slid that ice cube up my thigh, when he kissed me in a place where Dave would never kiss me, when he teased me with the flick of his tongue . . . was that real? It had felt more real than anything. And at the same time it hadn't felt real at all.

I look back at the table. It's made of a dark-stained wood that's been polished to within an inch of its life. It's solid, dependable, useful. It's real. Just like Dave.

Mr. Dade is the first man who has ever made me come while I was standing up. He's the first man who's ever seen me naked while he remained fully clothed. Even now I can see him, circling me, assessing, planning, wanting. . . .

I squirm in my seat.

"Are you all right?" It's Dave's voice. The voice of caution and reason. The voice I should be listening to. "You seem . . . agitated tonight."

The word prickles my skin. "I have a new account . . . the biggest I've ever worked on. I suppose it . . . has me on edge."

"God knows, I relate to that. I'm buried these days, too. You know how it is."

I do. Dave's a tax attorney. Like me, he likes things he can count on, and you can always count on the overprivileged to cheat on their taxes. That's where Dave comes in. The rich give him the money they refuse to share with the IRS, and Dave makes their worries disappear.

As I watch him finish his meal, I realize that I want to be something he can count on. And I want him to make my worries vanish like the invisible money he hides away in tax shelters.

He eats his last bite and I stand up and walk behind him. My hands go to his shoulders and I begin to knead away the tension. "Stay the night, Dave."

"Hmm, I was planning on it." He lifts the glass of wine to his mouth while I lift my fingers and run them through his blond hair. Moving in front of him I straddle his lap.

"I want you, Dave."

"What's gotten into you?" he asks with a wary smile. The wineglass goes back on the table.

I lean forward and let my teeth graze his earlobe. "It's what I want to get into me that's important."

He doesn't respond. His hands go hesitantly to the small of my back.

This could be good. This could be real.

"You don't need to be gentle with me tonight," I whisper. Again my hand goes to his hair but this time I gather it in my fist and pull his head back so he's staring into my eyes. "I want you to tear off my clothes. I want you to hold me down while you press inside."

"Wait, you want . . ." His words fade off; I can feel his hands trembling against me.

"Mmm, I want a lot, ferocity, passion, animalism. . . . Overpower me. Tonight I want to be wicked." My voice is teasing and sweet. "Dave, will you *fuck* me tonight?"

In an instant he's pushed me off his lap; I have to reach for the table to steady myself as he leaps away from me.

"What's going on?" He appears disoriented and lost. "This isn't you. You never talk like this."

The sweetness is gone. His bewilderment is pushing him toward anger.

He's looking at me with . . . disgust. "You don't even swear!"

Shrinking back, I can feel the shame spiraling up my spine and taking hold of my heart. "I was . . . I just thought . . ."

I wither under the hostility of his stare. The power I felt only a second ago is gone. "I guess I'm just overtired," I finish lamely.

He hesitates. He knows that being tired doesn't explain anything at all but I can see he likes the simplicity of the excuse. He wants to accept it. "You're overwhelmed at work," he says carefully, testing his own ability to defy logic. "That's always exhausting. I know how it is."

"Yes," I say, although my voice is so quiet, it's unclear if he can hear me.

"I think we should call it an early night after all." He takes his jacket, pulls it on. His words are coming a little faster now as he implements his escape. "Sleep is what you need. I'll be back at . . . shall we say eleven tomorrow morning? I have a list of jewelry stores we should start with."

I nod. I can't speak. Not without crying. Dave wants to get away from the demon that briefly possessed me. He assumes it will slither away after I slip under the covers, alone in my bed.

He crosses to me again, and gives me a brief, gentlemanly kiss on the lips. It's the kiss of forgiveness.

My shame curls up my throat, choking me.

As he opens the door to leave, he turns back with a sympathetic smile. "We'll want to go to several of these stores before we make a decision. Weigh our options and all that."

Again, I nod.

"So don't forget to wear sensible shoes. I don't want you to be uncomfortable."

He blows me a kiss just before the door closes behind him.

Gently, I pick up his wineglass. I take a moment to appreciate the way the overhead lights make the pale liquid sparkle before I bring it to my lips. The taste is floral, sweet, pure. Angelic.

I let these notes play on my tongue before hurling the glass across the room.

I walk forward and step down on the mess I've made, enjoying the sound of shattered glass crunching beneath my sensible shoes.

IT'S LATE NOW. I've taken a shower, tried to rinse away the embarrassment and anger with a cheap shampoo. I went too far, that's all. Like the corporations I work with, I am multifaceted, complicated. And like the corporations, there are some departments of my soul that just need to be shut down.

But I do have my strengths. I'm good at my job. I can recognize untapped potential, see strength where others see nothing, and I can find ways to optimize those strengths until all anyone else sees is power.

I sit down at my computer, my hair wet and hanging over the white cotton of a short Donna Karan robe. The terry-cloth lining soaks up the moisture from my body and adds a softness that the night has lacked so far.

I send Mr. Dade an e-mail: "I need to meet with the director of your mobile phone security software division. Can we set up a meeting for Monday?"

It's an obvious area for growth. Already there's been buzz about some of the products they've introduced. It addresses a need, feeds into a society's fears . . . there is always so much profit in fear. Insurance companies, Hollywood thrillers, cars with more airbags than cupholders—they all bank on it.

My Mac chimes as a message pops up: an invitation from Mr. Dade for video conferencing.

My fingers hover over the keyboard, then move to the belt of my robe, pulling it a little tighter. I could ignore this. It's eleven o'clock on a Friday night.

I should have waited until I was dressed to send that e-mail.

I could dress now, put on a suit, pin up my hair, but who wears a suit while at home at eleven on a Friday night? He'll know I made an effort for him, not an effort to please but an effort nonetheless. He'll know the effect he's had on me, and that simply is not an acceptable option.

For some reason, rejecting the invitation doesn't feel like an option, either. And part of me knows that my thinking, my compulsion to press Accept, is no good. But I don't listen to that part of me. Not tonight. It's speaking with too soft a voice for me to feel the weight of its wisdom.

I press Accept.

Mr. Dade appears on my screen like an apparition I summoned from some dark imaginings. He's composed as he watches me from the comfort of his home. In the background I can see his bed. The duvet is a light, glowing orange that reminds me of flames.

"I didn't expect to hear from you," he says. "Do you always work this late on Friday nights?"

"It was just an e-mail," I say, trying to keep my expression cool, lofty, compensating for the intimacy of the white robe. "I wasn't expecting to conference. It was your invitation that was out of place."

"Ah, but it was a working e-mail. I assume you'll bill me for the time it took you to write it, and probably for the extra minutes it took you to think of it, and even to turn your computer on, probably. You choose your own schedule, Kasie. You chose this as a working hour, and right now you're working for me. It's my expectation that during the hours that you work for me, you make yourself fully available . . . to me."

The words excite me but I press my lips into a hard line that I hope will help me draw the line in the sand that is necessary here. "I'm always available to talk about work, Mr. Dade."

"You can call me Robert."

"If we were friends, I would call you Robert."

"And we're not friends?"

He leans back and for the first time, I can see the graceful curves of the chair he sits in. An antique, perhaps from the eighteenth century. It's a chair that speaks of domination and royalty, but mostly it speaks of money.

I understand money. I can handle it, manipulate it. I can handle this man in his ridiculously expensive chair.

"No," I say firmly. "We're not friends."

"Lovers then? What do you call your lovers, Kasie? Do you address them by their last names? Their first? Or do you turn to words that are a bit more descriptive in nature?"

"We're not lovers."

"Oh, you're wrong there. I've felt you beneath me, I've held those beautiful breasts, I've been inside *your* walls. I know where to touch you to make you lose control."

"It was just one night." I try to keep the chill in my tone but I can see that my line in the sand is now threatened by the tide. "An anomaly. I am not your lover now."

"Ah, but then why do you respond to me as if you are?"

The words penetrate. They toy with my nerves and strain my willpower. I look away from the screen. This is stupid. It's not in my plans. I've cleaned up the shards of glass from the dining room floor. Nothing else has to be broken.

"I want to meet with your directors, your engineers," I say, still keeping my eyes away from the computer. I need to steady my voice, my breathing. "I want to talk to them about your capabilities."

"Do you remember when you touched me here?"

I turn to look at the screen and with a graceful, almost languid ease he pulls off the black T-shirt he's wearing. He's perfect, beautiful, powerful; he runs his fingers over scratch marks on the skin that covers his heart.

Had I done that? I remember dragging my fingernails over his back but . . . oh yes, it was when he had pulled me from the wall and lowered me to the floor. He had gently pinched my nipples as I had pressed my hips against his, no control, just lust, desire, and that feeling . . . the feeling of him touching me, the feeling of him opening me up, thrusting inside of me until there were no words at all.

"Do you remember where I touched *you,* Kasie?"

I'm blushing now, and knowing that he can see that only makes me blush more. I reach for the lapel of my robe. I don't open it, just run my fingers over it, carefully hanging on to the last remnants of restraint I have.

"Open your robe, Kasie."

"I can't do that, Mr. Dade. I need you to stay focused. I have to talk to you about business . . . security . . . public perception . . . there are strategies that we can implement."

His mouth curves into a small smile and I lose my thinly held train of thought as I remember what those lips felt like as they traveled up my inner thigh.

"Oh, I'm very focused. And trust me when I tell you that I am implementing a strategy."

"I'm not your project, Mr. Dade."

"No, you're my lover, Kasie. And I'm telling you to show me where I touched you."

This is the time to take my hands away from my robe. This is the time to turn off the computer. This is the time to hold everything together—white wine, not whiskey; quiet dinners at home, not wild nights in Vegas; no more shards of glass.

"Open your robe, Kasie."

I pull on the edges of my lapel, my robe opens just a little wider, and he can see the inner outline of my breasts.

"A little wider, Miss Fitzgerald." He says the last words teasingly. He's mocking me, daring me. It's childish and should be *so* easy to resist.

I pull the robe open a little wider still. I look into his eyes and again I feel his power . . . but this time I feel it entering me. I can breathe it; it fills me, touches me, like a caress.

With steady hands I pull the robe all the way back. It hangs loosely from my shoulders. I hold his gaze, all trepidation suddenly gone. I roll my shoulders back, my fingers slip down to my nipples that reach out to him, hard and ready.

"You touched me here."

And now we're against the wall of the Venetian and again I can feel him, I can wrap myself around his fierce energy.

"Where else?"

My fingers move to the outline of my breasts before tracing a line down from my ribs to my stomach. "You touched me here."

And I can feel him kissing the base of my neck, that little hollow area where the flesh is softest and the most sensitive.

"Where else?"

My fingers keep going lower. He can't see where they are but he knows; I can see from his eyes that he knows.

And I feel him deep inside me. I burn to be on that fire-colored bed. "You touched me here," I gasp.

I know I'm affecting him. The power is coming from both of us now. His breathing is a little faster; his eyes convey a little more urgency. His own hands move below the screen and I know what he's touching, I know its details, know its strength . . . I want to feel it again. I want to taste it the way he tasted me.

"You entered me here," I breathe, feeling, stroking the dampness between my legs. He moans as I throw back my head, my control quickly leaving me. I can feel his eyes, almost as good as his hands, and oh his hands had been so good. And still, I touch myself, replicating his caresses. I am immersed in his desire, in my own.

"Kasie," he whispers. My name is the final caress I need. My free hand grabs the armrest of my chair and my hips push forward as I follow this dangerous path to its only possible conclusion. I hear him moan again. I know I'm not alone. I know what I'm doing, to him, to myself.

My body shakes as the orgasm comes with a convulsing and heartwrenching power. It's the final chord of an erotic rhapsody that leaves me with the mingled emotions of satisfaction and endless longing.

For a moment I don't move. My eyes are closed and the only sound is of my breathing and his. Across the city, by my side, he's everywhere.

And the little voice that had tried to talk to me before, the voice that comes from the part of me I should have listened to, now whispers in resignation, *You've broken another glass.*

My throat tightens and with a shaking hand I reach for my keyboard . . .

. . . and disconnect.

# CHAPTER 5

❁

I SIT IN MY living room, waiting. Waiting for Dave. Waiting for the chaos. Something is churning inside of me. A brew of disaster mixed with an impetuous desire. I have to get it out of me. Throw it in the sewer along with all the other toxic waste that dirties our lives. But what I can't do is add deceit to that bubbling pot of trouble. Dave has to be told . . . something.

I stand and walk to my window and stare up at a brightly backlit sky of gray. Can I blame Dave for my recent mistakes? I'd like to. Wedding jitters run amok, that's all. My subconscious telling me that his proposed union isn't as perfect as I once imagined. He had rejected me so easily last night, like he would a homeless person holding out a hand for change. Dismissed me with a smile, a polite expression of sympathy and repulsion.

It was rejection that stirred that brew, insult that spurred my rebellion. So I will talk to Dave. I'll face the music. And if the music is rough, I'll find a way to smooth out its edges, I'll unplug the electric guitars and dismantle the bass until there's nothing left but a soft, unthreatening tune that I can sway to.

It's not until the doorbell rings that I have second thoughts.

Dave stands on my doorstep with a dozen white roses. There had been white roses at the luncheon where we first met . . . six years ago. Forever ago . . . but right now the memory's close enough to touch. When he walked me to my car, we had passed a florist and Dave had insisted that I, too, have white roses; he bought me a dozen to take home. He had asked for my number then and I had been moved to give it to him. Most girls will give up something for a bouquet: a phone number, a smile, even anger. But, of course, the most frequent price for such a gift is the loss of one's resolve.

I move aside, let him in, and watch as he disappears into my kitchen, then reemerges with the roses arranged neatly in a vase. He finds the perfect place for them on my dining table.

Dave and I still haven't said so much as hello, but the roses are speaking with something more tangible than words.

"I overreacted last night," he says. He's staring at the roses, not me, but I don't mind the evasion. "I didn't want to move to LA, did you know that? I just did it for work."

I shrug noncommittally. He's told me this before but I don't see how it's relevant.

"It's such a gaudy city," he continues. "A place where the men smile at you with bleached white teeth and the women thrust their fake boobs in your face. Everyone here is aggressive, but the women . . . they act like men. Like drag queens with a lust for exhibitionism. They're not ladies. They're not you."

"I'm a lady?"

"But you're also strong," Dave adds quickly. He sits in one of my upholstered dining room chairs. "Strong, ambitious, controlled, quiet, beautiful." He pauses as he works to find a metaphor. "You're a concealed weapon. A pistol hidden inside an Hermès handbag."

I like the image.

"The woman with the Hermès knows that she can only reach for that gun when she needs to keep the wolves at bay. Only in cases of extreme danger. Because a gun in the hand is vulgar, common," he says. "But when it's kept neatly in a couture bag, it becomes something else."

As the metaphor is stretched, it loses its appeal. A gun that can't be handled becomes useless. It's denied its raison d'être.

But I see his point. Last night I wasn't the woman he wanted me to be, the woman I had always been with him, the woman he had fallen in love with. Last night the gun had come out of the bag.

"I overreacted last night," he says again. "But you scared me. Not because what you said was so extreme but because it wasn't something you would say."

He rises again, pulls a single rose from the bouquet, and extends it toward me. "Remember when I first bought you white roses? The day we met?"

"I had just finished graduate school," I say, nodding at the memory. "Ellis took me to her Notre Dame alumni event because the Harvard events weren't bringing me any interesting job offers."

"I remember the way you held yourself," he says, "your modesty and your strength. . . . As soon as I saw you, I wanted to be near you."

My eyes focus on the flowers as my mind travels back.

*Dave had looked good that day. Boyish, sweet . . . maybe a little awkward in his red pinstriped shirt and navy tie worn in a city where ties are reserved for car salesmen and bank clerks. But I liked that he didn't play by the LA-style rules. He stood out. He was a throwback to a time and place where educated men were expected to be gentlemen and elitism wasn't such a dirty word.*

*He was shy when we first started talking but he quickly gathered confidence as we delved further into our conversation. He said he would put in a good word for me with the global consulting firm I had once hoped to work for. They had declined to recruit me right out of Harvard but Dave's godfather was the company's founder. He could give me the perversely rare and exceedingly cultivated second chance.*

*And then he started to tell me about himself, how he had been living in LA for two years. He hated the smog, hated the traffic, hated the people and the Hollywood culture. But he liked his law firm and loved the wealth he was able to coax out of the city's Armani-stitched pockets. It would be irresponsible for him to leave just so he could live in a city more to his taste.*

*And right then I knew Dave and I were alike. He followed the rules. He was responsible, pragmatic—he wasn't governed by temptation or rash whims. Dave was steady. And standing there by his side, a Harvard grad with a mountain of student loan debt and not a single job offer from a company I had any desire to work for, well, steady seemed nice . . . even sexy.*

*And I had wanted to be near him, too.*

He pushes the rose farther forward so now the petals are touching the base of my neck. The gesture brings me back to the present.

"Don't change, Kasie," he says. "You're the only thing about this city that makes it bearable. When I'm with you, I feel like I'm not really so far from the town where I grew up. When I'm with you, it feels like home."

And now he takes another step forward; the rose remains where it is, delicate petals against my skin. "Don't change. Please don't change."

This is the man whom I wanted to blame for my own misbehavior. This is the man whom I betrayed twice in one week. This is the man who sees me as I want to be seen. In his eyes I'm a lady, a deadly weapon in a designer bag. Dave sees the aspiration of what I want to be while Mr. Dade sees the woman I've been running from. Dade sees the version of me that I tried to bury in a garment bag.

I should have seen that, should have understood before I accepted the invitation to digress.

I have never had to search for my role in life. It's always been assigned to me. By my parents, by my teachers, by this man with his white, white roses. My sister chose a different path. No one in my family talks about her anymore. Like the ancient Egyptians who would erase the images and names of the gods who had fallen out of favor, my family has simply erased my sister from our lives. I live the life I'm expected to live and I'm loved for it. Why change patterns now?

"I'm going to buy you a ring today," Dave says.

And I nod and smile.

STORE AFTER STORE, ring after ring, none of them feels right. One's too heavy, another too murky. Diamond after diamond, each one is sharp enough to cut glass. Each one of them speaks to a convention that dates back to the fifteenth century. A history splattered with blood and greed. There are more innocent traditions. In colonial times, men would give women thimbles as an expression of eternal companionship. I wouldn't know what to do with a thimble.

But I'm not sure I know what to do with a diamond, either.

"Maybe another stone?" I suggest, eyeing the bold red of a ruby.

The woman behind the counter smiles the smile that all salespeople smile when they smell money. "It's untreated." She pulls the ring out of the glass case and hands it to me. "Just pulled out of the ground, cut and polished."

Dave wrinkles his nose. He doesn't like the sound of this but I'm entranced. I hold the gem up to the light.

"All rubies have their little imperfections," the saleswoman continues. "Incursions of rutile needles. We call them silks. The ruby is a more complex stone than the diamond. Their imperfections distinguish them."

Silks. I warm to the term. Even the imperfections are made to sound elegant.

"We want a diamond," Dave says definitively. "It's more . . . pure."

I don't know if that's true. Decades of oppression of South Africans versus the brutish military dictatorship of the ruby-rich Myanmar. Injustice and pain all for pretty little stones that are supposed to symbolize love. Still, maybe that's fitting when you consider the actual nature of love.

"Would it be so inappropriate for us to do something different?" I ask Dave.

Dave hesitates. I can see the conflict in his eyes. I know he's measuring the size of his guilt over last night's rudeness against his true wishes.

But the guilt wins. "If you really want the ruby, you should have it." He kisses my cheek and slips his arm around my tensed shoulders. "I want you to be absolutely and truly happy."

As I slip the ruby onto my finger I wonder if it's wise to wish for anything as fleeting and insubstantial as absolute happiness.

• • •

HOURS LATER AND minutes after Dave has gone off to play racquetball with one of his firm's partners, I sit at home, contemplating . . . well, everything.

I don't have the ring with me. The price had exceeded the budget Dave had carved out. So we had walked away; he told the saleswoman he wanted to think about it, and she had assured us both that she would talk to her manager to see if she could get us a slightly lower price. Dave told me it was just the first step in a bargaining process, that the markup on gemstones was so high, *not* haggling was an act of audacity. But I would have my ring. He would put it on my finger and it would stay there . . . forever. Just as we had always planned.

I roll the word around in my head: *forever*. I don't know what that means.

I grab a *Forbes* magazine from the coffee table and start flipping through it, but I can't focus.

There isn't a single logical reason why I shouldn't marry Dave. He's doing everything he's supposed to do. Getting me the ring I want in exchange for my agreement to be the person I've been for my entire life. All he wants is for me to abandon my recent vagaries of nature. Compromises are the support beams that hold up every relationship.

My compromise is only to give up a part of myself that I'm already uncomfortable with.

So why does that seem so impossible?

Suddenly I'm tired. I close my eyes, lean my head against the back of my cream-leather armchair.

I can see Mr. Dade's face against the darkness of my closed lids. I can feel him, sense him. I feel a throbbing that's becoming familiar.

This is not good.

I get up and walk to the kitchen and pour Evian into a crystal water glass. Fantasies are normal. I know that. Is this really so different from fantasizing about an actor, a rock star, a male model staring out of a Diesel jeans ad?

Yes. Because I have never touched the actor, the rock star, the model.

I've never taken off my robe for those people. I have never asked them to take off my panties. I don't know what their fingers feel like.

I want to close my eyes but I can't because *he's* there. It takes conscious effort to keep him out of my head. Keeping his image away is as challenging as winning at arm wrestling. If I relax, if I let the strength of the memories overpower me, I'm lost.

I sip the water. I know I'm a little lost already because while I can still keep his image away when my eyes are open, I can't push away the memory of his touch. Even now, as I try, I get wet.

I unbutton the top of my jeans and cautiously slip my hand in.

When I touch myself, I jump, surprised by my own sensitivity. I shouldn't be doing this, thinking about the wrong man, remembering . . .

My phone chimes and I jump again and quickly look around the room as if there could possibly be someone there to see me. I remove my hand and rinse it under the warm water of my kitchen faucet. Then, with my jeans still unbuttoned and loose around my waist, I leave the room and find my phone next to the roses on the dining table.

And printed across its screen is Mr. Dade's name. Just a text, a request that my team meet at his office on Tuesday at 9:30 a.m. for a tour of the facilities. There's nothing there to bait me, worry me, delight me . . . nothing but his name.

Yet that's enough to do all that and more.

I press my fingers against the touch screen: I want to meet earlier.

A moment passes, then two before he answers in the form of a question: How early can your team be here?

They'll be at your office at 9:30 am this Tuesday, I reply, then pause before adding: I'll be there at 8:00.

Another moment of silence as I wait for his response. Time is stretching out as the knots tighten in my stomach.

And then there it is, his answer summed up in one word.

Yes.

# CHAPTER 6

❀

ON TUESDAY I walk into the dark glass building. My heels click against a marble floor as I approach the elevators, and with each click my pulse speeds up, just a little but enough . . . enough to remind me that I might just be in over my head.

I don't hesitate or look at the board to verify his office number. I know where I'm going; I'm just not clear on what I'm going to do when I get there.

There's a waiting area outside his office but there's no one sitting at the assistant's desk. The door is open for me and I can see a cup of coffee and a small box of pastries sitting on a side table by the window, seemingly forgotten. And then I see him, at his desk, his head bent over some papers. Drops of water in his salt-and-pepper hair catch the light and hint at a recent shower.

I stop a moment and picture that: Robert Dade standing naked in the shower, water washing over him, his eyes closed, lost in his own thoughts and the feeling of the warmth against his skin, quiet, vulnerable to the world. I imagine myself sneaking into the shower behind him, running my fingers through his hair as he tenses with surprise, then relaxes into my caress. I imagine sliding soap-covered hands down his back, to his ass, around his hips, and then stroking his cock until he's clean and hard and perfect.

The sharp inhale of breath is enough to bring his attention away from those papers before him. He looks up at me, sees the color of my cheeks, and smiles.

I dig my fingernails into my palms and try to focus on the pain.

I've had days to think this through. I'm not here to engage in fantasies. I'm here to end things. I'm here so I can make a clean break and be the woman I want to be. The signs in national parks tell us to stay on the path. If we wander off them, we may get lost; we might crush the very things that brought us to the park to begin with.

I walk into the office, determined to stay on the path, even as I close the door behind me.

Looking into his eyes I can read an encyclopedia's worth of information. He wants me. He's curious. Like me, he doesn't know what to expect and he wants to know where the line is today, the line between pulling me in and pushing me away.

"It's going to stop," I say.

"*It?*" he asks from his seat.

My voice is even and so much cooler than my warming cheeks. "No more transgressions, no more mistakes. It's done. Dave and I . . . we've decided on a ring."

"Dave." He says the name carefully as he rises and steps around his desk but not in front of it, still looking for that line in the sand. "That's his name?"

I nod in acknowledgment. "He's a good man. Kind, considerate . . . he buys me white roses." The words are shooting out of my mouth like arrows but I have no aim. Not one has come close to hitting its mark.

"Then he doesn't know you very well."

"He's known me for six years—most of my adult life."

"Which means there's no excuse for his ignorance." He takes a step forward. "White roses are pretty but they have nothing to do with who you are. You're more of an African violet. Have you ever seen an African violet?"

I shake my head.

"It's a flower that often comes in the deepest of purples, the color of royalty." He studies me, folding his arms casually across his broad chest. "Its petals are velvety; they actually seem to want to be touched. And at its center, its core, the very spot where the bees can coax out its nectar, it's a vibrant gold. Its sensuality isn't cartoonish like the *Anthurium* and it's not as clichéd as the orchid, which is too fragile to be compared to you anyway. The African violet is strong, enticing, and its beauty can be seen, but to fully appreciate its depth, it needs to be touched. It's a very intricate flower."

"No," I say. "I like traditional roses. I don't care if they're common. They're simple, elegant . . . sweet." I straighten my back but don't meet his eyes. "It has to stop," I whisper. "No more mistakes."

"We haven't made any mistakes. Everything we've done was considered and deliberate."

"No, I didn't think it through. I was . . . overwhelmed."

He smiles again. I like his smile. I like the way it makes him look younger and mischievous. I like the way it heats the inside of my stomach . . . and other parts of me.

"I didn't carry you away from the blackjack table," he says. "You walked with me. You ordered whiskey."

"It was just meant to be a drink."

He takes another step forward.

"You rode the elevator to my room."

Another step.

"You made yourself comfortable, accepted a glass of very expensive Scotch."

Another step.

"And when I tasted that Scotch on your skin, you grabbed my shirt."

And another. His hand reaches forward as he grabs the front of my white silk blouse. His other hand goes to my hip, then slides to my belly, then lower.

I gasp as he cups me.

"You asked me to take off your panties."

The skirt I'm wearing is too loose today. It allows him too much access. I feel his hand press against the cloth that separates skin from skin, applying just the right amount of pressure. I dig my nails deeper into my palms but the pain is dulling, becoming insignificant in the face of other sensations.

"Ask me to stop and I will," he says quietly. "But don't tell me that *it's* going to stop. This isn't an *it*. This is *you* and this is *me*. We've always had the option of restraint. We've had the power to say no." He lessens the pressure of his hand. "Or yes," and with that word his hand begins to move, back and forth. I feel myself respond, my hips aching to move along with the motion.

"Ask me to stop, Kasie, if that's what you want. All you have to do is ask."

"Mr. Dade," I whisper before breathing, "Robert."

"Yes," he says. The word doesn't sound like a question. It's a proclamation. A statement of what is and what isn't.

I grasp the hand that still holds my shirt, I look into those eyes, I read what's there.

"Robert Dade," I say quietly, "stop."

His hands fall away. Without breaking eye contact he takes a step back. My breathing is still irregular. I wait for my arousal to dissipate. But it doesn't. It just shifts, morphs into something else.

Something that feels a lot like power.

I smile.

Walking in a half circle around him I find myself stopping when his back is to me. I close the distance I had just asked him to place between us.

I shouldn't. But I do.

I let my fingers move up into his hair, just like in my fantasy. And just as I predicted, he tenses and then relaxes.

"You took my jacket," I whisper into his ear.

I hook my fingers around his sports jacket and pull it off him before deliberately dropping it on the floor. I can see his beautiful form and I press myself against him, crushing my breasts into that area below his shoulder blades, where his muscular back begins to taper down to his narrow waist.

"This will be the last time," I say. "This morning will mark the end. This is the last time I'll stray from the path."

He turns and looks at me. He's trying to find the connection between my words and the small smile that plays on my lips.

"This is the last time," I say again, backing up to his desk. I'm a little nervous and I'm shocked by what I'm saying, what I'm wanting, what I'm doing.

"This is the last time," I say one more time as I lean back against his desk and open my legs. "So let's make it good."

And in less than a second he's on me. His mouth is crushed against mine as he pulls my hair, his hand reaches up my skirt, and I feel him roughly pull my panties aside before his fingers plunge inside of me. This time I don't resist. His mouth tastes both bitter and sweet. His fingers start to move faster and I gently bite his lip and struggle to hold back my moans.

I start working on the buttons of his shirt. I'm desperate to touch him, every part of him. I don't want to leave anything to the imagination or to the memories I've spent so many hours reliving.

This is the last time, and I'm going to make it good.

And now his chest is bare and exposed, mine to stroke and taste. As his fingers continue to move, my mouth moves to his neck, taking his pulse with my tongue. When his thumb slips back up to my clit, I moan again, and this time I'm not quick enough to suppress the sound.

He can't see my face as my mouth moves down to one shoulder then across to the other, shoulders that seem as strong as the shoulders of Atlas. No, he can't see my face but he can feel me react as the orgasm begins. My whole body shakes with its impact.

I'm pulling off his belt now, unbuttoning his pants, reaching for what's waiting for me. As his pants fall to the ground my fingers slide to the base and then trace a line right up that vein to the ridge that marks the beginning of the tip.

And now it's his stifled moan that teases the room. It's *his* breathing that is out of control as he undoes my shirt, unhooks my bra, runs his hands up my breasts, gently pinching my nipples as he kisses my hair.

I take off my skirt all by myself. I want to give him this and I want to give myself everything he has to offer. The experience needs to be not just tactile but visceral. I'm breathing him in, feeling his touch. . . .

I want to taste him.

I lower myself to my knees and let my tongue dance over his erection, loving the way it hardens even more, yearning for me, waiting for me, begging for me.

When I take him in my mouth, he makes a sound that reminds me of a growl.

The effect I have on him increases my eagerness, my sense of urgency, my need. As my mouth continues to work, my hands move up and down his stomach, his hips, his legs.

And then, he pulls me away. Lifts me back up onto the desk, pushes my thighs apart, stares into my eyes for just a moment before pressing forcefully inside of me.

I cry out as I instantly come again. I'm filled with him, his taste still on my lips, my hands grasping his shoulders as he moves, pushing in again and again. His eyes return to mine, and this time he holds my gaze. I can't look away. My hips have found his rhythm and greedily rise to meet each thrust as if daring him to go further. He pushes my knee to my chest, giving himself a new advantage.

And as my third orgasm explodes through me, I feel him shudder, feel him coming, feel the intensity of us.

As we stay there, pressed against each other, the room smelling of coffee and sex, I hear him mutter . . . perhaps to himself, perhaps to me, "Last time, my ass."

FIFTEEN MINUTES LATER I step back out into Mr. Dade's waiting room, alone, fully dressed but still smoothing the newly made creases out of my blouse. I don't look up to see Mr. Dade's executive assistant until I sit down on the sofa.

She has dark auburn hair and big green eyes that remind me of king-size marbles. And she's watching me. I suck in an audible breath of surprise and she replies with an inquisitive smile.

How long has she been there? Did she hear us?

But does it matter what she heard? The point is she *knows*! Those green marbles weren't reflecting the image I had so carefully crafted for the people around me. Instead she sees a woman driven by the basest of impulses, a woman who snuck into an office building at eight in the morning so she could fuck her new client.

*A woman who takes what she wants.*

The words are coming from a little voice inside my own head. It's not a voice that I'm very familiar with. The angel on my right shoulder defeated the devil on my left eons ago. But now the devil speaks. It's the angel who struggles to find her voice.

"Would you like a glass of water?" the woman asks. She tilts her head to the side, causing her auburn hair to fall over one shoulder.

I nod silently and her smile widens as she leaves the room and then returns with a clean glass and a bottle of Smartwater.

"I'm Sonya," she says as I reach for the items. She doesn't let go right away. When I look up at her, she's staring at the buttons on my shirt. I've missed one. I quickly take the water and glass and put them on the side table before scrambling to fix the problem.

I can discern the essence of the questions she's working so hard to repress. Her now empty hands flutter as if she wants to assist with the buttons.

"It's a beautiful silk," she says, quietly watching the quick work of my fingers.

*She wants me.* The knowledge springs up inside of me like a geyser. I stare at her impatient hands, her marble eyes. Mr. Dade's assistant wants me.

And astoundingly, that makes sense to me. I have never felt this desirable, this enticing, this potent. I've never been with a woman. I can't fully imagine it. A woman's skin is too soft, her touch too delicate.

Mr. Dade had pulled my hair, lifted me up, entered me. . . .

No, I can't imagine being with a woman . . . and yet I understand her desire and it electrifies me in all the places she wants to touch. I glance at the closed door of Mr. Dade's office. Her desire makes me want to open that door and ask him to take me again—against the wall, on his desk, on the floor. I almost laugh when it occurs to me that the one place we've never made love is in a bed.

The green marbles have rolled in another direction. I recognize the embarrassed blush on Sonya's cheeks. "I don't know if he mentioned it," she says, following my gaze to Mr. Dade's door, "but he has a meeting at nine thirty."

"Yes," I say, finally trusting myself to whisper a few words, my buttons now all neatly hooked. "With me and my team."

"You're his nine thirty?" She walks back to her desk and checks her computer screen. "Kasie Fitzgerald?"

I nod.

"Ah," she says, sitting down, "you came early." Apparently struck by her own unintentional pun, her mouth twitches with the effort to keep from giggling.

Her amusement does not sit well with me. The unaccountable confidence I felt just moments ago wanes and I press my legs together so tight the muscles of my hips and thighs shoot up little daggers of pain in protest. I may be desired but I have also risked humiliation.

Pride and shame smash into each other, causing an avalanche of less comprehensible emotions. I want to go home, lock the door, and try to make sense of the battle going on inside me.

But I had told my team to meet me in the waiting area outside Mr. Dade's office. So I drink my SmartWater and try unsuccessfully to wash down the confusion.

I refuse to look at Sonya as the minutes tick away. I pretend I don't see her when she knocks on the door of Mr. Dade's office and asks him if there is anything she can get him. I wonder if he's as embarrassed as I am, but the assured and professional tone he uses with her carries no discomfort. I'm the only one unnerved.

She returns to her desk and tries to flash me a conspiratorial smile but again I ignore her. I tense even more when I hear familiar voices coming from down the hall. My team of four files into the waiting room like a pride of lions on the hunt, with Dameon, the only man on my team, hanging back and letting the women take the lead. Nina, Taci, and Asha are my women. Their movements are slow, almost languid, but there's stealth there. They're taking it all in, trying to spot the company's weakest links. They're hungry and they're ready to pounce on anything that smells like opportunity. But they don't see me . . . or rather they do but they don't see my details. They don't see the crease in my shirt that is almost gone now. They don't see my clenched fists resting in my lap. All they see is Kasie Fitzgerald, greeting them one by one as they walk in. The only thing that strikes them as unusual is my hair that now hangs loosely around my shoulders. It contradicts the severity of my suit and it's a style my coworkers have never seen me wear. They all take a moment to throw me a compliment along with a curious look. I thank them for the former and ignore the latter.

When Mr. Dade walks out, I rise and rigidly accept the hand he offers me.

"Miss Fitzgerald, it's so good to see you again."

His teasing smile is disconcerting. I want to check to see if anyone else notices but I don't want to give myself away. "May I introduce you to my team?" I ask.

He nods and I go around and give him the names of my colleagues. He greets them with his casual confidence and clipped words of greeting before turning his smile back to me. "I have to say," he says to the room in general, "your boss has impressed me. Her enthusiasm and passion give me hope that you can help bring Maned Wolf to the next level."

I glance quickly over at the assistant, who is now biting her lip. But my team doesn't notice anything unusual.

I breathe a quiet sigh of relief for that small blessing and replay Mr. Dade's statement in my head. I'm more taken with the word "boss" than I am with the subtle innuendo. This is *my* team. I have never had one before. I've finally been given control!

But when we follow Mr. Dade out of the waiting room, as he begins the tour, I replay other things in my head—the feel of his hands between my legs, the kisses he placed in my hair.

And as I think of these things, I look back at the assistant. She's watching me, almost wistfully, almost admiringly. *She* sees my details. And in this moment I realize that control is becoming increasingly out of reach.

## CHAPTER 7

✿

ROOM AFTER ROOM, office after office, Mr. Dade leads my team through the winding corridors of his life. And it's clear that this really is his life. Evidence of that is in the way he describes his products with a boyish giddiness that I haven't seen before. It's evident in the way he caresses the plans given to him by the engineers he introduces to us. Not as intimate as the caresses he shared with me earlier but loving nonetheless. I hear it in his easy laughter as we chat with his marketing team over a lunch meeting in the conference room. He knows the names of every employee and knows exactly how they fit into his operation. He recites their duties to us with the enthusiasm of a man reciting the stats of his favorite football players. My staff takes copious notes as do I. But even as my pen glides over my notepad my eyes continue to flicker up to him. Everything about him fascinates me. Even the way he moves as he leads us to our meeting with his other top executives.

"Keep in mind that this place is more than just a company to Robert and me," his VP says good-naturedly as he shakes my hand, then Asha's, then Taci's, and so on. Mr. Dade stands a step behind him, owning the room without saying a word. "Particularly for Robert," the man continues. "His house? That's Robert's home away from home. But this is where he really lives. *This* is his true home."

The statement takes me off guard. My career has always been a huge part of my identity. I'm driven by success, motivated by failure . . . but the company that employs me . . . was there ever a time when that place felt like home?

Mr. Dade laughs softly and shakes his head. "You're not much better, Will. If I'm here for seventy hours of a week, you're here for sixty-eight. It's why your wife hates me so much."

Their banter is good-natured and kind. More than that, it's brotherly. Tom Love, Nina, Dameon, were any of them family to me?

I watch as my team flashes plastic smiles and nods encouragingly at this man, Will, who is now rattling on about projections and corporate ambitions. I don't know these people. Yes, I know their strategies, their work ethic, their level of intelligence, but I don't know what makes them truly unique. I don't know how long that wedding ring has been on Taci's finger or who put it there. I don't know why there's just a tan line where Dameon's band used to be. I don't know what pictures are inside that Tiffany's locket that always hangs around Nina's neck.

And they don't know me. If they did, they'd spend more time wondering about why my hair is down.

The only one of them I've ever spent any time wondering about is Asha. She has a seductively dark energy, darker than her brown Indian eyes or thick black hair. Her dress is tighter than anything I would ever wear to the office but her conservative blue blazer makes it acceptable. Still, you have to wonder what happens when she leaves the office and takes off the blazer. Does she live another life?

I wonder, but if I'm right, it would be hypocritical for me to fault her for it.

Mr. Dade is looking at me now. I feel it without having to return his gaze. The man can slip inside of my head as easily as he slides inside of my body. He looks away, toward the VP's desk, not so unlike the desk I had been on just over an hour ago—eager, wet, his.

I cross my arms over my chest self-consciously. I'm in a room full of strangers; what would these strangers think of me if they knew? What would they think if they saw? Would they look at me the way Sonya looked at me?

Images dance inside my mind, too quick for me to catch or suppress. I see myself on that desk, with a room full of my coworkers.

I imagine them watching as he undresses me; I see their eyes follow the path of my silk blouse as it floats to the floor, the first item in a continued cascade of fabric until I'm clothed in nothing but the cool air and the warmth of Robert Dade's touch. I hear the soft murmurs of our audience as Robert explores my body with his, as he opens me up with his hands, his mouth. . . . I sense them moving closer as I succumb to every kiss, every stroke and caress. And they watch as Robert growls his desire and enters me. Beams of pleasure shoot through my body, then his; we rock with the impact as the room sighs and gasps. I'm completely exposed to all of them. And in that moment they understand me. All of me. Not just the ambitious businesswoman who advises the world's CEOs, not just the polite lady who knows which fork to use while dining at the city's five-star restaurants. Now they know that the same woman who can lead them to power and success, the same woman who can conquer every professional challenge, can unleash a delectable chaos when she is touched just the right way by just the right man. . . .

I shake myself out of it, stunned by the outrageousness of my fantasy and even more unnerved by the idea that the man who is now standing across the room from me could possibly be the right man. I glance over at him and I see that he's still looking at the desk. His eyes dart back and forth as if he's in REM sleep with open lids. He, too, is seeing things on that desk that aren't there.

That wasn't just my fantasy. Without sharing so much as a gesture of communication, we had shared the same sort of vision.

This man who I had met less than a week ago: I know him better than Nina, Asha, Dameon, or Taci. I know what he wants.

He wants me.

He sighs quietly. I'm the only one who notices the slight rise and fall of his chest. He walks across the room, idly, seemingly without purpose. But I know better. He crosses in front of me. No more than a foot separates us in that fleeting moment of passing as he moves to the window. It's the tiniest signal, a little gesture to let me know that he wants to be near me. What surprises me is that what I see in his face is more than desire; it's frustration, determination . . . maybe even confusion that matches my own. Will, still talking, still answering the questions of the team, glances in Robert's direction as he passively stares out the window. The deep lines that are etched across Will's forehead deepen further. This isn't Robert's normal behavior. He's reacting to some invisible element that Will can clearly sense but not feel.

*Ha, you just thought of him as "Robert" rather than "Mr. Dade."* My little devil relishes in my increasing familiarity with this man who has unleashed her. My angel just quietly shakes her head and thinks of Dave, the man who buys me roses and rubies.

"So your main focus is optimal positioning before your initial public offering?" This from Asha. She's looking at the VP, but I sense that she's particularly tuned in to Robert.

"Timing is everything," Robert says quietly. He turns away from the window and smiles at Asha but the smile has a hint of melancholy. "We need to project strength, and the vulnerabilities need to be buried so deep, no one will be able to dig them up for years. We can't have the big investors perceiving us one way and the smaller ones another. That would only lead to conspiracy theories about insider trading and unethical practices. We must be universally seen as a giant."

"Every company has their weaknesses," Asha counters. "If you seem too good to be true, investors won't believe in you."

"They will believe because they want us to live up to the myths they've already created for us," Robert explains. "Our job is only to help them see what they want to see and be who they want us to be."

I stare down at the hard, gleaming wood floor beneath my Italian heels. Yes, I know Robert Dade better than anyone else in this room. I understand him because, at least on some level, I understand myself.

# CHAPTER 8

❧

"H<small>E'S AN INTERESTING MAN</small>," Asha says as we walk to our cars. The rest of the team has parked in Maned Wolf's parking facility but I parked a few blocks away on the street. I didn't want anyone noting how early I had arrived. Asha apparently parked near me for reasons I can only guess at.

"He was so enthusiastic for the first half of the tour," she continues, "and then . . . something happened in that office."

The wind is picking up, lifting my hair, chilling my neck. "I didn't notice," I say. My car's in sight now. I reach for my keys.

"You did," Asha says, "and now you're denying it. I wonder why?"

I turn my profile to the wind so I can look at her. I hadn't expected her brazenness and I speculate on whether or not a confrontation is brewing. But she doesn't say any more until we reach my car and even then she only adds a cheerful good-bye as she continues her walk to her own vehicle.

Asha started at our firm only weeks before I arrived. All these years I had quietly admired her mystery. Only now does it occur to me that she might be dangerous.

I get in my car, grip the wheel, and breathe, waiting for my thoughts to catch up to my actions. Looking up at my reflection in the rearview mirror I touch the freckle that I forgot to cover up this morning. When did I become so careless? When did I become one of the lost?

But that's an easy question to answer. I got lost at the Venetian in Vegas.

If I want to find my way, I have to retrace my steps. Find that path I strayed from, rediscover the joy of being loyal to one man. If I can mentally retrace my steps, I can leave this insane detour behind.

At eight I'm meeting Dave for dinner, but that's well over three hours away.

I pick up my phone and call Simone.

WHEN I GET to Simone's condo, it's just short of five o'clock. She waves me in. On her beige couch are leopard-print throw pillows; on the walls, framed black-and-white photographs of women and men dancing, the sensuality of their movement caught in a split-second pose.

"Can I get you something to drink?" she asks. "Tea? Sparkling water?"

"Maybe a cocktail?"

She pauses a moment and looks out the window at the smoggy blue sky. She knows I rarely drink before sunset. It's a rule my mother taught me when I was young. "Drinking is for the moon," she would say as she poured her wine. "Darkness hides our smaller sins. But the sun isn't so forgiving. Light requires the innocence of sobriety."

But how innocent had I been when I drank water in Mr. Dade's waiting room, fixing the buttons on my shirt? How many sins have I already committed in the brightness of day? The rules are changing and I need a cocktail to deal.

Simone disappears into the kitchen and returns with two glasses, one for her, one for me. The clear liquid does have the look of chastity but the bite of something much better. I take several sips and lower myself onto her sofa. She places herself on the armrest by my side.

"You always tell me your secrets," I say. One of those leopard throw pillows presses against my back.

"And you never tell me any of yours," she replies lightly.

It's not true. I told Simone about my sister once. I told her about her blinding brilliance and her energy that was as powerful as it was frightening. But Simone didn't know those confessions were secrets. For her a secret was something no one knew, not something everyone was trying to forget.

"I never had any secrets before," I say, using her definition.

"Before." She says the word carefully, tasting its meaning. She curls a lock of her golden hair around her index finger like a ring. "You know, secrets and mysteries, they have . . . weight. I've enjoyed traveling light."

"What kind of weight are you carrying, Kasie?"

When I don't answer, she changes tack. "When did you start having secrets?"

"In Vegas," I whisper.

"I knew it!" Simone leans forward and places her glass on the coffee table with a triumphant thump. "You were different when you came back to the room—"

"I told you, I had a drink with a man in the bàr with glass walls."

Simone swats aside my words like irksome flies. "There was more." She gets up as if standing over me will force out my story a little faster. "When I left you at the blackjack table you were still that woman without secrets. And now?" She shrugs.

"Now I'm something different." I turn my focus inward, gathering up the courage to continue. "I betrayed him."

"Dave?"

"Yes, Dave. He's the only man I have the power to betray."

Simone turns out her left leg, shifting her weight forward to her toes. She looks like the immobile dancers on her wall. "It was more than a kiss?"

"Yes, more than a kiss."

A slow smile forms on her lips. "You slept with a stranger."

I look away.

"You did it! For just one night you were young!"

"No, I was irresponsible."

She arches a blond eyebrow. "There's a difference?"

I make a small gesture of concession to her point. "The thing is, he's not a stranger anymore."

And now both her eyebrows reach for new heights. "You're having an affair?"

I wince, disliking the word. It's common and ugly.

And it fits perfectly with my actions of the last week.

"He hired me to consult for his company. Even when I'm not talking to him"—I glance up at the photographs—"he dances around in my head. I've been doing things I never thought I would do. I think things I never thought I would think. I don't know who I am anymore."

"That's easy," Simone says, sitting by my side and slipping my two hands between hers. "You're a woman with secrets"—she studies my eyes, my lips, my hair—"and you wear them beautifully."

I pull away. "It's just my hair, I'm wearing it down."

"No, it's the secrets, giving you color, brightening your eyes . . . you look more . . . human somehow."

"I didn't look human before?"

"Always beautiful, but a bit statuesque. . . . Do you remember the statues we saw during our college trip to Florence? They were fantastic . . . but as grand as he is, I can't imagine making love to Michelangelo's *David*. Too hard, too cold, too . . . perfect."

I laugh into my glass. "I have never been perfect."

"But everyone thinks of you that way. It earns you admiration. . . . Now your inner human is showing and it sounds as if it's earning you something . . . warmer."

"I slept with him today."

"At his place or yours?"

"In his office . . . on his desk." I'm surprised that the admission makes me grin.

"Shut. Up."

I look up at her and for the briefest of moments I bask in her envy, allow myself to indulge in the gratification that comes from my newfound audacity.

"You made love on his desk," she repeats. "It sounds like a fantasy."

I shake my head. "That's the thing, I did it and then I fantasized about it *afterward.*"

"But it was better than a fantasy," Simone corrects. "It's a memory now, and it's yours to keep."

"No." I shake my head. "In my fantasy I . . . added things." I swallow the rest of the burning liquid and tell her my imaginings . . . the image of him entering me while my team looks on. The words are hard to get out but I need to tell someone whose mind might be unconventional enough to explain the shift in mine.

"I imagined myself having sex in front of the people I work with!" I finally exclaim. "It's a little extreme, don't you think?"

Simone stares at me for a moment and leans back against the opposite end of the couch. She stretches her long legs toward me so she now has the repose of a Roman who might be fed grapes by beautiful slaves.

"Remember when I used to date Jax?"

I nod. Jax flies into my head with his wavy dark hair and impertinent brown eyes.

"While I was with him I developed this fantasy. . . ."

" 'Developed a fantasy,' " I repeat. The phrase sounds so purposeful, as if she spent her nights laying out a structure for her future daydreams.

"I still indulge it from time to time. I'm lying out on his deck on one of his lawn chairs, flat on my stomach, wearing nothing but my bikini bottoms. I don't hear the knock on the door, or the footsteps of his friends." Her voice is slowing, lowering, changing texture. "He leads them out to the deck. . . . I try to get up with some bit of modesty, my arm covers my bare breasts as I walk to them, shake their hands. I lead them to the living room and they all take a seat. Jax asks me to get each one of them a beer from that little bar area of his. I lean down and take the beer out of the mini fridge, try to open it without revealing too much, but every once in a while they get a glimpse. I'm pouring an ice cold beer in a glass for each one of them and now I serve them . . . wearing almost nothing."

· "And then?"

"Jax asks me to sit next to him. He doesn't want me to get more clothes. He wants me to be there with him right now. And so I oblige. He's already turned the television on; it's the Lakers as it always is with him. . . ."

I can see by the glazed look of her eyes that she's not with me anymore. She's by Jax's side . . . wearing almost nothing.

"His hand falls to my leg and I shiver as it moves up and down . . . in front of all these men." She shudders and suddenly I'm self-conscious. I shouldn't be seeing this. I was not invited into this room full of men.

"Jax tells his friends that I am the most orgasmic woman he's ever been with. He tells them he can make me come with a touch."

I close my eyes and turn my head. I'm not seeing Simone anymore. I'm not seeing Jax. I'm seeing Robert Dade, his hands sliding higher and higher up my inner thigh.

"He hands one of them his phone, asks him to record us . . . he even invites his friends to record it on their own phones if they like, so they can see me climax whenever they want. I'll be in their pocket, exposed for their pleasure."

I suck in a short breath. This isn't my fantasy but I understand it. I feel the cameras on me, feel the stares.

"The bikini is only tied together with pretty little bows placed on each hip. He unties the knots, lets them see me, and then, as they watch, as they film me, he touches me, moving his finger slowly then faster and faster. . . . I can't control myself anymore. I'm writhing around in my seat as they watch. I let the fingers of one of his hands explore my depth as his other hand pulls my arm away from my breasts. And the men, they keep watching, keep filming closer and closer as I come. . . ."

Her fingers scratch against the fabric of the couch. I don't have to look at her to know that she is now completely lost in this reverie. But then so am I.

"One man comes closer, he sees everything, they all do and I know I shouldn't like it but I do. I know what Jax is doing is wrong, displaying me like this, touching me like this in front of all of them, but knowing that only makes it all more intense. And in front of their eyes, in front of their cameras I come . . . they watch and Jax makes me come . . . I come in front of a room full of men."

She and I open our eyes at the same time. "That's a fantasy," she says softly. "I would never do it. Not in front of Jax's friends . . . definitely not with all their cameras trained on me . . . but that's the joy of fantasy. There are no rules, no limits, no consequences, no judgment. Just irreproachable pleasure."

I sit with this for a moment, delighting in the idea that something so scandalous can be irreproachable when contained inside the mind. But then I am not so constrained.

"I slept with Robert Dade, more than once." Reluctantly I step out of the ethereal mood Simone has cloaked us in to acknowledge this reality. "There will be consequences."

"Yes," Simone agrees. "But sometimes consequences are good . . . even when they don't seem that way at first."

"I'm engaged to another man."

Her eyes fall to my hand. "No ring yet?"

"We found one. . . . Dave wants to see if he can get the jeweler to lower the price."

Simone's smile fades, the haze of recent pleasure slips away. "How many millions does Dave have in his trust fund? Four? And he's making, what . . . a hundred and twenty thousand a year at his firm?"

"About half that for the former, almost twice that for the latter," I say but quickly add, "He's conservative with his money. I like that about him. He's never reckless."

Simone brings herself into a more erect position, moving slowly like a woman approaching a potentially explosive subject. "Has he ever said the words, 'Will you marry me?'"

"That's not really the point—"

"Maybe not, but did he say them?"

I don't want to answer this question. It will paint Dave as cold, as cold as the statues Simone compared me to. But I came here for honest advice and so I force myself to give an honest answer.

"He said," I begin, falter, and then let the rest of the words spill out in a rush: "He said 'I think we should go ring shopping.'"

Again she nods, no judgment in her eyes, just thoughtfulness. "Did he talk about wedding dates?"

"We haven't gotten that far."

"Has he told his parents? Asked your father for permission?"

"Our parents don't know yet . . . but they all assume we'll get married eventually."

"You're not engaged."

"Simone—"

"Not by any definition of the word," she says, more forcefully now. "Maybe you will be, but you're not engaged now. Something is pulling you into this affair. Maybe it's your attraction to this Dade guy or *maybe* it's your fear of settling down with the wrong man."

"Dave and I have been together for six years. How could we have made it that long if we were so wrong together?"

"Maybe he was right for six years . . . but will he be right for the next sixty? Your subconscious is telling you something . . . and your body wants to explore your options. You're not engaged yet, Kasie. Find out what this is with your fantasy man. Allow yourself time to explore. If you don't . . . if you just marry Dave without even indulging your alternatives . . . you could end up divorced. Worse yet, you could end up being duty bound in a marriage to a man your subconscious tried to pull you away from."

"You're trying to provide me with excuses for the inexcusable."

"If you marry Dave, if you smile at him and tell him he's the only man you want . . . if you look him in the eyes and tell him you're sure, if you tell him those lies while standing at the altar . . . will *that* be excusable? If you care about him, doesn't he deserve a wife who's sure she's making the right decision in marrying him?"

"But I'm lying to him now."

"You're making sure," Simone says between sips of her cocktail. "You've been dating for six years, you're not married, you're *not* engaged, and you're not living together. If there was ever a time to explore . . . just to be sure, this is it. It's your last chance."

I know what she's saying is wrong. It's against every ethic I have. But her logic is so appealing, so sinfully freeing. That's the thing about sin; once you fully embrace it, you don't have to worry about doing what's right anymore. You can do whatever the hell you want.

It's a slippery slope that I sort of want to get off.

Sort of.

"And if I decide I don't want to do it that way?" I ask, again lifting my eyes to the quiet dancers. "If I decide I need to let Robert Dade go . . . Simone, how do I do *that*?"

She exhales and slams the rest of her drink. All traces of the Roman noble are gone as she morphs back into the quintessential modern girlfriend I need. "I haven't seen Jax in three years," she says, "but I still have the magnificently twisted fantasies he inspired. I keep them under my pillow, in my pocket, tucked inside my bra. They're always within easy reach. You can keep this Robert Dade or you can let him go. But the memories and the fantasies are yours forever. . . . There are some gifts that just can't be thrown away . . . even when we try."

# CHAPTER 9

THE ATMOSPHERE AT Scarpetta is light. High ceilings, neutral colors. Even after the sky's turned black, the dining room feels as if it's being filled with soft sunlight. It's what I need for this moment as I sit across from Dave. He's talking to me about work, about family, about rubies—did I know that you can no longer directly deposit income into Swiss bank accounts and expect to avoid American taxes? Did I know that his mother just got a new mare whose coat is the exact color of a patchy gray sky? Did I know that rubies were actually more expensive than diamonds?

The talk is light like the room. Among teasing reminders of the expense of his devotion, he shares bits and pieces of his world with me, never suspecting that I might be hiding bits and pieces of mine. Every word is spoken with the casual intimacy that comes with trust. And for a little while I forget that I can't be trusted at all.

But as the appetizers are replaced by entrées, and the entrées replaced with cappuccino and dessert, I find that acting is an exhausting hobby. How do those celebrities do it? How do they smile at their costars and recite their lines with all the assigned emotion without once giving away hints of who they really are, the person beneath the character, beneath the stardom, beneath the image? How do they have the energy to keep *that* person tidily under wraps? I stir a white line of sugar into the froth of the cappuccino. We've fallen into one of our silences. I used to love this moment, the moment when you can sit quietly with the person you've chosen to be with without exchanging a word. It's a showy testament to our comfort with each other. But I can no longer sit with silence. Silence is the pathway to my darkest thoughts that have no place in this light-filled room.

"Dave." I whisper his name, afraid of what I'm in danger of giving away. "You don't just work with men at your firm."

"Of course not," he confirms.

"Some of the other lawyers . . . or your clients . . . are they beautiful?"

The question takes him off guard. He dips a small spoon into our *panna cotta,* making a little nick in its smooth surface. "I don't pay attention to things like that."

It's an odd response. You don't have to pay attention to see beauty any more than you have to think about air to breathe.

"Have you ever been tempted?" I press.

"No." The word comes out quick and so hard, it's almost bruising.

The truth never comes to anyone that quickly. People usually consider the truth before speaking it. We think about how to best phrase it and roll it out slowly in hopes of weaving a good story. Lies come easier.

*No.* It's a lie he didn't need to tell. We're all tempted now and then, right? The only reason to lie is if you gave in to that temptation. I should know. I feel an odd twinge in my gut, quiet jealousy that has no right to be there.

"Maybe just once?" I say, testing the edges of the conversation, trying to find my way in. "Maybe you, just for a moment, noticed the way a woman's hair hung around her shoulders, noticed how a coworker occasionally licks her upper lip, maybe just once you thought about what it would be like to touch her hair or taste—"

"I said no." The lie is firmer this time. Not so much a bullet as a border fence. I can almost feel its unyielding surface as I try to press up against it.

"I'd forgive you," I say. My jealousy is growing but I like the way it feels, I like what it says about my feelings for Dave. "I want you . . . I want *us* to be human," I continue. "I don't want us to think of one another as statues anymore."

He looks up from the dessert, making eye contact for the first time since I veered us toward this precarious topic. "I have no idea what you're talking about."

"I'm talking about silks," I say. I place my hand on the table, inch it forward, but he makes no move to take it. "I'm talking about the little flaws in a ruby that make it unique. I know you're not perfect. You know I'm not perfect. I was just hoping that we could stop pretending that we are."

"I know you're not perfect."

It's meant to be a slap in the face, his acknowledgment of my imperfection without any acknowledgment of his own. But I don't feel the sting of his words. They touch me differently. I see the unintended compliment. And I see the evasion.

"I'd forgive you," I say again. "Even if it was more than a temptation. Even if it was a mistake."

"I don't make those kinds of mistakes." And then he softens. He finally reaches for my hand and gives it a quick squeeze before releasing it. "Maybe there have been times when I've been a *little* tempted. But I'd never act on those impulses. I'm better than that, Kasie. You know that, right?"

I flush. This time no insult is intended, but I feel his superiority. He's better than that . . . which means he's better than me.

"I'm buying you a ring," he continues when I take too long to answer. "I'm tying my life to yours. There are no temptations worth recalling, I promise."

I run my finger around the rim of my cappuccino cup. It's a pure white, like the tablecloth, like the roses Dave bought me. "There's something I need to talk to you about," I begin. And I know I'm going to do it. I'm going to say the words, bring my sins into this brightly lit room where we can both see them clearly.

"We're tying our lives together," he repeats, but now there's a pleading laced into the phrase. "We don't have to dwell on imperfect moments. Okay, maybe our past was a ruby." I look into his brown eyes. I see his silent request. "But that was the past. We don't have to talk about . . . what were they . . . silks? Our future won't have those. Our future can have the clarity of a perfect diamond."

The future never has any clarity. At best it's like that mare his mother just paid a fortune for—it's colored like a patchy gray sky. But as usual Dave isn't talking about the way things are. He's talking about the way he wants to see them.

And isn't that what we all do? We choose our religion, our politics, our philosophies, and we see the world in a way that fits within those chosen confines. And if certain glaring facts don't fit neatly into our belief systems, we just ignore them or see them differently. We *make* them fit even if it means we have to squeeze them into completely unnatural shapes.

Dave is a man with secrets. I don't know if they haunt him or not but I know he doesn't want to look at them, which means that maybe, just maybe I don't have to look at mine.

I smile and take a bite of the *panna cotta*. It feels smooth on my tongue and it tastes pure.

I'm beginning to understand why so many people like the simplicity of diamonds.

# CHAPTER 10

❁

I T'S MORNING. THE office visit with Robert, the fantasies with Simone, the strange dinner with Dave: it's all in my rearview mirror. Just a big tangled mess of crazy that I'm ready to leave behind. Today is new and I'm feeling steadier on my feet. Yesterday I wasn't prepared for everything that was thrown at me. . . . I wasn't prepared for my responses. Today I'm ready for anything . . . and now that I know the full extent of what that means, I'm a little excited, too.

I mentally go over my calendar. Asha's putting together a report analyzing Maned Wolf's recent foreign investments. Nina and Dameon have domestic while Taci's focus is on the effectiveness of recent marketing and PR campaigns. People are in awe of Maned Wolf but it's not at all clear that they trust it. I'm supposed to be looking at the big picture, trying to put the pieces together so I can give Robert Dade a list of recommendations of what should be done before going public and a timeline in which to do it in. Of course they're just recommendations. The only worth they have is measured by the trust Robert puts in me.

Robert Dade is not in awe of me, but I do think he trusts me.

Just the thought of him is delicious. Two weeks ago I didn't know what it felt like . . . to be pressed against a wall, to be propped up on a desk, to be made love to on the floor of the Venetian. Two days ago I didn't have the mental image of me, in his office, on my knees. . . .

Two weeks ago, the length of a lifetime, I didn't know that you could feel completely vulnerable and completely powerful all at once.

The guilt creeps in, numbing some of the pleasure of my reminiscence. My angel and devil are at war again. The devil has framed my memories and is holding them up for my inspection, knowing that I want to indulge and massage them . . . and massage the man who made me feel these things.

But my angel . . . my angel is screaming. She wants the images to burn.

But shouldn't it be the devil who advocates the burning of memories? Roles are getting reversed. What's a woman supposed to do when her angel starts using her devil's tools?

What's a sinner supposed to do when all her devil asks her to do is face the truth, both of her actions and the way she feels about them?

Because the truth is that I don't regret any of it. I just *want* to regret it. I can't confess my sins in the spirit of contrition. Absolution is completely out of reach.

*Last night Dave lied about never being tempted. Was there more he was lying about? Did his lies free me to explore my possibilities?*

I shake the thought out of my head. "I'll just do my job," I say aloud. Surely that isn't wrong.

I go to my bedroom and open up my closet. A sea of dark skirts and trousers and light-colored blouses greets me. I'm instantly bored. Why don't I ever buy anything more lively? Who says I have to dress like a prep school librarian?

Impatiently I push aside garment after garment until I find the suit Simone gave me for my birthday last year. She had dragged me to her favorite boutique and thrust me into a dressing room before throwing a pair of gray pants and a matching blazer after me. The color felt natural but the fit was different. The pants clung a little closer than I was accustomed to. The curves of my legs, my hips . . . it was all there. And the jacket cinched at the waist, emphasizing my figure. The top had been too much, tight, black, sheer; when I stepped out into the store to look at myself in the three-way mirror, I realized exactly how sheer. The blazer prevented me from being truly indecent. And yet I did feel a *little* exposed as I stared at my reflection. I remember thinking I looked autocratic, lustful . . . maybe even a little dangerous. A man came out of the stockroom, no more than twenty. I could actually feel his struggle as he pulled his eyes away from me. He had wanted to look longer. He had wanted to examine me with more than his eyes.

And for just a moment I had been tempted to take off the blazer. Would he have been able to turn his eyes away then? How would it have felt to have a stranger see me like that?

Well, now I knew the answer to that question, didn't I?

I had never worn it outside of that store. I had told Simone I wouldn't even as she handed the cashier her credit card.

But I would wear it today.

I found a top that was a little more appropriate, a black silk camisole. It was cut high enough to avoid any accusations of promiscuity yet the fabric against my skin had a sumptuous feel.

And then I take that sheer top, the one I know I can never wear, and fold it up in some tissue paper and put it in my briefcase. I don't know why. I just want it near me.

I stare at the woman in the mirror, her hair loose around her shoulders, commanding, sensual.

"I want to know you," I say to her.

And in response she smiles.

AT THE OFFICE the stares are only a little less intense than the looks I had gotten in Vegas. Tom Love raises an eyebrow as I pass him in the hall and flashes me an approving smile.

"Go get 'em," he murmurs.

The directive excites me. Today I feel ready to take on the world.

But when I get to my office, it's not the world that's waiting for me, but a message from Dave's secretary asking me to call him. Dave always calls me directly. He never has his secretary do it unless there's something he needs to tell me that he doesn't think I'll like.

I don't sit, but stand in front of my desk as I dial the number. I don't bother with the middleman, but call his cell directly.

"Kasie, I have a meeting in five minutes—" Dave begins but I cut him off.

"Then tell me what you need to say quickly."

I don't mean for the words to sound so harsh but for once I'm not interested in smoothing things over. I see the red flag being waved in the distance and I'm ready for the fight.

It's *almost* arousing.

"I spoke with that saleswoman today . . . the one with silver-streaked hair from that jewelry store—"

"The one who showed us the ruby."

"Yes," he says hesitantly. "They're not being very flexible about the price."

I don't say anything. I stare down at my bare ring finger. We can afford the ruby. We can afford to pay for its alluring imperfections.

"And I was thinking," he continues, "I was thinking of you . . . and then I thought of this absolutely beautiful estate ring in the window of a store by my work. . . . I stopped by there right as they opened this morning. It's really perfect, Kasie. So I went ahead and put a deposit down on it so they'll hold it until you can come and see it. It's more *us* than the other ring anyway."

My bare finger curls into my palm, leading my other fingers to do the same as I slowly make a fist.

"It's a diamond—"

"But I'm not moved by diamonds, Dave," I interrupt. "If we can't get the ruby ring we saw, surely there are others . . ."

"Trust me, Kasie, this diamond ring . . . it's different. I mentioned that it's an estate piece, right? It's classic and elegant but it's also original, completely one of a kind. Just like you."

*Just like me.* I stare down at the suit I'm wearing. Would Dave even recognize me today? He thinks I'm a concealed weapon in an Hermès bag. He thinks I'm a bouquet of white roses.

He thinks I'm diamonds even after I stood before him and flat out told him I'm rubies.

"Look, I gotta get into this meeting. I'll call you tonight, okay?

We'll meet up after work tomorrow and I'll show you the ring. You don't really want a ruby for an engagement ring. Trust me, you'll end up regretting it."

I hang up the phone without another word.

He doesn't know me.

But then this morning . . . that woman in the mirror, the sensual power broker, the stranger who sleeps with strangers, the woman who scares me and intrigues me . . . how *could* Dave know her? *I* don't know her.

I run my fingers over my lapel. It's not a smooth fabric, but it's not unpleasant to the touch, either. It's thick and a little stiff, what you might expect from a man's jacket, but its cut is so decidedly feminine. It reminded me of a philosophy course I took in college. The professor had explained the true nature of yin and yang. Yin and yang weren't dualities but simply complementary opposites: the feminine and the masculine, the passive and the active, the unseen and the manifest, the moon and the sun. And it all had to tie together within a greater whole to be part of a compelling and vitalizing system.

I giggle at the idea that my suit could be part of something both compelling and vitalizing.

But I stop laughing when I think of myself in those same terms. Those early Taoist philosophers, they didn't think of the dark being bad and the light being good. It had nothing to do with morality at all. They just thought of them as two essential parts of a whole.

I wonder what it feels like to be truly whole. Is that what's happening to me?

Because while I don't feel quite as guilty as I should, I do feel a hell of a lot stronger than I ever have before.

Well, all right then.

I CALL MY TEAM into my office and get their updates, tell them what leads to follow and which bits of information can be brushed aside. They take notes, drink my words, accept my instructions without challenge. Only Asha hesitates, her own calculations slowing down her absorption of mine. At least that's my perception. She's studying me too intently; her comments seem to swirl around whatever it is she's really thinking. She is most definitely a threat. I'm sure of that now.

But she's the one who is truly in danger. She doesn't know who I am. I'm sensual, I'm commanding, I've been touched by a stranger.

It's only later in the afternoon that I remember that this isn't the woman I'm supposed to be. This isn't the picture I had in mind when I kissed Dave good night yesterday, pleading exhaustion.

And I haven't spoken to Robert today. We haven't so much as exchanged an e-mail and yet he's with me, luring me in new directions, providing me with a springboard for new temptations.

I haven't spoken to Robert Dade today but it doesn't matter.

My devil is winning.

❀

# CHAPTER 11

I WORK LATE, WHICH is hardly unusual for me. I'm the last one in the office. Even Tom Love left more than an hour ago. But I'm feeling energized. Blame it on the suit . . . or the sex. I laugh to myself. Yes, it's more likely the sex than the suit.

In my hands and covering my desk are statistics, facts, and numbers. I'm using them as building blocks to craft Robert's professional dreams.

And if I succeed, what then? What if I manage to chart a path for Maned Wolf's complete market domination? What if I gift wrap that particular treasure map and lay it at Robert's feet? Would he be amazed? Would he worship me?

But that's not what I want. I like the way Robert sees me. There's a gritty realism to his affections. Our attraction to each other is almost brutal . . . and yet our lovemaking never has anything to do with distress or affliction.

What I want is for him to thank me, with his eyes, with his mouth, with his tongue. I want him on his knees, not in worship, but in service.

These are the thoughts I'm having when my phone rings.

It's him. As usual, his timing is . . . opportune.

"Where are you?" he asks.

"I'm at work, playing with numbers . . . for you."

"Oh, I doubt your motives are completely altruistic." His voice sounds gravelly through our shaky connection. It has so much texture, I feel like I should be able to see it.

"No," I admit, "I do take some pleasure in it."

"There is nothing more spectacular than the vision of you in a state of pleasure."

"Now, now, Mr. Dade, is that an attempt at some kind of sexual innuendo?"

There's a pause on the phone. I know his thoughts. He hadn't expected me to be this playful. I told him I would never let him touch me again.

But I'm rubies. Not diamonds. I'm not sure of what I want anymore and my awareness . . . my *acceptance* of that uncertainty feels like a triumph.

And triumph makes me playful.

"You're done with work for the day." It's not a question.

"Am I?"

"Meet me out front."

The line goes dead.

Without hesitation I stack the papers filled with numbers into a pile. It's not as organized as it should be but a little carelessness feels appropriate.

I take off my blazer and open my briefcase. Inside is the sheer shirt.

I take off my camisole and then my bra before putting on the top.

My heart is pounding in my ears as I shrug back into the blazer. There is no pretense this time. I know what I'm going to do. I don't know if it's going to be the last time or not. I don't care. My body wants to explore and this time I don't feel the need to deny it.

I make my way down to the street and it's only a matter of minutes before Robert Dade pulls up in a silver Alfa Romeo 8C Spider. Its sleek lines and elegant power fit perfectly with my mood. He doesn't say anything as he gets out of the car and opens my door for me. It's not until I'm in the passenger seat that I hear him say, "I like your suit," before slamming the door.

It's been ages since I've been in a sports car and I've never been in one like this. The seats hug me like a lover while at the same time keeping my posture erect, ready to react to whatever adventures the vehicle might bring me to. Everything is silver or black. No bright colors are necessary for this beautiful beast to be the center of attention.

Robert Dade gets in beside me.

"Where are we going?" I ask.

Robert turns to me, the key in the ignition, his hand on the leather-cloaked steering wheel, the engine rumbling. "To my place."

I answer with a smile, then shift my eyes to the road as we roar away from the curb.

I've never asked Robert where he lives. I assumed Hollywood Hills, Santa Monica, perhaps somewhere among the mansions of Beverly Hills. But he lives in West Hollywood, on a hill, above the hustle and bustle of Sunset on a windy little street no one would think of traveling if they didn't know someone who lived there. The homes are impressive yet far short of astounding. But then the dark hides the more subtle elements of their design, so it's hard for me to make judgments.

And the truth is that they could never hold my attention, not even if they were each five stories high with gold-plated awnings. That honor now belongs exclusively to the man by my side. He's been driving the car in sports mode the whole way, gently adding pressure to the paddle shifters occasionally to take fuller control of the ride. I sense his thoughts are racing much faster than the car. He wants me here but he doesn't trust it. I sense it in his refusal to turn his head in my direction, as if I might be scared away with a look. I can tell by the way he holds on to his silence, as if one wrong word might awaken me to my previous declarations.

But I'm not changing my mind and as he opens the automatic gates with the touch of a button, I reach over and let my hand slide over his thigh and then up, letting him know my intentions, my desires, my willingness to go forward.

He breathes out of clenched teeth as if it's all he can do to keep himself from grabbing me, pulling me out of my seat, and taking me right here in the street, before we even have a chance to get to his intimate little driveway.

But like the car, he restrains his power and pulls us delicately into the driveway, then into the open garage waiting for us.

There is no other car there, though there is a motorcycle. It's not chic or dignified like the Spider. There're no special chrome accessories or add-ons to speak of. The seat has seen better days. Mud clings to its narrow black tires.

I love it. I love that this man with his exquisite car has a motorcycle that emanates nothing but rugged and gritty masculinity. Again I look at Robert's hands: beautiful, rough, strong but at times so very gentle.

Yin and yang. And as he puts his hands on my face, as he holds me still, as our eyes lock and my own hand coaxes out another primitive and powerful reaction, I feel our wholeness.

"I don't often invite people over," he says. "I don't entertain. But ever since Vegas, I've wanted to bring you here."

"Why?" I ask. "You've had me in your hotel room, your office, on the screen of your computer . . . why do you need me here?"

"Because," he says, then pauses as he searches for an answer. "I've been inside your walls," he says slowly, "and this is the only way I can think of to bring you more fully inside of mine."

I'm unsure of how to respond, so I wait for the kiss I know is coming. It starts soft but then quickly becomes more demanding—his tongue sliding against mine. He holds my head still and I press my breasts forward, trying to bring myself closer to him. My hand toys with him. I have no patience. I want him, every part of him, now. His erection is full and complete and I wonder if anyone has ever made love in a Spider.

But Robert pulls away. He removes my hand as he takes a breath to calm himself and bring his body back under his control.

Well, partially under his control. His body, like mine, aches to explore.

He gets out of the car and I wait as he comes around to open my door. Again we fall into silence as we step into the driveway. The house doesn't look like much. I can see only a wall and a door that looks like it leads to . . . maybe a small closed-in front yard? Maybe nothing at all.

But when he opens it, I am greeted with everything. The entire city is beyond this wall. A view that stretches to the beaches of Santa Monica. We stand on top of a hill, feeling a thousand miles away from the lights that decorate the vast city beneath us. But, of course, we're not so far. Only a two-minute drive to Sunset, where the hot dog restaurants complement a few strategically placed nightclubs.

I feel his fingers dance up and down the back of my neck, sending shocks of heat through my nervous system. The house that goes with this private front yard is to my right. It's built onto the slope of the hill, which is why it's virtually invisible from the street that leads to it. Stilt beams hold it up, fragile-looking things that have the strength of Greek gods.

I let him lead me through the front door; the home has walls of windows and I imagine what it must look like in the daylight: bright sunshine illuminating dark wood. But for now the only light is the light of the city. He finds a dimmer switch and gives me enough illumination to see the room's design a bit more clearly. The place is hardly immaculate but it feels comfortable. There's bold and abstract artwork on his walls.

One painting in particular draws me in. I can't say for sure if it's of lovers or even if the figures depicted are fully human. But it has the essence of unbridled passion. Two beings hold on to each other as a swirling mass of color and utter confusion appears to try to tear them apart. But they're stronger than the anarchy; their desire is more brilliant than the colors.

Robert steps up behind me, presses against me. I can feel his strength; I can feel his desire pressing into my back.

I stare at the painting as he unbuttons my blazer. The might of the painting is in the two embracing figures. That's what matters.

The rest is nothing.

My blazer falls to the floor.

Slowly he turns me around and takes me in. My nipples are hard and strain against the sheer, tight fabric of my top. He traces the outline of my breasts.

"You're magnificent," he says.

I slip out of my heels. I have to crane my neck to meet his eyes but I don't mind. My hand reaches for the button of my pants and with no effort I pull them off. The only part of my suit that I'm wearing now is this scandalously sheer shirt.

"Look at me," I say quietly.

He steps back, his eyes slowly traveling up my legs, to my panties, to my exposed breasts, to my neck and my lips, and finally my eyes before they reverse their journey on the way down.

"Do you see who I am?" I ask. "Or do you just see what you want?"

I see a flash of understanding as he brings his gaze back up to meet mine. "I see a woman who can be incredibly authoritative and a woman who is exposed. I see that you are as forceful as you are tender, absolutely brilliant, and just a little bit naïve."

"What else?"

"I see . . . I see that you have the courage to face your fears. You're a little bit scared right now, aren't you?"

I answer with only the slightest nod.

"What are you scared of, Kasie?"

I tremble even as I smile. "You tell me."

"All right." He takes a step forward and caresses my body with his stare one more time. "You're scared of the part of yourself you have begun to unleash."

"Partly."

"You're scared of how much you want me. Maybe you're scared because right now I can do almost anything I want to you without your issuing a single protest because you know that the things I want to do are the things you want to happen."

I swallow, hard. But I won't look away from him. He takes another step and runs his hand up my inner thigh until he presses against my panties, only the thinnest fabric between his fingers and my clit. I know this dance now but I still gasp as his fingers begin to move.

"I see who you are, Kasie," he says. "And it's the only thing I want to see."

My legs are shaking and I reach forward and grab his shirt, holding on to him out of both necessity and passion.

"Take me to your bedroom," I whisper as the shivers take over every part of my body. "I want to make love to you on your flame-colored bed."

His hand moves away and in a moment I'm up in his arms, being carried like a princess down a discreetly placed flight of stairs. The room he leads me to is massive, easily as big as the living room above us. I see his desk with his computer. I see the expensive chair.

In the center of it all is the bed, which I feel as he lowers me onto it. I feel it against my skin as he removes my panties. But when he takes off his shirt, his jeans, and all the rest . . . well then I can only feel him . . . the pressure of his muscles as they press down on top of me. His lips as they devour my neck. I pull off the sheer top. Every inch of my skin must touch his. The flames are not coming from the bed but from inside me. My hand goes to his erection and I feel my own potency as it twitches in my hand. Every ridge is familiar to me now. I know how to touch it to make him go crazy and I toy with him, enjoying the staccato nature of each breath he takes. But I don't object when he pulls away, lowering his mouth to my very core. I shake as his tongue plunges deep inside of me, tickling me, making me wetter than I have ever been before. I can't keep quiet. I moan and cry out as I grab on to the comforter beneath my arching back, almost pulling away, almost afraid of the intensity of what he's making me feel. But he holds my hips still, refusing to let me go, using his thumb to pull my skin taut around my clit so he can lick and taste every hidden corner, forcing me to experience what I'm afraid of and what I long for.

The orgasm is so strong, I think it's going to split me apart. I have no control. I don't even have the ability to want the control I've lost. I don't recognize the guttural sounds that are coming out of my mouth. I have no power to resist when he comes back up, hovering over me, taking a long, hard look at my trembling naked body before kissing me, his taste mingling with my own. I feel his erection pressing up against me but he won't enter. He's teasing me and my desire is driving me absolutely wild. I struggle to push myself down, struggle to force him inside but he grabs me by the arms and holds me in place. I have to wait, and the wanting, the lust, the impatience . . . it's bringing the intensity to heights I hadn't even known it could reach.

"Please," I say, arching my back, trying to touch my breasts to his chest. "Please."

"You are the only woman I know who is as sexy when she unapologetically takes what she wants as she is when she pleads for release."

I can't engage in conversation right now. Can't remark on the peculiar compliment. All I can do is listen to my body. The flames are consuming me.

"Please," I say again. "I need you."

And now he's the one who groans and in an instant he pushes into me. I cry out, unable to do anything but experience what he's giving me. Every thrust brings on new sensations. He releases my arms, and my hands run up and down his back, around his neck, through his hair, then down to his ass. I have all of him but I want more.

And he can do what he wants to me because what he wants to do is what I want to be done.

And as he presses deeper and deeper inside of me, another orgasm comes. And this time he comes with me. Our cries intermingle into one primal chorus.

And as he relaxes, as I feel the complete weight of him on top of me, I think of the yin and the yang.

And in that moment I truly feel whole.

# CHAPTER 12

T EN, FIFTEEN, PERHAPS even twenty minutes pass. Or is it years? It's hard to tell. I've lost all sense of time and space. Reality was left tucked away somewhere in my office. This moment, lying in Robert's bed, is not part of the space-time continuum. He's beside me; his eyelids are half-mast as he stares up at nothing. Our breathing has only now become steady. He seems mellow, even peaceful, nothing like the man who held me down as he pushed inside of me, his desire as fierce and unrestrained as my own. No, the man by my side is quiet, tender, and maybe a little vulnerable.

Tentatively I let my hand move across his chest. It's a subdued gesture that speaks of a different kind of intimacy.

He smiles a lazy smile, his eyes still staring up toward the high ceiling. "I'm actually craving a cigarette right now," he says.

The comment takes me off guard. "You smoke?"

"A long time ago, yes. I haven't thought about smoking for ages but . . . a cigarette after sex is calming, it brings you back to earth, and after *that*, I don't know if I'll be able to find my way to earth again without at least one to navigate me."

"I hate cigarettes. I hate how the scent of the smoke lingers in people's hair and clings to their clothes for days. My first lover was a smoker. I'll never be with a man who smokes again."

"Damn, okay," he says, the mischievous twinkle returning to his eyes. "How do you feel about cigars?"

I take my pillow and hit him over the head with it. He laughs and tries to fend me off but I straddle him and hit him again and again as he playfully begs for mercy. Finally, I toss aside the pillow and grin down at him. His hair is ruffled and he looks so young despite his salt-and-pepper hair . . . almost innocent.

He's observing me, too, drinking me in. "You're so free right now. You're beautiful when you're free."

I feel a twinge. I'm not free. Not yet. I haven't officially ended things with Dave.

But I don't want to think about that right now. I want to think about this man underneath me with his mussed hair and easy smile.

I lean over and kiss his lips. "You see, if you smoked, I wouldn't be doing this."

"That is the best anti-smoking campaign message I've ever heard in my life," he replies.

"Yes, well the American Cancer Society can have their tactics of fear and guilt. Me?" I lean over and kiss him again, letting it last a little longer, making it just a little more intimate. "I believe in positive reinforcement."

Robert's hands move up to my waist as I continue to kiss him, his mouth, his chin, his neck. The sweat from our most recent lovemaking still clings to our skin but I feel him harden against me as my path of kisses continues south.

What I'm feeling . . . it's unfamiliar—carefree, playful, light. . . . I feel light.

God, have I ever felt light before?

My mouth reaches his hips and I feel his hands in my hair, I feel the radiance of his anticipation.

He said he saw who I was. He said that's the only thing he wants to see.

I let my tongue flick across the tip of his erection. His breathing is no longer steady.

Yes, Robert Dade does make me feel powerful, vulnerable, light . . . and sometimes a little scared.

But I don't feel scared now.

My tongue travels to the base and then slowly up, over each

ridge. He is at full attention. Looking at him I'm amazed that I was able to welcome the full length of him into my body without even a bit of discomfort.

But there is never any pain when I'm with Robert. Even when he holds me down, when he pulls my hair, presses me into a wall, even when he tells me what I'm not ready to hear, there's no real pain.

I take him more fully into my mouth, my hand wrapping around the base of his cock while my other hand touches the tender flesh behind it. He groans as I move up and down, tasting him, knowing him.

Nothing about this feels wrong. No distress or conflict. The pleasure doesn't leave any space for regrets.

I love his taste; I love what I can do to him. I can literally feel him throbbing against my tongue. He leans forward, pulls me up, but I stop him from flipping me over.

"No, no, Mr. Dade, this is my ride now. I make the rules."

"Is that so?" he breathes, his smile appreciative, caring.

"Mmm, yes. Now, would you like to have sex with me again?"

"God yes."

"Really? That's funny, because I don't think I heard the magic word."

And now his smile widens to a full grin even as his chest heaves with desire. "Please."

"Please?" I repeat. I'm straddling him again, my hands pressing down on his hard chest, my own nakedness completely uncovered. "I was looking for 'abracadabra' but I suppose 'please' will suffice." And as he laughs I lower myself onto him.

And then the laughing stops . . . but not the smiles. As I ride him slowly then faster, his hands on my waist, my head thrown back, his eyes on my body, the smiles stay until the passion is so strong that our mouths stop working that way.

But the smile inside me never falters.

And I know without a doubt that his inner smile matches mine.

• • •

HE WANTS ME to stay but I'm not ready for that. Too much un-
finished business. For years I've loved the idea of belonging to a
relationship. I liked the rules, cherished the confines. But now I'm
tickled with thoughts of freedom. I know I have to end things with
Dave yet I'm not ready to be Robert Dade's official anything. I want
to ease my way into the relationship the way you might ease yourself into a cold swimming pool. Start with getting your feet wet,
wade in up to your waist, wait until the water feels a little less shocking, and then throw yourself in.

I'm wading in, but I'm not ready to fully immerse myself yet.

I get dressed while he watches me. He wants to pull me to him
but instead he reluctantly pulls on a pair of jeans and a T-shirt. My
eyes wander away from him long enough to take in a few more details of the room. There's the expensive chair that he had sat in while
he watched me remove my robe from miles away.

My eyes move past that to the floor-to-ceiling windows. The city
of LA is always the most beautiful at night. It's as if the stars that
can't be seen in the sky have fallen to the ground and paved the
streets with their brilliance. I give Robert a sideways glance. "Have
you always lived like this?"

"Like what?"

"Um, in affluence? In totally hedonistic opulence? Have you always driven cars with values higher than the GDP of third world
countries?"

He laughs and shakes his head no. My eyes keep moving; this
time it's a framed photo of a couple that catches my attention. The
frame is a little out of place. It's made of an inexpensive wood that's
on the rustic side. I pick it up and see a woman who looks like she
might be Latin . . . Mexican, Argentinean, maybe even Brazilian . . .
I can't quite tell. I can see that she must have been beautiful at some
point. She has that thick, dark hair and a bone structure that plastic
surgeons wish they could re-create. But even in this old photo—
more than twenty years old, easily—you can see the dark circles.
You can see the slight sag in her shoulders and you can see how the

man by her side, his skin as white as vanilla ice cream, is helping to hold her up. But he's tired, too. Look at the way his skin folds as he looks up at the camera. Look at the heavy smile as if the effort of saying cheese is almost too much.

"My parents," Robert says as he comes up behind me.

"They look like they love each other," I say, putting down the frame.

"They did."

I hear the change of tense and understand the meaning. "I'm sorry."

"It's all right," he says with a sigh, leaning against the dresser. "It's been a long time."

"May I ask what they died of?"

"Oh, various things." His voice is suddenly weary, like his father's smile. "But mostly it was misplaced trust and disappointment. When taken in excess, disappointment can kill."

I don't know how to move forward in this conversation so I wait to see if he is going to volunteer more. When he doesn't, I give him a nod and turn away from the photo, find my shoes, one by the corner of the bed, the other kicked clear across the room.

"How about you?" he asks as I fasten the straps around my ankle. "Are your parents still around?"

"Alive and well," I say, scanning the room for my purse.

"Any siblings?"

I pretend not to hear him. "I can't find my purse. I did bring it inside, didn't I?"

He studies me for a moment. He knows I'm purposely ignoring his question but senses that this is not the time to push me. After all, I've already gone out on a limb tonight. I'm so far outside of my comfort zone, I might as well be in Mozambique.

And I hadn't planned on ending up in Mozambique. I don't know the language or the laws and I'm completely unfamiliar with the currency . . . but, God, is it ever beautiful here.

# CHAPTER 13

THE NEXT DAY flies by. I can barely keep track of the hours, minutes, or seconds as they tumble into one another and roll past me. My team brings me their research, outlines of reports, ideas, concerns, and observations—all so I can weave them together into one beautifully cohesive presentation. It's not an easy task and under different circumstances, it might have stressed me. But it doesn't. I can't be touched. The whirling around me is just buzz. It's the confusion in Robert's painting and I'm the lover, the strong one who can't be thrown off balance. I study the profit margins of Maned Wolf's European operations and I feel his kisses gently brushing against the back of my neck. I study the projections of the cyber securities division and feel him take my hand and press it into the mattress beneath us. I read the plans for new products and I smell his skin, feel his breath, sense his presence.

I'm obsessed.

And when Barbara buzzes my phone to tell me that Dave is calling, I almost refuse to take it. A hundred excuses play through my mind. I'm in a meeting, I'm out to lunch, I'm on the other line . . . or maybe I just don't want to deal with the pain I'm about to inflict.

"Hi, how you doing?" His voice sounds apologetic, caring. Four benign little words but it's all it takes to open that little door in my heart and usher in the guilt.

"I'm a little busy right now," I say vaguely. Maybe there's a way to get him to break up with me.

"I'm sorry, I don't want to interrupt your day. But look, I know you're upset with me right now and . . . well, if we could just talk it out. Tonight? At Ma Poulette?"

"I think I might need to work late." If I could just convince him I'm not worth the effort. How do you get a man to give up on you after six years of commitment?

My cowardice is overflowing.

"Please, Kasie . . . just . . . I really need to see you tonight. You know the restaurant, right? The new one in Santa Monica? I'll pick you up at seven thirty?"

Every statement is a question. He's trying to appease and smooth the road ahead of us.

I hesitate as my thoughts twist themselves into shapes even I can't make heads or tails of. I'm not on the road Dave is smoothing out anymore. The ground under my feet is loose gravel. There's a sense of impermanence to it. And if I get hurt along the way, I don't know if there will be anyone around to help me find my way back. This is the option I'm choosing. I'm pretty sure it's the right choice for me but I can't figure out why that is, so how can I explain it to Dave?

And do I really have to?

My cowardice has a strength that my earlier euphoria can't quite match. The only thing that is clear for me is that I owe this man something. At the absolute least, I owe him dinner.

"I'll see you at seven thirty," I say.

Perhaps by then I'll be brave again. . . .

God, I hope so.

THE DAY LOSES the surreal quality it had before. Suddenly I'm in it, rushed, critical, and as impatient as the second hand of the clock, always rushing to get to its next place. After a marathon of meetings, Barbara tells me that Simone called; she said it was important. But Simone's idea of important usually involves a sale at Bebe. Besides, there's no time to call her back. I rush home and get ready to break a man's heart.

When I answer the door of my home for Dave at seven twenty-five, I'm wearing a white knee-length dress, sleeveless but not too low cut. It would befit any politician's wife. My hair is back up; pearls wrapped in gold decorate my earlobes.

"You're perfect," Dave says as he offers me his arm.

Ah, that word again. I'm beginning to really hate it.

But I don't say that as he opens the door of his Mercedes for me. It's a nice car and it makes the statement Dave wants it to make, one of unobtrusive wealth and comfort. I think about the rush of adrenaline I felt as Robert's Alfa Romeo rumbled beneath me, remember the thrill as it accelerated through the murky LA night.

Do those thrills last? Would I want them to?

But those aren't the questions I'm supposed to be considering. I need to tell Dave the truth. Maybe over dinner, or before it, or after—maybe in the car on the way home. What is the etiquette for betrayal?

The guilt in my heart has a voracious appetite. It's feeding off the leftovers of last night's happiness.

One foot in front of another. That's all. If I pace myself, everything will be fine. I will take care of this one grotesque task and then, in time, Dave will heal and I will feel carefree again, like I did in Robert's arms. Yes, fine, I've broken rules, Dave's rules, my parents' rules, my own rules . . . but rules are made to be broken.

That was my sister's favorite cliché . . . until she decided that rules should never be made at all.

More thoughts of my sister tug at the edges of my mind but I won't give them the attention they're demanding.

I cast a sideways glance at Dave. He looks good. I think I detect the faintest hint of cologne, which is unusual for him. He's been working through the same bottle of Polo Blue for the last five years.

He's wearing the sports coat I bought him from Brooks Brothers, Italian linen dyed the color of a warm cashmere tan. It suits him beautifully.

And for the first time I notice the way he's gripping the steering wheel as if it's the only thing keeping him tethered to the earth. Is he nervous? Does he sense the shift in me?

I study his expression but for once I can't read it. His eyes are glued to the road, his lips pressed together in something that could be determination, could be apprehension.

I give up and try to relax into the plush leather seats. My phone vibrates in my purse but I ignore it. I'm afraid of how I'll react if it's him. Afraid of what Dave will see in my face.

One step at a time.

I'VE NEVER BEEN to Ma Poulette before but I don't like the name. It's a silly pun, playing off the French word for "hen" and one of their terms of endearment. But English speakers will fail to understand it and French speakers will fail to be amused by it.

Still, the interior is nice. Dimmed lighting complements a bucolic charm. There's an exposed brick wall here, wooden accents there. Dave gives his name and the hostess looks down at her list. She hesitates for a moment, her finger touching what I assume is our reservation, and when she finally looks up, her eyes linger on mine for just a moment too long and her smile is wistful.

Something's up. This isn't just a simple dinner.

Suddenly I want to get out of the restaurant. But I can't make myself do it. That's the funny thing about cowardice. People think it makes you run away and hide but it's more likely to be a facilitator of something darker. It's the emotion that allows you to be passively led to places and fates you would otherwise reject.

And so I am led—the hostess in front, Dave's hand on my arm guiding me. The patrons we pass blur together as we're led to a closed door . . . another dining room, I'm told. Something more intimate.

One step at a time, I think as I listen to my heels click against the hard floor.

The hostess opens the door. As we step in, I see them all: his parents, my parents, a few college friends, one of the partners from Dave's firm, his godfather, Dylan Freeland . . . who is also the cofounder of my firm. Inexplicably, Asha is a few steps behind him. And then there's Simone; her eyes are wide and reflect the fear I'm feeling. She shakes her head and I know what she wishes she could say: *I called. I tried to warn you. You chose the wrong time to stop listening.*

"I wanted everyone we love to be here for this," Dave says softly as all these people smile at us, clutching their own loved ones' hands, waiting for the magical moment.

Dave lowers himself to one knee. I can't move, can't even look at him. My gaze is glued to my feet. One step at a time.

He reaches into that sports coat, the coat I bought him, the coat that will now have more significance than I ever meant it to have. I won't look. I squeeze my eyes closed. I don't want this diamond. I don't want to be Dave's white rose.

"Kasie," he says. His voice is confident, insistent. Reluctantly I open my eyes.

It's my ruby. The very ruby Dave and I had looked at, with all its delectable silks and passionate red glow.

"Kasie," he says again.

He got me a ruby. Something inside me softens.

"Did you hear me?" he asks, a slight touch of nervousness in his tone now. I look up, see the approving smiles of my parents, see the encouragement in the eyes of our friends.

"I asked you to marry me," he says. I think he's said it a few times now. I had lost myself in the ruby, in the cowardice, in the simple ease of being led to a once-rejected fate.

"You bought me a ruby," I say, my voice sounds so quiet, so re-moved. "You're asking me to marry you."

Our friends, our coworkers, our family . . . they're all represented here in this room. Some came from far away. They all expect to hear the same answer.

I meet Dave's eyes and smile wide, for him, for our guests.

"You're asking me to marry you," I say one more time, "and my answer is yes."

# CHAPTER 14

❀

C HAOS.

I don't know how else to describe it. The cheers that erupt are so out of sync with my emotions. Every handshake and tearful congratulations frightens me. This should have been a private moment between two people: me and Dave. Even in the best of circumstances I would have wanted it that way.

These are not the best of circumstances.

I see Simone standing in the corner, her normal effervescence nowhere to be seen. She and I share the secret, my secret, and it hurts her as it demolishes me.

My mother's arms are around my neck, her tears against my cheek. "We're so proud of you!"

"I didn't do anything, Mom," I protest. "This dinner, the proposal, it's all Dave."

"And who chose Dave? You!" She laughs. "Honestly, I look at you and the choices you make, and I know we made good choices with you." She pulls away, looks me in the eye. "This is good," she says. "*We* are good."

I hear what's not being said. The life I lead—at least the one the world knows of—is a vindication. It excuses a failure that none of us talk about. My rational and responsible choices are an announcement to the universe that anything that happened with Melody wasn't my parents' fault. It was her, not them. After all, look at Kasie! Kasie is perfect.

My mother takes my hand in hers as my father shadows her, smiling his approval.

"An odd selection," she says, looking at the ring. "Why not a diamond?"

"It's not what she wanted," Dave answers, pulling himself away from his colleagues.

"It's not, but you said you wouldn't offer me what I wanted," I remind him. "Just yesterday you refused to hear me."

Dave grows serious for a moment and then with a gentle excuse to my parents pulls me aside. "Up until tonight I haven't handled our engagement well."

"No," I agree. "Neither have I." I flush as I think of what an enormous understatement that is.

"I never actually proposed. I didn't say the words. I took all the surprise out of it."

I glance around the room. "Surprise" can mean so many things. There's the surprise of fortune and then there's the surprise of miscalculation.

"I wanted to correct that," he explains. "So I led you to believe I wasn't getting you this ring so you would be all the more excited when I did. I brought our family here to surprise you to make up for not surprising you with the proposal itself. Otherwise, to propose after the fact . . . after we had already been ring shopping . . ." He shrugs. "It would have been a formality. I wanted to give you romance."

I see his point. I get it. I look back at my parents. They're hugging. My traditionally stoic father is as teary as my mother.

They're proud of me. They're proud of themselves. I'm living the life they want me to live.

Because really, somebody has to.


MORE HANDSHAKES, MORE toasts, the champagne is flowing. . . . I can't grasp the moment. Dylan Freeland approaches. He embraces

Dave and gives me a more formal kiss on the cheek. "I trust you'll take care of this young man," he says. "He's like a son to me."

The grin on my face feels ugly and misshapen. I don't like this meeting of worlds. It's an unsettling reminder that my personal life is loosely tied to my professional prospects. The tightrope I'm walking isn't as strong as it's supposed to be and only now do I fully realize that there is no net.

I excuse myself. I need air. I press my way through the crowd. Every step I take brings another congratulations from a new voice. I quicken my pace. I feel nauseous and dizzy as I look for the door, the exit that will lead me out of my nightmare.

I finally reach a patio but it's not empty. Asha stands there, a thin cigarette in her hand. "We're not supposed to smoke," Asha says in lieu of a greeting. "Not even on the patio." She takes a long drag and lets the smoke out through the side of her mouth. "But sometimes you just *have* to break the rules. Don't you agree?"

I stand on the other side of the patio putting as much distance as I can between me and the smoke that carries the promise of cancer.

"I'm surprised you're here," I say.

She shrugs. "Dave called the office. He wasn't sure if there was anyone you were close to there, anyone at all whom he should invite. Funny he should have to ask. Anyway, I told him there wasn't . . . just me."

"We're not close."

"No, but I was curious."

I try to maintain my focus. She's wearing a tight-fitting black dress with a cutout back revealing a half circle of smooth brown skin. We're like cowboys in a Western except we wear our white and black hats in the form of dresses and we've traded our guns for other deadly but less tangible weapons.

But then perhaps my white hat should be colored light gray.

"Do you have a problem with me?" I ask her. I'm not sure I care about the answer. This night is filled with demons more frightening than her.

"No one has a problem with *you*, Kasie," Asha says before inhaling again. "You were given your job as a gift from a grateful lover and now you'll be married to both. You're blessed."

"No one gave me my job," I counter. "I pulled a string to get an interview, that's all."

"True." She takes an empty glass and drops the cigarette inside. The smoke curls up and rises out, making the stemware into something of a witch's cauldron. "You're very good at your job, too. Just be careful. Because the problem with strings is that if you keep pulling them, things unravel."

IT'S ANOTHER HALF HOUR before Simone catches up with me. She pulls me into the bathroom and checks for feet under the stalls. "What are you doing?" she hisses once our privacy is ensured.

"I couldn't reject him in front of everyone. Our family, our friends, his colleagues . . . I couldn't."

Simone breathes out her frustration. "I underestimated Dave," she mutters more to herself than to me.

"He can be very romantic."

Simone looks up sharply, studies my expression, and seems unhappy with what she finds there.

"So what now?" she asks, her tone harsh, demanding. "You'll reject him tonight? Tomorrow?"

"I don't know."

"After the witnesses have gone and you've reclaimed the stage?"

I look down at the ruby. I see my parents' faces. I think about the exuberance outside of this restroom. I think of Dave and his desire to do things right.

Once upon a time I had wanted to do things right, too. I had believed in black and white, right and wrong, good and bad. The truth is, I'm not really a Taoist. I just learned enough about the religion to pass my college exam. I learned enough to romanticize the philosophy when it's convenient. I've never had a comfortable friendship with ambiguity.

"We are good," my mother said, but she didn't know how wrong she was. I've gagged and bound the angel on my shoulder and given my devil my mind and body as a playground.

Can I go back? Do I even want to?

"I don't know," I say. It's an answer to both Simone's questions and my own. I tried taking one step at a time but now I don't know what direction I'm supposed to walk in. So I stand in the bathroom, weighed down by secrets and jewelry, looking for bread crumbs to lead me back to a path that doesn't terrify me.

The bathroom door opens. It's Ellis, the woman who I went to school with during my undergrad years, the woman who took me to the luncheon where I first met Dave. We rarely see each other anymore . . . maybe three or four times a year for a reunion lunch, but tonight she treats me like I'm her best friend in the world.

"I'm so happy for you!" she gushes as she brushes past Simone. "I always tell everyone I know that you and Dave are the perfect couple."

And as she embraces me, I hear Simone mutter to herself, "Perfect, like the statues of Italy."


DAVE DRIVES ME HOME. My ring needs to be resized. It squeezes a bit too tightly.

I've given my answer but have yet to make my decision. My world is upside down and backward like that. And it's my fault. I can no more blame Robert Dade for the complexities in my life than I can blame a fierce storm for knocking down a poorly made building.

"Are you happy?" he asks, and I nod and smile because I don't know what else to do.

He pulls into my driveway and turns to me. "May I come in for a nightcap?"

The word takes me off guard. It's old-fashioned and formal, the kind of thing a man asks for with an ironic smile on a third date. But Dave has been with me for six years, touched my bare skin more frequently than my favorite perfume has. Tonight he pledged to spend his life with me. He's past the point of having to drop hints to charm his way into my home.

Still, I don't question it. So much has been strange between us lately, maybe this new twist in his vocabulary is simply in keeping with our new awkwardness. So I lead him in and as he watches from the doorway of my kitchen, I select a sweet port from my small collection of wines and two fragile glasses for us to drink from.

But before I can open the bottle, he puts his hand on mine. It's a light touch and yet . . . it holds a different kind of weight.

"It's been a while, Kasie."

I stare down at the unopened bottle.

"Ten days since we've made love," he continues.

"Ah, you've been counting," I tease but there's a tremor in my voice. Has it really been that long? Why haven't I noticed?

Because it hasn't been ten days for me. It hasn't even been a day. In the wee hours of the morning I had been with Robert Dade.

Dave moves his hand to my wrist, his fingers pressing gently down on the little vein that gives away my speeding pulse.

How can I do this? How can I be with two men within twenty-four hours? How can I call myself anything other than a slut after that?

I focus my eyes on the port, not even allowing myself to blink, as if even the slightest movement of my lids might produce tears.

"Let me pour us something to drink?" I ask meekly. My guilt has made me timid. It makes me blush and tremble.

Dave sees all this, he feels my racing pulse . . . but he reads it differently. He leans over and tenderly touches his lips to mine. It's a soft kiss, loving, and as he quietly opens my lips with his tongue, I yield to him, raising my arms and wrapping them around his neck as he pulls me closer. Some of my fear subsides. This feels simple, comfortable, secure. God, do I crave a sense of security right now.

And I like the way Dave holds me, like I'm precious and worthy of admiration.

It's so dissimilar from the uncontrolled passion that shoots from Robert's fingertips. I remember him biting my lip, holding my arms above my head while tenderly kissing my neck, pressing me up against the wall as I welcomed him inside me. . . .

I pull away from Dave. "A drink," I say weakly. "I want us to have a drink together first."

Dave's confusion is clear but it's the hurt I see that tears at my heart. I lean forward and place a closed-mouth kiss on his jawline. "Just one drink first. I want you to taste this port."

He nods and walks out of my kitchen.

How many times have I seen Dave leave a room? It never bothered me before. But now the sight of his retreating back hits me like an ominous omen. I have to take three deep breaths before I can steady my hands enough to effectively dislodge the cork.

I find him on my sofa. He doesn't look at me as I hand him his glass. The wine is such a deep red it's almost black and now even that innocuous detail seems telling. The room is suddenly filled with signs and every single one of them is alarming.

Another deep breath, a few more silent words of reason to help me pull it together.

Dave finally raises his eyes, his pain sharpening into something that resembles an accusation. "Are you still mad at me?" he asks.

I stare back, blankly.

"I shouldn't have left you that night," he continues. "The night you straddled my lap and asked me to . . ." His voices fades off and he looks away again. "I apologized with roses. But if that's not enough, just tell me the price for moving past it. Because this"—he vaguely gestures with his hand at everything and nothing—"this is hell."

"I'm not charging you for a miscommunication. I'm not angry."

"But something's off," Dave observes. "When I put my arm around your shoulders, you don't lean into me the way you used to. It used to be that when I reached for your hand, your palm would just naturally melt against mine. Now it's as if our palms don't fit together the way they used to. I asked you to marry me tonight in front of everyone in the world who matters to us. Is it too much to ask that we celebrate and . . ." Again, his voice fades.

I almost don't recognize this man. I've never seen him miserable. I did this to him.

"Dave," I say his name carefully and sit by his side. But I don't reach for him. Instead I sip the rich sweet notes of wine and try to find an explanation that will help rather than destroy.

"Did I scare you that night?" he asks. "Please tell me I didn't. I want to make you feel safe. It's my job. Please tell me I didn't mess up something so fundamental. Please."

"No, you make me feel safe," I say quickly. "Always." I study the contents of my glass before taking another sip.

"Then what is it?"

I don't answer right away. I'm busy gathering up my scattered bits of courage. This is the moment. I know that. It's now that I need to tell him.

"Is it your sister?"

The non sequitur jars me, throws me completely off balance.

"You know we're a week away from her birthday. Melody would have been thirty-seven, right?"

How on earth did we get *here*, from talking about the troubles in our relationship to talking about Melody? She has no place in this exchange.

"She died two days after her twenty-second birthday, right? That means we're approaching the fifteenth anniversary of her death."

I don't respond. The conversation we had been engaged in ripped at my gut but *this* conversation is untenable. I know why Dave and I are having problems; that's on me. But to try to blame this new distance between us on Melody would be worse than anything I have done so far. And it would be worse than all her sins combined.

"You were thirteen when she died," Dave is speaking slowly as he tries to remember the details of a story that I so rarely tell. "It was a suicide."

"*No,*" I spit out the word vehemently. "It was an accidental overdose." I say this as if that isn't a kind of suicide. Cocaine, ecstasy, tequila, men: my sister used them all to feed her self-destruction. Every line, shot, and brutal crush was no better than a violent slash of a knife.

And yet she said she loved them all. Her love of excess and reck-lessness was only matched by her hatred of structure and tedious commitments.

She accidentally overdosed. My mother said she brought it on herself.

Dave doesn't say anything. He doesn't want this to be a mono-logue. He had hoped I would hold his hand. He wants me to once again lean into his embrace and tell him he knows me better than anyone else.

But this was not a reminder that will lead to that kind of affec-tion. At the moment it's hard for me to think of him at all because, *at the moment*, I'm not his fiancée. I don't even know him. We've never met.

At the moment I'm nine years old and I'm staring out my bed-room window at a girl named Melody who can't stop dancing. She's dancing in the front yard to music no one else can hear.

It will be the last time I will ever see her. She came home to ask our parents for money and when they refused to open the door, refused to even acknowledge her presence, she had danced.

But I'm not going to talk about those things to Dave or anyone else. Instead I drag myself back to the present and pull my lips up into a small, practiced smile before I wrap my hand around his knee and stare up into his eyes. "This isn't about her," I say. "It's not even about us. It's about me being ridiculous."

"Ridiculous?" he repeats as if struggling to find a way to apply the word to me.

"You were right to walk out on me that night," I continue. "I wasn't acting like myself. Wedding jitters maybe. But it wasn't right." I lean into him, the way I used to, the way he wants me to. "There's no percentage in being crazy or out of control."

He brushes my cheek with the back of his hand. "You're not like any woman I've ever met in my life. You're my Kasie, and you're perfect. I said you weren't that night we ate at Scarpetta's. I lied."

"No, that was the truth. But I'm sure there have been other, nicer lies that you've told me over the years. We all lie, occasionally," I say. "And we make mistakes."

"I suppose so," he says uncertainly.

"Maybe what differentiates the good from the bad is that only some of us . . . when we lie, when we make a mistake . . . maybe some of us can pull it together and . . . and fix things."

Again I feel the tears well up as he kisses my cheek but this time I let a few slip from the corners of my eyes and I don't protest as he tastes them.

*You're not like any woman I've ever met in my life.*

His words . . . and I like them. I like the idea of being completely unique.

It means that I'm nothing like her at all.

His kisses have traveled up to my forehead and then down again to my mouth. I don't object as he takes the port glass out of my hand and places it on the coaster resting on the coffee table. I don't pull away as he unzips my dress, pulls it off my shoulders, cups my breasts. I don't challenge him as he cautiously removes my dress entirely and folds it over the arm of a chair along with his own sports coat and shirt. I don't say no as he lowers me down on that sofa and lies on top of me, careful, oh so careful not to hurt me, bruise me, cause me even a moment of discomfort. He cherishes me. I feel it as he brushes his fingers over my stomach. I feel it when he kisses my hair; I feel it in the warmth of his smile. This is where I'm supposed to be. These are the rules I have chosen for my life. I had no right to offer myself to Robert Dade. He has no place in my personal life or in my thoughts.

And as Dave kisses my forehead, I try to ignore the images, the memories . . . I try to forget that only this morning I had lost control.

# CHAPTER 15

DAVE STAYS OVER. Of course he does. It's hardly the first time. It's just that we haven't been spending the night together for a few weeks. I've forgotten the feel of it. His gentle snores are jarring to me now.

I turn on my side and look at him. His mouth is slack as he sleeps.

Dave and I had been going out for a week before he kissed me, three months before we made love. He said he didn't want to rush me, that he knew I wasn't that kind of girl. I didn't have the heart to tell him that I hadn't waited half that time with the men before him. My first had been when I was twenty. I had been so desperate to get rid of my virginity, I hadn't cared that he smelled of cigarettes, that he spoke in clichés, that he barely looked at me as he forced his way in. My second lover had been a smart, tall, beautiful lacrosse player with roaming hands and a roving eye. The pain of the breakup had been sharp but fleeting. There had been plenty of Kleenex left in the box once I was done crying.

But Dave is different. He respects me. He thinks I'm precious. He honors me with outdated romantic notions.

And to top it all off he helped me get the job I wanted.

Dave has given me so much, it makes sense that he'll be my first forever, the first thing in my life that will be more than a stage.

That constancy has value, right? Certainly more value than the illicit secrets that weave themselves into my dreams at night. I can never make love to Robert again. Never. I will force him out of my life.

Now if I could only force him out of my head.

• • •

IT'S ONLY 7:00 A.M. and I'm handing Dave his lunch and a travel mug full of a deep-bodied coffee before his unusually early conference call. He's surprised; I've never made him lunch to take to the office before. It's a Norman Rockwell kind of move, which is good. I need to incorporate a little Norman Rockwell morality into my life.

He kisses me on the forehead and I feel the completeness of his affection. As I watch him leave, I feel something else, too, something that springs from deep within me. I want it to be love.

But it feels a lot like obligation.

I was in Dave's debt before, what with the job and his frequent kindnesses. But now that I've betrayed him, I owe him so much more, more than gifts or favors. I owe him happiness.

Almost an hour later, while I'm dressing for work, my phone rings and Robert's assistant's number pops up.

No, that's wrong. It's Mr. Dade again. I have to find a way to turn him back into a stranger.

"Miss Fitzgerald?" Sonya's inquisitive voice melts through the phone. "Sorry to call so early."

"It's fine." I sit on the edge of the bed wearing nothing but a matching bra and panties with the phone pressed to my ear. I feel exposed, which is silly. Sonya can't see me. But she does know things about me that others don't and I'm reminded of this when she tells me in a tone that is a little too intimate that Mr. Dade is requesting a meeting away from his office.

"13900 Tahiti Way, in Marina del Rey," she says. There's something about this address that thrills her. I can tell by the way she whispers the numbers.

"What's there?" I keep my own tone flat, emotionless. I want to wipe her memory away. . . . Has she imagined me with him? Has she imagined me with her? Did I call out when Robert let his fingers slide over my clit, when he kissed my neck, my breasts? . . .

Did she hear me when I lost control?

"Oh, I just figured you two had already worked out the details. . . . I didn't ask specifically which part of the marina. . . . I mean, it's not my business."

And with that comment I know that she heard everything, imagined everything; to her I'm not just an associate of Mr. Dade's. I'm the woman he fucked on his desk and it doesn't matter what tone I use, what outfits I wear . . . she'll always know me for my indiscretions.

I hate her for it.

I hang up the phone without another word. But then nothing else needed to be said. He knows I'll come. It's my job, my addiction, my temptation . . . it doesn't really matter if it's lust, ambition, or just plain ol' curiosity that'll get me there.

All that matters is that he knows I'll come.

A trickle of foreboding works its way down my spine. I know where my place is now. It's with Dave. I had my last hurrah with Robert Dade.

I'll go to the meeting for the sake of ambition and in spite of the lust, which I will have to repress. I'll go to the meeting to say good-bye.

I select a Theory suit, not as provocative as the clothes I wore the day he last saw me but significantly more stylish than my regular garb. I pair it with a satin blouse that could pass as menswear if it wasn't for the fabric. He will not shake me.

Or if he does, he won't see it.

It's not until I'm in the car, plugging the address into the navigation, that Sonya's words come back to me. The marina?

For a split second I consider removing the keys from the ignition. Why would I meet this man at a marina? The location is too soft, too romantic, whispers of too many fantasies of just sailing away from it all.

But he knows I'll come and so I turn the key.

I PULL INTO the parking lot lining the peninsula. Moorings holding pleasure craft are surrounded by high-rise condos and hotels. It's fantasy meets urban reality—an appropriate metaphor for my current predicament. But I can't have both. I have to give up the fantasy.

My cell buzzes with a new text message. It's from him. He simply tells me where to park, where to walk, which gates to open. The text is eerily well timed. It's as if he has a sixth sense when it comes to me.

I study his words again. He's instructing me. Just as he instructed me that one night in Vegas . . . just as he had instructed me when he had watched me through his computer screen. But perhaps these instructions are more benign?

No, not benign. Nothing about Robert Dade is benign. And neither is my eagerness to follow his directives.

As I walk away from my car to the gate that he told me to walk through, the Ritz-Carlton to my left, the ocean to my right, I find myself wondering what he'll ask me to do next.

It's hot; the jacket comes off. Even satin isn't right for this setting but it'll have to do. I follow the steps and go down the dock, passing sailboats, restaurants, tourists, and palm trees until I find the place where I'm supposed to turn . . . toward the horizon. And I see him, standing on top of a small yacht, wearing another cheap T-shirt, charcoal gray this time so it matches his hair; his jeans are faded. . . . I can't tell if they're old or simply designed to look that way. Doesn't matter.

I walk to him, just as he asked, but stop when I'm still several feet away from the boat.

"Are we meeting in the yacht club?" I ask from the dock.

"No, come aboard."

I'm pained by how much I want to heed his request. I want to let him take me on yet another adventure. I want to follow my devil's lead.

But I shake my head. "There are plenty of restaurants for us to have our lunch meeting."

He studies me for a moment. "Is everything all right?"

It's a good question. Maybe it isn't right now but surely it will be if I just stay strong. I press my lips together and give a stiff nod.

"If I come down there, I will not be a gentleman."

He's teasing but the threat scares me anyway. Everything has changed. I am now officially engaged and everyone, my friends, my parents, my colleagues, they all know it. If Robert does anything to give me away, the consequences will coat my world with humiliation. I can't even let myself think about it.

"I could turn around and leave right now," I say. The wind picks up and lifts my hair with a silent force. I wore it down again and I'm getting used to the way it feels when it moves. I'm getting used to the way Mr. Dade's words move me, too, and that's a problem. I will myself to turn away from him. "I'm not here for that, Mr. Dade."

"Ah, so we're back to formalities." There's a question there. He doesn't understand the degree of the shift. He thinks I've just gotten a little scared . . . or that maybe I'm teasing him back.

"I think . . . for a lot of reasons, we should strive for a more . . . professional decorum. I . . . I'm afraid I let things get a little too familiar. It won't happen again."

He pauses, studies me. "I assume you've heard the story of the boy who cries wolf?" he asks, deadpan. "You realize that you don't have a lot of credibility in this area."

"I'm serious this time."

"As opposed to last time, when you were just joking?"

"I'm not getting on the boat."

I roll back my shoulders and meet his gaze. I wait for the anger, the hurt, the bewilderment that must be coming. But his poker face is flawless. I can't predict what hand is about to be played. . . .

Until he smiles—it's the smile I get when I realize I'm playing chess against a worthy adversary. It's the smile of someone who knows he's about to win against the best.

"If I come down there, Miss Fitzgerald, I will kiss you"—he raises his hand as I start to protest—"and I won't stop there. I will touch you the way you want me to touch you."

"Quiet!" I hiss.

I look around self-consciously. I don't see anyone on the nearby boats but that doesn't mean anything. We're in public, his voice is strong, I can't count on the ocean breeze carrying his every word out to sea.

"You do want that, don't you, Kasie?" he says, his voice keeping the same steady volume—the tenor low, insistent, confident. "You want me to touch you right here, in full daylight so that everyone in that bistro only a stone's throw away would see you. You want the audience. You want me to pull off the mask in front of everyone."

"I can't get on the boat," I say, but now it's my voice that's getting weaker. He has no right to say these things to me . . . and I have no right to want them.

But the fantasies are tiptoeing into my consciousness. On the desk in front of my team, on the couch in front of his friends . . . walking through a casino wearing a Herve Leger dress, everyone looking at me, seeing me as the woman I'm not supposed to be.

"Come aboard," he says, softer, kinder. "Nothing will happen that you don't want to happen. Remember, all you have to do is say no."

Hadn't I said no? Hadn't I said *I can't get on the boat*? Wasn't *can't* the same as *no*?

But it wasn't. *Can't* spoke to what I was capable of doing and what I wasn't. *No* wasn't about capabilities; it was about desire.

I had no desire to say no.

Carefully, I find my way onto the boat.

He meets me, kisses me innocently on the cheek, but his hand slips between us and I gasp as he applies a slight pressure to the one spot that will always give me away.

"I didn't come for that," I say, stepping away.

"No, you came to work." He walks over to a bottle of Sauvignon Blanc that's been chilling in a bucket. "You would never come here just because you want me to touch you again, although you do. You wouldn't come just because you feel alive when you're with me. You wouldn't come because I'm the only one you can be your true self with. But for work? Yes, for work you'll always come."

He pours a glass of the white wine and offers it to me. The drink reminds me of Dave. I shake my head.

"I'm not my true self when I'm with you. I don't know who I am."

"That's the problem," he says, taking the wine for himself. It's the first thing he hasn't tried to push on me since I arrived. "You don't know who you are. You even had me describe you *to* you last time we met and you *still* can't figure it out. Normally that would be enough to make me lose interest. Self-awareness is sexy. Delusions are not."

The sun is at my back and yet I reach into my bag and pull out my sunglasses. I sense that I'm going to need as many layers of protection as possible. "You think I'm delusional?"

"At times. It doesn't suit you."

"If it's such a turnoff, maybe you should back the fuck off."

Robert Dade bursts into laughter. It's an easy laugh with just a touch of opulence. It softens my edges and makes me want to step toward him rather than away.

"Like I said, I would. But the thing is," and with this it's he who takes a step forward, "the woman who you really are . . . the one who you keep so tightly under wraps, the woman who is only allowed out when she is touched a certain way, made to feel certain things . . . that woman is so damn compelling . . . I can't seem to turn away."

*Turn around and leave. Tell him that the engagement has been announced.*

But I don't say a word. My voice was carried off with the wind.

"I want that woman," he says again, taking another step. "And not just in the bedroom. I want to know what she's like over a candlelight dinner. I want to see her on the beach. I want to know what it would feel like to walk beside her talking about the thoughts you never let her share."

"I'm getting married."

"To a man you don't love."

"He's the man I want."

"What a seductive little liar you are."

I lift my chin and strike him with a defiant glare. A flash of respect . . . I see it in his eyes . . . but then maybe it's always there. Respect for me in those hazel eyes of his . . . but then it's *not* for me. It's for this woman he thinks I'm hiding from him. A woman I don't want to be.

"I want Dave Beasley."

"Do you?" His voice is gentle now but it's impossible to miss the hint of sarcasm. "What exactly do you want him to do to you?"

"Don't be crude."

"Do you want him to keep you in line?"

I don't answer. Robert is very close now. If he takes one more step forward, we'll be touching.

But he doesn't. Instead he circles me the same way he did in that Venetian hotel room.

"Do you want him to suppress your true nature? Keep you on the leash you made for yourself?"

"Shut up." My whispered tone contradicts the meaning of the words. I feel him behind me although he still isn't touching me.

"Do you want him to confine you? Are you afraid you won't be able to do that job all by yourself?"

His breath tickles my ear as he moves to my right. I wait for him to complete the circle but he doesn't. He just stands there at my side, facing me. If I lean in, just a little, the top of my head will touch his chin. My shoulder will touch his chest; my hand, his thigh.

I continue to stare straight ahead, thankful for my dark glasses. They mute the colors that are just a little too bright today.

"Look at my hand," I say quietly.

He pauses, perplexed by what seems like an odd request. But then he sees it, lifts it up so the light hits it just so.

"He bought me a ruby," I say as he studies the stone. "Not a diamond ring, a ruby."

"Whose idea was that?"

Again I don't answer.

"It was yours." He says the words with the tone of pleasant surprise. And now he does reach out. He moves my hair away from my face. I don't turn to look at him.

"You let the woman you're trying to destroy pick your ring."

"This isn't *Sybil*. There is only one me."

"Oh I know . . . and it's you, the only true you, that I want. Not the facade who smiles sweetly and pretends that she's some white rose . . . delicate, bland, weak."

"Did you call me here for a business meeting, Mr. Dade?"

"I want to tear that facade away." He lifts his hands and clutches at the air around my body as if he could literally pull away some invisible force field. "I want to throw it in the ocean where you'll never be able to get your hands on it again. I don't want you on that leash, Kasie. I don't want to confine you, I don't want to control you. I want to set you free."

"Says the man who practically blackmailed me into boarding this boat."

"Ah, yes. But that's different. For now it seems I have to practically blackmail you to do what you want to do. I want you to do those things on your own. I want you to indulge your desires the way you indulge your ambition."

"Don't be stupid."

"If you did, you would be unstoppable."

"I love him."

He hesitates. He hadn't seen that coming.

"I love him," I say, louder this time.

"Ah," he murmurs. "That lie is less alluring."

"You had *sex* with me." My voice is even, cold. "You know my body, you even know how to make it sing . . . but that's just chemistry. Dave knows my past, he knows how I think. . . . You know my body, Mr. Dade. Dave knows *me*."

"I doubt that."

"He knows where I come from."

"I'm sure. Just as I'm sure he knows where *he* wants you to go."

"No. He wants what I want. Not because he's trying to accommodate me but because *we* really do want the same things. That's what makes us compatible. You're the one pushing me. What you and I have . . . it's just . . . just . . ."

"Chemistry," Robert finishes for me.

He steps away, takes a seat on one of his deck chairs. He drinks his wine a little too fast. Is he nervous? It's not an emotion I've ever associated with him before.

"Do you know what chemistry is?" he asks.

I shrug but in my mind I answer the question.

Chemistry is the sparks that ignite inside me when Mr. Dade's fingers brush against my neck. It's the quickening of my pulse when he kisses that same spot, tasting my salt, licking that delicate patch of skin. It's the throbbing I feel between my legs when his hands travel from my shoulders to my breasts, to my stomach . . . lower. . . .

"It's the study of atomic matter," Robert says, pulling me out of my thoughts. "It's the description of how different chemical elements react. But more important it's the study of the makeup of those elements."

"I think I should go."

"In order for two elements to react to each other, they have to meet," he continues. "They quickly latch on to and, in some truly primitive way, recognize the details of the other element that will lead to a chemical reaction."

"I have no idea what you're getting at."

"We wouldn't react to each other the way we do if we weren't able to sense something fundamental about each other's nature. When I saw you . . . when I touched you, I sensed that there was something in the very makeup of who you are that would cause me to react in ways that I simply wouldn't, *couldn't* react to others. We're baking soda and vinegar, Diet Coke and Mentos—"

"Scotch and soda?"

He smiles at my unexpected contribution to his monologue.

"I don't know that Scotch and soda actually cause a chemical reaction."

"Maybe not," I admit. But now I'm thinking about the cool, mild sting of the Scotch when he had dabbed it between my legs, I remember the taste of it on his tongue.

Chemistry.

"I love him," I say again. The sun is getting higher in the sky. I feel it beating on my shoulders. A small bead of sweat rolls down from my hairline. *It's the sun I'm reacting to.* I say the words to myself. *It's the sun . . . not the heat.*

"I almost believe you," he says. For a moment I think he's hearing my thoughts as well as my words.

"You should believe me." I brace myself, find my courage, and tear my eyes away from the horizon to meet his. "I have never lied to you."

"But you lie to him."

"I love him," I explain. "Everyone lies to the people they love. They're the only ones worth the effort."

"Then you must love yourself very much."

Something catches in my throat. I don't know if it's a giggle or a scream.

"Does Dave love this freckle as much as I do?" He stands again, puts his finger on the freckle that rests above the scoop neckline of my shirt, right where my breast begins to swell.

"Do you shiver when his hands slide to your waist, when his hands slip underneath the silky fabric of your top?" His hands are on my waist; his thumbs slide underneath the bottom of my shirt so that they now press into my flesh.

"Does he make you tremble when he pulls you to him?" His hands move to the small of my back and apply just enough pressure to move me forward, into him. "When he lifts you up." I'm in his arms; my feet are lifted from the ground as I cling to him. "When he takes you—" He's carrying me down into the cabin, through a kitchen, a living room, into a bedroom. . . .

And just as he predicted, I shiver.

He has left his words on the deck of his yacht. In the cabin there is just the sound of each one of our breaths mingling together to create a pressing but jagged rhythm. As he lowers me onto the bed, I forget. Dave, my work, my ideals . . .

. . . and I remember . . . the kisses, the taste of him, the feeling of him inside me.

I exhale as my shirt falls to the floor; my bra isn't far behind. I gather the blankets beneath me into my fist as he grazes his teeth over one nipple, then the next.

Some feelings are almost too strong. They can't be harnessed. Some desires can do nothing short of overwhelm.

I arch my back as his hand slides up the inside of my thigh.

I can't think. . . . I won't think. . . . Just the quiet scent of his after-shave screams seduction to me now.

My pants are still on but they might as well not be. They offer no protection from the heat of his touch as he presses his hand into me.

His radio is on, playing softly through the speakers—classic rock; the genre fits him. He's the grit of Jimi Hendrix and the eerie mystery of Pink Floyd and the groovy elegance of the Doors.

He has the top button of my waistband undone; I feel my pants loosen as he pulls the zipper down and the air on my thighs as he pulls them off me.

"Stairway to Heaven" is fading into something else . . . ah yes, the Rolling Stones. It's "Ruby Tuesday."

Rubies.

My eyes open and suddenly I can see, not just the room around me but the path I'm on. I reach down and cover his hand with mine just as he's about to pull my panties off me.

He pauses, hoping that the gesture isn't the stop sign he senses it is. But I keep his hand still, gripping it firmly, not with passion, but with resolve.

"Kasie," he says, looking into my eyes.

"I love him," I say. The boat sways ever so slightly; Mick Jagger croons good-bye to "Ruby Tuesday." "I love him . . . and that's not just a feeling, it's a decision."

"You're choosing prison over the unknown."

"We're all in some kind of prison," I point out. "But I can pick my cage, and the cage I'll live in with Dave is gilded."

And with that, I pull away, sit up, and reach for my bra, the remnants of his touch still warm on my breast, my body still aching for him; my devil is still pulling me toward him. . . .

But I've made my decision. This is not my place. Robert is right; he is the unknown. And I reject the adventure of discovery. Maybe my life with Dave really will be a sort of prison but it's the Ritz-Carlton compared to the dingy prison of my guilt.

"Don't go," he says.

I whirl around. I'm still wearing nothing but my undergarments but I feel an invisible armor building up around me, shielding me from the attacks of temptation. "Why are you doing this?" I ask. "Why me? Is it that you want what you can't have?"

"I thought . . . I hoped I could have you," he says quietly. "Every taste of you intensifies the craving. Like the Turkish delight the White Witch gives to Edmund in Narnia. I just have to have more."

"So that means you're Edmund, a modern metaphor for Judas, and I'm the personification of evil."

"No," he says with a sad smile. He stands and carefully lifts my shirt and pants from where he dropped them on the floor, but he doesn't hand them to me. Instead he holds them like they're a treasure, or a last hope. "My metaphor isn't holding up. Obviously what we have isn't anything like a children's fairy tale. What we have is . . . darker, richer . . ."

"It isn't right."

"But it's us."

I shake my head, staring at the shirt in his hand. I could pull it from his grip but I'm not ready. I can't bear the idea of being so aggressive and violent in this moment. He will never see me in any other form of undress again. I'm determined to make sure of that.

But I do want him to see me now. I want him to look at me one more time. I didn't cherish that last touch; I didn't predict my own fortitude. But I want to feel his eyes on me. I want that to be a memory I can fall back on when life gets so rough, fantasies become hard to conjure.

"You think you know what you want, but you don't," I whisper. "You think you want me but what you want is a string of stolen moments like this one. You think you see through my facade but you can't see that the facade is as much a part of me as the wildness beneath. You don't want me."

"But you can get rid of the facade."

"Don't you get it?" I scream. Suddenly I'm not the Harvard-educated businesswoman, I'm not the fiancée of a young lawyer from an old family. I'm anger, desperation, frustration, unrequited passion.

"I don't *want* to get rid of it!" I grit my teeth against the violence that's welling up inside. "You're asking me to toss aside my thick-soled shoes and walk barefoot by your side, but look down, Robert! The ground we're walking on is covered with rusty nails! I want my protections. They *are* part of me! I love them more than I love the . . . the savagery of my underlying nature and I want a man who loves the part of me that I celebrate! Why can't you see that?"

"Because I'm a savage," he says simply. But his eyes are sad; there is no savagery on display.

"Then find yourself a woman raised by wolves. I was raised to be civilized."

"This is your definition of civility?"

"We have business, Mr. Dade. Shall we get to it?"

He sighs, "Ruby Tuesday" is gone, and its absence adds a small chip in my resolve that I can ill afford. I hold out my hand.

"Give me my clothes."

He hands them to me without any resistance.

"You and I, we're not the good guys," I say as I slip back into my pants. "We did something wrong."

"If you do this," he says, watching me carefully, "if you marry a man you don't love, you will not only hurt me but you will damage yourself. And most important, you'll *torture* him."

I pause but only for a moment. "I'm doing what I need to do." The floor is cold under my bare feet.

"I think if you listen to me for even five minutes, you'll realize that you have choices."

I look up at him. There's so much he doesn't know. So many secrets and skeletons. And I no longer know if I'm running away or being led to a fate. All I know is that I'm going to survive. It's more than my sister was able to do.

He examines me; his hazel eyes draw me in as they always do. "There are things you want to tell me?" he asks.

I smile despite myself. No one has ever been able to read me so easily and I've known this man for less than two weeks.

He nods. "I'm going to go up to the deck, pour two glasses of wine. I hope that once you've dressed we can talk."

"Oh, now you want to talk? So it's really not just about sex?" I say with only partial sarcasm.

"I told you, I want to know you in every way. I'm going to go up to the deck. If you come up to talk, then I'll know that at least there's some hope that you'll let me."

And with that he leaves the cabin. I listen to his footsteps fade away only to hear them again after he goes above board and starts to walk the deck, which is now acting as my ceiling.

With a jolt I realize that Robert Dade is no longer pushing me. He's not trying to tempt me or overwhelm me.

Robert Dade just asked me if we could talk.

Like I would talk to a normal person? Have we ever done that? It's always been passion and teasing and excitement. Have we ever just sat down and had a conversation that wasn't about work?

No.

But maybe we could. The possibility bewilders me and then quickly builds up a mysterious appeal. We could be more than the roar of a sports car, more than a rash night in a luxury hotel.

I close my eyes for a moment. The images that swirl before me are different from the fantasies I've entertained over the last few weeks. In these imaginings, I see Robert and me sitting side by side at a movie theater eating popcorn. I see us poring over the *Wall Street Journal* and *LA Times* while eating Sunday brunch. In my fantasy, our brash impulses are supported by a bond that is every bit as strong as the beams that hold up his decadent house on the hill.

Robert is the man who unlocks my inhibitions and revels in

their display. But if in addition to all that he could also be my friend and my partner . . . if he could be a man who willingly walks with me on firmer ground, maybe, just maybe that would change things.

Robert has always appealed to my devil, but what if I gave him the chance to befriend my angel?

If he could, then maybe, just maybe I could be a woman who has it all.

Little sparks of hope ignite inside my heart but the ringing of my cell phone jars me out of my musings. It's coming from my purse that sits discarded on the floor.

It's Dave's ringtone.

I pull out the phone but don't pick up, letting my cool and collected recorded message greet him. I can't talk to him now, not while in this place and certainly not before I have more time to sort through my thoughts and emotions.

But then I hear that he's sent me a text. Which he never does.

```
I know where you are, I know what you're doing.
```

I try to make sense of the words. He can't mean . . . how . . . The next text comes.

```
I'm supposed to call Dylan Freeland soon. He
doesn't know what you're doing . . . yet. But
if you don't get off that boat and meet me
by your car in five minutes I will make sure
Dylan, our families, EVERYONE knows.
```

I stare at the screen, my eyes wide and unblinking. Dave has never threatened me before, not with anything, let alone the destruction of my career. But then I have never betrayed him like this before.

I look down at myself; my pants are wrinkled and my shirt's still in my hand. I'm shaking. I'm ruined.

Another text.

```
Leave him, now. I'm giving you one chance.
Take it. Take it or I'll take everything.
```

I have never felt so cornered or more scared. It's not just that he could cost me my job. He could cost me my entire professional reputation. He could cost me my parents' respect. He could take away their conviction that we, as a family, are good.

With unsteady hands I put on my shirt, gather up my purse, and go above board.

"Kasie," Robert says, his tone so soft I could curl up in it like a blanket. "We just need to talk for a bit. You don't have to leave. We don't have to play these games. . . ."

But his voice fades off as I walk past him without stopping. I get off the boat and walk away. I can feel him watching me. He thinks I've made a choice. He thinks I'm running away from him.

But I'm not. I'm not even being led. I'm being pushed.

And it occurs to me that I have never ignored him before. My lack of response to his conciliatory words might actually be the one thing that will keep him from pursuing me. It may be the thing that makes him give up.

The thought makes me stumble but I keep walking, away from the boat, away from the pier and the horizon, back to the parking lot where I can see Dave. Even from a distance I can see his anger pouring out of him, burning the pavement, setting fire to any sense of security I have left.

"I could make you pay," he hisses when I'm close enough to hear.

"Dave, I'm so sorry. . . ."

"Shut up." He holds out his hand. "The keys to your car, please."

Without a word I give them to him.

He unlocks the doors. "Get in the passenger seat."

I do. He gets in the driver seat and with a screech he peels out of the parking lot, away from Robert Dade. . . .

And toward God only knows what.

# PART 2

---

*Exposed*

---

# CHAPTER 16

❈

ELEVEN DAYS AGO I met a man with strong, beautiful arms and salt-and-pepper hair. Robert Dade. We were in Vegas and he bought my attention with a smile. We talked, first at a blackjack table, then at a bar, and later in his hotel room.

I should have thought of Dave when Robert sat down by my side. Dave, the man who I've been dating for six years, the man who wants to make me his wife. I should have remembered my commitments before I opened my body for Robert on that Vegas night. But Robert, he unleashed an animal from within me, one that clawed his back and bit his neck. I didn't know what kind of beast it was. I didn't understand the chaos it could unleash.

And yet that chaos had been so sweet. Like ice cream after a lifetime of dieting.

How many times have I tried to say good-bye to Robert Dade? In Vegas, in his Santa Monica office, on the screen of my computer . . . every time I've ended up breathless, naked, caressed by his eyes and his hands. All he has to do is say my name, Kasie. . . . That's it. That's all it takes to make me tremble. "Kasie," he whispers and I throb.

Robert thinks I'm strong. He says he wants to free me from my self-imposed confines. He says he wants to walk by my side on the beach, have dinner with me, and celebrate the little pleasures that make up our lives . . . together.

He says he cares for me, not the woman who I like to show to the world, but the woman who lies underneath all that, the woman who refuses to be suffocated with the expectations of others.

He told me all that as we stood on his boat.

In my mind I'm still on that boat in that moment. Yes, that's the reality I choose to believe in. I give Robert my hand and he whispers words of reassurance. He tells me we can be together and no one needs to be hurt. We're just two people; we don't have the power to conjure deadly storms or turn the whole universe inside out. We're just two people falling in love.

He tells me we can run away, just for a little while, and that when we come back, everything will be set as it should be. I'll still have my position at the global consulting firm where I've steadily risen through the ranks; my career path will still be assured. He will still be the CEO of Maned Wolf Security Systems, my firm's biggest account. We will work together, play together, be together.

We don't have to feel the pain of guilt and consequences. Only pleasure. As if to demonstrate that, he reaches out to me. Brushes my cheek with his hand. Hands that are gentle and rough.

He's built things with those hands, delicate woodwork and powerful companies. He runs those hands through my hair and tugs just slightly.

"Kasie," he says, and the cage is opened.

I feel his mouth on mine as his fingers slip between my legs, applying just a little pressure . . . just there against my clit. The fabric of my clothes feels flimsy and weak against the heat that we generate. I wonder if I'll take them off or if they'll just melt away on their own.

But Robert answers the question when he pulls my shirt from me, cups my breasts, pinches my nipples as they strain against my bra. We're on the deck of his boat, docked in a slip in Marina del Rey. People can see us. I can feel their eyes as they shift from the ocean to the fire. They're watching him undress me, watching him touch me and I just don't care.

Because I'm with Robert. Because I know that when I'm with him, I'm safe.

He pulls me to him as he gently sucks on the curve of my neck. I can feel his erection press against my stomach; I feel myself getting wet as I anticipate welcoming him inside. People are watching as I pull off his shirt and reveal a perfect body, hard and chiseled with the artistry of a sculptor. People are watching as he opens my bra and lets it drop to the deck.

I lie back on a deck chair . . . had that been there on the boat?

It doesn't matter. In the reality I choose, it's there and I can recline all the way back, half naked, inviting him to take me here in plain view. Let them watch. Let them take pictures for all I care. None of them matter. This is my world; I choose what rules are to be followed and which will be burned. I lie on this chair and I smile as I feel Robert's fingers working on the buttons at my waist, smile as I feel him pull my pants off me, gasp as his fingers brush against my soaked panties.

"She's magnificent," a man murmurs. He's all the way over at the end of the pier, but I can hear him perfectly. He's never seen anyone like me. He's never seen someone consumed by this kind of passion and power.

I watch as Robert pulls off his belt, his eyes never leaving mine. He is oblivious to our audience. He sees only me, the woman he wants, the animal he's unleashed.

As he strips down I find myself breathless. He's the reason the Greeks decided that the human form was worthy of worship. His desire is on display and I reach for him but he doesn't immediately oblige.

Instead he kneels before me, pulls down my soaked panties, opens me with his tongue.

I arch my back and cry out. I'm so tender now, so ready. More people have come to watch. Women and men. They touch me with their eyes as surely as Robert Dade touches me with his hands and mouth. His tongue continues to toy with me, moving slowly at first and then faster as his fingers plunge inside of me, making the experience complete.

This time it's me who runs my hands through his hair, me who tugs as an overwhelming desire pounds through my body. My hips are raised; the orgasm is coming, I hear the whispers of the onlookers, hear the clicks of their cameras as I explode, unable to contain myself for even a moment longer.

And then Robert pulls away, smiles. . . . The lounge chair I'm on seems wider now, sturdier, too. He straddles me, lies on top of me, presses his cock against my core . . . but not entering, not yet.

He looks into my eyes as I silently plead and the audience holds their breath. They share my anticipation, share my need, and when, with a hard thrust, he pushes inside of me, I feel their approval as my entire body rocks with the force of him.

I move my hips with our rhythm. I run my nails down his soft skin, feel his hard muscles, feel him push himself farther and farther into my body.

He pulls my leg over his shoulder and drives in deeper still. His eyes never leave mine. I can feel his breath, smell his aftershave on my skin.

I can barely contain myself; the passion is too much but he holds me still, pinning my arms above my head as he sometimes does, forcing me to do nothing but receive this pleasure as the world watches.

Now every part of me is palpitating as he leads in this erotic dance.

"Robert," I moan his name, the only word I'm capable of saying, the only word I can think of in this moment.

He smiles and speeds up the rhythm. It's the final push I need. Again my back arches, my head thrashes from side to side, my breasts reach up, my nipples brush against his chest as I cry out again, and this time his voice joins mine as we climax together, there on the deck of the boat.

People are watching, but they can't touch us. We're too powerful to be bothered by their attention. We don't even bother to acknowledge them as we try to catch our breath, holding each other, drenched in our sweat.

People are watching, and they see me, see the woman Robert sees, see the animal, the strength, and the vulnerability. But I don't see them. Everything right now is the man who is on top of me, breathing deeply. He looks into my eyes and I know we are safe.

"I'm falling in love with you," he says.

And I smile.

THAT'S THE REALITY I want to believe in, but as I lie in Dave's bed, untouched but completely violated, I find that the fantasy doesn't have enough substance for me to hold on to. It floats away into my subconscious, waiting for sleep to come where it can live again.

But I know sleep is a long way off. Dave is snoring by my side, seemingly at peace. Yet how is that possible? How can he be peaceful after the violence of our last encounter?

Because I didn't choose to stay on the boat. I left Robert standing on the deck. I walked away as he called my name.

Dave had found out the truth. Robert doesn't know this, but I left because I got Dave's text. He was waiting in the parking lot for me, and he was ready to use the new information he had gleaned to humiliate me at work, with my family . . . he was threatening to make my nightmares come true.

I went to Dave to stop him, yes. But more than that I went to Dave because I owed him. I needed to make up for the hurt I had caused by choosing Robert.

Had I done that? Was he satisfied in his revenge? Maybe yes, maybe no. Dave would say there had been no revenge. He would say he was helping me.

Months ago, on some cable news channel, I heard a terrorist interviewed by a reporter. He had hostages, but he called them "guests." On cue, the hostages nodded their heads and sung the praises of their captor. He was the perfect host, they said. They loved every moment of their forced imprisonment.

Had those words scraped at the captives' throats?

I'm not a hostage in the Middle East. I know Dave has no plans to kill me. Physical torture is not in my future.

But I do understand what it feels like to have to praise the man who is intent on making you suffer. I know the humiliation and the impotence. I felt it when I talked to my parents earlier in the evening before they took a flight back home. With the phone pressed to my ear I thanked them for coming out to the "wonderful" surprise engagement party Dave had thrown me. I looked down at the red ruby engagement ring on my finger, a ring I once coveted, and told them I couldn't wait for the day when I would become Mrs. David Beasley.

Dave stood in front of me the whole time and fed me my lines.

I felt it when I texted my friend Simone to tell her that Dave is my choice. I texted because I didn't think I could speak the word "choice" without crying. In truth, my choices are gone. They vanished when I got off the boat, handed Dave the keys to my car, and let him drive me to my prison. He drove and I sat in the passenger seat wringing my shaking hands, like a hostage. Like a liar.

It's not just my parents who love Dave. Dave is the godson of Dylan Freeland, the cofounder of the firm I work for. "He's like a son to me," Mr. Freeland had said at my engagement party. It had been a subtle reminder that my career and my love life are not as separated as I'd like them to be.

And Dave knows the secrets of my family . . . he knows about my sister who lost control as she recklessly danced with self-destruction. He knows that she used her own irresponsible impulses to the same ends as Cleopatra used her snake and Juliet used her dagger. He knows I wanted to be different from my sister.

He knows that I failed.

And so he drove me to his home and for ten minutes we stood in his living room without exchanging a word. I had wanted to break the silence but I couldn't find a way to add actual gravity to the words "I'm sorry."

So in the oppressive stillness we had stood across the room from each other. I had tried to meet his eyes, but the ferocity of his glare had forced my gaze downward. He's barely five foot ten but in that moment his anger made him taller, more menacing.

He had stood there, in front of his fireplace, holding on to the mantel as if he intended to tear it from the wall.

"You're a whore."

"I made a mistake," I said feebly. "I . . . I think I got scared. I wasn't sure about marriage. . . ."

He took the Waterford vase on the mantel into his hands, stared at it before hurling it across the room. It crashed into the wall behind me . . . too far away for me to think that he was aiming for me.

But still.

"You're a whore."

"Dave, I'm so sorry—"

"I don't want your apologies." He took a step forward. He has blond hair and pale blue eyes, gentle colors that are tainted by brutish enmity.

I did that to him. It's my fault. "If you don't want my apologies," I said carefully, "what is it that you want?"

"I want you to admit it."

"Admit what?"

"That you're a whore."

He stepped closer.

The last time I made love to Robert, it had been in his home. He had held me afterward. We had giggled and shared the casual details of our lives. He had been kind and loving, a perfect and compelling balance to our rough desire.

I feel guilty as hell . . . but I don't feel like a whore.

"I think," I said quietly, "that you should give me my car keys. We should talk about this when you're calmer."

My steadiness had brought him to a new level of fury. He grabbed my arms and pushed me up against the wall.

When Robert had me up against a wall, it had been exciting . . . but that had been the touch of frenzied ardor.

Hate is a very different thing.

Dave's violence affected me in ways I couldn't have predicted. It's like I came out of myself. I wasn't the woman he had pinned against the wall but simply a bystander, watching, observing. I saw Dave, and the more enraged he became, the weaker he seemed. I hurt him, I betrayed him, I was wrong.

But his reaction makes me think that maybe I had cause.

"I need you to let go of me."

Dave hesitated. He wanted to hurt me. Maybe he wanted to hurt himself, too. But unlike me, Dave has mastered self-discipline.

He took several steps back and looked away as he gathered up his willpower. I can't help but admire him for it.

"My keys," I said again.

He continued to stare at nothing . . . or maybe he was staring at the past. Maybe he was seeing all the missteps that led us to this place.

"I told your mother that it could have happened to anyone," he said.

I froze. "You spoke to my mother?"

"This was years ago," he clarified. "We were visiting them in their Carmel home during the Pebble Beach car show. You, your father, and me . . . we all went but your mother pleaded out. A migraine, she said."

"I remember."

"I left you there with your dad about an hour into it. I've never been into cars and you two don't get a lot of alone time. I came back to your parents' house and there was your mother, sitting on her cream-colored couch in her vacation home, photographs scattered all over the coffee table. She was crying."

"What were the pictures of?"

"Your sister."

"Those photos don't exist."

"Did she tell you that she destroyed them along with the memories? And you believed her?"

I hadn't answered. I knew everything of Melody's had been discarded. Her clothes given to Goodwill or thrown in the trash, her old stuffed animals thrown into the Dumpster, her diaries burned with the photos . . . I saw them do it. I watched them as they found a thousand little ways to spit on her memory.

"She kept some," Dave says gently. "If you were able to see outside yourself, you'd have known that your mother isn't so callous as to destroy all of it."

There are some insults that can't be brushed off. That was one of them.

"Your mother told me she's haunted," he continued. "She wanted to know how she failed and I told her that all we had to do was look to you to know that whatever demons consumed Melody were of her own making. If it was your parents' fault, you would be out of control, too."

I didn't want to hear any more.

"Your mother told me your sister was a whore. I told her you were nothing like that."

That's when those mutinous tears escaped, rolled down my cheeks, and left streaks in my foundation.

"How will she live with this, Kasie?" he asked. His voice had grown soft even as the words had grown harsh. It was like being caressed with barbed wire.

"She doesn't have to know," I had pleaded.

"If we split up, she does. I'm not like you. I don't believe pretty lies are better than hard truths. Maybe your parents won't fail you now the way they must have when you and your sister were children. Maybe they'll help you, because God knows you need help. . . . If you don't get it . . . think of what happened to your sister, Kasie—"

"That's not fair."

"At the very least they need to know that they can't trust you. They need to know you're a liar."

"I lied to *you*," I screamed, my calm disappeared—memories of Melody, of the pain in my parents' eyes, of the confusion around her death . . .

As I lie by Dave's side now, it's hard to remember he's supposed to be the victim and I the outlaw.

"I cheated on you, Dave," I had said, not quite as loudly this time. "It doesn't mean I'm going to lie about other stuff. It doesn't mean I can't be trusted."

"And I'm sure that when Melody was first caught doing vodka shots at fourteen, she insisted that it didn't mean she couldn't be trusted to resist drugs. You know the saying, once a cheater, always a cheater? Well, that's not basic enough. Cheaters are liars. It's a perversion. A pervasive problem that colors everything you touch. You're a liar, Kasie, and you can't be trusted. Not by me, not by anyone, because now we know that when it serves your purposes, when your . . . *pleasure's* at stake, you *will* lie."

"Dave—"

"Your parents should know that," he continued. "Your employer, too. The team that works for you should definitely know that. They should know that you've been fucking your client. They should know that you got down on your knees and sucked his dick to get the account. After all, your actions affect them. It's their account, too. They should know that when he tires of your attentions—and he will tire of you—they should know why he's taken his business elsewhere."

"Oh God, please, Dave—"

"And if your parents, your employer, your coworkers, if they all decide to reject you, cast you out the way your parents cast out your sister, you shouldn't be angry, Kasie. They have the right to protect themselves. They have the right to choose to spend their time with people who have better values and judgment than you."

"Dave, I'm begging you—"

"Are you?" he asked. His eyes seared into mine but I couldn't read them. I don't know that man who stood before me, who sleeps by my side now.

Maybe I don't know myself, either.

"Are you *begging* me, Kasie?" he asked again. "Do you want my help?"

I didn't know what to say. It was easier when he was being violent. I'd have preferred the blows of his fist to the stabs of his words.

"I want to help you," he said. "You don't need to be Melody. I can help you find your way back. If you let me help you, no one will need to know what you did. Do you want that?"

I nodded, unable to talk.

"Good. That's what I want, too." He walked over to me, stroked my face with the back of his hand. I stood motionless. I felt sick.

"I want the woman I fell in love with. She's still in there; I know it. You know it, too, don't you?"

Another nod, another tear.

"Good, good. Because if we're going to get her back, you have to acknowledge the problem. You have to acknowledge what you've become."

I squeezed my eyes closed. I thought of Robert Dade. I thought of his smile, of his warm hands and kind words.

"I need you to say it, Kasie. I need to know that you realize the full extent of your debasement. I need you to acknowledge where you're at so we can start to get you back to where I . . . where *everyone* needs you to be."

"Dave," I whispered. His name is acidic against my tongue. "Please don't—"

"Say it, Kasie. Say it so I don't have to expose all this. Say it so we can get back to where we were."

I opened my eyes. I wanted to come out of myself again. I wanted to be the bystander.

But I was in this now and I didn't see a way out.

"Say it." The look on his face was as cold as it was expectant.

Pain, hate, totally futile anger, memories of Robert Dade's kisses, memories of peace . . . But that's gone now. I did this; I gave away all my power, my freedom, my moral compass. With so much already lost, how can I expect to hold on to my pride?

"Dave . . ." I choked the word out again, "Dave . . . I'm a whore."

And he smiled as I crumbled.

❀

# CHAPTER 17

DAVE DIDN'T TOUCH ME that night. That's good, because if he had, I might have killed him. I would have wanted to stop myself, but I don't always get what I want.

For instance, I hadn't wanted to stay at Dave's but he had insisted. I know why. He didn't want me to go to Robert. He wanted to watch me, control me, keep me in line.

It's odd because only a few days ago I had wanted to be controlled; I didn't really care how much of that control came from within and how much came from without. As long as I was able to stay on the predetermined path, I was good. I had so many goals: success in my career, respect from those in my industry and from those I love . . . but mostly, my goal was not to be Melody. My sister had rejected all the paths available to her. She had sprinted through the trees, pushing aside branches, ignoring the thorns that scratched her skin, oblivious to the living things she crushed under her feet.

Robert had told me that if I chose Dave over him, I would be choosing prison over the unknown. I had countered that we all live in some kind of prison. At least the cage with Dave is gilded.

But as I stand over his bed, watching this man I once loved sleep, nothing in this room seems to shine.

Again I think of violence. I think of putting a pillow over his head and not letting go. Would he be able to fight me off? What if he couldn't? Could I cover up the crime?

I blanch, shocked at the darkness of my thoughts. It's not even

6 a.m. I have to get out of here. Because if Dave is right, if I can't be trusted to resist temptation, then we both have a problem.

I sneak over to his dresser. I haven't spent the night here for so long. We always stay at my place. I live closer to my office, and to his, too, for that matter. But there's another reason I prefer my place. My home . . . it breathes. Even when things were good, I had found Dave's house to be a little stifling. Nothing's ever out of place. Books and CDs are alphabetized and the corners of every sheet are pulled and tucked with military precision.

But once in a while he would convince me to stay over and for those rare occasions I had some things, including some gym clothes, tucked away in the one drawer Dave has allocated for me. In the closet I find my tennis shoes and I shove them onto my feet as Dave continues to snore.

ONCE OUTSIDE, I start running at a criminal's speed. My form reeks of panic, not athleticism.

But as I get farther away, I slow to a more rhythmic pace. My heart races, though my breathing is measured and I find my stride. The air is crisp and fresh; the pounding of my feet drums up a slew of new ideas.

For the first time I wonder if there is a third way. A different path, one that may have a few bumps but no chasms. If I tread carefully, I can avoid most, if not all, of the thorns. Dry leaves crunch under my rubber soles as I pass the pale yellow and cream homes of Woodland Hills. Every front lawn is perfectly maintained, every door protected by its own security system.

There are thorns and there are *thorns*. I don't think I can survive humiliation or the pain my affair would cause my parents. I know I can't survive the public destruction of my career.

*They should know that you got down on your knees and sucked his dick to get the account.*

It's not true but it won't matter. My master's degree from Harvard Business School, all of my hard work and professional accomplishments, it'll all be cast off into the riptide of public opinion. My entire career will be pulled out to sea and lost forever.

And my parents will blame themselves, and they will erase me from their lives the same way they erased Melody.

Others have faced ostracism—for example, women in difficult nations who have stood their ground, walked away from husbands even though such action was considered the ultimate act of shame; men who have stood up and proudly admitted to being gay even though they knew it would get them exiled by their community, their church, their family. There are political activists who have spoken out when everyone around them insisted they toe the party line.

These are the heroic men and women of our time. But they have the moral advantage; I don't.

I am a capable, tenacious woman; a survivor through and through. But I have never been brave.

The realization cuts at my gut. If I can't produce courage, then what? Will my cowardice bind me to Dave forever? Will I have to let him touch me?

Once upon a time I thought Dave was a decent lover. He's gentle, caring . . . he always looks into my eyes as he climbs on top of me. Always kisses me as he pets my thighs, a polite request for entry.

Robert never really requested anything. He always made sure I knew that all I had to do was say no to get him to back off, but aside from that he just went for it. I liked the way he pinned me down. I liked the way he held me still with a look before claiming me, pressing himself inside of me . . .

. . . loving me.

Is Robert falling in love with me the way I'm falling in love with him?

I stop in the middle of an empty street. Sweat trickles down my spine. I've run a few miles but I'm not even close to feeling sore or tired. My body barely registers the effort. I am strong. I am a coward.

But I'm also smart. It's my intelligence that has opened doors for me in the past.

Maybe I can use it to open my cage.

I squint at the rising sun, note how it makes my engagement ring glow, reminding me of fire and blood. It's a beautiful reminder of the hell I'm in. Reluctantly I turn my back on the light and return to my prison, a new, less frantic determination in my gait.

When I get there, Dave's awake and eyes me suspiciously as I burst through the door.

"Where were you?"

I hold out the fabric of my soaked apparel for his inspection.

"Obviously I was running."

My impertinence brings a crease to his forehead. Apparently he doesn't think I've earned the right to show him anything but deference.

"You know how lucky you are?" he asks.

This gives me pause. "Lucky?"

"I'm giving you a second chance. It's more than you deserve."

It's a stupid, clichéd threat, but he's betting that I'll be too scared to call him out on his ineloquence or even remark that I don't want this "chance." I only want his silence.

I push past him without a word, but when I'm halfway up the stairs I stop and turn. "I have a question."

"Yes?"

"You found me at the marina."

"I did."

I walk back down the stairs. I keep my eyes lowered hoping that humility will be enough to elicit the answers I need. "You need to know that nothing happened on that boat. I stopped it even before you called me. I went to the marina to end it."

He still doesn't believe me. My truths have the same intonation as my deceptions so he rejects it all.

"Nothing happened on that boat," I say again.

"And before that?"

I lower my head farther, letting my hair fall in my face. "I've made mistakes . . . but no more, Dave. I'm not going to let my impulses rule me."

He laughs. There's no warmth in it. "You don't think I'm buying this, do you?" He turns his back on me, which is better.

"No. I know it'll be a while before you'll believe anything I say," I admit, and I mean it. The concoction of guilt, fond memories, and unspeakable anger make my feelings for Dave complicated. I take a deep breath, take a step forward, stand behind him, close enough for it to feel a bit intimate. "But no more lies, all right? I promise. From now on we'll both be honest with each other."

He whirls around, once more the predator. "There is only one pretender in this room. Only one of us acted the slut."

The jagged edges of my rage puncture my heart as I cozy up to him. "I know how angry you are . . . I know I have . . . things to make up for. And I know we need to talk about what happened. Can you tell me how you found me yesterday? You came to the marina, we took my car back here . . . and yet your car is in the garage."

He's silent; a malicious smile plays at the corners of his lips.

"Who drove you to the marina?" I ask softly. "Who else knows?"

He wanders past me toward the kitchen, forcing me to follow him for my answer.

"It's hard, isn't it?" he asks as he reaches for a coffee cup.

"What's hard?"

"Being kept in the dark."

I don't answer. I wait a moment as he pours himself a fresh cup of coffee from his coffeemaker; he's only made enough for one cup.

I force myself to turn and leave the room. I'll find out who knows. I'll think my way out of this.

But as I climb the stairs toward the shower, I realize that the questions are piling up. I need a solid strategy, I need to know who else knows . . .

. . . and I need to figure out Dave's motivations. If he hates me, why does he want to keep me? Control? Or something else?

I go into the bathroom, close the door, and peel my clothes off as I warm up the shower.

The door to the bathroom opens and I turn to see Dave looking at me. I recoil, grabbing a towel and holding it up against me.

"You're my fiancée," Dave says, taking a step forward and pulling the towel from me. His gaze oozes over naked skin. "And this is my house," he adds.

I hold up my head, resist the urge to cover myself again. I stretch out my fingers, keeping my hands stiff as boards so they don't curl into fists.

Dave quickly tires of his game and turns away, walking back toward the door. "Besides," he says, calling casually over his shoulder, "it's not like I'm seeing anything you haven't shown to any man who asks."

I bite down on my lip as the door closes. Maybe I can find courage in hate.

# CHAPTER 18

When I get to my office Barbara, my assistant, is at her desk. She gestures for me to approach; culpability and concern color her expression. "Mr. Dade is in your office."

No one is allowed in my office when I'm not there. Each consultant here has too much confidential information nestled into our files to be so careless.

But it's hard to resist Robert when he tells you what he wants, so I know he's basically forced Barbara to give him entry.

I take a pad of paper off her desk and scribble down a series of menial tasks that I say need her immediate attention; all of them require her to be away from her desk. I stand there until she leaves, knowing that I bought myself at least a few minutes of privacy. Once she's gone I walk in to greet him.

Robert Dade is leaning against the front of my desk, his arms crossed over his chest, his legs crossed at the ankles. He's relaxed, patient, beautiful. Everything I would expect from him. His eyes meet mine as I step toward him, letting the door close behind me.

I feel a rush of confessions press up against my clenched teeth. I want to tell him about the desire that bubbles up when I look at him and that his being here makes the shadows a little lighter.

I want to ask him to touch me.

But instead I look away. "We don't have an appointment."

"You're working for me," Robert points out. "My business can bring your firm millions. Do I really need an appointment?"

But it's not a question. Just a gentle admonishment.

Quietly I lock the door, something I almost never do, but at the moment, interruptions can be dangerous.

"So, you've made your choice," he says as he wanders around the boundaries of the space, taking in the pale yellow walls and company-approved artwork.

"I told you, I'm with Dave."

He looks at me sharply, more curious than angry. "Say that again."

"I'm with Dave."

"You're saying his name . . . differently."

I laugh; I want the sound to be buoyant, but the heaviness of my mood adds unwanted weight. "His name has always been Dave. There's only one way to pronounce it."

"That's not what I mean. Before when you spoke of him you sounded . . . determined. He was your decision. Now . . ." He lets his sentence drop off and waits to see if I'm going to fill in the blank. When I don't, he walks toward me, and I don't move. I don't even blink as he brushes my hair from my face.

"What is it, Kasie? What's changed? You seem . . . scared."

"You know what I'm afraid of," I hiss. "I don't want to lose who I am. Dave keeps me grounded. You . . . you're . . ." I hesitate. I want to say that he's the tsunami that turns land to sea but I can't get the words out. I *want* the land that I'm standing on to be destroyed. He'll hear that in my voice. So instead I turn my eyes away. "I can't do this, Robert."

"No, you're repeating old lines," he says quietly, studying my face. He leans in so his mouth is near my ear. "Tell me."

He's only touching my hair but every part of my body reacts. I feel myself warming, feel my breath catch in my throat. I feel the throb.

"Tell me," he says and I close my eyes. "Are you afraid?"

I reach for him, take his shirt in my fist, feel the comfort of these waters, the quiet power of him. His lips move away from my ear and I feel the tip of his tongue sliding down my neck, tasting me with gentle precision and purpose. Instinctually I move into him as his hand rises to my breast.

I want him. I want to get lost in him. My fist opens and my fingers slowly, almost unwillingly, wander to the buttons of his dress shirt.

His tongue has moved back to my ear and I gasp as he pulls me closer again. His fingers in my hair, holding me in place as another hand moves lower, past my breasts, to my stomach . . . lower . . . I feel his hand slip between my thighs and press up into me.

"Let me in," he whispers. "Not just here," and with that he adds more pressure, sending a jolt of pleasure through my body. "That's good," he says as I begin to tremble, "but I want in here, too." And he kisses the top of my head. "Tell me what you're thinking."

The buttons of his shirt finally give way and I place my hand over his bare skin. His heart is beating a little too fast, as if urging me forward. I turn to him and look into his eyes. There's something there that I haven't noticed before. Something inside the desire. Is it concern? Need?

Love?

His hand is still between my legs and I lean forward and let my lips brush against his; my eyes stay open and he becomes a blur of lightly tanned skin and black lashes. His fingers start moving and with each stroke I feel things fall away—fear, thought, confusion—until all I'm aware of is the feeling of him.

Without a word he pulls away his hand and moves it to the waistband of my pants. I feel it loosen as he unfastens the buttons, slips his fingers inside the cloth of my panties, already wet for him. When he finds that little spot, I dig my fingernails into the skin of his chest.

"We're not over," he says and I respond with a moan. "Did you think we were? Do you think I can't see the invitation in your smile, in the way you shiver just slightly when I get near? You think I can't hear it in the quiet that comes when you can't quite get yourself to deliver the scripted denial or well-wrought protest? I can read your body like a blind man reads Braille."

He lifts one hand and slips it under my shirt, over my bra, lets his fingers slide over my erect nipples. "Did these get hard the moment you saw me?" he asks.

I bite down on my lip, afraid that if I speak I'll admit the truth.

"How long did it take you to get wet?" he asks. "Did it happen when I first spoke? Was it before I finished my first sentence?"

I shift just slightly so I can look into his eyes yet again. Yes, there it is, that unidentified emotion that doesn't match his words. Maybe need, maybe love.

I want to tell him the real reason I left the marina but I don't dare. I know he can sense that there are unspoken words, feel that something is being held back.

With our eyes locked his index finger plunges inside of me. My fingernails dig in deeper.

"What do you want?" Robert asks. "Do you really want Dave?"

I rest my head on his shoulder as his finger continues to thrust its way inside my walls, again and again. I shudder as he kisses my neck.

"Or do you want me inside of you, Kasie?"

I nod my head still against his shoulder.

"Then I'm going to need you to come now." His fingers become more insistent; his free hand pulls me to him tightly, roughly. Something like a whimper escapes my lips.

"Come for me now, Kasie. Right now, I want to see you."

I can hear people passing the office outside in the hall. I don't dare make another sound. My nipples pressed against him, I reach up and pull his hair, frantic for release but so afraid of giving myself away.

"Oh God," I whisper.

"Not good enough," he says insistently; the intensity of his touch increases; he steps forward, moving me with him until I'm pressed against the wall with nowhere to go.

"Someone will hear," I whisper.

"I don't care."

I look away. I should be angry the way I'm angry with Dave but I can't think. All I can do is react, and what I'm reacting to is . . . exceptional.

One hand slides into that small space between the wall and the curve of my back. He forces it lower, down to my ass, and he manages to press me to him in an even tighter hold than before. Another finger slips in. I let out a small cry of excitement. I see his eyes move down my body, demanding, but where Dave's eyes scrape, Robert's penetrate. They reach in and pull at the internal flames that are consuming me. They make the fire brighter, stronger.

"Oh God," I say again and then quickly cover my mouth.

But Robert takes away my hand, holds my arm captive as he brings his eyes to mine once again. "Try to lie to me now, Kasie. Try to tell me it's him who you want and not me."

I try to look away but I can't quite make myself do it. I feel his erection against my stomach, rigid and strong. I bite my lip so hard I can taste blood but even that isn't enough to silence me as his thumb moves up to caress my clit.

It brings me over the edge. Another cry, a little louder this time. I don't care who hears. I can't care. I have no awareness of anything that isn't Robert or me.

I grab him by his open shirt. "I want you. Make love to me, Robert."

"Yes." His voice is a growl of pure desire. "But you have to leave him. I want to make love to you knowing you're mine."

I close my eyes, my erratic breathing makes speech difficult. "Just make love to me. Please."

"Promise you'll leave him."

His hands are still stroking me, gently now, keeping me in the folds of passion but holding me back from another complete release.

"I . . . can't."

And with that he lets go of me. In an instant he's across the room as I remain pressed against the wall, gasping for air. Instinctually I extend my arm toward him, as if for balance, but he's out of my reach.

He's out of reach in every way.

"I thought you were through with betrayal," he says quietly.

My pants are loose around my hips, my hair disheveled and around my shoulders. I try to gather my thoughts but the suddenness of the mood shift has the room spinning. "Robert, you don't understand—"

"I understand enough," he says curtly. "I understand what I have and what I don't."

"It's not that simple!"

"It's always been exactly that simple."

I'm still trying to catch my breath as he buttons his shirt.

The earth is off its axis. Nothing's going the way it's supposed to. Slowly, over the span of silent minutes, my breathing becomes more measured. I straighten my clothes, turn my gaze to the windows, and stare at the graying skies. "You're both bullies," I say quietly.

Robert turns. "Excuse me?"

"You think you know what's best for everyone, always. You tell me I should be more independent, and then you bristle when I don't make the choices you want me to make."

"I have never bullied you," he points out. "I would never raise a hand to you, or even consider it."

I shrug, a sudden melancholy making me tired. "Some bullies use fists, some blackmail or verbal intimidation. Others use pleasure. You know how to make me . . . feel things and you use it to control me . . . except you can't, can you? You can make me call out your name but you can't make me jump when you call out mine."

Robert's face hardens. "You think so little of me?"

"I think so little of men."

He studies me. "Yesterday, after you left the yacht, you fantasized about me."

I don't answer but I feel myself blush.

"I know you, Kasie," he says with a sigh. "I know that even when I'm nowhere near you I'm inside of you. I can touch you with a thought."

"So touch me," I say quietly. "Touch me with your thoughts, with your eyes, your hands, your mouth and let me touch you." I walk over to him; I want to stay strong but there's a need in me that I can't harness. "I can't be yours, not right now, not in the way you want me to be. Everything's complicated. But I do want you, Robert." I look down, see that he's still hard. I reach for his hand, let my tongue flicker over his thumb. "You see? With us it can be simple."

He smiles, almost wryly, and takes a step closer. "God knows I want you. I want to make you call out my name so loudly they'll be able to hear you in Orange County. But," and with this last word he pulls his hand from mine and uses his fingers to lift my chin, keeping my gaze, "it will be on our terms. Not just yours and certainly not his."

"Is this revenge?" I ask. "I walked away from you, and now you're walking away from me?"

He shakes his head; I can see that he feels my fatigue, that he's unwillingly making it his own. "You know damn well I'll never walk away from you. You're the one pushing me out the door."

He runs his hands over his own shirt, smoothing out a few remaining creases. And then he walks away. "I have some new product development in the hands of my engineers. More user-friendly security systems. Marketing thinks it has significant potential. I'll send over the data."

I grit my teeth. Only Robert can switch from passion to business so easily. They occupy the same space in his heart. It's the foreplay and the cuddling. Usually it is for me, too, but not this time. Not when every statistic and every kiss is a challenge.

"Your team will need to reevaluate some things based on the new developments. Take one more week," he says. "That should be enough time for you to figure out how you want to handle things. Shall I e-mail your managing partner to inform him of the change?"

"No," I mutter, "I'll tell Mr. Love."

"Very well." He smooths his lapel one more time. "And then after that our business will either be through or not, depending on your determinations."

I don't miss the double meaning although he keeps his voice professional, his posture relaxed. "Oh, and Kasie? Just so you know"—he reaches for the door but doesn't open it as he makes direct eye contact one more time—"I fantasized about you last night, too."

# CHAPTER 19

✿

A S I STAND there in my empty office, frustrated and unsatisfied, I wonder, should I have told him? What if I had? Would he have rescued me?

I break out into a bitter laugh. This isn't a fairy tale. Robert can't get on his white horse and permanently seal Dave's lips. I walk around my desk and fall into my seat. The quiet of the room is taunting me, reminding me that I can't even risk a scream.

I reach for my appointment calendar and flip through the pages. I've always been a good planner. I still believe that if given time, I can outsmart Dave. I can get out. But I can't risk Robert confronting him, thereby giving Dave more ammunition for his plot. I'll figure out why Dave wants to hold on to me and how he discovered my secrets. . . .

. . . And then I'll discover his.

I'll discover his secrets and I'll gag him with them. I'll find his lies and weave them into a rope to bind his hands and feet. I'll make him every bit as helpless as he thinks I am now.

*You betrayed him first.*

It's the voice of the little angel on my shoulder. She's feeling neglected lately. And why should I start listening to her again? She wants me to stay where I am and ponder things back into stasis. My devil is more proactive.

For instance, right now my devil reminds me to find out how Dave got to the marina.

He didn't drive there and there was simply no way Dave would use public transportation. Yesterday had started with him saying he had an early-morning meeting. But what if he didn't? What if he had waited in someone else's car, parked discreetly on the street, just waiting to follow me?

A cab? No, probably not. Los Angeles is not New York, where the yellow cabs stream through the city streets like so many migrating salmon. In LA cabs of any color stand out, and if one had been parked on my street as I pulled out of my driveway, I would have noticed.

So someone had driven him. One of his coworkers or friends? But Dave would not have allowed himself to be humiliated in front of someone whose opinion he cared about. A private detective? Could Dave have had a professional follow me?

I look down at my appointment calendar again. I have a meeting with my team in forty-five minutes. I idly read the names of those who are reporting to me for this project: Taci, Dameon, Nina, Asha. . . .

Asha.

The buzzer for my intercom goes off and Barbara's voice breathes through the speakers, letting me know that the long list of menial tasks I heaped upon her this morning has been attended to.

"Come into my office, please," I say and then sit back as the door opens and she tentatively approaches my desk.

Barbara has been my assistant for as long as I've been here. Before that she was the assistant to a man who worked here as a consultant for ten years. She claims to be content with her quiet place in the corporate world, saving her energy for her husband and children at home. I've overheard her waxing poetic about the joys of having free time and a rich family life. I don't understand her enthusiasm. It's within the unstructured mess that qualifies as my free time that I stumble and thoughtlessly submit to whims that will later come back to haunt me. I love my parents, but my family life has been rich only in tragedy and denial. Barbara's view of the world is as foreign to me as that of a tribesman in the Brazilian rainforest. But while

I may not be able to relate to her, I certainly respect her strengths, one of them being her keen powers of observation.

"Did Asha come to work yesterday?"

"Yes," Barbara says with a definitive nod.

Ah, she did. So she couldn't have been the one to ferry Dave about. I sigh and place my chin in my hand. "All right, my team will be meeting in here at the end of the hour. Just hold my calls until it's over."

Barbara nods again and starts to turn before stopping. "Does it matter that Asha showed up late?"

I lift my head. "Excuse me?"

"She wasn't here in the morning. Apparently she had some kind of appointment. But she was here by noon, and I think she stayed late."

"Noon," I repeat.

"Is that important?"

As important as the timing of Judas's departure from the Last Supper.

I sit back, measure the likelihood of the duplicity. "Two days ago, Dave called the office . . . he was planning a surprise party—"

"Oh, did that go well?" Barbara asks hopefully. "He called me but I couldn't think of which of our colleagues to recommend as guests, since you really tend to keep your personal and professional lives separate."

I wince at that. "Why did you tell him to invite Asha?" I ask.

Barbara gives me a funny look. "I told him no such thing. Asha came up to my desk just as I was hanging up. She had sent me some report that she wanted me to print out and have on your desk for the next morning. She asked me who had been on the phone and I told her. That's all."

"That's all? She didn't talk to him? He didn't invite her to the party?"

"Not that I know of . . ." Barbara's voice trails off. The rapid blinking of her eyes gives away her nervousness. "I did tell her about the party . . . and I mentioned that it was a surprise party. She didn't spill the secret ahead of time, did she? I guess I shouldn't have told her about it at all, but it was such a grand romantic gesture . . . and Ma Poulette is supposed to be a fabulous restaurant. I just had to talk to *someone* about it. Did I make a mistake? If so I'm so sorry. I didn't mean—"

I hold up my hand to stop her. "Barbara, you didn't do anything that merits an apology." And I'm beginning to suspect that what Asha has done is so extreme that all the apologies in the world won't make a damn bit of difference.

"Let Asha know that I need to see her."

"Before the meeting?"

"Now."

A few minutes later Asha walks in, all grace and conceit. She's been expecting my summons and it's her anticipation that gives her away.

I stand at my desk and gesture to a chair. Carefully she takes it, her eyes scanning the room, looking for something she apparently isn't finding.

"Did you hear I was leaving?" I ask.

Her mouth twitches, the slightest giveaway of the smile she's suppressing. "I've heard nothing. Are you?"

I reclaim my seat, lace my fingers together. "So Dave didn't tell you?"

Ah, there it is, a flash of worry. "Dave . . . your fiancé? Why would Dave tell me anything? I barely know him."

"But you knew him enough to get him to invite you to our engagement party."

She shrugs, suddenly bored. "Only because he called the office to see if there was anyone from here he should be inviting. I told him he should invite me. That was the first time I've ever spoken to him." She leans forward; her dark eyes are pools of mystery and cynicism. "Are you leaving, Kasie?"

"He called the office," I say, refusing to allow her to drive the conversation. "Did he call you specifically?"

"No, he called your assistant," she says, now clearly exasperated. "Why does any of this matter? Have you been asked to leave or not?"

I smile. Asha's off her game. Today she's more impatient than devious. "I never said anyone *asked* me to leave. Why on earth would you come to that conclusion?"

She hesitates; her error was a stupid one. Unworthy of her. I watch as she gathers her thoughts, calms her mind, and draws herself up. "You would never leave of your own free will," she says simply. "If you're leaving, it's because you've been asked to."

"I'm good at my job, Asha. You acknowledged as much the other night. So again, why would I be asked to leave?"

Again a shrug, but this one more practiced. She's thinking, perhaps wondering how far she can backpedal before I have her crashing into a brick wall. "Politics are funny" is the phrase she settles on. "Sometimes people . . . perfectly competent workers, are let go because they don't fit within the structure as well as it was originally presumed they would. But I'm just speculating, Kasie. You're the one who suggested you were leaving."

"Did I suggest that?" I ask. I keep the sarcasm light, almost playful. "And here I thought I just asked a question," I say with a smile. "I'm more than a competent worker, but let's not spend time debating things we both know. In fact . . . now that I think about it, there's a lot of things we both know, aren't there?"

"I'm not following."

"Well, let's see." I get up from my seat again. My anger is intense, but I like the way it feels. I like the way I'm able to give it shape, form it into a weapon of torture. It's a slow torture, delicate and feminine . . . it has artistry. I imagine myself holding a pretty little scalpel and rubbing it gently against Asha's throat. "We both know you shouldn't have been at that party unless of course you came with someone else. I saw you hanging out with Mr. Freeland. Was he your date? Your way in?"

"Did I give Freeland my affection in exchange for a party invitation? No," she says, and now it's her turn to smile. "I don't mix sex and commerce. Do you, Kasie?"

I stop. This is more audacity than I expected, even from her. "Are you asking me if I'm a prostitute?"

Asha giggles. It's a surprisingly appealing sound, almost seductive in its daintiness. "Don't be silly," she says. "You're an honorable woman. You wear a rather expensive engagement ring to prove it."

I glance down at the ring. It squeezes too tightly.

"Besides," she continues, "prostitutes have sex for profit. Not you. Although after you started dating Dave, you did get a very profitable position here—"

"He got me an interview. I got the job."

"And then you also got us a very profitable account, didn't you?" Asha asks sweetly. Her voice is the spoonful of syrup used to mask the bitterness of a crushed pill. "You got that all by yourself. No help from Dave at all. Mr. Dade just handed it to you."

I don't answer. Instead, I wait to see how far she'll push. Is her hatred enough to make her careless? Has she been spying on me, even before that day on the boat? Or is this all presumptions and speculations?

"What did you tell Tom Love?" she asks. "That you met Mr. Dade in the security line at the airport before flying home?"

"Yes," I say. I have my back to the wall while she looks up at me from the chair I ushered her into. This is my office. I'm in the position of strength here. But the dynamic is unstable.

"It's funny, because I've never gotten into a conversation with anyone I didn't know while in those security lines. Everyone's so focused on getting their keys out of their pockets, their watches unstrapped from their wrists, it's not really a let's-get-to-know-each-other kind of place, is it?"

"For every rule there are exceptions."

"True," Asha agrees with a nod. "And for every crime there is a criminal. When Mr. Dade called to tell Tom he wanted consultant Kasie Fitzgerald to head a team to help him prepare his company for a public offering, he had a different story of your first meeting. He said that the two of you had spoken at a blackjack table."

I raise my chin as if the gesture could increase my height. I need to be above this, but I don't manage it. Her words cut as they were meant to. Tom never told me that my tale contradicted the true story he had apparently already gotten from Robert.

What else had Robert told him? Had he told Tom that we had ended up in his room? No, he wouldn't have shared any of those secrets. For a brief moment my mind betrays me, bringing me back to that night, forcing upon me the recalled feeling of when the man I only knew as Mr. Dade had taken a Scotch-soaked ice cube, briefly touched it to my clitoris, and then licked the liquor off me with the flick of his tongue. Images of his hands on my hips, his head in my lap as I grabbed the back of my chair, my skirt up around my waist . . . I had never done anything like that before.

I was paying for that now.

I could try to convince Asha that Robert is the liar. I could tell her that he had made up a false tale of how we met to insinuate things that never happened, as some men are apt to do.

But I can't do that. I can't load my shame onto Robert's shoulders. Yet the price of the truth exceeds my means.

"I didn't feel the need to tell my boss that I occasionally dabble in gambling," I say, hoping the excuse doesn't sound as lame to her as it does to me. "Some people don't approve."

"Tom Love approves of anything that brings him business, and your time in Vegas definitely did that."

"Asha, where were you yesterday morning?"

"I was in a car," she says, leaning back in her chair. "With your fiancé."

And now I see that I've approached this all wrong. I had assumed she wouldn't want me to think of her as a snoop, as someone so desperate to undermine me she would scurry after me, looking for bread crumbs, clues that could lead her to greater sins. But I'm the only one here who cares what people think. I'm the only one looking to hide my flaws with layers of icing. Asha cares only about power.

And that one fact gives her all the power in the world.

Her lips spread into a Cheshire grin. "Do you think I fucked him?

Dave, that is. Would that upset you? Or would it just even the playing field?"

She stands up, crosses to me. She stands close, too close. "I would never fuck Dave," she purrs. "I'd fuck you, though. Tell me, Kasie, have you ever been touched by a woman?" She reaches forward and brushes her hand against my breast. I jump back, shocked and completely thrown. When I asked Barbara to invite Asha into my office, I had a plan. I had set a trap for a wolf. I hadn't understood that the predator I faced was a viper.

"I'm not a lesbian, not exactly," Asha explains, answering a question no one had asked. "It's more like authority, privilege . . . entitlement that I'm attracted to. I like to strip it away like so much unneeded clothing. I'd love to see you naked, tied to a bed, your body responding to my touch even though you wouldn't want it to. I'd love to see you completely vulnerable with no semblance of control. Then again, you're completely vulnerable now, aren't you? And if there's anyone in this room with control, it's me."

Is Asha trying to commit career suicide? She reports to me! If I told Human Resources what she's saying to me now . . .

My cheeks heat up as what she already knows comes crashing home to me. Her smile is gentle, almost sympathetic.

"You're not going to tell anyone about this conversation, Kasie. You can't. One of us cares about her personal reputation, and I can destroy it with a word." She leans her shoulder against the wall next to me, too close but not touching me. "I bet you made yourself vulnerable to Mr. Dade. That's a man who can make a woman beg; I'm *sure* he can make you beg. And I bet that man is hung. Guys with big, rough hands like his always are. I bet your pussy's sore for days after he's done with you."

"Get out of my office."

"But you're the one who asked me to come, didn't you, Kasie?" she asks. "You brought me here to toy with me, find out what I know. Well," she says, inching even closer. I turn my head away but I can still hear her whisper, a malicious seduction that makes me shiver: "What you've found out is that I know *everything* and now it's my turn to play."

She pushes herself off the wall and starts to walk toward the door.

"I don't have as much to lose as you think," I call after her. "If Tom already knows what I've done, as you suggest, then he's known for a long time. And I still have my job. Nothing's changed for me here."

"Ah, but Tom is comfortable with corruption as long as it works to his purposes. But even he knows that if Dylan Freeland, the founder of our company . . . the fucking *godfather* of your fiancé, ever found out, your office would be mine."

"So why are you talking to me?" I ask. "Why not tell the world?"

She shrugs. "Because this is fun. And if Dave hasn't exposed you yet, it's because he's giving you another chance. He'll back up any lies you spew. It'll be his word . . . and yours and Robert's against mine. I wouldn't stand a chance. But if you slip up again? And Dave finds out?" She wags her finger at me. "That's when the real fun begins."

She smiles again, knowing everything she said is perfectly clear and totally ambiguous. Then with another shrug she says, "See you at the meeting!"

I watch her leave and then, with the wall pressing into my back, I slide to the floor; my knees come to my chest and I bury my face in my hands.

# CHAPTER 20

❀

I DON'T KNOW HOW I got through that meeting. Every one of Asha's comments and questions were completely appropriate. Her composure was perfection. Mine, not so much. I knocked over a bottle of water on my files, I tripped up on my words, I had to ask Taci to repeat her proposal for Maned Wolf's international repositioning twice.

The problem was not what Asha knew. The problem was that Asha didn't lie. She treasured the viciousness of complete honesty. She used truth as a weapon every bit as much as I used lies as a shield. That meant that if anyone ever asked Asha the wrong question . . .

Even now as I sit in my office, alone among a pile of paperwork, the thought makes me shudder. When did I become the fly in the web? But no, that's wrong. The fly is an innocent. I am not.

Most of my coworkers have already gone home. Barbara left ages ago, but I'm still here, as is often the case. This office was once my sanctuary and I hope that in my solitude I can find a way to recapture that feeling.

Daylight is fading behind a smoggy sunset. The sky is a brilliant combination of pinks and lavenders. That's the thing about smog. It's toxic and according to the American Cancer Society it can even be deadly. But when framed the right way, at just the right moment it can make everything beautiful, and you forget. You look up at those colors as the sun rises and declines and you forget that the very thing that is enhancing the natural light, the thing that makes everything look so intensely beautiful, is slowly killing you. Eventually the sun gets a little higher and you see the ugliness of it. But by then it's too late. You've been pulling it into your lungs for hours. It has you. It's in you. That's it.

I wonder if my affair with Robert Dade has been a little like that. Intense, brilliant, beautiful . . . but now it's killing me. I've lost control and for me, for my entire life, control has been my oxygen.

I stare intently at the colors, wishing they would stay. What if I had never met Dave? What if I had found this job that I have loved so much on my own? What if when I had met Robert in Vegas, I had been free? How would things have proceeded? Would we have dated like a normal couple? No, nothing about Robert Dade is normal. But still, we would have become a couple. I'm sure of it. We would have traveled together—sometimes hiking up the Mayan pyramids; other times making love in "The Hotel of Kings" in Paris, the Tuileries Gardens below our window.

But I'm being too conventional in my thinking. We could go to Nice, to the Musée Marc Chagall, rent out the concert hall for a private performance. Not something the Musée would normally agree to, but Monsieur Dade could make it happen.

A small band of musicians is waiting for us on the stage as we walk into the room bathed in the blue light streaming through the stained glass. A pianist sits with his fingers poised over a baby grand that would be completely unremarkable if the lid of the piano wasn't open to reveal painted lovers rising into a blue-gray landscape. Around them are villagers, a quarter of the size of the lovers. They don't attempt to match the couple's grandeur but they seem to rejoice in the warmth that emanates from them.

Robert leads me past rows of empty seats until we are in the front of the room, just a few feet from the stage. He steps away from me only to extend his hand in my direction, his palm up, offering a universal invitation that he reiterates with words when he asks, "Will you dance?"

As I take his hand the band starts to play and we begin to move.

The bass is so low, its vibrations tremble against my skin as I follow Robert's lead in something that resembles a waltz but is different enough to make it uniquely ours. I throw back my head and laugh as I'm twirled around the room, wrapped up in blue light and Monsieur Dade's arms.

But then he stops, right there in the middle of the floor, and with a slow smile, he tells me I'm beautiful. Lifting myself onto my tiptoes, I kiss his lips, lightly at first but then his hand moves to the back of my head, pulling me in closer.

The music soars with my pulse and we begin to dance again. But this time it's different. Our shirts drift to the floor as the sonata ends, bringing us to a new, more rhythmic melody. Then comes his belt, my skirt, everything, until we are dancing naked through the hall. A red dove on painted blue glass seems to swoop down on us as his tongue parts my lips. The music beats through me as we sway. I feel him get hard against me. The musicians don't even seem to notice us; that's not their place in this dream. They are only required to provide Robert and me with a soundtrack for our passion. And as he lowers me to the floor, as I roll on top of him, straddle his hips, and feel him push inside of me, I know that, in the ways that count, it is just the two of us. I ride him slowly, moving with the tempo.

The musicians have the stage. We have each other.

Robert's hands slide to my waist, guiding me, moving me so I can feel the full length of him inside of me. Painted memories of Chagall's youth seem to fall from the sky as Robert sits up. He's still inside me as I sit facing him in his lap. For a moment we don't move; we just take a moment to feel what it is to be connected, with our bodies, with our eyes, by an emotion that is so much bigger than either one of us.

And then the dance starts again. I gasp as his hips buck against mine, splitting me open until it feels like it's not just him but the music itself that's inside of me, moving through me, resonating against every nerve ending to make me frantic with desire.

With one decisive movement he flips me over and I cling to him as he begins to pull out only to enter me again with a forceful thrust and a gentle kiss. "I love you," he says, and I respond in kind.

He positions one of my legs above his shoulder. "Follow my lead," he whispers.

And with that he thrusts again and my world is filled with ecstasy. The music, the art, the man who makes my heart pound . . . it brings me to the brink of nirvana and as Chagall's lovers swirl in their blue light I come with a cry that echoes through the room.

His sweat is mingled with mine, my nose is filled with the scent of our sex . . .

. . . and we're not done.

He turns me on my stomach and again he enters me. On the ground I can see fragmented reflections of blue, a cool contrast to the red heat inside me.

As he pushes farther and farther inside, his hand strokes the length of my back with a subtle pressure that brings me to crescendo. And as I come again, I hear him cry out, too. We climax together in the blue light of Chagall's concert hall, surrounded by music.

My name is on his lips and it's what I hear as he lays his head between my shoulder blades. "I love you," he says again as the musicians transition to a quieter song.

And in the perfection of that moment I know it's true.

Just as I know the sunset I see right now is beautiful.

But like my fantasy, it's fading. Darkness is coming.

The door opens to my office. I don't turn to see who it is. I know just by the way my ring seems to get heavier on my hand.

"The workday's over," Dave says; his voice is laced with his newfound cruelty. "Get your stuff together. I have plans for us."

CHAPTER 21

WE DON'T SAY much as we crawl along with the late rush-hour traffic of the 405. Dave keeps his eyes on the road, his hands on the wheel. I can smell the smoke of cigars on his clothes. He stopped by his men's club before coming to me, sat in a leather armchair, chortled while some stockbroker told him a dirty joke, basked in the glory of being one of the elite. But whatever cheer he derived from those interactions fell away as soon as he got within touching distance of me.

I want to tell him that if he's truly repelled by me, he should just let me go, spare us both. But I know it's not that straightforward for him. There's pride involved and maybe, to use Asha's word, *entitlement*. There's more, too, emotions and motivations I can't yet read, but I'm too tired tonight to dip deep into that brew. I rest my head against the passenger window and wonder how long I can extend the silence.

"I talked to your parents today," he says.

And I can feel the smog in my lungs.

I force my brain to start running through the facts rather than giving in to the panic that's ebbing its way in. Dave is not like Asha. He can lie. He could be lying to me now. He has every reason to want to unnerve me.

"You called them," I say, making my words into a statement rather than a question. If I'm wrong, he'll smirk, inadvertently giving me a clue as to what's going on. If I'm right, he'll think I know him better than I do.

But of course I don't know him at all. The man sitting by my side is little more than an ice sculpture of the warm human being who used to hold me through the nights.

Dave doesn't smirk. Instead he nods, almost reluctant to acknowledge the accuracy of my statement. Perhaps he wants to keep me guessing about everything.

"Do you want to know what I told them?"

It's funny, but I don't think I've ever heard menace and hope mingled together like that. He wants so badly for me to take the bait. He wants to win the game. For him this is a sporting event, one that he's only beginning to master.

For me it's a war.

"Only if you want to tell me," I say, a false retreat as I work to lure out the truth.

He gives me a sharp look. "I guess it doesn't matter. Obviously I told them enough to keep them from calling you."

"Is that obvious?" I ask. One more bullet deflected.

"What do you mean?"

"Well, aren't you trying to prove a negative? You're assuming they didn't call me after your conversation, but you haven't actually asked me if that's the case." I reach over and take his hand, ignoring the frostbite sting of his touch. "If you truly want to help me, like you say, then you need to communicate with me honestly."

Again the silence comes as Dave keeps his eyes on all the brake lights ahead; they're like the intent red eyes of demons watching a show.

"Things are supposed to be a certain way," he says after we've rolled through another quarter of a mile. The statement isn't meant for me; it's not exactly like he's talking to himself, either. This has the sound of a prayer, like he's gently correcting God, reminding the universe how to act.

My hand is still on his, keeping the force field down. "What did you tell my parents, Dave?"

"I am so incredibly angry with you." Again I'm not sure if the words are meant for me or God, though undoubtedly they ring true for both of us. "I'm not going to let you go, but I can't let *it* go, either. They say love and hate are the opposite sides of the same coin but I never understood that expression before. I never got it. Now I do."

I withdraw my hand. If this is what's beneath the force field, it's not worth my time. "This isn't a coin toss," I say. "If it was, I'd pick it up and flip it back to love." I snap my fingers and then smile down at them wistfully. "It would be that easy."

He doesn't say anything and keeps his eyes on the highway. "I told them you were acting like Melody. I didn't need to say much more before they speculated on the details themselves."

I freeze. That bullet hit. My throat begins to constrict. But . . . "If you had told them that, they would have called me."

"I told them not to. I told them I'd set you straight . . . or not."

"I don't understand." *And if it doesn't make sense then it can't be true,* I want to add. It can't be true. I won't allow myself to even entertain it.

"Your mother thinks she did this to you. Maybe she did. She's hysterical. Your father probably agrees but he won't say as much. Since they think they're the cause of the problem, they're letting me be in charge of the solution."

I feel myself color. "You think you're in charge of me?"

"Yes. They're disgusted with you, Kasie. They think you're nothing better than a common slut fucking her way to the top. After we spoke, your father actually speculated that you might have been granting favors to some of your professors."

"Shut up."

"Tell me, how did you get an A in physics when you don't know the difference between fission and fusion? Did you stay after class? Crawl under his desk, rub yourself against his leg like a dog in heat?"

"I earned every grade I got."

"But *how* did you earn them? In sweat? Was it the papers you put on the professors' desks that pleased, or was it the view of you bent over their desks, arching your back, offering your body as a door prize?" He shakes his head. "I think the saddest thing I ever heard was your father saying that it might have been better if they hadn't had children. I don't know, Kasie—they could be done with you. Just like they were done with the disappointment they spawned before you, even before she died."

*I can see my father sitting at the kitchen table with my mother. I hear him running through the filthiest of possibilities as my mother gets smaller and smaller in her chair. They don't know I'm there, standing outside the room, peeking in. I only turned nine a few days earlier; my birthday party had ended badly right after my father had caught my sister and some man together in her bedroom.*

*"She was high, Donna," he says to my mother. "My guess is that he gave her the drugs. That's what she was doing, she was paying him with the only currency she has. And she did it during Kasie's birthday. She taints everything she touches. We have to kick her out. I won't have that kind of depravity in my house."*

*"She's our daughter." It takes me a moment to realize it's my mother speaking. She sounds so different. The polish has faded from her perfect diction and her words are laid bare, the desperation on display for all to see.*

*"She stopped being our daughter when she became a whore."*

*Is there a tremor in his voice? Is he struggling with his proclamation? I don't know. All I hear is the definitiveness of the sentence. I hear the condemnation. Only yesterday we were innocent, my sister and I. Her oddities were eccentricities; she was a handful. My father needed to take her in hand; that's all.*

*But now she's a whore.*

*Whores are nothing.*

*Whores can be cast out, punished, hated. I'm watching my father learn to hate my sister.*

*"Not under my roof," he says, and I wonder if I'll ever see her again.*

I reach for my handbag, but Dave stops me with a look before asking, "What are you doing?"

"I'm calling my parents."

Dave opens his mouth to protest, then stops and shrugs. The traffic is lightening as I fish out my cell and dial the numbers of my father.

It's hard to hold the phone; my palms are slick with sweat and my eyes are already misting over.

My father picks up. "Kasie?" he says, surprised. Perhaps he didn't think I'd be brave enough to call.

"Dad, I . . . we need to talk. I know . . . I know how angry you must be with me."

There's a long pause on the other end of the line and I anxiously try to think of a way to proceed.

"Kasie, is there something you're trying to tell me?" he finally asks. His voice is cautious . . . and confused.

"You . . . you don't know why you might be angry at me?" I look over at Dave. He's grinning.

"Have you done something?"

I pull the phone away from my ear. Part of me wants to laugh with relief and hysteria and pain. Dave's playing a game. I'm fighting a war. He's winning and I'm dying.

With a shaky hand I bring the phone back up. "I just realized that I didn't spend much time with you at the party and I didn't even offer to drive you back to the airport the next day. I've been horribly neglectful."

"Which is why you had Dave call us," my father says; his voice isn't guarded anymore. It's relaxed; he's pleased with my apology for what he sees as a minor offense. "Dave explained how things are at your work right now. You do what you need to do, honey."

"Okay," I say numbly.

"Dave's a good man," my father says thoughtfully. "He's . . . decent and he comes from a good family. I really like him."

"I know," I say.

Dave pulls us into a new lane and we pass a stream of cars slowly making their way to an exit.

"We're proud of you, Kasie. We're proud of the choices you've made in your life. And please don't worry about being caught up at work. Your mother and I completely understand. And it's not forever, right?"

"Right."

"Good! So soon you'll be the sweet, attentive daughter we all know and love. Just make sure you don't neglect that man of yours. He's a treasure, too."

*Trust, sweet, love* . . . these words seem loaded to me now that I'm living in a world of deception, bitterness, and hate. Dave's clearly enjoying my unraveling. He's savoring the sour taste of my betrayal, letting the vinegar slide around on his tongue before swallowing it, and now I can smell it on his breath and seeping out of his pores. It defines him.

I say good-bye to my father, doling out enough pleasantries in the process to distract him from the sadness he might hear if he bothered to listen too closely.

I look at Dave. He's still smiling but his smile doesn't seem to be attached to the rest of him. His shoulders are rigid, his eyes are hard, his hands grip the steering wheel like it's a rifle someone might try to pull away from him.

"I'm sorry," I say. For the first time today I mean it. "I'm sorry I made you so very sad and so horribly angry."

The smile stays plastered in place but his shoulders rise even higher. "Just because I didn't tell them this time doesn't mean I won't. Your father won't forgive you."

"Dave, you don't have to let this happen."

"What?" he says with a short laugh. "I don't have to expose you?"

"You don't have to let my misjudgments change who you are."

He's quiet for a moment; we switch from the 405 to the 101 and the traffic slows once more. "When you took off your clothes for him, when you let him touch you in all the places where only I was supposed to be allowed to touch you . . . was that a *misjudgment*?"

"Perhaps I should have chosen a different word but—"

"Like when a track and field athlete hits the bar during a vault . . .

or a quarterback tries to throw the ball to a teammate only to miss his mark and have it intercepted . . . that kind of misjudgment?"

"We're not arguing semantics while we stomp on each other's hearts."

"No, we're not arguing; I'm asking you a question. I'm giving you an opportunity to explain yourself."

"I've already done that."

"Have you?" He turns to me. The traffic has stopped . . . an accident perhaps. Someone's carelessness has destroyed property and lives.

"I had wedding jitters . . . I got scared—"

"So you slept with someone else. You fucked a security blanket? Rubbed it between your legs, that made you feel . . . safe?"

"Dave—"

"Because I can do that, if that's what you need." With a jerk of his hand he plunges it between my thighs, roughly rubs the fabric against my vagina. The man driving the SUV in the next lane, bored and weary, looks over at the wrong moment. He sees where Dave's hand is, makes eye contact with me, lifts his eyebrows.

I grab Dave's hand and pull it away. "Knock it off."

"Ah, so when he fingers your pussy, it makes you feel safe, but when I do it, you find it repulsive."

"When you do it in hate, yes, it's repulsive."

"You want to be touched in love?"

"Yes."

"Then make me feel love."

Perhaps it's the accidental sincerity of his tone. I turn in my seat, try to study his expression, but his eyes stay stubbornly on the road. There's something tragic in what he's said.

"I don't know if I can make you feel that."

"Does he love you?"

I hesitate before answering. "I don't know. I don't even know if it matters."

"And you?"

"You're asking if I love him?"

"Yes . . . no . . . I . . ." His voice trails off and he blushes slightly, embarrassed by his own fumbling response.

The traffic in our lane starts to move. The witness to Dave's brief assault falls behind us, making the memory nothing but a shrinking image in my side mirror. "What do you want to know, Dave?"

"I don't think love can just disappear," he says, as much to himself as to me. "And yet what you did . . . we had something . . . it was big. How can you be so cavalier with something that had so much substance?"

I don't have an answer.

"You think I'm trying to torture you," he says quietly. "Maybe I am. Maybe I want you to experience a tenth of the pain you've caused me. But I don't believe the love we had just disappeared. I don't believe that the woman I love has evaporated."

"I'm here, Dave. I didn't evaporate."

"No, it's not you. A whore in sheep's clothing . . . in *her* clothing. It's like a split personality or . . . or a mental breakdown."

"You think I've gone crazy?"

"I think you need to be saved." He takes a deep breath. "I'm going to do that. I'm going to be your hero whether you want one or not."

And like that, he's going from tragic to insane. He's still the captor asking his prisoner to sing his praises, but maybe all captors are a little insane. What does it matter if someone is fanatical about religion, politics, or love? Fanaticism is what it is: crazy, misguided, and, in a weird way, honest. Fanatics believe their own bullshit.

"I understand now," he continues. "You have . . . needs . . . things you have to get out of your system. I'm going to help you do that. We're going to use the depravity that's infecting you to our advantage. I'm going to bring you back to the woman you were, the one I want to marry. By the time I'm done, that's who you'll *want* to be. You'll see how your current path only leads to degradation. You'll crave purity."

I shake my head. I didn't know an affair could push someone

over the edge like this. It's like he thinks he can turn our lives into a modern-day version of *The Taming of the Shrew*.

"Tonight," he continues. "We'll start tonight."

I don't know exactly what that means but I know what it *might* mean. The idea of being with Dave now, having him touch me, having him push his dick inside of me, looking at me smugly as I squirm underneath him . . . I can't do it.

"You are so angry with me right now," I say softly. "I don't want to . . . to be with you until you feel some degree of kindness toward me."

"You don't think I do?" he asks, but it's a rhetorical question. We both know I'm right.

"Then we'll start slow," he says. "A dinner at home. Cook me dinner the way you used to do. Dress up for me. Show me that you're at least willing to make an effort."

I turn toward the window. I'm tired. I don't have the energy for any of this. But Dave had been making a point when he lied to me about telling my parents. He was letting me know what he could do. If I don't make an effort, why should he hold his tongue? Why should he do anything for me at all?

"I'll cook dinner," I say quietly.

"And you'll let me select something pretty for you to wear while you serve me?"

*While I serve him.* I have to tell myself that he's only talking about dinner . . . but of course the wording was more carefully crafted than that. I've given my confession and this is the penance he has chosen for me. Instead of appealing to God, I'm meant to appeal to him.

So I nod. It's only dinner, only a dress. I'd rather recite the Rosary a few hundred times, but perhaps that wouldn't be appropriate. It seems silly to try to bring something sacred into hell.

❁

# CHAPTER 22

W HEN WE ENTER his house I head straight for the kitchen.
Dave probably thinks this is submission but really I just
want to get away from him. I'm not a spectacular cook but I'm not
horrible. I pull out the ingredients necessary to make a quick-and-
easy stir-fry and try to forget the day. The counter is covered with
fresh vegetables and two small frozen lamb loin chops when Dave
walks in. He stares at the meat, seeing an insult there. He doesn't
much like red meat but had bought the lamb in an attempt to please
me. Months ago, a lifetime ago, he had tried to surprise me with a
meal . . . which he mangled terribly. We had laughed about it and I
had ended up making us pasta.

But he hadn't thrown away the remaining uncooked loin chops
and I *do* like red meat . . . and I'm the one cooking this time. I pull
out a large chopping knife and lay it carefully on a cutting board.

"The dress is on my bed. Go ahead and change."

"I'll change after I make dinner," I say as I reach for some extra-
virgin olive oil and a microwave-safe plate for the defrosting.

"No, change now. It will make me happy."

He's a million miles from happy. If he was happy, I'd have the
man I once cared for, even if I don't love him.

I suck in a sharp breath. And like that I finally admit the evil
truth. I never loved the man I agreed to marry.

I only wanted the life he provided, the orderliness, the structure, the predictability. That had all seemed so important. Funny
how those "attributes" have lost so much of their appeal. Perhaps it

wasn't the betrayal that turned him inside out. Maybe it's the lack of love that's transformative. Maybe it's the distance between what we want and what we have that sculpts our behavior.

A dress won't fix anything, it certainly won't make either of us happy, but since I don't know what will, I do as asked and go up to his room to change.

The dress makes me laugh. It's ridiculously provocative and clearly something he picked up today. It's black and off the shoulder. A strip of solid fabric covers my breasts but below is sheer black mesh, which will reveal my full midriff before meeting another band of solid fabric that forms the micro-miniskirt. I saw a photograph of a pop star wearing a similar dress to the VMAs or something like that, but I doubt Dave knows this is a knockoff of a piece just slightly less tacky. For Dave, this probably constitutes lingerie.

I squeeze into the dress. It's skintight and oddly flattering but it's also a little slutty. Much more so than the Herve Leger dress I wore in Vegas the night I met Robert Dade. One glance in the mirror tells me that I'm going to need to change out of the bikini panties I'm wearing and into a thong.

I fish through the few items of clothing I have stored here to see if I can find one.

"You won't be able to wear underwear with that," Dave says.

I whirl around to see him standing in the doorway.

I smile slightly. "Are you trying to humiliate me?" I ask.

He shrugs, giving away the answer in his silence.

I won't give him the satisfaction. Not over a dress worn within a private residence. "Why would I be embarrassed? Only yesterday you saw me in less."

I let my hand slide over my exposed stomach and then up my skirt. It takes effort to wriggle out of my panties without flashing him, but I manage it and then throw them at Dave, who catches them in one hand. He looks mildly embarrassed and slightly aroused.

I walk up to him, lean in, and say with a singsong whisper, "If you touch me, I'll kill you."

And then I walk past him to make dinner, leaving him with an erection he's going to have to take care of all by himself.

It's a struggle to prepare the lamb with my movements restricted by the unforgiving fabric. My guilt over what I've done is slowly dissipating with each one of Dave's pathetic attempts to debase me. While Asha's attacks are polished and executed with a vicious grace, Dave's moves are clumsy, only hitting his mark by the occasional stroke of luck. The single advantage he has is that, unlike with Asha, I'm still not clear I fully understand what motivates him.

And what does he have to lose by calling my parents or his godfather right now? Is he stringing me along until he does? Am I playing for salvation or time?

The oil in the frying pan pops and sizzles as I sprinkle in bits of bloody red meat. I turn the knife on the vegetables, slicing through them with precise and violent movements.

I've been fighting like a civilian, wildly swinging at anything that resembles an enemy. I need to be the soldier. I need a battle plan.

As I wield the blade across the cutting board, I wonder if the violence will remain in the form of metaphor. How far can I be pushed before I snap?

Twenty-five minutes later dinner is nearly ready but before I can reach for a single plate, the doorbell rings.

I hesitate. This doesn't feel like coincidence. I look down at my dress. It was one thing to wear this in front of Dave but someone else?

And then an odd thought crawls into my brain. *What if it's Robert Dade?*

*I imagine Robert bursting through the door. He doesn't see Dave, only me. "You don't need to do this for me," he says. And just like that I realize that it's always been about us. Dave isn't important. I turn my eyes to Dave and watch as he fades away, like an apparition or a shadow destroyed by the light.*

It's an indulgent fantasy, one I don't allow myself to entertain for more than a minute but it's long enough to excite me. My heart beats a little faster; I feel a small ache of yearning. . . .

It's pathetic, really. The chances of it being him at the door are slim to none. He doesn't even know where Dave lives. He's not here, so why am I feeling these things?

*I know you, Kasie. I know that even when I'm nowhere near you I'm inside of you. I can touch you with a thought.*

The doorbell rings again, pulling me out of my fantasies and reminiscences. But by now I already feel a slight moisture between my legs.

I shouldn't have removed my underwear. Self-consciously I walk to the entryway of the kitchen as Dave approaches the door.

"Who is it, Dave?" I ask.

He looks over his shoulder with a smirk. There's malice in his eyes as he flings the door open.

Tom Love stands there, a bottle of wine in his hand and a puzzled look on his face. "I wasn't sure if I was supposed to bring something," he says to Dave, speaking hesitantly as if he's unsure of what he's walking into. "I didn't expect the invitation."

And then Tom's eyes dart to me. He takes in the dress and his mouth goes slack, his eyes wide . . . and then a devious smile.

"What exactly am I being invited to?"

I feel the embarrassment start at my toes and then crawl up my legs through my very core until it wraps around my lungs and squeezes with the crushing power of a snake.

"Remember I said your boss would be joining us?" Dave asks. He approaches me; each footstep has the hollow echo of spite. "When I put together our engagement party, the only people from your firm who you even knew well enough to invite were my godfather and Asha. Afterward, I realized that most of your superiors don't know anything about what you're like outside of the office. I thought we should give Mr. Love a glimpse." With this his eyes fall to my hem. I'm tempted to pull on it, try somehow to make the dress longer but it would be useless. If anything, pulling it would bring the top a little too low, exposing the pink areoles that surround my nipples. I'm hyperconscious of the wetness between my legs, I can feel it trickling down and I squirm slightly wondering how to best make my retreat.

"I won't be joining you," I say quietly. The declaration is met by a sharp look from Dave and a surprised one from Tom.

"You're not?" Tom asks, stepping in and closing the door behind him. His eyes move from me to Dave, then back to me. He takes in the dress appreciatively, but the leer is gone now that he's beginning to understand what this is and what this isn't. "You didn't know Dave invited me."

I shake my head, but Dave drapes a heavy arm over my bare shoulders. "No matter; she made enough for three. Kasie's not a big eater."

I imagine scratching his face with the ring he forces me to wear. Red blood on a red stone.

"I won't be joining you," I say again, but suddenly Dave's arm gets tight as he pulls me to him.

"But you must join us, Kasie," he says. Again the image of a snake leaps to mind. Dave speaks with the serpent's voice. "What will Tom and I talk about without you? It will all just be business, like that account you've been working on or something. Maned Wolf, right— Mr. *Robert* Dade?"

"Ah," this from Tom as he gently places the burgundy wine on the table. I sense the dawning of understanding, but not surprise. He keeps his eyes on the table, perhaps studying the metaphorical puzzle pieces that have just been exposed to him.

"We'll need three plates," Dave says definitively. The role of master was not tailored for him. It's a size too big and he seems more vulnerable within the fabric of the character. Like a boy wearing his father's clothes.

And yet this bullet has hit its mark. I report to Tom, and although I respect his professional abilities, I don't like him. I don't like the way he molds ethics and morality to support his ambitions. I don't want him to see me dressed like this, the skirt barely covering my hips, the neckline exposing the curve of my breast . . . this was never meant for Tom's eyes.

And Dave's threats were not subtle. Tom understood the nuance as well as I did. He had figured out that my relationship with Robert was more than platonic long before he arrived for dinner. But that doesn't mean I want to discuss it with him. It doesn't mean that I want to be faced with the shame of his knowing . . . and judging me. Was he like Dave? Did he, too, think I was a whore?

"The plates," Dave says.

I turn and walk into the kitchen. The reverberations of my pounding heart are so powerful it makes my whole body shake. How could I have done this to my life? And for what? Sex with a stranger? An illicit affair? Had I actually thought it was worth the risk?

Had it been? The memories flicker in front of my eyes in rapid succession: flirting over Scotch, energetically talking business at a restaurant, playfully hitting him with a pillow while he laughs, being in his bed, his weight on top of me, his hands on my hips, gently lifting them so he can plunge deeper into me, his hand slipping to my clit; he toys with me as he continues to move inside me. I can't catch my breath . . . I don't want to. . . .

*What am I doing?*

I have a crisis on my hands. My fiancé is treating me like a tramp in front of my boss and I'm fantasizing about my lover?

*No,* my devil answers, *you're just remembering why it was worth it.*

I try to shake the thoughts out of my head and split the stir-fry into three portions.

*Robert's hands are on my breasts, gently pinching my nipples.*

I pull out three wineglasses.

*I feel Robert's kisses forging a path across my shoulders.*

I hear the low murmur of male voices coming from the dining room as I carefully select the utensils. My nipples are hard and pressing against the fabric of this hateful dress.

I take a deep breath and center myself. I'll take my time in here. Let the fantasy run its course, let it fortify me. When I make love to Robert I always begin by feeling vulnerable and end by feeling strong. I need to reach that point of strength tonight.

"Kasie."

I turn swiftly, surprised by the sound of Tom's voice so close. His eyes immediately go to my chest and I cross my arms over my breasts in hopes of hiding the evidence of my train of thought. But the action only pulls the dress higher, and I quickly lower them, hoping he didn't notice that I exposed everything in a moment.

He turns his head away, his eyes on the floor.

"Where's Dave?" I ask.

"I just got a new Porsche, told him he should go and take a look at it."

"You didn't go out with him?"

"No. I locked him out."

The admission shakes me out of my embarrassment and into something that resembles shock and awe . . . and admiration. "You locked him out of his own house?"

"I did." He's still looking at the floor but I can see the smile.

Maybe I like Tom after all.

Unless . . . I look down at my silhouette, feeling self-conscious once again.

"Why did you lock him out?" I ask. "If you think something's going to happen between you and me—"

"What, are you telling me that I can't have sex with you in your fiancé's house while he's locked out on the front porch banging on the door?"

I don't want to show my amusement, but it's hard to hide it.

"Look, sex with you under those circumstances, under *any* circumstances, would be awesome, but it's not going to happen. I know you don't want me here," he says.

I swallow but don't answer.

He shifts, suddenly gangly and awkward. "I also can't sleep with you because you're engaged to my boss's godson. I don't think he's going to squeal on me for locking him out; he's gotta have some level of pride, but sleeping with his fiancé while she's cooking him dinner? Yeah, that might get him to make a phone call."

"You're smarter than me," I say quietly. "I've done some things that I . . . I didn't think through. Things that could get me fired."

Tom lifts his eyes to mine. "I know what you've done . . . not the details, but I know . . . and I don't care." He lets that sink in, then breaks into a silky smooth laugh. "Actually I do care. I'm glad you fucked Robert Dade. If I had thought fucking him would get us the Maned Wolf account, I'd have fucked him, too. I'd have to have a lot to drink first but . . ."

A giggle bubbles up in my throat. Everything about this moment is preposterous.

Yet Tom's smile fades as he presses forward. "Thing is, Kasie, if I had known that *your* fucking him was going to get us the account, I would have encouraged you to do it, and if you had let me in on what was going on, I would have helped you hide it from Dave."

The giggle dies, the bubbles popping under the pressure of my disapproval even as my own hypocrisy drums against my temples. He's only saying he'd do the things that I've already done.

"I didn't have sex with Robert to get ahead," I say quietly.

Tom shrugs, indifferent to my motivations. It's the result that pleases him. "I'm just saying that if Dave's godfather wasn't Dylan Freeland, it would be a win-win for everyone."

I watch Tom with new eyes, seeing for the first time how his indifference to morality can serve me. There is no judgment here, just hard practicality that rules his actions and a little lust that he restrains with admirable skill.

"Mr. Freeland is a great businessman," Tom continues thought-fully. "But unfortunately for us he's an even better family man. If he finds out you cheated on his godson, you're out. He'll find an appropriate excuse. We have clauses in all of our contracts about behavior with clients, the importance of protecting the firm's reputation, etcetera, etcetera. He'll say you traded sexual favors for an account and that'll be it. It'll become a matter of public record; Freeland will make sure of that. Your life will get harder."

As the word leaves his mouth, he winces and shifts his weight uncomfortably. The movement draws my attention downward, making me aware of his physical state and his unintentional pun. With effort I manage not to roll my eyes. It's silly really, getting so excited over a dress. He could go to any beach to see women wearing less. And if I was any other girl, he would leer or dismiss me as a common slut or perhaps not notice me at all, write me off as another LA, club-going exhibitionist.

It's the rarity of seeing me vulnerable, of seeing me revealing what I have consistently concealed, that disarms him. He knows I'm not wearing this dress by choice, and, because of that, I sense that he wants to be repelled rather than aroused by the sight of me . . . a sight he has no right to see. It's a flash of decency in a cold storm of cynicism.

But his body is not cooperating with his whims of conscience and I can't blame him for that. I can blame Dave, but not him.

Carefully, I clasp my hands in front of me. It feels like every movement moves the dress a little higher. "What can I do?" I ask.

Tom's eyes flicker to my hemline before going back to the floor. "A counterattack."

"Against Dave? How? He hasn't done anything that will turn Freeland away from him. I have nothing on him that will compel him to keep quiet."

"You're not being imaginative enough," Tom says. "Facts can be bought just like any other commodity. Sometimes by barter, sometimes with currency, but they can always be bought."

It's then that we hear the pounding on the front door. Tom sighs and shakes his head. "He'll wake the neighbors with that racket."

It's only eight thirty, but the point's a good one. Tom walks to the foyer, I follow a few feet behind and hang back as Tom opens the door, revealing Dave on his own doorstep, his face an intriguing shade of crimson. "You locked me out on purpose!"

"I did no such thing," Tom says, the lie light on his tongue. "I have no idea how this happened."

Dave's eyes shift to me. "What exactly did you two get up to?"

I almost laugh. He calls Tom here to see me in a state of undress and now he's worried that Tom might have touched me with more than his eyes? Again, I'm reminded that, like me, Dave is an amateur when it comes to ruthlessness.

Tom sees the humor in this, too, and a small smile plays on his lips. "Are you worried that I've already sampled what you've brought me here to taste?"

Dave looks stricken. Control is a slippery thing and his grip is weak. I see the way he's looking at me. The hostility he shoots from his eyes almost hurts.

Almost. That's the thing about cruelty: as with most venoms, when they are taken in continuous but small doses, one can build up an immunity to it.

"I don't think I'll be staying for dinner after all," Tom says. He turns to me, conspicuously dismissive of the man in front of him. "The wine on the table is all yours . . . although I'm sure you need something stronger."

"I'll walk you to your Porsche," I say.

Tom nods. "Take your key first. That door lock is temperamental."

Yes, in many ways Tom is smarter than me. His vision isn't clouded with emotion or pain. I grab my keys from my purse on the console and follow him to the car.

"He's angry. He doesn't want to let you go," Tom says while we walk down the pathway, Dave's glare pressing against our backs. "No man in his right mind would."

His car is painted a uniquely dark, metallic silver that reminds me of the tinted mirrored windows that make up the high rise that holds Maned Wolf's offices. He pauses at the driver's-side door, his keys pressed into his palm. "Will you be safe?"

I look up sharply, consider his features. Concern is not an emotion I've seen him wear before. "Dave won't hurt me," I say.

"He's hurting you *now*, Kasie. This is abuse."

"I know . . . but what I meant . . . he won't lay a hand on me, Tom."

"I can take you home," he says carefully. "Or if you like, I can take you to *him*." I flush and Tom smiles wryly. "Would feigning ignorance be better?"

I nod. The reflection of my figure in the car's metallic paint is distorted and fragmented.

"Very well; as far as I'm concerned Dave is the only man you've been with in years. Your relationship with Mr. Dade is purely professional. See," he says as he unlocks his door, "facts can be bought, sometimes for as little as a smile."

*But I'm not smiling.* I keep the thought to myself as he gets in and I watch my reflection in the shiny silver exterior shift, change, and disappear as he drives off.

When I get back to the house Dave is still in the doorway, his fury weakened with uncertainty. I move past him, wait for him to close the door before I turn to face him.

"I am stronger than a dress. I'm stronger than all of this." The words are flat, without inflection. These are simple truths that don't need enhancement. "Did you think Tom Love would forget who I am? Did you think he would see me in this dress and treat me differently than the woman he knows me to be? I've been working with him for five and a half years."

"Yes," he acknowledges. "And I've been your boyfriend for six. But as I said earlier, I don't know who you are. What I do know is that the clothes you used to wear don't seem to suit you anymore. This does."

I feel the cheap fabric clinging to me, feel the air between my legs, reminding me of my exposure. I should feel vulnerable right now, but at this moment I simply don't. He's weak, desperate. I feel no more vulnerable before him than I would feel in front of a bird with broken wings.

"Is this how you wish to define us now?" I ask him brazenly. "With you constantly trying to bring me down and with me rising above it?"

"Seriously, Kasie?" he hisses. "Look at you! You're dressed like a tramp!"

"And yet Tom didn't see a tramp." I take a step closer. Some foolish impulse takes over and I add, "Robert didn't see me that way, either."

"You're bringing him up to me? In my home?"

I smile. In a Victorian novel he would have added the words "You dare?" and with a raise of an eyebrow I answer the unspoken question: Yes, I dare.

But I need to be careful here. The moment Dave gives up, the moment he thinks all his attempts at torture will be fruitless, he'll end this thing with a phone call. And Tom was right in his predictions. If he exposes me to those who care about such things, to people *I* care about, he will pull away my newfound courage like the peel off an orange. I'll lose everything.

So I soften my tone, offer him a treaty rather than a punch: "I don't think you see me that way, either. I think you're angry. But I think that maybe you meant it when you said—"

"When I said what?" The words come out like venom from a spitting cobra.

"When you said you wanted me to make you feel love. I think you want to love me again."

He takes a step closer, hesitant at first, then another and another, each move becoming a little more confident and a little more aggressive. "He was different from me, yes? Edgier? Rougher? More dominant?"

"Is that what this is about," I ask, almost weary, "dominance?"

"Give me a chance." His right hand slips to the back of my neck and holds me in place. "I can give you what you want." His left hand reaches for my breast.

I slap him in the face.

Slowly, his eyes never leaving mine, he lowers his hands and moves to the side, picking up his keys from a low table in the foyer.

"Where are you going?" I ask as he opens the coat closet.

"I'm going out." He smiles sardonically before adding, "I need space to consider whether or not I'm going to destroy you. Don't wait up. It'll take some thinking."

The air's prickly. I may have pushed him too far. But he's taking away my options and the violence he keeps pumping into my heart is hard to discipline. "My car's still at work," I say quietly.

"You won't need it," Dave says decisively. "I want you to stay here tonight. Your obedience may be the only thing that saves you."

I don't argue this time. There's no point. I simply stand there as he exits.

And in my mind my new fantasy is that he never comes back.

# CHAPTER 23

❀

I STAND ALONE IN the foyer for seconds, minutes, a brief eternity of time as I try to decide on a mental journey that will take me away from this place. What shall I fantasize about now? Swimming through the mellow waves of the Mediterranean? Dancing in New York? But my mind stays stubbornly in the here and now. A few days . . . how many lifetimes have I packed into that small space of time?

I lean against the wall, suddenly dizzy. It seems impossible that I'm at risk of losing to such an unskilled adversary. I'm just not used to this kind of struggle. My opponents have always been my own desires and memories, the war an internal one. And even in that war, my opponents were the conquistadors. They overcame my defenses and occupied my mind with colonial ambitions, bringing me to this hellish reservation where subjugation and servitude are the most obvious means of survival.

I hear footsteps approaching outside of the door. What could Dave have forgotten? Perhaps an insult or threat that he had neglected to throw my way.

I back away and watch as the doorknob moves, just a fraction of an inch this way and then the other. Why doesn't he just turn the key?

But as I watch the doorknob continue to jiggle, I realize I have another problem.

The person at the door doesn't have a key.

The person on the other side of the door is breaking in.

I move quickly, not caring how high my skirt hikes up, not caring what's exposed. As long as I'm able to keep this new nightmare at bay, the dress is inconsequential.

I reach for the dead bolt, but it's too late. The door swings open and I find myself backing up as quickly as I moved forward, wanting to run but knowing there's no use.

But then the intruder isn't a stranger at all. It's Robert Dade.

He takes me in with only the quickest movement of his eyes and then he moves past me, into the living room, standing in the center, his fists clenched at his sides, his ferocious energy flooding the room.

"Where is he?" he asks.

His back is to me, which is fine. My anger, shame, and humiliation have me burning tonight and he looks a lot like kerosene.

"He's out. How did you know I was here? How did you even know where Dave lives?"

"Your boss called me."

Well, there's an unlikely hero. I almost say it out loud but sense Robert isn't in the mood for small talk. His posture reminds me of a stalking tiger ready to pounce.

"When will he be back?"

It's not so much a question as a demand for information.

I've had enough of demands.

"I can take care of this, Robert. I don't need you."

He pivots, his fury slamming into my frustration.

"Go upstairs and get out of that dress. You're better than this. You should know better than to accept the role of Dave's slave."

"I'm not a slave."

"Take off the dress!"

I stand my ground. I feel a little like a student in Tiananmen Square standing defiantly before an oncoming tank.

He breathes out aggravation through clenched teeth but then, as his eyes shift, so does his focus. There, on the side table, he sees the framed photo. It's of Dave and me in kinder days. He's wearing a navy wool crepe suit with a quiet silver tie while my hair is slicked

back into an intricate chignon bun. There's an almost elderly sophistication to the jewel-necked suit I'm wearing, the light sheen of
the fabric and the ruffled peplum being the only hint toward a softer
form of femininity. Dave has his hand on my back and I'm smiling
serenely at the camera. It's an image that could have been ripped
from the pages of *Town & Country*. We're perfect.

Roman statues, that's what Simone had compared us to, perfect
and cold.

Robert picks up the picture, examines it more closely. "I'm not
sure I know this woman."

"I know her." I move behind him, peeking over his shoulder to
see the photo. "I just don't know where she went."

Robert puts down the picture frame. "Let her stay lost." He then
turns to me, the edges of his anger mildly blunted by concern. "I
won't let him do this to you."

"I don't think you can save me and . . . I'm . . . I'm not sure I want
you to."

A flash of pain flickers across his features. He reaches out, cups
my cheek in his hand. "You can't ask me to just let this happen. I
won't do that."

I feel a sudden rush of confusion. If he can help me, why
shouldn't I let him? Is it because I don't want to admit to being a
damsel in distress? Do I really value my bruised and battered pride
over my freedom? What convict ever insisted on making an unas-
sisted prison break?

But as much as I want Robert, I can't help thinking that his affection might be infinitely more dangerous than Dave's hostility.

"Take the dress off," he says again. "I hate that it's touching you.
It's like he's holding you tightly from a distance."

Yes, I want to say, holding me in an embrace of humiliation. I
take a step back, moving away from Robert's touch. I continue my
backward stride, Robert following me, letting me set the pace. It's a
strange tango in which the woman leads . . . if only for the length of
a few bars of music.

I lead us to the dining room. The table had never been set and it now stands bare, except for one unopened bottle of wine, a reminder of Dave's failed plans and my minor victory. I move the bottle to a chair.

"He's not here," I say and I reach down to the hem, pull it up over my hips, my stomach, my breasts until, with a little effort, it's gone and I'm standing there, completely naked, before my lover. "He's not touching me," I say. "No one will touch me without my invitation. If anyone tries, they'll pay for that mistake. But you're going to have to let me exact the price. Me. Not you."

Robert stares at me. His eyes are hungry, but I still feel his vexation. Yet it's not aimed at me. He's pointing it toward the night, toward the unknown part of town where Dave sits, making decisions about my life. "I won't just turn a blind eye, Kasie. That's not who I am."

I hear him but I'm not fully listening. I'm looking at the table. In its polished surface I see the night Dave had planned for me. How far would the game have gone if Tom had cooperated? And Asha, how far did she plan to push me? Did they all see me as weak? Did they think I would surrender all my power so easily?

"Kasie, did you hear me?"

I ignore the question, redirect his energy to my liking. "Would you like to touch me, Mr. Dade?"

His breath catches in his throat. I can still feel the anger but it feels even more distant now, allowing him more room to explore more pressing passions.

"I asked you a question." I let my fingers run over the table. I'm playing a very dangerous game. I don't know when Dave will come home. I don't know what Robert will do to him if he does reappear. I don't know if this will be the act that breaks my world to pieces. I'm risking everything for a moment of pleasure, to celebrate a fleeting victory. But I'm beginning to think that life is about passing moments and small celebrations. Without them there's only pain, fear, ambition, and, for some of us, foolish hope.

"He wanted me to serve him and Tom Love at this table," I say.

"He wanted me to play the part of the submissive. He wanted to control me. He didn't get what he wanted. I won. Will you help me celebrate, Mr. Dade? You're invited."

Robert doesn't move right away. But when he does, it's swift, closing the distance between us in seconds and pulling off his shirt so that our bare skin presses together in a raw embrace.

"I want you to take me here," I whisper as his teeth graze my shoulder. I pull off his belt. "I want you to take me on the table where I refused to serve him."

"Are you sure?"

"Yes," I say as his belt falls to the floor. "You're invited."

And then I'm being lifted into the air, laid back on the table, like a delicacy meant to be savored.

He strips off the rest of his clothes and I take him in. His muscles create little hills and valleys across his chest and stomach. His arms and thighs are equally strong and enticing. This is a different kind of perfection. He's sculpted but not like Michelangelo's *David*. He's made of something much more vibrant than marble. He's a song with a pounding beat and a roughly melodic tune. His erection reaches for me, another blatant reminder of his vitality.

He leans forward, runs his fingers across my stomach; it seems he's tracing the letters of a word there—"lust," "love," it's hard to tell the difference, his touch shoots over me so fast. I breathe in the scent of him as his fingers continue their dance up to my throat, resting there, right under my chin. He studies me the way one would study an eclipse, expectant but awed. And his fingers keep moving, this time down to my breast; he caresses the area around one nipple and then the next, so different from Dave's intrusive touch.

Besides, I stopped Dave. And if he tries to touch me again, he'll again feel the sting of my refusal. He will never get anywhere with me. Not by design or force. He is not invited.

But Robert is, and as his fingers travel down to the curve of my waist, my hips, his hands gently pull apart my legs, opening me up; I feel my body silently restating that invitation, reinforcing it with the dampness between my legs, with the erratic pace of my breathing. He lifts my leg, kisses my ankle, then slowly moves higher. Each kiss is a little different. Here, where the muscle of my inner thigh begins, he sucks, just slightly, and here, as he travels upward, his tongue flicks out to taste the salt on my skin. Here, as he comes closer to my core, the kiss becomes gentle, almost innocent, a direct contradiction to his clear intent.

I reach my hands into his hair, try to draw him higher, but he will not be rushed. He lets the anticipation warm me before his mouth reaches its destination.

But when it does, when I feel his lips wrap around my clit in an open-mouthed kiss, that's when the kerosene truly meets the flames. I grasp the edges of the table, anchoring myself to its solidity. Again images of what was supposed to happen here flash through my head. Me, exposed, serving men against my will.

But the image comes crashing down as I feel his tongue press inside of me, penetrating me, then pulling out, then tasting again. His hand slips beneath my hips, lifting me for his benefit and mine.

There are no images anymore. I'm blind to all of it and like any blind woman my other senses are heightened. The feeling of his hands pressing into my flesh is a unique ecstasy. The flicks of his tongue are like jolts of electric delight; the sound of my heart beating is thunderous and beautiful.

My orgasm is almost luxurious in its decadence, like a fine champagne bursting from its bottle.

In a flash Robert pulls me forward. As he stands I remain lying on the surface of polished oak, my straight legs supported against his chest. I feel his erection against my thighs, eager for entry. I grant it by lifting my hips; his hands quickly reach to hold them in place as my back rises with them into the air.

He enters me again and moves slowly, the gratification of this steady, cadenced hypnosis. This is what it is to *feel* beauty, to experience the texture of bliss.

For a moment I think I hear music like I heard in my fantasy but it's only our mingled breathing, his growls harmonizing with my cries of rapture as he drives into me again and again.

What if Dave comes home? What if he sees Robert making love to me in his house, on his table where I have served him coffee, where he would have me sit by his side, the perfect subservient wife?

He'd broadcast the news to the world, to my family, and to my employers.

But as Robert grinds against me, I find that I don't care. This is my rebellion. It's a day of sunshine amid a season of rain and I will not waste it.

And then the dance shifts. He releases me, pulls away, lays me flat on the table. For a moment I'm confused, disoriented. I'm not ready for this to end.

And neither is he. He pulls me up so now I sit before him as he stares. The intimacy of a look can have its own tender eroticism. I link my legs around him, lean my weight back on my hands. The summons could not be clearer. With a single thrust he's inside me again but this time he reaches new depths. I cry out as he leans forward, his teeth nibbling my ear before his tongue seeks out the nerve endings there.

"He's never going to touch you again," he whispers as he speeds up his rhythm. The table vibrates with our movement but it's sturdy and strong, stronger than the rules I once set for myself, stronger than the threats of my enemies, stronger than my restraint that crumbles the moment Robert enters a room.

"I am the only man you will ever make love to again."

I feel myself tremble as my muscles begin to contract.

"I'll have you in his house, in mine, in your office, in a thousand beds all over the world. But this," and now he pushes into me with even more force, "this is mine." Again I cry out as yet another orgasm rips through me. And I feel him join me, feel him coming inside me, feel him throb as he claims me in the only way a man can really claim a woman.

I stare up into his eyes and gasp the word, "Yes."

We cling to each other for minutes that feel like seconds . . . or days. I listen to his breathing, feel his heartbeat, smell his cologne. . . .

"You're coming with me," he says. His voice isn't demanding. He's just stating a fact.

I run my fingers over the back of his neck and stare at the white walls of Dave's dining room, silently saying good-bye to my prison.

## CHAPTER 24

I DRESS IN THE CLOTHES I wore to work but before Robert and I leave Dave's house, I fold up the offensive dress neatly and place it in the middle of the dining room table. Robert nods his approval. He doesn't know about the note I put inside the flimsy fabric. A small piece of white paper with some words written in cursive:

> *Do what you will but I can't take this anymore.*
>    *You miss the woman who was loyal, I miss the man who was kind.*
>
>                    *Good-bye,*
>                    *Kasie*

Robert expelled the fog from my mind. I felt it seep from my pores, mingle with the sweat of our lovemaking, and then it just evaporated. Robert thinks I'm going to trust him to save me. Dave will think I'm throwing caution to the wind.

They're both wrong. I'm still at war. But now I'm ready to fight like a warrior.

But even wars have moments of quiet—moments when the gunfire's so faint, it could be the popping of balloons. I feel that ephemeral peace as we drive away in Robert's Alfa Romeo, a car that resembles art and smells of power. We don't speak. Instead I enjoy the movement of his hand over the gearshift, cherish the way he caresses the leather-covered steering wheel. I'm almost jealous that the car should be the beneficiary of such firm and loving handling, but it'll be my turn soon.

I've been to Robert's home before but when we finally walk through that front gate . . . when I see the entire city sparkling back at me with excitement and anticipation, I can't help but feel a little alarmed by the grandeur of the view. He leads me inside and I find that I feel awkward and a little shy. Last time I had been here we had made love in his massive bed over and over again, but afterward we had talked. It had been so comfortable. I had been at ease. I wonder if he expects that I'll be able to go back to that place. I can't of course. Not yet.

He seems to understand, or maybe he just sees the blush on my cheeks and senses that delicacy is needed. He almost formally ushers me to the deep brown leather sofa in the living room and then disappears to get me something to drink.

I sit rigidly, wondering if he'll bring me a Scotch, the dangerous cocktail that had started it all.

But I need a clear head tonight. The battle is too close for that kind of indulgence.

When Robert comes back with a large green mug, I catch the scent of hot chocolate and I eagerly take the mug into my hands, sipping the bittersweet flavor with relish. It's such an innocent drink, I wonder if I deserve it. But I hope I do. I hope to absorb some of the sweet, childlike qualities. I want to feel just a tiny bit of that innocence.

Robert sits by my side. "I'll talk to Dave tomorrow."

"No," I say simply. "That's my fight."

"Love tells me that Dave might use our affair to get you fired."

For a moment I'm puzzled, and then I realize he's talking about Tom. That's the only Love that can tell him anything practical.

"I'll stop that from happening," Robert goes on. "Even Freeland won't throw away my business out of loyalty to his maggot of a godson."

"Asha knows, too," I say.

"Asha?"

"You've met her. She's on my team."

Robert shrugs, not understanding her significance. "It won't matter what she knows. The world can know. It won't affect your position. I'll—"

"You'll see to that?" I say, finishing his sentence, my tone harsher than I had intended it to be. It's no use. I can't internalize the sweetness of the chocolate, only the bitterness. I stare into the darkened fireplace. "She thinks I only got this job because I was sleeping with Dave, the maggot of a godson you're so eager to confront."

"So?" Robert says, still not grasping the problem.

"So now she'll think that I'm only keeping my job because I'm sleeping with you."

Fresh comprehension sparkles in his eyes. "Who the hell cares what people think, Kasie? They don't matter. Only you and I do."

"If that was true, the world would be other than it is. If that was true," I say, each word growing a little more testy, "we'd be gods. Osiris and Isis. Zeus and Hera . . . but that's not quite right, either, is it? After all, even they had to give the other deities some consideration."

"Are you angry with me?"

I almost say yes but then realize it's not true. Not exactly. "I'm angry because I want everything to be as simple as you say it is, and I'm angry because it can't be. It's my fault. I can't be seen as the office slut. I need respect to do my job. I need respect to be able to breathe."

"They'll respect you when you excel. All anyone needs to do is watch you work to know that you deserve your position."

"But they won't see me. They'll see what I've done and they'll train their eyes to see the whore Dave and Asha believe me to be."

"Tom Love knows you better than that."

"And will Tom be in his job forever? Will I always report to him? Can you promise me that?"

Robert leans back into the couch, holds me with his gaze. "Yes, I can. I can make sure Tom never has any incentive to leave his position. I can shape the world to your liking. Money and power are the only currency you need if the goal is to pull the strings of industry. I have both. Let me buy you some peace of mind."

I want to laugh. He's going to make it rain and, like a stripper, Tom is supposed to get on his knees and scoop up the falling dollar bills. I suppose Robert would expect the same of almost anyone whom he threw money at. Maybe someday he'll expect it of me.

But he can't buy my parents' approval. And he can't buy the respect of my colleagues. He can just give them incentive to hide their true feelings. I'll always know what they'll be saying behind closed doors. And I can't allow Robert to force Tom into a stagnant career. Eventually I'll be reporting to someone else, another man or woman who will wonder what I'll do to earn my next promotion. I'll be given clients who expect to be allowed to play with me during our meetings, to show me off to boardrooms of hungry men ready to fuck the woman who's known for whoring her way through the business world, handing out sexual favors like they're business cards.

Robert's far from stupid. If he allowed himself to think, he'd see how impossible it all is. But he's not thinking; he's feeling. He says he wants to reshape the world, and in the late hours of the night, not long after making love to me on another man's dining room table, he's sure that he can do it.

Tomorrow reality will rise with the sun. But probably not tonight. So I swallow my pessimism with my chocolate and gently put my hand on his knee. "I'm tired," I say. "Take me to bed."

Perhaps the hot chocolate imparted some innocence to the night after all, because for the first time Robert and I slip into bed together without tapping into the ocean of sexual energy that always lies between us. Instead he gives me one of his shirts to change into and under the sheets we curl up into each other. He's asleep now and his breathing has a steady, soothing quality that quiets my anxiety. For a brief minute I can almost believe in his false promises. It feels like I really can be safe here, in his arms, inside his palace of capitalist riches. Isn't this what I've always wanted? Security, wealth, success?

Yes, but I want those things to be real, not facades. I want the success to be mine. I can't share in Robert's dreams if I don't pursue my own. Reluctantly my thoughts turn to Dave. I can see now that my relationship with Dave was never right but I also see why it had so much appeal. His dreams seemed to dovetail with mine. We seemed to complement each other. He was better connected but I was arguably better educated. Yes, he was a lawyer with a degree from Notre Dame but I have a master's from Harvard Business School—and no Harvard graduate will ever accept the idea that there might be a better education available than the one he or she got, no matter what *U.S. News & World Report* says about Yale.

But what held us together for so long were our common goals. We both want respect. He wants respect within the old-money world the men in his family have always traveled in and I simply want respect within my family and in the business world. Self-discipline is the attribute I've tried to nurture and refine while he has tried to exercise control over the external, his home, his social circle, me. I fear failure and rejection, even my own impulses. He fears helplessness, ridicule, the reckless wantonness of the city.

I smile in the dark. It's that last part I'm focusing on now. In that knowledge is the key to everything. Getting respect from those who frequent Dave's elite men's club with its prohibitive membership fees and ingrained superiority complex requires a different set of rules. I picture the darkened rooms that make up those establishments that officially allow the admittance of women but never make them feel welcome. I see the cigars held by men with manicures and pedigrees. I hear their whispered interactions. In that world there would be no shame in demanding the subservience of a woman. These are stories Dave could tell with relish. But there is shame in losing a woman to another man. There's shame in being abandoned. Dave is asking me to humiliate myself in exchange for his silence but I haven't yet asked him to pay for mine.

I know what Dave wants, and what he's afraid of. I know how to hurt him.

Carefully I slip out of Robert's firm grasp. He stirs, waking enough to see that I'm getting up but not enough to ask where I'm going. I tiptoe to my purse, pull out my cell, and read the text I know will be there.

```
Where the hell are you?
```

That sent an hour ago. Then another sent after twenty minutes more had passed.

```
Kasie, really, where are you?
```

And then ten minutes after that:

```
I understand you're upset. We just need to talk.
Please respond.
```

I smile. My aim is getting better.

I hear Robert stir again but his breathing quickly falls back into the quiet pattern of slumber. I take my phone into his bathroom. I close the door and flip on the lights, blinking a few times to adjust to the illumination. The room is about the same size as my first apartment. There's a sunken bathtub with water jets, a spacious shower with transparent glass walls, a mirror that lines the space of almost an entire wall . . . it's decadent as hell.

And then I catch my reflection. My hair is a tumble of waves that fall over my shoulders; my eyeliner, not properly removed before bed, is now mildly smudged, giving me a careless, sultry look. I hold Dave's text in my hand while wearing Robert's shirt on my body. Who is this woman?

*I'm not sure I know this woman,* he said.

. . . and I responded, *I know her, I just don't know where she went.*

I stare down at the phone. The device itself is the only thing that's

familiar to me right now. It has my photos, the numbers of my con-
tacts, old e-mails, and so on. It's filled to the brim with reminders of
the life that I destroyed. And I destroyed it for the man whose shirt
is still on my back.

The devil works in mysterious ways.

But I can't dwell on it anymore. It'll drive me insane. So instead
I type in a response to Dave.

```
Yes, we should talk. Let's meet before your squash
game tomorrow night. In the restaurant next door
to the club.
```

I press Send and wait, one minute, then two and then the response comes:

```
You don't need to go out of your way. We can meet
by your work.
```

I smile. He has just shown all his cards, confirmed all my sup-
positions. I look back up at the mirror; there is one small thing I
recognize in this woman smiling back at me: her intelligence.

```
No, we'll meet by your squash game. It's easier.
```

This time it takes him only seconds to respond.

```
Do you have your car? How will you get there?
```

He's placed the target on his heart and I load my weapon.

```
I have someone who will give me a ride.
```

I giggle as I send this last message, knowing exactly what images
are playing through Dave's head. He sees me walking into a restau-

rant in front of all his friends. He sees Robert Dade by my side, a man stronger, more successful, better looking, a man who surpasses him in every way that matters. He sees himself as the cuckold as we sit down across from him, Robert's hand on the leg of the woman whom Dave once boasted to have as his own.

In this vision he is the one cloaked in humiliation.

The Balance of Threat. It's a theory of a highly esteemed Harvard professor. The idea is so simple, it's beautiful. Independent nations' behavior will be determined by the perceived threat of other nations. Where people miss the genius is that they focus on the wrong word, *threat*. But threats are finite. They can easily fall apart when a bluff is called. The word that holds the power is *perceived*. Perception is everything. I have no interest in threatening Dave the way he has so openly threatened me. I want my threats to be unstated but intrinsic in my messaging. I never said it would be Robert driving me to the club. I never said I would try to show him up to his friends. I want to let his imagination do my work for me because the demons within will always have more influence than the demons without.

Finally he responds with a text that reeks of fear and frustration:

```
I don't want to meet by the club.
```

I take a deep breath. This is where I turn fear into panic.

```
I am going to be at the club tomorrow at 5:45 pm.
If I don't see you, I will ask your friends as
they arrive where I can find you. I'm sure if I
explain the situation, they'll help me. As you
said, we need to talk.
```

As I read his response I imagine how it would look if it were written by hand. The letters would be shaky and uneven; his sweat would stain the paper. His text says:

I'll meet you inside the restaurant. I'll find
a table in the back. Please, let's make this
private. This is about the two of us, just us.

I don't respond to this last message. If I did, I would have to explain his error. This isn't about the two of us at all. It's about something bigger. It's about concepts and perceptions, power and grief. It's about the line between fair retaliation and offensive vindictiveness. It's about winning and losing.

It's about war.

I smile to myself, flip off the lights. A small night-light illuminates things enough for me to find my way to the door.

And when I open it, he's standing there before me. The dark silhouette of Robert, naked and strong, his form vaguely outlined by the weak light. He looks down at my hand.

"A little late to make calls, isn't it?"

"I was just checking my e-mail," I reply.

"My seductive little liar," he says softly.

I open my mouth to defend myself but stop. "Must we tell each other all our secrets?"

"No, I enjoy a little intrigue." He steps into the bathroom, puts a hand on either side of my face, holding me still. "I don't insist on knowing everything."

"So nice of you not to insist," I say, the note of teasing light, mingled with a strong dose of anticipation. I close my eyes and feel his hand move into my hair.

"You laugh but there are things that I do insist on." I open my eyes again. It's still so dark. His details are lost, making him a man of mystery. I lift my hand, let my fingers outline his features.

"I insist that you stay safe," he says. He drops his hands to my thighs and then up to the curve of my bum. "I insist that those who would hurt you be dissuaded." His hands keep moving up, to my waist. With a sudden movement he lifts me up and I instinctively wrap my legs around his waist. I can see his hazel eyes twinkling in the shadowy light.

"I have a plan," I say. "No one will hurt me. Your lover is a warrior."

"Are you now?" he asks. "Perhaps my warrior will join me in the shower."

He lowers me onto the counter, unbuttons the shirt I'm wearing, strips it off me quickly. It's almost one in the morning. Having shower sex right now is completely impractical.

But now we're riding the waves of our impulses, and instead of drowning, I swim.

He leads me into the glass-enclosed shower area, turns on the water, and pulls me into a kiss. As the water washes over us, I feel his hand on the small of my back, feel him grow hard against me.

I pull away, smile. "Your warrior's hungry," I say.

I lower myself to my knees. I kiss the side of his hip, brush my fingers against the tip of his erection.

"Kasie," he groans. His cock twitches ever so slightly.

"Is that for me, Robert?" I ask. "It seems impatient."

This time I let my index finger trace the vein that travels from the base to the tip, moving my finger up and down, lightly, taunting and tantalizing.

"You were made for me," he breathes.

"Maybe. Or perhaps it's the other way around."

Again he reaches into my hair. He pulls just a little. I raise my eyes up to his.

"Kasie," he growls, "now."

There's something in the way he says the word . . . it invites no argument; it's presumptuous in its authority.

And it makes me want to immediately follow the instruction. I wrap my lips around him, take him fully into my mouth, one hand on the base while the other reaches between his legs, finding that place that makes him shudder. I hear him groan again as I move my hands and mouth in unison, back and forth, up and down. His skin glistens with the warm water, the muscles in his thighs tense, and I pause long enough to trace the tip again, this time with my tongue, before devouring him. Everything is slick and wet and utterly amazing.

I can tell he's getting close to losing control and with a bit of re-luctance I let him pull away. He pulls me to my feet, kisses me again, gently before whipping me around and bending me over. I reach down, press my hands into the floor.

The penetration is so deep I cry out in both pleasure and sur-prise. I feel the water rushing down my back, through my hair as he grasps my hips and thrusts inside me again and again. Even with him in me I ache for him, and it's that aching that brings me rapidly to the brink. The orgasm comes so hard and so fast my legs shake with the pleasure of it. But Robert supports me within his grip as he continues to thrust. I gasp, predicting his imminent release, but then he stops.

"No," he breathes, "I want to see you."

He releases me and I stand again, finding my balance before turning to him.

Robert wet is a beautiful sight. With grace I didn't know I had I raise one leg and wrap it around his waist, balancing myself against him.

"Now," I say.

And immediately he's inside me again. The warm stream beats gently against our skin as we lock each other in a kiss. He moves inside me, one hand supporting my leg and the other on my ass; my breasts are pressed against his chest. We're intertwined, connected in every way possible. I keep my eyes closed so all I can do is feel— the water, him, the ecstasy. It's a greedy and indulgent romance and as he presses into me, slides his tongue against mine, I moan.

His rhythm increases. "My warrior," he whispers as his breath mingles with mine.

"Always," I respond.

He explodes inside of me as the water washes over us. In that moment I am the happiest warrior on earth.

❀

# CHAPTER 25

WHEN I WAKE UP the next morning, he's sitting by my side, looking down at me. Slowly I remind myself of where I am, that I am again in his shirt. I feel the gentle pressure of his fingers on my hip, only a thin sheet separating skin from skin.

"You don't have to go," he says softly.

I don't fully understand his meaning. Is he referring to a specific location or is he talking about something grander, a declaration of us and what we can be?

But he quickly brings me back to earth with a troubling clarification. "You could work from here today. They don't need you there. I'll talk to Love, maybe Freeland—"

"I can't let you do that," I say. He already knew I was going to say that. I can tell by his tone, which carries only the faintest notes of hope, like violins that are all but drowned out by the heavy brass sounds of resignation.

"I told you last night, I will not sit back and watch as he victimizes you. That's not how I live."

I pause to consider the phrasing. It's not how he lives. There's something telling in that . . . but something I can't quite place.

"I can win," I say, pushing these thoughts aside. "I'm stronger than Dave. Smarter, too. I can win."

"Not if you play by the old rules."

I shift uncomfortably in the bed, moving the sheet down to my waist. "You don't believe in rules?" I think of my sister, I remember her dancing on a table, shedding clothes like so many restrictive social conventions.

Robert smiles; his eyes flicker to the window, the port of entry for the hazy morning light. "There are so many old adages about winning. To the victor go the spoils, the history books are written by winners, and so on. But there's only one truly meaningful benefit to winning. You see, to the victor go the *rules*. I believe in rules, Kasie. I believe in them because in my world I *am* the winner. The rules are mine to set. What I don't believe in is playing by other people's rules."

The arrogance of that is enough to wake me up. I look at him with clearer eyes. What does it mean to truly be a power player? I wouldn't know; neither would Dave. It took me a day and a half to figure out how to get out from under Dave's thumb. Today, at 5:45 p.m., I hope to have that situation a bit more under control. Asha will be harder, she'll bide her time, sharpen her weapons, hit me when I'm the least protected. But Robert Dade is different. He dominates the world in a way that I don't fully understand and it occurs to me that if I give in to my feelings for him the way he wants me to, he'll dominate me, too. And the danger here is that with Robert I might not look for the escape.

I will lose myself.

Like now, for instance. See the way he looks at me? Like a jaguar looks at a mate. Without making a sound he roars for me. How easy has it been for him to get me to forget my many protests and reservations? How easy was it for him to make me risk everything for him?

There's a shift in the air. His hand reaches for the sheet and carefully he pulls it back. It's just me, in his shirt, my hair covering the pillow. I sense his frustration, see that it's mixed with a strong desire. It's a hazardous cocktail.

I sit up, draw away from him. "I need to go home and change my clothes. Will you drive me or should I call a cab?"

There is a strain in our connection. His mouth twitches slightly as he swallows instinctive demands. "I'll take you."

He gets up and leaves the room. He's exercising self-control by not trying to control me. But I wonder how long that will last.

AN HOUR LATER we're parked by my front yard. I don't have my car here. It's in the parking lot below the office building I work in. But I don't bring up this inconvenience. I don't want to risk people seeing him driving me to work. I'll find my own way. Just like I've found my own battle tactics.

I turn in my seat, a little hesitant, a little hopeful. "There's a plan . . . one I've already set into motion."

"All right," he says, nodding his approval before he's heard a single detail.

"I need your presence for it to work. I need you to be at this restaurant." I pull out one of my business cards and scribble down a name and address before handing it over. "I'll be meeting Dave there after work."

His smile spreads a little wider. "You want me to come?"

"Yes," I confirm, "at around six. Dave and I will already be seated by then. I'd like for you to come to our table and greet us, then choose a table for yourself. It doesn't matter where."

"You want me to be inconspicuous?" he asks; there's an undertone of humor to his question. I doubt Robert has ever been inconspicuous in his life.

"No, I just want you to be close by but at a different table. I won't be long. I should be leaving within fifteen minutes of your arrival, alone. I just need Dave to know you're there as . . . as backup." *As a perceived threat.*

Robert nods, warming to the idea quickly. "Six o'clock, I'll be there. But, Kasie, if he so much as raises his voice to you, I won't stay at my table. He will have to deal with me. It won't end well for him."

I hesitate. Coming from the lips of another man, that statement would imply that a physical fight was possible—a barroom brawl as it were.

But I don't think that's what Robert means. I am anxious to win this war with Dave but I don't want to completely annihilate him. I want him to rebuild a life without me. It's easier for the victor when the vanquished sees a path out.

But if Robert gets involved, if he handles things his way, I don't think Dave will get the chance to do that. I don't think Robert fights with a gentleman's grace, following civilized rules of engagement. I suspect he fights like a colonial power, decimating those who hold the territory he hopes to claim. If I win this war my way, Dave will lose me. If we fight Robert's way, Dave will lose everything.

"He won't raise his voice to me," I say carefully. "If he sees you're there, it'll be enough."

Robert nods and I lift his hand to my mouth, kissing his palm. "Thank you," I say.

His eyes roam over my features, my hair, my neck . . . I feel an unwelcome shudder of excitement as I wonder where this will lead. I don't have time for romance and yet something inside me knows that if he insisted, if he tried to take me right here, in his car, in front of my house, in view of all my neighbors and friends, I might not refuse even though part of me would want to.

It scares me and yet the thought is exhilarating. Why is that? How can I fight so hard for freedom only to be enticed by captivity?

"Go in the house, get yourself ready," he says before leaning forward, gently kissing my lips. After a moment he pulls away. "I'll see you tonight at six."

I feel him watch me as I walk to my door, hear his car pull away as I go inside.

As I head upstairs my mind idly goes back to my undergraduate philosophy class. The professor's favorite quote was from Lao Tzu:

*Mastering others is strength. Mastering yourself is true power.*

A little part of me worries that Robert Dade has the strength to take away my power.

❀

# CHAPTER 26

A FTER A QUICK taxi ride I walk into my office with renewed confidence; I've tucked concerns about Robert and me into my back pocket and I've almost forgotten they're there. Things are going my way, I've chosen my weapons, selected my target. I have a plan. I'm ready for the day.

My team has sent me all their individual reports. Barbara has printed them and left them on my desk. I can see they've been working hard. Their reports are more thorough and precise than they were before. Our goal is to help Robert position his company for a public option and now as I study the numbers and strategies of his various divisions laid out in neat detail, I can see how it all fits together. The trick of my job is to know what to focus on. There are always more numbers than you need, problems that don't need an immediate answer, others that demand attention. But once you know what's important and what can wait, when you can see with the kind of tunnel vision that allows you to block out the background noise and zero in on the one instrument that needs to be tuned, that's when your job is practically done. I see it now: the marketing plan that would be best; I can see the path.

*I can see the path.* Surely that will be the mantra for the day.

I spend the first half of the day bringing it all together in a single report that will be submitted to Robert.

Tom walks into the office. As usual he didn't knock or give Barbara a chance to announce him. Barbara stands behind him now, a look of defeat weighing down her features. As usual I wave my hand in a gesture of casual forgiveness and she leaves us, quietly closing the door so we're alone.

He sits opposite me, his eyes flickering to my outfit. I'm dressed more conservatively than I have been for a while. Beige trousers made of a gentle fabric, a cropped blazer of a similar color closed over a long satin top that's the shade of platinum. I've accessorized with a long silk scarf that I've strategically draped and tied around my neck. The only skin that is showing is on my hands and face. But I can tell that's not what Tom's seeing. He's seeing the dress from last night and everything it exposed.

I look down at my desk, squirm slightly in my seat, then curse myself for doing it. I don't want to be reminded of that torture.

"Is the Maned Wolf report ready?" Tom asks.

I look back up at him, surprised. This is not the line of questioning I expected.

"I've just sent a final draft to my team and to you, and in an hour the team and I will have one more meeting to decide which parts of the plan will be presented by whom."

"Is that what he wants?"

"Who?" I ask, confused. "Rob—I mean, Mr. Dade? Of course that's what he wants. It's what he hired us for."

Tom raises his eyebrow. The question he doesn't have to ask echoes in my ears. *Is it what he hired us for? Or was it so he could claim you?*

The silent question leads me to memories of harsher, spoken statements.

*Prostitutes have sex for profit.*

Asha's words. I close my eyes and try to force them from my head. I didn't even know who he was when I met him. My actions were wrong but my motives had been physical, emotional, never monetary.

"Does he want the entire team to present the report or just you?"

I open my eyes. "I thought we were going to pretend that you don't know about . . . about my relationship with Mr. Dade."

"Yes, well I thought about that, and if he asks me to pretend, then that's exactly what I'll do because, after all, this is all about what *he* wants."

"Are you mocking me?"

Tom cocks his head to the side; he hadn't expected the question. "Why would I mock you? I like you and I respect you, although my definition of 'respect' might be different from yours. I'd respect a drug dealer if he did his job well."

"You have no morals."

He effortlessly shrugs off the accusation. "Look, Robert is the biggest client we have. I want as many Maned Wolf projects—and as much Maned Wolf money—as our division can handle. I know that I need you for that but I also need you to keep him happy."

"Are you seriously suggesting that I have to fuck him?" I snap, the profanity coming to my lips a little too easily.

He chuckles. "Of course not. That would be . . . what's the word you like to use?" He snaps his fingers a few times as if trying to remember. "Ah yes, immoral. No, I'm not saying you have to fuck him. I'm saying you have to *keep* fucking him."

"You're out of line."

"What are you talking about?" He shakes his head; his smile wavers. "I'm only asking you to do what you want to do."

"And I'll do what I want to do," I say simply. "But you have no right to expect it of me."

"Seriously?" He leans forward. I hear my cell ringing in my purse but ignore it. "Tell me, Kasie, do you enjoy your job?"

I don't respond. He knows the answer well enough.

"Do you think it's fair that I expect you to do your job?"

"That's different," I say, seeing the trap.

"Is it?" His posture is relaxed; he's sure of his footing. "You enjoy your work and I expect you to do it. You enjoy fucking your client? I expect you to keep that up, too. And yes, there may be aspects of your job and your affair that you think are beneath you. Tasks that you find demeaning. It's the nature of the beast. Work through it."

There's a shift in the wind that carries my mood in a new direction. Tom is supposed to be my ally but if he switches sides, I'm prepared to draw blood. "Wasn't it you who pointed out what will happen if Mr. Freeland finds out about Mr. Dade and me?" I ask. "Dave knows, Tom. You know that better than anyone. You should be encouraging me to find a graceful exit to the affair so we can all get out of this unscathed."

"Kasie, I'm getting out of this unscathed regardless. If you get fired, that sucks for me. Really sucks. You're an amazing consultant, hands down the best analyst I've got. There's a chance I'll be up for promotion next year and if I get it, you'll be partially responsible for that, and you'll probably get my job. But empires rise and fall. Kings and queens are overthrown and replaced with others, ones who use different titles, wear different crowns but are every bit as ruthless as their predecessors. We're all replaceable in the end."

Out in the hall I hear someone laughing, the hum of activity. "Are you threatening my job?" I ask.

"Don't be ridiculous." Tom's eyes idly travel the room. "My only goal is to keep the account. I'm sure Mr. Dade told you that he spoke with me last night?"

"He did."

"He's going to take care of Freeland, Dave, the works," he says, as he finally brings his attention back to me. "And if Freeland has a problem with Mr. Dade's terms, well he is only the *co*founder after all. Mr. Dade will put the right pressure on the right people. You'll keep your job as long as we keep that account and that means that it's most definitely in your interest to keep him happy."

My fingers slide over the surface of my desk. For me it has as much import as any throne. I earned my place here. Dave got me the interview, not the job. I deserve to have the assignment given to me by Robert even if he didn't know it at the time he gave it. "Mr. Dade and I have talked about this," I explain. "He will not be *taking care of* anyone. I will. This is my fight and I'm fighting it alone."

Tom's expression doesn't change; his face doesn't move. The only hint of frustration is in the way he squeezes the armrest of the chair, just tight enough to make the tips of his fingers go white. "That's not a wise choice, Kasie."

"It's the choice I've made. I meet with Dave tonight. By tomorrow he won't be a problem anymore. Freeland will never have grounds to attack me. It'll be done."

"And if things don't turn out your way?"

I press my lips into a thin line of rebellion. I will not entertain that scenario.

"Ah, no plan B? Well then we'll use mine: if you don't have it under control, we'll let Mr. Dade handle this."

"How? By telling the board of directors that they need to keep me on until he tires of me?"

"If necessary. But don't worry, Kasie. I doubt any man ever tires of you easily."

"I can't believe this," I growl.

"Really?" He frowns. "You're the one who got this ball rolling. And it's a nice ball. We're all going to get a lot richer because of your talents . . . *all* your talents."

Again I don't answer and Tom sighs. "Look," he says, his voice almost weary, almost angry, "I don't really care how this is handled, as long as it is. But let's face it, if you're handling this yourself, it's because Mr. Dade's *allowing* you to do so. That man holds all the cards. Which brings me back to my original question. Does he want the entire team to make the presentation or would he rather you give it to him personally in intimate detail? Because I swear to God, Kasie, if you have to dress up in a G-string and pasties and give him this report while rubbing your ass up against a pole in order for us to keep his business, then you better get out the company card and book it on over to Frederick's of Hollywood."

"Get out of my office."

"No."

I lean back in my chair. "You want to keep Mr. Dade happy? Fine. How happy do you think he'll be if I tell him you're harassing me?"

And now the smile is back. "That's my girl. Now you're thinking like the merciless businesswoman I know and love." He stands up. "For the record, I don't want to upset you. I want you happy, healthy, and available . . . to Mr. Dade. I'll be keeping in touch with him, too, but you'll always be the main point of contact—"

"Is that supposed to be a pun?" I snap.

Tom blinks, surprised, and then laughs, a full jolly laugh, like a perverted Santa Claus.

"My, my, aren't we paranoid these days!" he exclaims once the laugh has calmed to a chuckle. "But it's good. *Point of contact*—I'm sure Mr. Dade will remain very pleased with you." He shakes his head as he turns to leave, unaccountably amused.

"You know, you think the two of us are alike, but we're not."

Tom turns, waits for me to continue.

"I made a mistake. I got involved with someone when I was already involved with someone else. It was wrong."

"And I told you, I don't fault you—"

"But you should," I say. "The only reason you don't is because you have no decency. No sense of right and wrong. You're a womanizing narcissist who probably buys his romance off Craigslist. I screwed up. You *are* screwed up."

Tom waits a beat. He'd have a perfect poker face if it wasn't for the clenched jaw. But then he shrugs with forced casualness. "I'll call Mr. Dade and find out how he wants the report delivered," he says as he reaches for the door.

"Tom!" I say. He stops and turns toward me. "You don't need to call him. I've handled his account beautifully up to this point. All the Maned Wolf executives trust me. Do not undermine *the whole team* by interfering." I cross my arms across my chest purposefully to demonstrate my stubbornness. I think I see a gleam in Tom's eyes but I don't know what it means.

Finally he nods. "Very well, do things your way. Like I said, just keep him happy. If I hear from him that you're not, there are going to be problems. Not just from me but from the higher-ups." I notice that Tom's smile is harder now. I hit a nerve with my outburst.

"You really should stop crossing your arms in front of your chest like that," he adds.

"Excuse me?"

"It's just that it reminds me of when you crossed your arms in Dave's kitchen. You do remember that, don't you? When you were trying to hide how hard your nipples were but then the gesture accidently gave me a glimpse of your . . . *contact point*."

I feel my face burning. I get what he's doing. He's angry. He wants me self-conscious, less righteous.

But he also doesn't want to waste any more of his time. Without another word he turns and leaves.

I sit back down, try to wipe out the last few minutes of the conversation from my mind. Tom is wrong. Robert doesn't hold all the cards, and, yes, I *will* handle Dave after work.

But now Dave's only one of many enemies. The war has emboldened the terrorists, and despite the confidence I felt this morning, I still don't have enough weapons in my arsenal to fight them all.

✿

# CHAPTER 27

T HE DAY MOVES SLOWLY. The phone call I missed while talking to Tom was from Simone. From my recent silence she can sense that something's off. I send her a text promising to call tomorrow. I know I can't talk to her now, while I'm still reeling from Tom's audacity. I get through the meeting with my team. Once again Asha is on her best behavior. She gains nothing by antagonizing me and prefers to wait for her moment. Will it come soon? Will she find an angle that works for her?

But such thoughts are as useless as a straw hat in a rainstorm. I'm in the rain, I'm going to get wet, so what use is it to think about the sun?

I get through the day, get to the restaurant, and immediately spot Dave at a table in the back. I can see he ordered us each a glass of white wine and a calamari appetizer. We'll probably drink the former, ignore the latter.

I can see he's worried, sending furtive glances to the left and the right as if he expects an ambush to come in from the window rather than the main entrance. He acknowledges me with a sheepish nod as I sit across from him and offers an almost grateful smile.

"You're alone," he says. His relief shoots out of him like steam from a kettle.

"For the moment." I sip my wine. It's dry with hints of citrus. Dave looks a little ill.

"I-I went too far last night," he stutters. "I overreacted."

The words sound familiar. Not long ago I had tried to be a bit more aggressive with Dave, sexually, that is. I had behaved spontaneously, straddled him as he finished his wine, asked him to take me in words much rougher than the soft enticements he approved of. He had balked. Rejected me completely.

Then he apologized the next day. He told me he had overreacted because my behavior was so out of character. He didn't want me to change.

I see now how absurd that explanation had been. Everything changes. Everything. And really, all I had done was try to mix it up in the bedroom. If that's not change we can believe in, then what the hell is?

But there was something sinister there, too. He had walked out when I overtly tried to seduce him. He walked away the moment I tried to propose a new idea, as playful and inconsequential as it may have been. Dave has always tried to control me.

And it had been his controlling nature that had attracted me to him. I was afraid of freedom, scared of my own impulses.

I've changed.

"Kasie, did you hear me? I went too far."

"I heard you," I say mildly. At the corner table is a woman sitting alone, giggling. It takes me a moment to spot the cell phone she holds against her ear.

Dave gestures toward another table, this one closer to the front. Three men who appear to be wheeling and dealing over drinks. "They're members of my club," he says. "I would prefer we not make a scene here."

"Would you?" I ask. "I didn't come here to make a scene, but I do find it interesting that you would think I would care about what you prefer."

His eyes snap back to me. "You cheated on *me*. You betrayed *me*. I gave you everything. I got you that job—"

"You got me an interview."

"Which was more than you could have done for yourself! I bought you white roses, I gave you that ruby that you still wear on your finger! I *cherished* you!"

I shake my head. Clangs from the kitchen, a car honking outside. "You never cherished me. You cherished the idea of me."

"What are you talking about?" he snaps. "Have you lost it? Is this a game to you?"

"No, it's a war. I recognize the carnage."

"I'm going to tell Dylan."

I smile. In the end he's a child running to his elders to tattle. I glance toward the host stand . . . and there he is. Robert. He's speaking to the hostess but looking at me.

"I don't think that would be a good idea," I say slowly. "Telling, that is."

"I bet you don't!" Dave sneers. "You thought you'd just get away . . ." but his voice trails off, because he sees Robert, too, as he walks toward us. It's impossible to miss him. Robert has that kind of presence. He reaches the table, his eyes glued to Dave.

"So you're the man who is about to lose," he says.

I wince at the words. I don't mind antagonizing Dave, but I take offense at the idea of someone else doing it on my behalf. I hadn't minded so much last night when Tom took up my case, but that situation had been more urgent. Here in the safety of the restaurant, restraint would be welcome.

Dave opens his mouth to speak, but instead of intelligible speech he releases a series of fragments, "You must be . . . why . . . when did . . ."

Robert watches him with bemused condescension before placing a gentle hand on my shoulder. "I'll be at the table over there." He points to an empty table in the center of the room. It's a spot that will give him a perfect view of the entire restaurant and the restaurant a perfect view of him. "All you have to do is wave," he says, looking at me before excusing himself with a parting nod.

Dave's face is the color of a robin's breast. He fumbles with the fork sitting before him, lightly tapping it against the table as if testing to see how easily it will scratch.

"You brought me here to humiliate me," he whispers.

"You taught me well."

He stares sullenly at the table, taps the fork with a little more force. It's the metronome that sets the aural pulse for our meeting.

"It doesn't have to be this way," I say. "We could just stop hurting each other. We could call a truce, rebuild our lives, we could move on."

"Separately," he says.

I can't tell if it's a question or a statement. Either way, I confirm it with a nod.

"I needed you," he says. Again his eyes dart around the room, his gaze lightly landing on the woman with the brightly dyed hair before flitting to the man wearing expensive clothes and cheap tattoos, to the woman still laughing by herself to, at last, Robert Dade. "I don't like this city," he continues, his voice vibrating with emotion. "It's tasteless, brazen, it—"

"It scares you," I finish for him.

"I didn't say that," he snaps.

"No, you didn't, not in so many words. But you told me as much in a thousand little ways." He glares at me but allows me to continue. "You're from a world where manners are quieter," I say. "Where traditionalism still means something and modesty is an attribute, not a hindrance. You came to LA because of a job offer. You came thinking you could handle the glitter of Hollywood, the vivid diversity, the aggressive women, and the preening men, but you can't handle any of it, can you?"

Dave shifts in his seat; the fork continues its metrical pulse. I lean forward, determined to be heard. "So you tried to control your little corner of the city," I say. "You did it by joining clubs that disdain those who don't fit your old-school, ivory tower view of the world. You found a house in a neighborhood where the only diversity that can be seen is between the different makes of luxury cars. You've kept your home stark to the point of austerity as if to compensate for the wildness of the city and you chose me because I had the right look, the right mannerisms, and the right education . . . and because I let you control me. You told me who you wanted me to be and I poured myself into your mold and held its form for years."

He looks up at me now; he's pleading with me without saying a word.

"I can't do it anymore, Dave. I've changed. You can punish me for that if you like, but it won't do you any good. At best you'll embarrass yourself; at worst you'll become a laughingstock. Either way we'll be over. I am no longer well suited to live within that corner of the world."

The laughing woman finally hangs up her phone, and just like that, her smile disappears.

"You're holding on to me out of fear, not love," I finally add. "But unfortunately this relationship will never make you feel safe again."

Dave lets the fork drop back to the table, but he holds his silence. I nod, knowing he's giving me his answer. He won't be going to Freeland, he won't be fighting me anymore. This battle is over. He's letting me go.

Discreetly I take the ruby off my finger and push it in his direction. I'm careful about this. I don't want anyone else to notice. He scowls at the offensive piece of jewelry.

"I hate this ring," he mutters. "I hated it when you picked it out and I hate it even more now."

"Of course you do," I say; there's no judgment in my voice. "You want a woman who is comfortable with the easy transparency of diamonds, not the flawed passion of rubies."

"Silks," he says. "That's what the jeweler called the flaws in a ruby. I don't understand it. Why would you give such a pretty name to an imperfection?"

I smile and sigh. "I know you don't see the beauty in that. That's why we don't work."

I look down at my hands, now naked of adornment. "I *am* sorry

I hurt you. It shouldn't have taken an affair for me to find myself. I should have figured it all out by myself. I should have been stronger. I'm so, so sorry that you had to suffer for my weakness."

Dave nods curtly. "Will you leave together?" he asks.

I glance up at Robert's table. "No. He'll leave a few minutes after me. If you like, you and I can walk out together, for appearances."

He perks up slightly at that. It's the first thing I've said during this entire meeting that he's comfortable with.

He signals for the check and I pull out my cell and send Robert a text.

```
I'm going to walk out with Dave but then we're
going our separate ways, permanently. Everything
has been handled. No need to follow.
```

I watch as Robert glances down at his phone as a waitress brings him a cup of coffee. He reads as he sips, not bothering to put any cream or sugar in it. He takes it black. I didn't know that.

It's funny but that bothers me. How many other little details do I not know about the man who has redefined my life?

His response is quick and to the point.

```
You shouldn't be alone with him. I'll follow.
```

It's the response I predicted but I had hoped for better.

```
Everything is fine. He and I are done hurting each
other. I need you to trust me with this.
```

I press Send as Dave gives the waitress his credit card.

I can see Robert's frown as he reads. For a moment I question the wisdom of using him as my "perceived threat." It's a little like using a mountain lion as a guard dog. You have no real control over who and when it will attack.

But Robert meets my eyes from across the room and gives me a stiff nod before sending yet another text.

```
If I don't hear from you in five minutes I'm
coming after you.
```

It's funny because I know his interest is in protecting me but the text makes me feel like I'm the one he's targeting.

I put my phone back in my purse, smile at Dave. "Let's go."

He gets up first, stands politely by as I gather myself. We walk out side by side, past the tattooed man and dyed-haired woman, past Robert, only stopping briefly at the table filled with the wheelers and dealers who greet Dave warmly and me with the civility required.

Once outside we walk the block to where I'm parked. My ring is in his pocket; my keys are in my hand.

When we reach my car I turn to him. "We have things in each other's houses. Shall I bring your stuff to your place and pick up mine or visa versa or—"

"I'll bring your stuff to you, pick up mine," he interrupts. "If it's all right I'll do it while you're at work; Monday afternoon should work. I'll mail you the spare key you gave me . . . or—"

"You can just leave the key under that plant—"

"The potted cycad by the kitchen entrance—"

"Yes, the one I bought at Boething last year—"

"I remember."

We stop. He shoves his hands into his pockets, directs his attention to the passing cars. Good-byes are never elegant. There are always things left to be said, little memories that need to be shoved aside, littering our minds until time finds a way to discard them. Finality, which should be so easy, is always awkward.

"I guess I should go then," I say softly.

He nods, turns but then stops. "I had an affair, too."

I drop my keys. Confusion followed by a new sense of indignation. All the righteous anger he had thrown my way and he had been guilty, too? Was he kidding?

When he turns back to me I expect to see the triumph of a man who's delivered a knockout punch, but instead I just see sadness.

"Years ago and it only lasted a month. She was a college student doing a legal internship at my firm. You were acting a bit moody. When we were together you seemed . . . I guess melancholy is a good word for it. I thought I was losing you. And then this ambitious young woman with dark hair and light eyes . . . just like you, she comes to my firm, looking for role models, looking up at me with admiration . . . I was weak, I thought I was losing you."

"But when . . ." My voice trails off as a memory creeps to the forefront of my mind. "We had only been dating a year . . ."

"Yes, you remember that time, five years ago. You had been at your job for a few months and all of a sudden you pulled away from me. I tried to reach you with romance, little gestures of affection, but you didn't respond and I was too much of a coward to face the issue head-on."

*Too much of a coward.* Well, that was one thing Dave and I had in common. Except . . . "You did talk to me about it. We were at my place, finishing off a bottle of wine, and you asked if I was losing interest. You asked if you were the one making me sad."

"And you started crying. That was the first time you told me about your sister."

"It was the tenth anniversary of her death."

A bird lands lightly on the sidewalk by our feet, picks at some crumbs of crackers dropped there by those who had walked before us. "That's when you broke off the affair with her?"

Again he nods. The bird continues to feed off someone else's mess. "I knew when I heard the story of your sister that you were the perfect woman for me."

"Excuse me?" Again the indignation pounds at my temples.

"You say I'm scared, Kasie? Well, you were terrified. You were terrified by the very idea of being out of control, so much so that, yes, you let me set more rules for us, you allowed me to wield a lot of the control. If you felt the impulse to rebel, you squashed it all in the interest of *not* being Melody."

"You took advantage of my tragedy."

"Because you wanted me to."

The bird, now done with its snack, flies off to find the next course. Dave stares down at the remaining crumbs, shuffles his feet. "I knew we were in real trouble when you insisted on a ruby over a diamond."

"It's a small thing."

"It was enough to let me know that the current had changed." He reaches down to pick up my keys. I had forgotten about them. "I guess you're not scared anymore, huh?"

"I wouldn't go that far," I say as I take the keys from his hands.

"Well, at least you're not alone." He pauses before adding, "That girl I cheated on you with is married now, to some other guy who'd worked at my firm. I doubt she ever told him about me. I haven't seen her in years, but her husband and I travel in the same circles. I hear things. They have a baby now. Apparently she decided that a career in law isn't her thing. Too much ugliness and aggression. Now she's running the Sunday school at his church or something."

"It sounds like she would have been perfect for you."

"Yeah, maybe she would have been." He meets my eyes. His sadness is mixed with just a little bit of anger and maybe a few spoonfuls of regret. "I picked the wrong woman."

I stand outside my car and watch as he walks away, not to the club but toward some other destination. I'll never know where. The little minutiae of his day-to-day life is now off-limits to me. He's going to become a stranger.

Maybe he always was.

I turn my head, not wanting to see the moment when he disappears.

CHAPTER 28

❀

I'VE ONLY JUST opened my car door when I hear him call my
name. I turn to see Robert striding toward me.

"Where is he?" he asks; his voice is steady but I can hear the un-
dercurrent of aggression.

"He left. Like I said in the text, it's over."

He studies my face, then looks around to see if he can spot Dave.
"He's not going to give up so easily."

"Nothing about this was easy," I say.

"He'll talk to Freeland. He's petty like that. You just have to look
at him to see it."

"*Petty*'s the wrong word," I say, but I can't think of the right one.
The only word that comes to mind is *lost*. "He won't talk to Freeland."

"Why not?"

"Because he's like the rest of us, guided by self-interest. There's
nothing in it for him anymore. It serves him better to just walk away."

Robert shakes his head, unable to accept that any man would so
readily accept defeat. The wind blows, making the trees rustle above
our heads; leaves fall among the crumbs. Robert looks down and
lifts my left hand. "He took the ruby back?"

"I gave it to him."

A flash of approval, maybe even relief. "Let's go to my place.
We'll order Chinese food and talk. I know you want to trust him,
but we have to be prepared."

A dry leaf falls on my shoe. The tree doesn't need it. It has plenty
of other greener and healthier leaves to adorn its branches. This leaf

here is dead. It must have died on the vine, well before it detached itself.

But I wonder if the tree will miss it anyway.

"I think I'd like to spend the night at my place," I say.

"All right, I've never been to your place—"

"No, Robert, by myself."

For a moment I can see his confidence waiver, he thought my days of pushing him away were over. Maybe they are, but tonight I need to mourn for a relationship that died on the vine.

I put my hand on his arm. "Monday I'll come to you, or you can come to me if you like. But I'm tired, Robert, in so many ways. You need to give me a few days to recover."

He nods, understanding. "My car's parked in the lot on the next block. Walk with me there; there's something I want to give you."

I nod and walk by his side. At some point he takes my hand, rubs his thumb back and forth over my bare ring finger. It feels weird, holding hands in public like this. In fact, it still feels wrong.

But how much time have I spent fantasizing about being in a relationship with this man? Sailing away with him, scaling the Mayan pyramids, making love on the floor of the Musée . . . in my mind Robert and I have been a couple for some time now.

And yet I never imagined us walking down an LA street holding hands.

"Was Asha a problem today?" he asked.

"No, not Asha. Today it was Tom who treated me like a hooker."

The words came quickly to my lips before my mind had time to engage, before it could remind me of who I was talking to.

"Tom . . . Love? What did he do?"

This is a story that needs to be significantly watered down for Robert. I'm not sure why, but I sense that it would be best if I appear unfazed. Unfortunately I can't repress a shiver when I recall the interaction. "He's just being Tom, that's all. Now that he has confirmation about the nature of our relationship, he . . ." My voice trails off as I try to think of the best way to summarize everything.

"He what?"

"It's not a big deal," I say quickly. "It's just going to take some time to remind him that my personal life is none of his business. I can handle it."

Robert's grip on my hand tightens but he doesn't say anything. No verbal response is probably the best response I can hope for.

We reach the parking lot and I break out in skeptical laughter. "This is where you parked your Alfa Romeo 8C Spider?" The lot is a little run-down. Cars are tightly packed together, the wind pushes bits of litter over the gravel surface; it does not speak of luxury.

"I gave the attendant a little something extra to take care of it for me," Robert says and gestures to the far end of the lot where only one car is parked.

I try to speculate on how much "a little extra" is and I wonder if it's necessary. There's something intimidating about Robert, even when he's not trying to be. I can't imagine anyone trying to test him by screwing up his $300,000 car.

He walks me over and opens the trunk that is about the size of a hatbox. He pulls out a couple of dress shirts, considers them both before handing me one. "Sleep in this until I see you next," he says. He throws a fleeting look at the lowering sun. "Put it on as soon as you get home. Wear just my shirt, nothing else. Think of me."

I take it in my hands, lift it to my nose. It smells slightly of his cologne. I smile my consent. I will sleep in it, and thinking of him has never been a problem.

He opens the passenger door for me and tells me he'll drive me back to my car. I begin to protest, telling him that I'd rather walk, but he insists and I give in easily.

As he starts up the engine I realize that when it comes to Robert, I quite frequently give in easily.

WHEN I FINALLY get home, it feels oddly empty. I have lived alone since college, but before all of this, I was able to fill the empty space with plans and expectations. On the coffee table are travel magazines to help Dave and me plan our next vacation. And there on the wine rack is the bottle of expensive Merlot I planned to bring to a birthday party for one of Dave's coworkers. Upstairs is a calendar with each day jotted out in perfect detail with lunch meetings and date nights, next to it a list of potential clients I'd like to promote my firm to, earning their business and impressing the partners.

I still have the things, but they signify nothing. What was once travel research is now just a few periodicals with pretty pictures in them. What was a gift is now just alcohol waiting to be drunk. The calendar of planned days is now just paper filled with useless scribbles.

Perhaps the list of potential clients is still useful. After all, I'm pretty sure I'm right about Dave. He won't talk to Freeland. Maybe he was never going to. I don't think he can face the shame any more than I can. Asha is powerless without Dave's cooperation. Evil bitch that she is, she'll probably find somebody more vulnerable to torture. Tom will get himself in line in time, after he sees that I have everything under control . . .

. . . except for Robert. I don't have him under control. And of course I don't want to control him, but his unpredictability is unnerving. Perhaps I won't have time to approach new clients. Maybe he'll give me more and increasingly time-consuming assignments to fill up my days. He could keep me tied to him with ropes made of numbers and mergers.

I've draped Robert's shirt over a dining room chair but I go and pick it up again. I have nightshirts that are more comfortable than this. Later tonight, when I get tired, I'll change into one of them. He won't see me in the shirt, so there's no real need to wear it.

*Put it on as soon as you get home. Think of me.*

My hand goes to the scarf around my neck and I carefully pull it off, drop it on the table . . . a table not so unlike the one at Dave's house.

I do it only because my house is warm. I don't need the scarf. I don't need the jacket, either. I pull that off as well, drape it over another chair.

*Think of me.*

I had been laid out for him like a feast, right there on Dave's table. He had run his hands over my body, kissed me, tasted me. . . .

*. . . as soon as you get home. Think of me.*

I unbutton my blouse. I'm alone here. It doesn't matter.

He had pinched my nipples, made them reach out for him. My hand goes to my bra.

*Wear just my shirt, nothing else.*

The bra falls to the floor and he's there. I feel him in the air, hear him in the stillness; I hold the shirt to my face, breathe in the cologne so that now all my senses are engaged.

*I can touch you with a thought.*

Is he thinking of me now? Is that what I'm sensing? Him, reaching across the distance with a fantasy, like some warlock in a fairy tale? I pull off my belt, drape it over my jacket; my fingers fumble with the buttons that hold my slacks to my waist. He guides me, instructs me, compels me to go further.

*Wear just my shirt, nothing else. Think of me.*

I remove my pants; my panties are next; I clutch his shirt in my hand.

*. . . even when I'm nowhere near you I'm inside of you. I can touch you with a thought.*

I feel the throbbing between my legs. Slowly I loosen my grip on the cotton fabric, slip in one arm, then the other. The fabric is light, almost teasing against my skin. Goose bumps rise all over my body. Outside, I hear the wind knocking at my windows, clamoring for entry.

*. . . even when I'm nowhere near you I'm inside of you.*

I feel a jolt of electricity, a small spasm. I reach out for the back of the chair for support. My breathing is irregular. It's just cotton, just the trace of cologne, just the Santa Ana winds clearing away the haze, encouraging the fire.

*Think of me.*

I close my eyes, try to regain my composure. There are things

I'm supposed to pack, a loss I'm supposed to mourn. This isn't right. It's crazy. He's not here.

*I can touch you with a thought. . . . Think of me.*

I lower myself onto the chair, finger the fabric; I can feel him caressing the insides of my thighs, kissing my shoulder. I don't touch myself. I don't need to.

*I can touch you with a thought.*

His teeth graze my neck, his hands run down to the small of my back. I slide down farther in my chair, part my legs just enough. His tongue flicks back and forth against my clit, and I let out a tiny gasp as I writhe in my chair, running my hands up and down his shirt.

*Even when I'm nowhere near you I'm inside of you.*

I feel him enter me; my muscles contract as I lose myself in the ghostly fantasy. The wind quietly howls and I part my lips, tasting the energy that's in the air. He surrounds me, overwhelms me.

*Think of me.*

I feel myself on the cusp of losing control. There's an aching inside of me that's both erotic and torturous. It seems impossible that I could orgasm without the help of my hands, without his physical presence. But Robert is so much more than the flesh, blood, and muscles that compose him. He's a force, a phenomenon. He's power and intrigue, enticement and danger. He licks the hollow of my throat, strokes my thigh.

*Even when I'm nowhere near you I'm inside of you.*

The throbbing intensifies, I arch my back; his tongue is now on my nipples, his hands are in my hair, his erection fills me. Is this really happening to me?

*I can touch you with a thought.*

When the explosion comes, I close my eyes and give in.

# CHAPTER 29

❊

T HE SPELL FADES slowly over the following days. It stays with me in low degrees as I extricate Dave's life from mine. I put his things in boxes, making sure everything is neat and well folded. I leave it near the foyer but not in it. I don't want it to look like I'm pushing him out the door. He can take those steps himself. I pull the pictures of us out of frames and put them into photo albums that will be stored in the back of a closet with the old yearbooks and neglected skeletons.

But my mind's not fully engaged in the tasks. This was supposed to be a weekend for good-byes, the last nights for reminiscing, nights to indulge light tears and heavy thoughts.

But the last few nights haven't been those things, and that bothers me. What bothers me even more is that I've worn Robert's shirt each night. As soon as Los Angeles turns away from the sun, I slip it on. It's Sunday night and I'm wearing it now. Why is that? Robert's not calling to check up on me. He hasn't even sent me a text. Did he ever really expect me to put it on in the first place?

Yes . . . yes, of course he did. And he knows I'm wearing it now. That's why he hasn't called or texted. He doesn't have to.

So as I move from room to room in my lover's shirt, Dave, the man I've spent the last six years with, disappears. Like a minor earthquake that briefly wakes you up at five in the morning. You know you felt something but you can't quite figure out what that something was, or if it was real.

I don't think I want to know what that says about me.

I eat a light meal, try to distract myself with a little TV, open that overpriced bottle of Merlot, and try to become accustomed to the scent of Robert's cologne.

It's almost ten when my phone rings. Something tells me that it's not Robert even before I look at the screen. But I am surprised when I see Tom Love's name.

Ten o'clock on a Sunday night is not an appropriate time for him to call. My eyes scan the room as if looking for a weapon that will reach through a phone line. It's not until the last ring that I finally pick up.

"What," I say in lieu of hello. Really, considering how angry I am with him, it could have been a lot worse.

"Relax." Tom's voice holds the air of bemusement but I don't sense the smugness he had on Friday. "I'm calling to apologize."

"I should have you fired for sexual harassment."

"Probably. Look, I don't always phrase things right. Ambition keeps me moving forward but it can also addle my brain. I get so focused on what's to come, I don't think about what I'm saying in the moment."

I shift slightly in my seat, hold my tongue, wait for him to get to the point. I've worked with Tom long enough to know that if he's apologizing, there's something in it for him.

"It was wrong of me to ask you to continue your affair with Mr. Dade for the sake of the firm and it was ridiculous for me to suggest that you should do it for my sake. I know I could never pressure you into sleeping with someone you don't want to sleep with, and even if I could, I wouldn't."

"Bullshit."

Again a rueful laugh. "I guess I deserve that. But I am sorry for the way I spoke to you. That kind of talk is only appropriate in locker rooms and strip clubs; I should know, I've apparently spent enough time in both."

I sigh and pick up the remote, slowly scrolling through the news stations, watching with mild interest as they deftly interweave tragedy with entertainment. People die in the Middle East and a European prince wants to introduce an American-style Halloween celebration to the royal family. A man in New York kills his wife and children and Kim Kardashian gets another $600,000 appearance fee. The anchors slip from one story to the next with barely a pause, their smiles and frowns flickering off and on with the rapidity of blinking Christmas tree lights.

"I would like you to consider something, though," Tom goes on, insisting on my attention. He's been talking for a while now, bumbling through various forms of an apology, but nothing he's said has been remotely as interesting as Kim's $500 manicure.

"And what would that be?" I ask with a sigh.

"Don't keep your relationship going for the sake of the firm, but don't end it for the sake of pride. You like him, Kasie. If you didn't, you wouldn't have risked so much to be with him."

"I took care of Dave," I say coolly. "Just like I said I would."

"So he's not going to go running to Freeland, crying about his girlfriend cheating on him with the big, bad Mr. Dade? Well done! I underestimated you."

"Which is another thing you should apologize for." I sip my wine. An awkward young anchorman is relaying true stories of Stranger Danger.

"You're right, you're right," Tom says. "I'm sorry. But that doesn't change the crux of what I'm saying. No one is making you do anything, but don't throw an entire relationship away just to make a point."

"You're doing it again," I say.

"Doing what?"

"Underestimating me. Do you really think I can't see through this? You're changing your wording, not the message. You want me to keep seeing Robert Dade because it benefits you. My heart is of no interest to you at all."

"Now that's not fair . . . at least it's not entirely fair. I do want you to enjoy your romance because I like you. My apologies and advice are as legitimate as your accusations and anger. But at some point you're going to have to accept that we have a symbiotic relationship. If I advise you to follow your heart and you *listen,* everyone wins. Yes, my motivations are mostly selfish but I don't see how that changes anything."

This is probably as PC as Tom gets. That's not saying much, but the fact that he's trying is telling. "You really want more Maned Wolf accounts, don't you?"

"Well, aren't you quick."

I laugh despite myself. "I don't want to ever hear about that night that you saw . . . I don't want to talk about how that dress. . . ." I blush and grit my teeth, angry with my own embarrassment. "Just don't ever mention it again, all right?" I finally manage.

"Never," he says quickly. "That's a promise."

I wish I could make him promise not to think of it ever again, too. I could ask him to say he won't, but I'm so tired of lies and false denials. I know Tom has relived that moment a thousand times. I know in his fantasies he was not so honorable. I know that when he looks at me now, that image leaps to the forefront of his mind. My humiliation prickles my skin, makes me squirm a bit, but at least my humiliation is real. And for the first time in my life I'm able to acknowledge what I'm really feeling rather than denying it and pretending to have neater emotions.

"I haven't ended things with Mr. Dade. I have no plans to do so."

"You'll tell me if and when you do? Just so I can prepare myself and the firm?"

"That's a promise," I say, mimicking his words and tone.

I can almost hear Tom's smile. "You're a treasure, Kasie."

"Good-bye, Tom."

I hang up the phone.

On the television children are being tested. The journalist says that these tests prove that even the most responsible child will accept the invitation of a stranger if the incentive is strong and the lie is smooth. Children are impulsive, the journalist says. And when approached by a well-dressed, charming adult who speaks with authority, they will respond. They will forget what they've been taught, forget the warnings and follow the stranger to danger.

I look down at the shirt I wear as a nightgown, feeling like a child.

❦

# CHAPTER 30

THE NIGHT STRETCHES ON. Around eleven I go to sleep restlessly. My dreams are jumbled and disquieting.

*In one I'm in the back of a limo with Dave by my side . . . except he's a ghost; I can only see his outline.*

*"Did I kill you?" I ask as the limo takes one sharp turn and then another.*

*He just smiles with transparent lips. "There's so much to fear in this world," he says with a laugh.*

*Except it's not his laugh; he speaks with my sister's voice. Panicked, I try to get out, scurry to the other side of the limo, and attempt to open the doors, but they're locked.*

*"Silly." Her voice murmurs in my ear even though Dave has not moved. "It's not me that you have to be scared of! That would be like being scared of yourself!"*

*"I'm nothing like you," I say to her, to Dave, to anyone who will listen.*

*"Really?" the voice says teasingly. "Tell it to Mr. Dade."*

The dreams go on like that. Nightmares and phantasms, clashes with invisible opponents. I wake up a few times, tangled in the sheets as if I had been combating the bed itself. It's not until well after two that my mind finally escapes from the alarming images and lets me fall into a deep, continuous sleep.

When next I awake it's to the sound of classical music. My alarm clock, of course. I find it easier to start the day with the slow build of a sonata than the sudden scream of an electric guitar. I keep my eyes closed and let myself be drawn into the music. It's a Baroque piece of the eighteenth-century master Tomaso Albinoni, a personal favorite. The sound is low and alluring, decadent to the point of being sinful. I become aware of the feeling of Robert's shirt against my skin and let a small sound of pleasure hum through my closed lips, breathe in deep through my nose . . .

. . . and smell coffee.

Slowly, almost fearfully, I open my eyes. On my nightstand next to my alarm is a steaming cup of coffee.

And another is being held on the charcoal gray armchair of my bedroom, cupped between the hands of Robert Dade.

I don't move, don't sit up, don't say a word. I think about the dreams and nightmares I had had only a few hours before. This doesn't feel like a dream and yet it doesn't make sense that he could be here, holding one of my ceramic cups filled with coffee.

"You know he's a Venetian," he says, gesturing to my clock radio.

"I'm sorry?"

"Albinoni. He was a Venetian. It seems appropriate when you consider where we met."

I pull the sheets up to my chin. "How did you get in here?"

"As you may recall, I know how to pick a lock."

"I have a security system."

"I know. My company made it."

"Robert, you can't just—"

"You do remember that you told me I could come to you in a few days. It's been a few days."

I turn my eyes to the clock. "True," I agree, "it's also seven fifteen in the morning."

He sighs, sips his coffee. "Do you know how hard it was for me to stay away this weekend? Knowing that he still has a key to this place? Knowing that he could come here and try to exact revenge at any time?"

The music has taken on a yearning quality. Its melody keeps me calm. "Dave isn't a psychotic. He's a man who was hurt. That's all. He gave me back some of the pain I gave him and now he's moving on."

He studies his coffee, tilting it like a sommelier would tilt a glass of wine while looking for clues to its age and weight. "Putting you in that dress," he says, "displaying you in front of Love as if you were a toy or a prostitute . . . perhaps it's not psychotic but it does point to a . . . a demonic sensibility." He looks up from his coffee, locks his eyes on mine. "You think you know what he's capable of. You don't."

I groan and look up at my angled cream ceiling. It's early; I'm not thinking straight. But for him to break into my home to warn me of what Dave might be capable of seems ironic.

"Those boxes downstairs, those are his things?"

I nod.

"When will he be picking them up?"

"Later this afternoon." I turn on my side, flash him a pacifying smile. "I won't be here."

Robert nods his approval, walks to the bed, puts his coffee cup next to mine. "You won't see him alone again. It's not safe. If you need to meet him, you'll call me first."

"You don't have the right to tell me how to handle this."

"No?" He cocks his head to the side. "You'd risk your well-being just to be rebellious? Why do I doubt that?"

There's a gentle but mocking lilt to his voice. I bite down on my lip. I should kick him out. This morning he is a criminal. My angel is incensed. But my devil has Hollywood tastes and seeks to glorify the crime.

Perhaps it's I who has the demonic sensibility.

"Maybe you should take the day off," he suggests. "Work from my house. Give Love another day to reassess his behavior."

"No, I need to be at work. I can't let my personal stressors keep me from my professional responsibilities."

Robert doesn't say anything. Instead he pulls the sheet back, runs his eyes over his shirt that covers my body. "You did as I asked."

Of all the things he's said and done this morning, that one sentence is by far the most provoking. And yet it oddly thrills even as it alarms. The combination of emotions worries me. He needs to leave the room. I need to drink my coffee, get my bearings, find the good sense to chastise him for his magisterial behavior.

But I don't move. My request for privacy dies before it ever reaches my lips. Instead I lie here and wait for his next move, knowing deep down that if he demands, I will want to give.

Therein lies the danger.

With a firm but gentle hand he pushes me from my side to my back. "You can go to work today if that's truly what you want to do. But you're going to be late."

"I can't—"

He puts a finger against my lips. "You can talk later. Right now you need to unbutton your shirt. Show yourself to me."

It's a power game. Pride kicks in, and I almost refuse.

But I don't.

Something in the way he's looking at me, something in his tone . . .

My fingers fumble with the buttons of the shirt. It had been so easy to refuse Dave, but Robert . . . it's different.

The shirt is now undone, but it still covers me. A small strip of skin is revealed between my breasts.

He leans over, gently pulls the fabric back so that it lies on my shoulders and spreads out at my sides like the closed wings of a moth. He straightens his posture, stands over me as he studies the nuances of my figure. My breathing is irregular and I look away from him. I shouldn't want this. I shouldn't want to follow a man's commands. Not after what I've been through with Dave.

And yet.

"Spread your legs, Kasie."

I close my eyes. "I have to go to work," I whisper.

"Later. Spread your legs."

Is it because I know what it's like to have this man inside me? Am I like any addict, willing to humble myself for one more fix? Or is there a part of me that really isn't ready to face the music of the day?

Am I using a convenient sense of subservience to justify this small procrastination?

Does it matter?

Slowly, I open my legs. I expect him to touch me but he doesn't. Instead he circles the bed, wolfish in his movements.

"You want to handle things in your own way," Robert says, his eyes moving up and down my body with an unapologetic appetite. "I respect that. I will allow that."

*Allow* . . . I open my mouth to object but again he leans over, puts his finger against my lips. "As I said, you can talk later. But right now, I want you to listen. And you will do what I want, won't you, Kasie?"

My heart is pounding so loud, I wonder if he can hear it. He removes his finger and I remain silent.

Again his eyes roam over me, caressing my thighs and stopping there, right there between my legs.

"Are you wet, Kasie?"

I don't answer, partially because I don't know if he wants me to speak, partially because I'm embarrassed to admit that I am.

"Touch yourself," he says; his tone leaves no room for negotiation. "Reach between your legs; tell me if you're wet."

My hand twitches at my side, almost as if it's battling with itself, but my urge to yield is overwhelming. With an odd mixture of reluctance and anticipation I move my hand between my legs. My fingers slide over my clit and I jump, surprised by my own sensitivity. But I know he wants more. I slip one finger inside myself as he watches.

"Yes," I say quietly, almost meekly, "I'm wet."

He nods, satisfied with my answer. He reaches down, gently directs the movement of my hand. "Use two fingers," he says; his voice is kinder now but the air of authority is still prominent, "and use your thumb to rub your clit. When I tell you to masturbate, this is what I want you to do, unless I tell you otherwise."

And as he pulls his hand away, I do as I've been asked. My fingers plunging inside of myself as I further stimulate myself with my thumb.

"As I was saying before," he says, his eyes glued to me as I begin to writhe on the sheets beneath me, "I will *allow* it." He puts special emphasis on the word he knows will get under my skin but I don't think I have even the slightest ability to challenge him. I try to focus but my mind is clouded with confusion and ecstasy. Why am I doing this for him? Why does it incite me?

"However," he continues, his voice still calm, "if he tries to hurt you, if he tries to lay a single hand on you, I will step in. I will take care of him and I will decide how to do that. If there are lines that can't be crossed, I will erase those lines. I will keep you safe. You will not stand in the way of that."

I'm coming dangerously close to an orgasm, and somehow the thought of coming in front of him while he is fully dressed, so calm and so commanding, intensifies my agitation. I look away but he reaches over, guides my chin back in his direction. "Do you understand, Kasie?"

I nod but it's not enough.

"I need more than that. No, no, don't come yet," he says as I arch my back, the little control I have left slipping away. "I need you to answer me first. Tell me you understand."

"I understand—" I gasp.

". . . and you will not stand in my way."

"I will not stand in your way," I parrot. It's all I can manage.

"That's good." He sits on the side of the bed; he watches the movement of my hand with almost scholarly interest. "How close are you to coming, Kasie?"

"Oh God!"

"That's not an answer. How close are you?"

I try to look away again but again his fingers slip under my chin. "Answer me."

"I'm very . . . very close . . . to . . ."

My voice gives out. I can feel the orgasm that sits on the verge of bursting through me, but just then Robert firmly but carefully grasps my hand, stills it, and then pulls it away from my body.

"Not yet," he says.

My eyes widen in surprise. The shock of being denied when I'm so close is too much. Suddenly I don't care about the consequence of my submission. I don't care that he has taken command of me without having to fight me. I certainly don't care about how late I'm going to be for work. I need the satisfaction my fingers had promised. I try to move my hand back between my thighs but his hold is too strong.

"Please," I gasp.

"Please what, Kasie?"

I flush, my cheeks red with frustration and uncontainable longing. "Please let me come."

He smiles and kisses my forehead protectively. "Don't move; you're not allowed to touch yourself, not right now. Just wait."

He stands and again for reasons I'm not clear on I obey despite a growing desperation.

Slowly he takes off his shirt, then his pants. I watch him as I struggle to stay still. My body is on fire.

Finally he exposes his erection to me. I'm frantic to get it inside me, but instead he pulls me up so that I'm sitting back on my heels. He pulls my knees apart enough so he can see me completely and then pets my hair. "I know what you want. You want me to take you on this bed. You're desperate to come. But the blowjob will be first, Kasie. Understand?"

Again I nod and he smiles before gently pressing my head forward. I wrap my lips around him, my hand slides over the base of his cock as my tongue finds the veins and ridges, toying with the tip before taking more of him in my mouth. I hear him moan and the sound encourages me, electrifies me. I move back and forth, preparing him, hoping that my success will be rewarded with something even better.

Again he moans and then quickly pulls my head away. "Now," he says. And then he pushes me back on the bed and in an instant he gives me what I crave. He's inside of me, answering my body's pleas for release. My orgasm comes swiftly, tearing through my body like a tornado, making the room spin and my world buckle. He continues to move inside of me, grinding, biting my neck. I try to hold on to him but he holds my arms down and his strength is insurmountable.

"No one will touch you," he says, his voice so low I have to struggle to hear him. "No one but me."

He thrusts again and I cry out. He overwhelms me, pounding into me as I thrash beneath him.

Yes, this is a dangerous man. Dangerous because his power comes from my own desire and his power over me is increasing with time and familiarity. I can fight Dave, I can fight Asha.

But Robert Dade?

I stare up into his eyes. Can he read my thoughts? That quiet but knowing smile suggests it. I wrap my legs around his waist; his mouth moves down to my ear. "Kasie," he gasps.

He pulls out, flips me over, and enters me again. Again I cry out, my breasts crushed against the firm mattress. I grab on to the wooden bars of the headboard like a convict railing for release.

Again his mouth is by my ear as he pushes inside me again and again. "No one but me," he says again, his voice rasping as he struggles for a last moment of control. But as I push my hips back against him I know that his control is almost gone.

"Now," he groans and in that moment we come together. The sensation is so forceful and primal, it feels almost perilous.

I feel the weight of his chest on top of me as he finally collapses; I close my eyes and try to bring myself back to earth.

I might have been safer at Dave's.

# CHAPTER 31

❀

I'M ALMOST AN hour late for work. Barbara looks at me, surprised as I stride past her. I had forgotten to call to warn her of my delayed arrival, not something I've ever done before. But it's all right. I'm composed now. The hypnotic events of the morning have passed. By the time we had parted ways, Robert's voice had adopted his normal low and casually confident tone.

But as I sit at my desk, mulling over the contents of my inbox, a nagging sensation of worry distracts me. I lost myself earlier, I gave myself to him, my body, my will. . . . The angel on my shoulder, long neglected and ignored, raises her voice, urges me to run. Prays that I'll listen just this once.

But I can't run from Robert. Not now, not yet. Tom was right: it's not what I want. Obviously my relationship benefits the firm, my career, and so on, but as far as I'm concerned that's all beside the point. I can't run from Robert because I don't want to. I just don't have the necessary will to make my legs move.

Tom bursts into my office with his characteristic inconsideration. Barbara stands behind him with a shrug and a smile before closing the door behind him, giving us privacy.

"Tom, I'm sorry I didn't call to say I would be late; I—" but something stops me. The sheen of sweat that dots his brow, the flush of his cheeks and the rigidness of his jaw, it all adds up to no good. "Did something happen?" I ask.

"My apology wasn't good enough?" he croaks. I've never heard his voice take this tenor. It's thin, artless; it hints at an ocean of rage that threatens to submerge the entire building. "Was I not sincere enough?"

I shake my head, not understanding.

"I went too far Friday night, I know that. I apologized for that!"

"You did," I agree, then turn up my palms as a sign of confusion. "I'm sorry, Tom, I'm still not following. What is going on? What's upset you?"

"He took it away."

"Took what away?"

"*EVERYTHING!*"

The cry is so loud that Barbara hurries back in as if expecting to break up a fight. But when she sees Tom's face, sees the pain, she steps back out, closes the door again.

I wish she had stayed. Before me is a man so wrecked, it wouldn't be implausible if he told me someone had just broken into his home and killed his children, raped his wife, stolen all of his possessions.

But Tom has no children, no wife, and all of his possessions are insured.

As far as I know, the only thing Tom has, the only thing he actually *cares* about, is his job.

I fall back in my seat. The air seems to have taken on the sulfurous scent of foreboding.

"What happened?" I ask again. But I know. I know Tom will be leaving today with the remnants of his career here packed up into a small box. I know his heart has been crunched with the same callousness we use to analyze the numbers of a division that is slated for liquidation.

And I know who's responsible.

As Tom lets the silence do his talking for him, I shift positions; Tom has always been able to elicit in me a strange mix of derision and respect. And he didn't just step over the line on Friday. He obliterated it. If I wasn't afraid of damaging my own reputation, I could sue.

But that's the thing. I never wanted to sue. I was ready to accept his apology, as self-serving as it might have been. I was willing to take this on a day-by-day basis. I wanted to see if we could make it all work. Not doing so wasn't just bad for Tom. It was bad for me.

"On what grounds?" I ask weakly. "They have to have grounds, right?"

"The complaint of a client," he hisses. "Apparently I've made some disparaging remarks to some of the women who work for Maned Wolf, Inc. . . . . women I'm pretty sure I've never spoken a word to in my life—but they're all willing to sign affidavits saying I have. And then there are other companies who have brought their business here, smaller companies who have suddenly remembered that I was inappropriate with the women at their firms, too."

He stares at me, waiting for a response. My mouth opens but nothing comes out.

"It's a joke, of course," he says, then tears his eyes from me, turns to face the wall, raises his fist. "It's. A. *JOKE!*" With each word he pounds his fist into the wall. I can practically see Barbara on the other side of the door wondering if she should come in again.

He continues to stare at the wall. "It's a joke," he says again, softer this time. "I've never harassed a woman in my entire professional career."

"Wellll . . ."

Tom pivots slowly, sneers at me. "You?" He takes a step closer. "I said a few brash remarks the day after you flashed me your pussy."

I grow cold, my nails scrape against my desk. "I didn't flash you—"

"Tell me, if I hadn't locked Dave out of the house, if I had accepted his invitation to dinner, would you have served me? Would you have poured my wine while wearing a dress made out of the same amount of material as a washcloth? Would you have sat next to me, wearing no underwear, knowing how high your hemline was going to rise as soon as you hit the chair, knowing that I would be looking at you while you were *literally* half naked for the entire night? Would you have let Dave debase you in front of me, let him indulge his little revenge fantasy?"

Now it's me who turns red. The humiliation of that night shoots through me like the pain of a damaged muscle that's been reinjured. "There is no need—"

"Because that's how it seemed to me," Tom continues, cutting me off. "You felt cornered. You felt like you didn't have a choice. But I *gave* you a choice. That ass your fiancé was so eager to show off? I saved it! I left! I called Mr. Dade! I am not the bad guy here, so why the hell did you sic your fucking dog on me? Because I told you what you didn't want to hear?"

"I didn't *sic* anyone on you," I hiss. Slowly I rise to my feet. "I am grateful that you didn't act like an asshole when Dave tried to use you as a weapon against me. I'm grateful that you called Mr. Dade. None of that gives you the right to treat me the way that you did on Friday. But despite all that, I did not get you fired."

"You expect me—"

"I don't care what you believe!" I snap, not allowing him to finish his thought. "I told my lover about my day at work. That's it. Period. I have the right to do that! Everything I've done since I've last seen you I've had the right to do!"

"And can the same be said for him? Do you honestly believe he had the right to do this?" Tom blurts out the question with vehemence, but after it's spoken it hangs in the air like a sword above my head.

Tom seems to see the sword, too, and it calms him. He's apparently satisfied that he's shaken me. But with the calm comes a new melancholy. I watch as his shoulders drop, the red color drains away, and suddenly Tom just looks old. At least ten years older than how he looked on Friday when he laughingly and unknowingly sealed his fate.

He exhales loudly. It's a despairing and mournful sound.

When he turns from me he seems empty. After so many unexpected theatrics he leaves my office with the silence and weight of a ghost.

Tom has always been more of a troublesome ally than an enemy.

Like China or Saudi Arabia. Not governments I love, but countries whose value I recognize. As Tom would say, I recognize the symbiotic relationship.

And if this is a war . . . if it ever was, then Robert's a mercenary. He fights by his own rules, not those of a more honorable soldier, but he fights for me. I've paid him in . . . in what? Sex? Affection? Have I paid by giving him control of my own life?

I stand up again; my legs are wobbly but I manage to gather my purse and leave the office. "I'm taking the rest of the day off," I say to Barbara.

"Oh I know," Barbara says, smiling up at me. "Mr. Dade already called to say that you would be. He said he'd meet you at his place. I would have rung him through but you seemed . . . busy."

I stare at her, sure I've misheard. She takes a moment to lean forward, whispers conspiratorially, "I had no idea! He's so hot, Kasie!"

I stiffen; my throat constricts, so I answer only with a stiff nod before turning and walking away.

On my way to the elevator I run into Asha. She stops, offers me a thin smile that hangs in that no-man's-land between admiration and resentment. "I heard you're getting promoted to Tom's position," she says.

I freeze. Everything takes on a surreal quality. The shadows cast by the light take on the shape of specters and shadow-people.

"I'm impressed," she continues. "You did it. You won." She gives me a reluctant nod of deference. "To the victor go the spoils."

*To the victor go the rules.*

"I have to go." I push past her before she can say more. The elevator ride makes me nauseous. I know I'm not fit to drive but I get in my car anyway. I stay below the speed limit, hoping to give myself time to think. But it doesn't help. The only things in my head are anger, confusion, fear . . . fear of what?

But the answer to that is easy. I fear my protector.

When I get to Robert's the gate is open. I move into the driveway, pull my keys from the ignition, and carefully make my way through the gated front yard and into the house. Nothing is locked against me. Everything opens with a touch.

I find him sitting in the living room, reading some report. He looks up at me and smiles. "You're welcome," he says before turning his attention back to the papers in his hand.

I shake my head. "You think I'm here to thank you?"

"Why not? I've taken care of Tom for you. If Dave's a problem—"

"He won't be."

"But if he is," Robert continues, "I'll take care of him, too."

Behind him is a painting. I've admired it before. A picture of abstract lovers surrounded by a chaotic swirl of nonfigurative and colorful shapes that seem impotent in their efforts to pull them apart. When I had first seen it I had thought the painting was a testament to the power of love.

Now I wonder if it's just a testament to power.

"This is not how I do things," I say. "I don't live in a world where it's okay to destroy those who cross me."

"Trust me, you'll get used to it."

"I'm leaving you."

He finally puts down the papers, gets to his feet, moves to me. We're a foot apart now. I don't want to respond to him but my body won't cooperate. It's almost Pavlovian. He comes near me and my heart speeds up, my breathing becomes more shallow, and then there's the gentle throbbing between my legs.

I turn my head away, shamed by my body's betrayal, knowing that he can see it.

"You have told me it's over a thousand times," he says quietly. "It never is, Kasie. You've tried, but you can't walk away. At times you think you should but you don't. I told you I wanted to be with you when you were truly mine. Now you are."

"No," I say feebly, trying to find strength in repetition, "it's not how I do things."

With his hand he guides my chin back to him, just like this morning. He stares down into my eyes. "It's okay," he says. "I've re-shaped our world."

A small cry escapes my lips. I turn around and run to the door.

But even as I get outside, even as I climb back into my car and peel out of the driveway, I know I can't get away from him.

*Even when I'm nowhere near you I'm inside of you. I can touch you with a thought.*

I'm in trouble.

# PART 3

---

*Binding Agreement*

---

# CHAPTER 32

❦

SOMETIMES THE MOON looks angry as it rises above this
City of Angels. We are, after all, angels with guns, angels who
carefully recycle our Coke cans while dumping chemicals into our
heated swimming pools that we've built only a few blocks away
from the sea. So sometimes when the moon rises from the polluted
horizon it's an angry shade of red, a glaring reminder that we are
angels intent on creating an earthbound hell.

This is one of those nights. I'm up on the roof of the Griffith
Observatory watching the moon rise and I can feel its rage as my
own. Where is the slice of heaven I was promised? A life of peace
and honorably earned success? Where is the man I can rely on to be
ethical in his pursuit of greatness? What happened to the simplicity
of knowing with complete certainty what's right and what's wrong?

*You threw it away,* my inner angel says. *You listened to your devil
and chose a different path.*

It's true but I don't feel like claiming responsibility. The wind
picks up, raises my hair, and blows it back as I keep my eyes on the
red moon. I want the wind to cleanse me, to simply blow away the
mistakes and immorality.

But there are other things I want more. Like Robert Dade. When
he comes near me, I feel an overwhelming impulse to yield to him.
I thought that when I broke up with my controlling fiancé, Dave, I
would become the master of my own life.

But now it's just another version of the same thing. Dave controlled
me with guilt and shame, even fear. Robert controls me with a kiss.

One kiss on the nape of my neck, a hand on the small of my back, one caress up the inside of my thigh, that's all it takes. My body overrules the messages of my mind. I used to think that being with Robert was empowering but he directs that power.

I shiver as the moon rises higher, losing some of its crimson glare. I think of Tom, the man I reported to only yesterday. Is he looking at this moon, too? Tom was forced out of a job for no reason other than that he insulted me, and Robert found out. It's not what I wanted, and even if I had, revenge reaped by a surrogate is no revenge at all.

But when Robert touches me in just the right way, I forget. I forget what it is I want, or rather I forget that I want anything other than him.

If he were here right now, on this roof deck, with tourists and stargazers milling around the antiquated telescopes, would I let him touch me? If he stood behind me and slipped his hand up, cupping my breast, would I protest?

I swear, just thinking about him makes me throb. Perhaps he's the moon and I'm the ocean, my tides being pulled to new heights by the force of his presence.

The thought thrills and disturbs me. After all, the ocean is its own force, isn't it? It moves with the wind; it gives and destroys in equal measure. People love and fear the ocean. They respect it.

But without the moon, the ocean is nothing but a lake.

I need the moon.

I turn around and take the curving steps down to the base of the building. *Get a grip, Kasie.* But I don't know if I can. I can't control my tides.

# CHAPTER 33

I DRIVE FOR A WHILE before going home. When I do get there, I immediately spot his Alfa Romeo Spider parked in front of my house. It's impossible to miss. He blends in a little better, leaning against the outside of my door. His arms are crossed and his salt-and-pepper hair gleams with the slight dew of the night. I park my car but keep the engine running at a resting purr. Part of me knew he would come. That doesn't mean I'm ready for it.

But it's not my choice. So I switch off the ignition and carefully approach.

"You didn't let yourself in this time," I say.

He smiles ruefully. "I'm trying to find a happy medium between being protective and being intrusive. I thought not breaking into your home would be a good start."

I can't help but smile. "You're learning." I put my key in the lock, open the door, allow him to follow me into the living room. "Still," I say once we're inside and he's lowered himself onto my sofa, "you could have called."

"I could have," he agrees. "I didn't."

I turn to him. I don't understand this man. There are times when I'm not entirely sure if I like him. But, my God, do I want him. "What are you here for?"

"You're not leaving me," he says simply.

"You think you get to make that call?"

"I do." He cocks his head, smiles. "I would have to do something specific to give you the will to walk away. I haven't and so now you can't will yourself to do anything but stay."

"You haven't done anything specific?" I don't say the name Tom. I don't need to.

"Kasie." Robert sighs as if mildly disappointed by my lack of vision. "The way Tom spoke to you . . . the things he said . . . if one of his superiors had overheard him, would he have lost his job?"

"But they didn't overhear," I point out. "You're speaking in hypotheticals, choosing your truth. Tom helped me when Dave was trying to humiliate me. That's part of the story, too."

"And if Tom had thought taking Dave's side would have advanced his own interests, do you still think he would have helped you?"

"I don't know, Robert." I throw up my hands in exasperation. "Do you think Stalin would have helped defeat Hitler if he hadn't invaded Russia? Sometimes we don't need to analyze motivations. Sometimes we can just put our hands together and be grateful that the Nazis lost."

Robert leans back into the couch, his eyes brightened by my challenges. "I'm grateful that the Nazis lost, too, but I don't think that gives Stalin a pass."

"Tom isn't Stalin."

"No, Stalin deserved to die. Tom just deserves to lose his job." He glances toward the street as a truck rumbles by. "This is business, Kasie. Tom sexually harassed an employee and he angered a very important client. People get fired for these things all the time."

"But he wasn't fired for harassing *me*."

Robert waves away the point. "It would have been . . . *awkward* if the charges had come from you, and you didn't want to take that on. So I simply made sure the allegations came from other people."

We're going in circles and now I'm too dizzy to continue.

I stare up at the off-white ceiling above me. I have worked to keep the interior of my home simple, sophisticated, comfortable, but now this room feels complicated, untamed, and I am not comfortable at all. Everything about Robert agitates me. His voice vibrates inside of me like the beat of a rock song, bringing me alive, amplifying emotions that I might otherwise suppress. "I'm just out of a relationship," I remind him. "I spent years being controlled by someone else's vision of me and now you want to control me, too."

"No." He stands, moves to my side. "I don't want to control you." He lets his fingers slide under my chin, guides my face in his direction. "I *would* like to corrupt you . . . if only a little."

"Corrupt me?"

"Kasie, if you let me help you, we could have everything. The people who would mock you or try to make your life harder? They'll bow before us. Tom was a cautionary tale. We need those. People should know what happens to those who try to bring us down . . . to those who try to *demean* us."

"You're talking about a man's life."

"I'm talking about winning."

His hand slips to the small of my back and I instinctively lean into him, pressing my breasts into his chest. "I want you to stop interfering with the careers of my coworkers."

"Ah, but you want so many things," he whispers, grazing his teeth on my earlobe. "What is it you want more, Kasie? Fairness? Power?" He gently pushes me back against a wall; his tongue flicks against the base of my throat. "Me?"

I try to answer but his hands are on my shirt, pulling it from me, unbuttoning my pants, letting them fall.

He takes a step back, pulls his phone from his pocket, and points it in my direction. "I want this image. I want to be able to look at you when you're not with me."

I immediately feel my face warm and try to cover myself with my hands but he shakes his head. "No, leave your arms by your sides. You should never be ashamed to show yourself. By the time we're done no one will ever have the courage to question your audacity. They'll admire it."

My arms are at my sides but it's hard. This isn't right; I don't know why I'm allowing it . . . except that I want to allow it. "You're

not going to show this to anyone," I say. Is it a question? A statement? A request? I just don't know anymore.

I should be horrified . . . but the idea of being seen . . . audacity
without consequences . . .

I pull my hair back off my shoulders, lower my head to a co-
quettish angle . . . and invite the attention of the camera.

He smiles his approval and takes another picture before putting
the phone on the side table. He removes his jacket slowly, drapes it
over a chair as I stay pressed against the wall, held by an invisible
force.

Sitting down on the sofa, he motions for me to come to him.

I walk to him like a woman under hypnosis . . . maybe that's what
I am. Perhaps he's cast a spell.

I straddle him, wearing nothing but my bra and panties. His
hands cup my breasts. "Take this off," he says softly but with a note
of authority that's impossible to miss.

I remove the bra, let my breasts spill out. With languid, almost
casual movements he feels them, squeezing them slightly, toying
with my nipples until they become long and hard and needing.

"You're beautiful this way," he says. "We should designate a day
when this is all you wear, just these panties"—he puts his finger
inside the waistband, pulls the elastic. "We could have dinner like
this, watch television, chat over coffee with you wearing virtually
nothing, completely available for me to touch and taste."

And with that he leans forward, kisses my breasts while his
hand slips inside my panties, finding my clit and making me gasp.
"Would you do that for me, Kasie?"

I flush, knowing the answer should be no even as I nod.

"And what would you do for yourself?" he asks, slipping a finger
inside of me. "If I give you the world on a platter, will you take it?"

"Robert," I say. I want to explain, to tell him where he's wrong
but his finger begins to move. He covers my neck and shoulders
with kisses designed to provoke yearning rather than satisfaction. I
groan and instinctively buck my hips against him.

"Just wait, Kasie." His caresses become more demanding, I feel the orgasm coming. "They'll play by our rules and we'll change the rules as we please. All these worries you have about the opinions of others will have no foundation. No one will judge you, no one will dare."

With that another finger pushes inside of me and I come, right there straddling his lap. I shiver, grasping his shoulders, my fingers digging into the fabric of his shirt, pressing into his skin. I think I say his name but I'm so overcome that it's hard for me to know what I'm doing, what I'm saying . . . it's chaos.

It's spectacular.

He pushes me onto my back; the panties come off. He stands above me as he removes his clothes, watching as I struggle to catch my breath. He's naked now, his erection reaching for me, his hard, sculpted muscles only hinting at the real power that exists within. He reaches down and strokes my cheek. It's a gentle touch, as tender as it is sensual. "You are so beautiful," he says quietly. "Tell me you know that."

I don't know how to respond. I shake with anticipation as I reach for him but he takes me by the wrist, holds me off even as he steps closer. "Say it, Kasie. Tell me you're beautiful."

I squirm slightly and I try to turn away but he guides my face back to him. "Say it."

I press my lips into a thin line, look up at him through lowered lids.

And then something happens to me. I forcefully pull my arm away. As he observes me, his expression now questioning, I slowly raise myself up until I'm standing on my knees, my legs tucked back, my posture straight as I brazenly meet his gaze. "I'm beautiful," I say; my voice is assured, strong . . . and even to my own ears, seductive.

He smiles, kneels before me on the couch. He watches as in languid, luxurious movements I lie back, my knees still bent, my back arched. I reach my arms above my head as if posing for a poster. "I'm beautiful," I say again.

And he's above me now, his hands gripping my shoulders. I feel him hard, against the inside of my thigh.

"Now, Robert. Enter me now."

And with a moan he does, penetrating me in wide, circular motions. His hips grinding against mine as I hold my pose like a ballerina being lifted to the heavens by her partner. He's so deep now, thrusting with a straightforward force; he's hit every nerve, and like a quiet applause that builds to a roar I feel the orgasm taking over. I feel my walls contracting around him, holding him as my body trembles and a cry escapes my lips.

In that moment I believe all of it. I am beautiful and powerful.

And I will rule. If not the world then certainly this man.

With care I unfold my legs, so they stretch to either side of him. He lifts up, shifting his weight onto his knees to give me room but I don't wait for him to lower himself again. Instead I plant my feet and raise my hips, pressing my pelvis into his, forcing him inside once again. This time it's me who sets the rhythm, savoring the friction as I move my hips up and down in the air. I can see what I'm doing to him; his breath is shallow; his arms shake although I know it's not from strain. It's exhilarating.

And when he can't stay still anymore, he grasps my legs and while he's still on his knees, raises my legs to his shoulders. With one arm on either side of me he takes the lead once again. And again he is deep into my world, vulnerable and strong and awash in perfect ecstasy.

"I will give you everything," he breathes, "everything. And you will take it."

Outside the strengthening wind beats against the windows as I cry out; it's animalistic and almost frightening, completely delicious. I grab his arms, overcome with yet another orgasm, even stronger this time. And as the sensation rolls through me I feel him exploding inside of me, letting me absorb his power.

Power enough to conquer the world

Maybe even enough power to conquer him.

❀

# CHAPTER 34

I COULD HAVE ASKED him to stay the night. He could have requested it. But we both sensed that space was called for. I need to
let the high tides recede to something more manageable, less intense.

Otherwise I'm afraid I'll drown out the world.

We talked a little. I again argued that Tom shouldn't be rail-
roaded for a moderate infraction. But Robert cuts through challenges and concerns like they're paper and he's scissors.

My sister treated such things with similar disregard. Except she
did it with manic adrenaline and chemical vices while Robert does
it with confidence, disdain, and sheer strength of will.

But in the end won't the results be the same? Destruction, loss,
broken hearts? Isn't it possible that worries are like scabs? Ugly but
part of healing?

But then, what would I know about healing? I don't believe I
have any scars, just open wounds that I've learned to cover loosely
with Band-Aids.

Working through the pain and healing are completely different
things.

And here it is, morning, and I'm in my bed alone. I had tried to
sleep in my French terry gown but the tags and seams that never
bothered me before irritated my skin. My entire body is more sensitive now, after his touch. So I took it off, let the softness of my sheets
lull me to sleep.

As I stand, naked in front of the mirror, I realize that this is how
I'm going to feel all day. Naked, vulnerable, embarrassed. I can think

of no reason why Tom would have left quietly. By now what happened between me and Dave will be all over the office. And the focus will undoubtedly be on Mr. Dade's role in the breakup. Both Robert and my coworker Asha have assured me in their different ways that I will be moved into Tom's job. My professional achievements have been impressive but not enough to have earned that honor, so it'll be rightfully assumed that I earned it on my back. Those who are my equals today will report to me tomorrow but they will still see me as a slut who will make herself sexually available to any man who might advance her.

And how many men will test that theory? As long as I'm with Robert, perhaps no one. But without him every executive will feel that he has the right to take his place. They'll expect me to spread my legs for my career.

And of course there's Mr. Freeland, the cofounder of the company and Dave's godfather. Surely I've made an enemy of him. He has to tolerate me due to Robert's influence but for how long? On how many fronts will the attacks be coming from?

I should hate Robert for putting me in this position. But as I roll through the memories of last night, being underneath him, feeling him pulsing inside of me, remembering how he looked afterward, by my side, naked and perfect . . . well, I don't hate him.

So with shaky hands I pull on a conservative light wool suit in black paired with a white chiffon blouse that ties in a prim bow at the neck. Thin armor for such a battle but it'll have to do.

When I get to my office, Barbara is ready for me. Reports have been printed onto glossy stationery and held together in deep blue folders. I have a meeting in less than a half hour.

I go through my inbox. There's a memo announcing Tom Love's departure. Odd to think that was only yesterday.

The message explains that until Love's replacement is named (which will be within days) we are all basically being left to our own devices. If any of us have a question that needs an immediate answer or a project that needs the input of management, we are to e-mail Love's superior, Mr. Costin.

Love's superior. I can't help but smile at that. Those words could mean so many things. But my amusement quickly wanes as more pressing issues consume me. So they'll be naming Tom's replacement in days. And yet no one has even called me. Maybe Robert, Asha . . . maybe they're wrong. Maybe Tom's job will be offered to somebody else.

And if that's the case . . . I can't decide if I'd be relieved or profoundly disappointed. I should probably be the former, and if that's how it goes down, that's the emotion I'll show the world.

But deep in my gut? There will be a rage of disappointment. It shouldn't be that way but I don't think I'll be able to help it.

At nine thirty sharp my team files in to review and prepare for the Maned Wolf presentation. Taci, Dameon, Nina, and Asha all have their roles to play, details they will explain, questions they'll be prepared to field. But in the end they're just backup singers. Tomorrow is my day. I will be the one to rise or fall.

They're looking at me differently . . . but not with judgment exactly. All of them, with the exception of Asha, seem nervous. When I ask a question, they jump to respond, their eyes anxious; then they sigh quietly in relief when I toss out words of approval. There are nuances, of course. Taci appears a bit curious, Nina's apprehension seems tinged with disapproval. When I stand, Dameon's eyes seem to linger on where my skirt hugs my hips. When I send him a questioning glance, he immediately looks down at the floor, bending his head as if in prayer . . . or in shame.

They all know. But they're not testing me and they're certainly not mocking me.

They're afraid of me. And that fear seems to simultaneously repel and attract them. That should probably upset me. But there's really only one takeaway that I keep coming back to.

I'm getting Tom's job.

Dameon glances up again as I pace the room, going over the numbers. His gaze rises above my hips this time, to my breasts. He doesn't think I notice; he doesn't think I know what he wants me to do to him.

And that's the key, isn't it? It's about what he wants *me* to do to *him*. I can see he would never dare try to be the aggressor. His deference is tangible.

*The people who would mock you or try to make your life harder? They'll bow before us.*

The thought is unsettling. . . .

. . . And a little thrilling.

I know it shouldn't be but . . . well, I've never tasted this kind of power before. And oh, how many years have I hunted, fought, and cultivated control. And here, in a single act, Robert has given it to me.

I swallow hard, switch my focus to Asha. She's the only one whose attitude remains the same. Her dark eyes are attentive but give away nothing. She is the picture of calm and composure. Ironic since she's the only one here who deserves to be cowed.

A little of my confidence fades away. Not much, not enough to make me humble, but still. I roll my shoulders back, finish up the meeting. We have all the information we need for tomorrow's presentation. All that's left to do is to go back to our individual corners and practice our lines.

In the end I gesture with a silent hand that it's time for them to leave my office. And just like that, they file out. Taci, Nina, Dameon with a lingering smile. All obedient, all ready to please.

Again that little thrill . . .

. . . which is quickly squashed when it becomes clear that Asha is hanging back, waiting until it's just the two of us.

"Did you want something, Asha?" I ask when the others are gone.

"Is today my last day?"

The question hits me like an electric current, rendering me temporarily unable to speak.

We stand opposite each other, taking in each other's details. She, too, is wearing a black suit, but unlike me she's wearing pants and a stark white button-down shirt under the neat blazer. Her hair hangs down her back, the same midnight shade as her clothes.

"Why would you ask me that?" I finally sputter.

She meets my eyes but doesn't answer.

"Did you tell them I slept with Robert?"

Her mouth curves down into a grimace. "No," she says shortly. "I had hoped to hold that information over your head but it's obvious they already know. Perhaps Tom thought telling them would be his drop of revenge. Clearly it's backfired."

The idea of Tom retaliating makes me shiver. I cross my arms over my chest protectively.

"Is today my last day?" she asks again.

"Not that I'm aware of," I say. "But again, why do you ask?"

Asha studies my face before responding. "Your lover is setting the stage." Her voice is steady, emotionless. "He's picking the players, dismissing the actors who don't please him. It's what needs to be done before the curtains rise."

"And then what?"

Her lips curve into a Mona Lisa smile. "And then he can make his pretty little marionette dance."

A flash of anger but the cutting retort jumps to mind too late. She's already walked out.

I turn and look out the window. The sky is a dark gray; perhaps a storm is brewing. When I was a little girl, I was afraid of storms. But now when I think of a storm, my mind wanders to the ocean. Those choppy, white-capped waves creating a sense of excitement, danger, and most of all, beauty.

"I am beautiful," I say quietly to myself. It's funny because in the past I've always thought of beauty as a thing for princesses. But when I say the word these days, it feels different. It's like I've changed the meaning to something richer, darker, and considerably more sensuous.

"I am beautiful."

It's a mantra, a chant, an aspiration. I sit down at my desk. There's calm in the isolation of work.

I didn't know I wanted to be a business consultant when I was growing up but I knew I wanted to do something that involved numbers and strategy. In high school I fell in love with Einstein's beautiful equation, and as a child I used to love playing chess with my father . . . although he began to lose interest in the game when I was about thirteen . . . right around the time I started regularly beating him.

What would Melody have done with her life had she lived? Her dreams for the future were always a bit mercurial. One day she would want to be a dancer, the next an actress; once she pulled me aside and whispered that she wanted to be a jewel thief. She said she wouldn't even sell all the jewels she stole but just hide them in her attic until she had so many that when you climbed up in there the darkness would sparkle like a night sky filled with earthbound stars.

I was about seven when she told me that, and I remember the mental image made me giggle with delight. Melody was always making me smile back in those days. She was so fun and vivacious. I loved her. I think my parents loved her, too . . . just not unconditionally.

In the end, she took it all too far and like a supernova she ended up shining so bright that she burned herself up. And my parents just turned away from the spectacle, pretended it wasn't there, and focused on me. My light was never as impressive as Melody's, but it was steady, and that's what was needed for me to keep the love Melody had lost. My father told me not to shed tears for her. He said she simply didn't exist anymore, not to us. And so it was. At night I would bury my face in my pillow and fill it with tears. Still, I was cared for and she was just . . . erased.

Their rejection of her was even more terrifying than her death. After all, by then I already knew all about death. But it wasn't *until* then that I realized people could become completely invisible to those they love.

My parents don't even know that I've broken up with Dave. Obviously I have to tell them eventually but part of me is so afraid that if they see that my light is no longer steady, they'll erase me, too. And yet here at work I'm still the star everyone turns to, despite my mistakes . . . maybe even because of them. Like an alchemist Robert turns mistakes into rewards. He makes sure people see me and they don't get to turn away if I shine a bit too brightly. That's the reality of Robert that both attracts and scares me.

*They'll play by our rules and we'll change the rules as we please.*

That's a very different game than the chess I was raised on.

I try to push those thoughts out of my mind as I work, memorizing statistics, double-checking figures and percentages. At six, Barbara sticks her head into my office to see if there's anything else I need before she leaves, but I simply shake my head and wish her good night. Everything I need is in the folders on my desk. The tangibility of the numbers soothes me. They're something I can hold on to when everything else is upside down and backward. By the time I lock up my office well into the night, the building is dark and virtually empty.

Except.

The light in Asha's office is on. It's not entirely uncommon for her to stay late, but not this late. Not after the sky is completely black and the only other people in the building are janitors and security personnel. I should pass her door without a glance. How many times has she sought to undermine me, humiliate me, even dominate me? A thousand times. If you count today, a thousand and one. I should ignore her.

But her light is on and for some reason I find myself reaching for her door.

I don't knock. Instead I just turn the knob. I expect to see her poring over copies of the same files I've been studying or perhaps researching other companies, trying to find new ones to bring to the firm to enhance her status, but instead she's staring at the wall with such intensity, I wonder if she sees something I don't. An apparition maybe, or the hazy outline of a lost dream. Something other than white paint.

"I graduated in the top ten percent of my class at Stanford," she says. She hasn't even looked up at me. I shouldn't be here at this time in this place. I should have knocked. But none of that fazes her. She just glares at the wall and continues.

"I was recruited. This firm *wanted* me. They knew what I could do for them. I didn't need to sleep with anyone to get here."

"I never slept with anyone out of ambition," I say, acknowledging and correcting the insult, but this time without offense. I'm a bit too tired for a brawling fight. "Tell me something," I ask, "if I had, would you really have a moral problem with it? Is your bitterness coming out of disapproval or disappointment?"

She remains silent, waiting for me to clarify.

"If there was a man who could help you with your career," I continue, "someone you were attracted to, would you have made yourself available to him in exchange for his assistance?"

She shakes her head. "Not my thing. When I use sex as a tool, it's as a knife not a stepladder." She finally looks at me with a thin smile. "You use sex as a skeleton key. It opens doors for you. Your way appears to be amazingly effective."

Asha's taken her blazer off. Her white shirt is sheer against her light brown skin. She's of East Indian heritage but something about her transcends nationality. She's almost more of a concept than a person. She embodies cool, aggressive ambition, fierce sensuality, malicious honesty. . . . She adds femininity to sadism.

"I didn't want to get Tom fired," I say quietly.

"Why not?" Asha asks. "You're going to get his job. I heard it from a reliable source. The higher-ups probably thought it would look better if they gave it to you after you have your predictably successful meeting with Maned Wolf." She pauses, cocks her head slightly to the side. "Tell me, where did you run off to after you found out Tom had been let go? You left in such a hurry."

"I had to confront him."

It takes a moment for Asha to contextualize the words but once she does, a light, gentle laugh escapes her glossy pink lips. "Mr. Dade? You think what he did was unscrupulous?" She stands, crosses to me, her lips by my ear. "You have never been a beacon of morality," she points out. "You get no points for being conflicted if you constantly choose the path of wickedness."

"I haven't—" I begin but Asha cuts me off.

"You are wicked, Kasie." She reaches for me, tucks my hair behind my ear, runs her fingers up and down my back as I grow rigid. "You fucked a stranger," she says, her voice as gentle as a caress. "You betrayed your fiancé by taking Mr. Dade's cock in your mouth. You lied to Tom about it, to everyone really."

"You do remember that I can get you fired," I say tersely.

"Oh I know that's around the corner. Maybe not tomorrow, maybe not even next week, but soon. First Tom, then me, it makes sense. I might as well have my fun while I have the chance." Her hand slips down to my ass but then she steps away before I have a chance to protest.

"I will say that if I had been given the opportunity, I would have slept with your Mr. Dade." She walks to the window, puts her fingers against the glass. "When he walks into a room, he dominates it; it's almost impossible not to look at him. His form, the broad shoulders, the muscular build . . . and yet all that is nothing compared to his presence. He has a . . . a savage sophistication. He's Daniel Craig's James Bond; a young, sexy Gordon Gekko."

"He's Robert Dade," I say with a smile because while the analogies work I can't compare this man to another. His effect on my life is so unique and unexpected; he stands apart from the giant cinematic images of men wreaking havoc on fictional adversaries.

"Yes," Asha agrees. "He's Robert Dade and I'd be a willing and eager player in his bedroom games. Not because I want his assistance but because I'd like to see if I could break him."

I laugh, almost charmed by her arrogance.

"You don't think I could?" she asks . . . although maybe it's not a question. Her voice has no inflection. She turns back to me and shakes her head. "Your problem is that you have never fully understood the power of being a desired woman."

My mind flashes back to a night in Robert's bed. I had climbed on top of him, refused him until he said, "Please."

Asha smiles, reading my mind. "Power between the sheets

means nothing if you don't learn to extend its reach outside of the bedroom."

I look away. The room seems to be getting colder. I rub the back of my arms for warmth.

"You don't have to believe me," Asha continues. "It's in the stories of your religion. Adam and Eve, Samson and Delilah, Salome and her dance of the Seven Veils: they all speak to the same undeniable truth. If a woman truly wants something, whether it's having her man bite into an apple, bringing a divinely appointed superhero to his knees, or a Baptist's head on a silver platter, she can have it. A woman can have anything if she knows how to use what God gave her."

I start to laugh, but then . . .

*If I give you the world on a platter, will you take it?*

A Baptist's head on a platter. Is that really so different from what Robert is offering?

*Yes*, I tell myself, *because Tom is no John the Baptist and Asha is a far cry from a saint.*

Asha's fallen silent, giving me time to try to see the stories of the gospel through this new lens.

"If you knew how much power you have, you'd have courage," she finally adds.

Sometimes, when people name the thing you want, that thing gains texture. You can see it and therefore you're sure you can have it if you just do or say exactly the right thing.

That's sort of how I feel when I hear Asha suggest I can be courageous. It's what I want.

But in a moment the image fades away. Melody and her love affair with destruction and divorce from sanity, my parents and their complete abandonment of her . . . I have nursed cowardice all my life, hoping it would protect me from all of that when nothing else would. It's part of me now. I don't know how to expel the beast.

"I don't have any interest in helping you keep your job," I say, shifting my weight onto my heels, suddenly tired and resigned. "But I promise to do what I can to keep you from being fired over false pretenses. If you get thrown out of here, it'll be your fault, not mine, and not Mr. Dade's."

"You say that now—"

"—and I'll say it tomorrow." I turn and pull open the door. "Good night, Asha. Go home and get some sleep."

"I'm not tired."

"Then go to the park and pull the wings off butterflies," I say with a sardonic smile. "That seems like the kind of thing you would enjoy."

She smiles back, shakes her head. "Butterflies are too weak."

"Then shoot a coyote, whatever," I suggest. "But your workday's over. We all need our rest and if I'm going to be a dictator, I'm going to try to be a benevolent one."

As I walk out of her office I hear her gentle and appreciative laughter. For a split second I feel a jolt of camaraderie and forget that she's the personification of evil.

But no doubt she'll remind me of that in the morning.

As I step into the elevator I mull over her words. *Your problem is that you have never fully understood the power of being a desired woman.*

That's where she's wrong. Robert made me feel that power. When we make love, I always feel protected, frequently overwhelmed, but I also feel the power I have over him. It's an aphrodisiac that has become rather addictive.

*Power between the sheets means nothing if you don't learn to extend its reach outside of the bedroom.*

As the elevator makes its descent to the parking lot I realize that she might have a point. But I'm learning . . .

. . . and rather quickly.

# CHAPTER 35

❦

I T'S AFTER ELEVEN. I'm about to go to bed when I get the text.

`Video conference?`

The last time I had a video conference with Robert, whom at the time I only really knew as Mr. Dade, I had ended up naked, touching myself . . . it became a habit with us, not the video chatting but the rest of it.

But tomorrow I have to prove my worthiness in this meeting. I can't allow him to shake me tonight.

I text back.

`I can't.`

I don't say more than that. I shouldn't have to. He knows what tomorrow is, what it means.

He sends his reply.

`You can. Tonight will be innocent.`

I hesitate. *Say no?* I tell myself. *How can you have any power at all if you can't say no?*

But of course I can say no. Just not to him.

I turn on the computer; in a moment I see him, on my screen, in the chair in his bedroom. So far and yet so very, very close.

"Robert, I can't—"

"Tomorrow you and your team will be in my boardroom," he says. His voice is kind, almost paternal.

I smile. "It's not something I'm bound to forget." But then the weight of it hits me and I lower my head. "I have to remind them all of my capabilities," I whisper, pulling at the ends of my fingers like a nervous child. "They need to remember how qualified I am. Otherwise—"

"You will stand in front of me," he interrupts gently. "In front of my executives and your team and you will deliver your recommendations on how to strategically place my company up for public option. You will impress us. You'll show that entire room the aggression and fervor that you've shown me every time I've held you."

"It's hardly the same."

"It doesn't need to be that different. Every time you've been in my arms, in my bed, you have risen to meet my challenge and my passion. You can do that in different ways, in a different setting. You *will* show everyone why you're deserving."

That makes me giggle. "How exactly shall I do that?" I gently put my fingers against the computer screen, touching the image of his arms where, even from here, I can see the small scratches I left there during our last time together. "By making them bleed?"

His smile widens as he leans back in his antique chair. "I'd like to think you'll save your violence for me."

"Ah," I say, almost reluctantly pulling my hand away. My smile wavers. "You're assuming too much. You haven't seen the presentation. You . . . you may not like my proposals."

He cocks his head to the side, raising his eyebrows in a way that is both seductive and impish. "Take a chance."

I burst out in full laughter because it seems that lately I've done nothing but take chances.

"I promise you this," he says softly. "I won't pressure my executives to accept your proposals. Whatever reaction you get from them will be honest and I won't overrule them."

Ah, so there is no guarantee here. The realization actually relaxes me. This is the kind of challenge I've trained for. I get it and it's familiar. Right now, when everything in my life feels new and scary, *anything* that feels familiar is a blessing.

I roll back my shoulders, raise my chin just a little. "Sleep well, Mr. Dade," I say softly. "We both have a big day tomorrow."

"Good night, Miss Fitzgerald," he says, and with a small smile he disappears. My screen goes black.

But I still feel him.

Like the ocean feels the moon.

AND THE NEXT DAY I'm ready. I have to be, right?

"I'm ready, I'm ready, I'm ready," I repeat to myself as I pull the comb through my hair, ripping through the tangles, barely flinching at the pain.

I choose a black fitted skirt that hits a few inches above the knee and match it with a tight-fitting blazer with a peplum flare. Under that I'll wear my silk sleeveless top in a green that reminds me of the Everglades. It's so light you almost expect it to be sheer. It's an illusion, a hint of mysticism encased in the harsh realism of a business suit. I'm making a statement.

"Today's my day," I say again to the mirror.

My reflection looks back at me, doubtful.

I grab my briefcase, my grip a little tighter than usual, and walk out. No need to go to my office. My team will meet me at Maned Wolf.

As I drive there I think about the name, Maned Wolf Security Systems. A little research has taught me that the maned wolf is the largest canid of South America and, thanks to its long legs, it stands taller than any wild canid in the world. It bites the neck of its prey, shakes it violently until it's limp. But unlike other wolves, this one doesn't form a pack. It claims a large territory that it roams and defends with only the help of its mate. Together they work to keep all threats and challenges to their authority at bay. The maned wolf mates for life.

But for all its height and aggression, the maned wolf is considered a vulnerable species. It's hunted.

Driving now through Beverly Hills I decrease my speed and wonder if Robert sees how much he resembles this animal. I think Robert's a vulnerable predator. And I could be his mate, helping him rule and expanding his territory.

But we'll still be vulnerable.

Eventually I reach his Santa Monica building. Tinted glass walls stretch up to the sky as if appeasing this city's need to see its own reflection. I park on the street, straighten my posture, and breathe. My team knows that I've slept with the man we'll be presenting for. They're judging me. If I mess this up and still get a promotion, I'll invite nothing but disrespect and derision. I'll have to turn down the promotion, maybe even leave the company.

That simply can't happen. I swallow hard and walk through the doors of the massive building. I stride past the security desk and on up to the conference room. I'm ten minutes early but people are already in their places. My team sits with the Maned Wolf executives all ready for my performance. Only Robert is missing. I walk to the front of the room. Taci has everything set up for the PowerPoint presentation.

I stand in front of them all and idly reach for the laptop that stores the visuals I'll be using. I wonder if anyone else notices the slight tremble of my fingers. The executives flip through their iPhone apps, read e-mails; a few grace me with quiet smiles. If their thoughts are lewd, they hide them well under their bland, almost disinterested expressions. I've spoken to every one of them over the last few weeks but none of them address me now. They all just wait.

And then he enters the room. The energy immediately shifts. Everyone lifts their faces to Mr. Dade but as his eyes stay trained on me, the others follow suit. The intensity of the attention hits me like a wave of heat from a controlled explosion. I click on to PowerPoint and begin.

I start with market trends, boring stuff to most but not to me. The trend of the market is a mathematical manifestation of the expectations and values of an entire class of people. The ticking numbers of the Dow can tell you if thousands of people are feeling hopeful or scared. Are they pulling their money out, hoarding it like one would hoard water before an impending disaster? Are they investing in pharmaceuticals, predicting that more of us will find solace in a pill? But the trends that are relevant to Maned Wolf are even more interesting. Their alarms and safeguards can give the insecure a sense of safety. So the question here is, will investors be attracted to the market value of fear?

And the answer is, *always*.

I walk them through the different aspects of their business that will appeal to investors and find the areas that will mean little to them. Protection details for foreign nationals in dangerous countries is a division that should be downsized. Too much risk. The profitability of fear is continuous, the profitability of death is finite.

Everything can be reduced to a number.

The executives are more alert now. They watch as I point to different areas of the graph. My fingers no longer tremble. I can feel their eyes, but Robert's gaze has a distinct texture. It's velvet against my skin.

I go over the numbers of their R&D department. This is an area that needs to grow, but their marketing department needs a makeover. New hires will be needed here; layoffs will be needed there.

When it's reduced to numbers, I can be ruthless.

Dameon has forgotten that he needs to keep his eyes to himself. I can feel his gaze, too. But it's not like earlier. His desire doesn't stem from what he knows about my relationships. It stems from my power. I'm a force.

Asha's looking at me, too. The power excites her. She wants me, to touch me in the most intimate ways. She wants to be the hunter who can bring down the predator, tie me up and display me for all to see.

And these executives . . . they *all* want me. And their desire is not an insult. It's a gift.

Image and branding is Taci's area, and I step back and allow her to temporarily take the floor. But I know the attention is still on me.

What if I let them all have me? What if I made them work for my affections, *made* them bend to my will, agree to the implementation of all my plans? What if I rewarded them for it?

I imagine it now. Dameon stands up, crosses to me, waiting for instruction while Robert nods his approval. This isn't betrayal. This is strength. It's the kind of power that allows me to do anything I want anytime I want. No one dares object.

I imagine myself stripping Dameon down. I remove his jacket first, then his tie, dropping them unceremoniously on the floor while he stands quietly compliant. I slowly unbutton his shirt as he faces the room; Nina smiles as I expose his carefully sculpted, slender torso; run my fingers along the outlines of his muscles, his pecs, his abs, his narrow waist. "Take off the rest," I say, standing back, watching as he obediently pulls off his belt, then his pants, and finally the boxer briefs. He's slimmer than Robert, a little less bulk, and his youth gives him a fragility that can't be shaken by his daily workouts. His erection gives away his desire. He looks to me, hope lighting up his brown eyes as he waits for his next instruction. I put my hands on his shoulders and press down until he lowers to his knees, waiting.

Again I look at Robert. He smiles as I raise my skirt to my waist, lower my panties just enough.

"Taste me," I instruct, and immediately I feel the caress of his tongue splitting me open as my milky desire runs over his tongue.

The VP stares at Dameon, envy coloring his face. I nod at him, beckon with one hand, and he immediately complies, coming behind me, pressing himself against me; I can feel his erection as he sucks gently on my neck even as Dameon continues his ministrations. My eyes are now locked with Robert. This time it's Asha who must attend to me. She, too, walks behind me, running her fingers through my hair, up and down my arms. She wants more but this is all I will allow her. This is my party. I make the rules.

Robert smiles; he understands. His eyes speak his requests; to please him I allow Asha to unbutton my shirt, unfasten my bra. The VP gets to his knees and strokes my thighs as Dameon's tongue plunges inside of me. I shudder, my head falls back slightly, the pleasure is intense. But my eyes stay with Robert. Slowly he gets up, walks around the table, stealthy, confident, demanding. He stands in front of me.

"Step aside," he says, and the other players in this game fall away, none of them fully satisfied but knowing that they are not allowed to protest. He runs his hands over my hips, my stomach, my breasts as I work on his belt.

And then in a flash we're up against the wall, in front of everyone. My legs wrapped around him as he thrusts inside me over and over again. I cry out as the room watches, waiting to see if they might have a turn.

But they can't. I'm Robert's and he's mine. We make the rules and the excitement of that is almost as intoxicating as the feeling of Robert's erection inside of me driving deeper and deeper. He steps back, pulling me with him so only my shoulders are against the wall now and I rotate my hips, grinding against him, bringing him to new levels of ecstasy. From the corner of my eye I can see Dameon itching to join in.

Just when I think I'm about to come, Robert stops me, lowers my legs to the floor, and turns me around. He gently presses down on my back and I bend over, putting my hands on the wall. I moan as he enters me from behind. I turn my head so I can see the room. The VP is touching himself as he watches us. Asha looks angry and envious. Taci squirms in her seat, shy but desirous.

And Robert's hands stay on my hips as he thrusts harder and harder. I'm shaking now as I brace myself against this wall, feeling him, seeing them. One of his hands slides up to my breast, he pinches my nipple before bringing his hand down, between my legs. I'm so wet; he knows that, everyone here knows that. They all want to touch and taste. But this is just for Robert. He touches my clit, moving his finger slowly at first then rapidly, playing with me even as he presses inside of me.

I scream as I come; the sound is too raw and unrestrained to be considered a yell. I feel him come inside of me, filling my body even as he fills my mind with a new sense of dominance, influence, control.

Yes, control. That slippery thing I thought I was losing. Now, in this moment it once again occurs to me that this man who has tried to control me has given me more control than I've ever had before. Is it an illusion? Or is it actually real this time?

I set aside the questions as Taci finishes her part of the presentation and I take the stage again, a secret smile on my face.

Today this room filled with an attentive, eager audience is mine to dominate . . .

. . . and I am his.

✤

# CHAPTER 36

A T THE END of the meeting the executives have agreed to everything. Implementation will be their responsibility but I've set the direction. Robert urges each of them to question me, to give their honest opinions. But I have answers to everything. They're satisfied.

I know Robert's about to give me more work, another project, another reason why I'll be required to report to him but no one will question whether or not I'm deserving.

As I file out with my team, Robert and I don't touch but there's something in the look we exchange . . . the pretense is fading away. They can all see that. It doesn't matter. They know and they can't do anything about it. Asha trails behind me; I can smell her sense of defeat and it's invigorating.

I've given my team the rest of the day off but I go back to my office, where Barbara tells me I've been called to the eleventh floor. The CEO, Sam Costin, wants to see me. I don't hesitate. I know I'm about to be offered a promotion and now I'm ready to accept. I take the elevator up and announce myself to his receptionist, who tells me to wait.

This is the first time I've ever had a formal one-on-one meeting with Mr. Costin but I know that he always makes everyone wait. It's one of the ways he demonstrates his authority. And yet as I lower myself into the brown leather chair in his reception area, I find that the directive unnerves me, brings me down from the heady sense of supremacy I had only a moment ago.

The thought stops me. *Supremacy*? Was that what I was feeling?

I glance over at the receptionist; her hair is tied back in a low pony-tail, a black pearl ring clings to her index finger while her hands fly over the keyboard of her computer, her disinterest in me palpable. Do I really think I'm better than this woman? *Really*? Do I think I deserve more of her attention?

The minutes tick by slowly and as she continues to ignore me I find myself less inclined to believe that I do. I stare down at my own bare hands. I haven't worn a ring since I gave Dave back the beautiful ruby he gave me. What else had I given away that day? My pragmatism? My modesty? My humility? Am I really ready to part with so much?

"Mr. Costin will see you now," she says.

The phone hasn't rung so I can only assume that she's reading something on her computer screen that lets her know it's my time. Then again, it isn't really my time at all. It's Mr. Costin's. He may have called the meeting but he is still doing me a favor by keeping it. That's what I'm meant to feel.

I open the door and step inside. Mr. Costin sits at a mahogany desk; behind him is a wall of windows. I have a view from my office. His is better. His head is bent as he reads some report. I'm treated to a view of his bald spot, not his face.

"Close the door," he instructs, and I quickly do so. He contin-ues to read as I tentatively approach his desk. I consider sitting but think better of it. Instead I stand there and wait for him to greet me . . . and tell me what to do.

At last he looks up. His eyes run up and down my suit, his expres-sion impassive. He's not an unattractive man. He has high cheek-bones and a strong jaw but his eyes are too light, a very pale blue that makes him look perpetually icy, even cruel. "You've changed your style," he says wryly. I have a feeling he's talking about more than just my clothes.

Uneasily I shift from foot to foot. He leans back, seeming to enjoy my discomfort. Finally he sighs and gestures to a chair.

"Sit."

It's the kind of command you give a dog and it shames me that I so quickly obey.

"We had to let Tom Love go," he says. "But you know that."

I nod, swallow hard, and stare at my lap.

"Tom was an asset," Mr. Costin continues. "All of his departments were performing well, including yours."

Again I nod. What was once confidence is now anxiety. I can feel my heart pounding against my chest. It's so loud, I wonder if Mr. Costin can hear it.

"The business world is a brutal one," he continues. "Survival of the fittest and all that. And the fittest isn't necessarily the strongest. There are many incredibly strong animals who have fallen victim to extinction while the weaker monarch remains protected by her colors, beautiful and toxic. Funny how that works, isn't it?"

I consider challenging him, but when I look up and meet his eyes I think better of it. I shrug awkwardly, suddenly ashamed of my brighter colors.

"You came up here expecting me to offer you Tom's job. Am I right?"

Again I shrug and hope he doesn't notice the flush creeping up my cheeks.

"For God's sake, if you're going to act like a shy kindergartner, I'm going to have to treat you like one. Use your words, Kasie."

I clear my throat. "I have heard rumors . . ." But my voice trails off. I don't have any idea how to proceed. I thought I knew what was coming, but I don't.

"Now that's an interesting way to put it." Mr. Costin steeples his fingers and smiles. "I've been hearing a few rumors myself. Shall we compare notes? Do tell, Kasie. What have you been hearing?"

I squirm slightly. "I heard that you might be about to offer me a promotion," I say. My voice is as thin as a monarch's wings.

"As rumors go that's probably one of the more innocent ones I've heard in a while," he notes. "Most of the rumors circulating around this company lately are more . . . salacious."

Now I know he can see my blush. I straighten my posture. I have to hold my own here. I need to look like a woman who deserves a promotion, not, as Mr. Costin just implied, like a scared little girl. "Are you considering me for the job, Mr. Costin?" I manage to sound a little more composed this time.

But my composure is tenuous, more so when Mr. Costin takes his time answering me, studying me with those cold eyes. "Maned Wolf has business relations with many of our clients and Robert Dade is a personal shareholder in the rest. He has more pull and influence in the business world than any other man in LA. I had to let go of Tom because keeping him could have cost us all of our accounts. I wasn't given a choice. I don't like it when people take away my choices, Kasie. Do you understand that?"

I nod.

"Your words!"

"Yes, Mr. Costin," I say quickly. So much for being powerful and in control. This roller coaster of emotion is too extreme for me. I want to get off the ride.

"I also like Dylan Freeland, the cofounder of this company. He may no longer be that involved in the day-to-day operations here but he is still a key player in all our major decisions. Do you know what it was like for him? Being cornered? Feeling like he has to make decisions to elevate someone who caused pain to those he loves while ruining a man who has always served his company—the company he *built*—with honor?"

Honor. Tom Love doesn't deserve to have the word associated with him. And yet I hadn't felt comfortable with his firing, either. It hadn't been based on his sexual harassment of me; it had been based on lies. I have no defense against Mr. Costin's attacks.

I force myself to hold his gaze. I can see there's more he wants to say. Insults and accusations that he's working hard to hold back. He's yet to accuse me of sleeping my way to the top even though that's clearly what he thinks I'm doing. He hasn't told me that I fucked around on Mr. Freeland's godson only to then get rewarded for opening my legs to a client. Does he want to call me a bitch? A slut? What would he do to me if he wasn't afraid of repercussions?

And that's when it dawns on me, he *is* afraid of repercussions. His anger has no teeth. I lift my chin. Sticks and stones. I can bear this. I *have* to bear this. It's no less than what I deserve and, honestly, *it can't hurt me.*

"If Mr. Freeland is upset, I'm truly sorry about that. I'm sorry you're upset, too," I add, "but that was never my intention. I've worked here for six years and none of my clients have ever had a complaint."

"I wonder why," Mr. Costin says dryly.

Again I squirm. He says so much without saying anything at all. Still I push forward. "I just led a team on a major project for the first time. While I realize that most people who are moved into a supervisory position such as Tom's—"

"You should refer to him as Mr. Love. You owe him at least that respect, don't you, Kasie?"

I wait for the sting of that insult to fade before I continue. "I realize that normally, someone stepping into Mr. Love's managing partner position have led more than one team, but if you talk to the executives at Maned Wolf, I think you'll find that I did an exemplary job. I believe we'll have that account for quite some time along with many lucrative projects."

"*Quelle* surprise."

Behind him I see the city laid out. The tops of buildings and little cars that look to be no bigger than matchboxes crawl through the crowded streets. Everybody is going somewhere and everybody has to deal with the irritation of the traffic and the long stoplights. But eventually they'll get to where they want to go. The trick is not to let the road rage get to you.

"Do I have the job, Mr. Costin?"

Again he waits before answering but this pause isn't as intimidating as the last one. We both know his choices have been taken away.

"Start tomorrow," he says coolly. "You have a lot to learn. Your entire experience here has involved things like Corporate Finance—risk, marketing and sales, and so on. You have zero experience with Health Care Systems and Services, Media and Entertainment, or Travel Transport and Logistics and yet those are three of the four departments that will be reporting to you now. Your protector won't do you a lot of good if you screw up this company beyond repair."

"I don't have a protector."

Mr. Costin flashes me a sarcastic smile. "We all have protectors, Kasie. Gods that we pray to for help. A lucky few of us get the attention of one of the earthly gods. They're more easily seduced. But then you know that, don't you?" He glances at his watch and sighs. "Go home, come back tomorrow ready to learn. I assume that tonight you'll need to do some more worshiping, because without your protecting god, you don't *have* a prayer."

I dig my fingernails into my palm but then force myself to release my fist and smile at Mr. Costin before leaving his office with the quiet humility he seems to want from me.

But I don't leave the building as he requested. Instead I go to my office and start to organize. I hadn't asked if I would be moved into Tom's office; Mr. Costin hadn't exactly invited those kinds of questions. So odd to get a promotion from a man who hates you. And it's odd that only a few months ago I couldn't imagine anyone really *hating* me any more than I could imagine anyone completely loving me. I just hadn't viewed myself as the kind of person who inspired those kinds of extreme emotions. But now the word "hate" comes up a lot in regard to me. Dave, Tom, Mr. Costin, perhaps Asha . . . how is it possible that after so many years of playing it safe, I'm now inspiring such contempt?

I don't like it. I never wanted to be the Bond girl who destroys lives for lovers and profit. But I *have* always aspired to power, and perhaps it's the meek who inspire more charitable emotions. If so, isn't strength worth the price of animosity?

The strong can't be erased.

And what of love? Does Robert love me? Or is this something else?

As for Mr. Costin . . . well, if he's right about the amount of in-fluence Robert has, I could have his job as easily as I got Tom's. He must know that. So in his case it's his fear that makes him hate. It's so conventional, it's not even interesting. The only part that gives me pause is that I'm the one he fears. The head of this company fears me. That's . . . different.

I drive home that night thinking of the moon and the ocean. Together they can do so much damage.

❀

# CHAPTER 37

I DON'T WANT TO invite Robert over tonight. It's not just that I need space this time. Things are getting out of hand, but the most frightening part about it is that his ideas, propositions, and philosophies that I *know* are unethical are becoming more and more alluring.

So I don't reach out to him. Instead I make myself a salad, open a bottle of wine, and cry. Maybe it's because this isn't the life I imagined. It's so much more and so much less. Eventually I call my friend Simone. She doesn't berate me for evading her for weeks on end. Instead she simply listens to the notes of emotion in my voice and tells me she's coming over.

She arrives holding a bottle of Grey Goose by the neck. She studies me, standing in my doorway like an expectant trick-or-treater. I've changed out of my suit into a long silk robe; my hair hangs loosely over my shoulders. "Wow," she says as she finally enters, walking past me. "What a difference a month makes."

I follow her into the kitchen, where she leans against the counter holding the vodka against her heart. I study the label depicting white birds flying over a glass sky. "What do you mean?"

"Well, let's think," she says solemnly as she opens the bottle. "You were a good girl dating a controlling asshole and then you had an affair, and then you got engaged to the asshole, broke up with the asshole, and coupled up with your lover. All that in less than thirty days?" She raises her blond eyebrows. "That might be Guinness worthy."

"And exactly what world record would I be setting?"

"Most transformation ever achieved by one Harvard grad during the month of March? Can we make that a category?" she asks. She hops up on the counter. "Do you have ice cream?"

I hesitate only a moment before going to the freezer and pulling out a pint of Stonyfield Vanilla. Simone unceremoniously digs out scoops for both of us and drops them into my blender before drowning the ice cream in the clear alcohol and blending it all together into something that reminds me of false innocence.

"You've already been drinking," she notes.

"Yes," I admit.

"But you'll drink more?"

I nod and she smiles, pouring the drink into two gracefully curved water goblets. "That's a change, too. Tell me, Kasie, does this mean you're finally willing to relinquish some of your precious control?"

"I've been relinquishing control to Dave for years."

"True." She sips her drink, purposely giving herself a milk mustache to make me smile. "But that was like getting on a merry-go-round. You may not be controlling the plastic horse, but you know where it's going. That ride's over, so I guess I'm asking, are you moving on to the controlled thrills of the roller coaster, or are you ready to leave the amusement park altogether and try skydiving?"

I shake my head. "You thrive off risk; I don't."

"Oh? And what makes the newest rendition of Kasie Fitzgerald thrive?"

It's a complicated question and I meditate on it as I swallow the sweet taste of sin. I think of what it feels like when Robert is inside of me. I think of the energy he fills me with, the intensity. In those moments the world becomes brighter even as the darkness inside me is expelled. In those moments I'm skydiving, breathing in the clouds, relishing the thrill and danger of the fall. Perhaps that's what it is to thrive.

Or is it when I hold the corporate world in my hands? It's no wonder that I fantasize about sex while mastering a boardroom. It's a different but related thrill. Falling versus flying. And what about Robert's proposal . . . and it is a proposal, controlling the world, making up the rules as we go and forcing others to bend to our whims. He's proposing that we reshape the universe, make ourselves gods. If I were to give in to that, which of course I could never do, would I thrive?

"You don't have an answer," Simone whispers. Her voice is hushed and touched with awe. "Things really *have* changed, haven't they? Not too long ago you had an answer to everything."

I laugh out loud. "I *thought* I did." The drink is making my consonants softer, a little harder to understand. "Turns out I didn't even know the questions!"

Simone reaches forward, brushes my hair back behind my shoulders, then lets her hands slide down the edges of my silk lapel. "Relax," she whispers. "You're beautiful when you're vulnerable."

"And when I'm strong?"

"You're gorgeous." Simone's hands float back down to her sides. I'm seeing the room through a soft-focus lens. Simone is the one who is gorgeous as her fingers stroke the stem of her glass. Her life has always been luxuriously simple. My eyes follow her hair down to her neck, where for the first time I spot the small bruise that's been left there. A mark of triumph left by a recent lover. "Who gave you that?" I ask, knowing that whoever it was probably won't be around for long. Simone has a habit of choosing easy, unambitious men who can act out her fantasies without touching her mind. It's fun at first, until it gets boring.

She raises her fingers to the mark and smiles reverently. "My first ménage à trois." She giggles. "I think his name was Joseph and she called herself Nidal. It's a lovely name, isn't it? Nidal. A boy's name given to a girl . . . it suits her." She lets the word slide around on her tongue.

I hesitate. I'm not the only one who is changing. Simone has never crossed that line before. "Did you . . ." My voice trails off, unsure of what to ask. "What did you do?" is the question I finally settle on. I'm not sure I want to hear anything she's too scandalized to volunteer. After all, Simone isn't scandalized by much.

"It was Nidal's idea. She's a DJ at Divinity."

"Divinity?"

"You haven't heard of it?" She puts down her glass and raises her arms into the air, stretching her back as she reaches for the sky. "It's a little club on Melrose. Divinity. A funny name, isn't it? It's sort of a reminder of why people go to clubs. To dance, drink, and flirt until reality and all sense of mortality just sort of melt away and we all feel a bit like divine beings. Deities of the night."

I look at my own glass. I'm not drinking because I hunger for a taste of the divine. I get that every time I lay my lips against Robert's. I feel it when I lie beneath him, when he enters me and throbs inside of me, and I hear it every time he whispers my name.

On the contrary, I'm drinking because I want to touch the part of myself that is endearingly clumsy and human.

"It scared me at first," she admits. "Nidal always flirts with me but I never thought anything would come of it. I told her I didn't swing that way." She pauses before adding, "Then she started asking me questions I didn't have answers to."

"Like what?"

"She asked if I was afraid I'd lose myself. She wanted to know if I thought I'd be changed if I let another woman touch me, if I liked it. She wanted to know if I thought it would muddle my sense of identity, my definition of femininity and sexuality. It was all very philosophical and I began to wonder . . . what *am* I afraid of?"

"But you've never mentioned being interested in women before," I note. The thick, creamy concoction coats my throat and stomach, making me happy. Happy for this mild intoxication and happy to be distracted from my life by one of Simone's titillating but innocuous adventures. "Perhaps it wasn't fear that held you back, just lack of desire."

Simone laughs. "But I'm always desirous of adventure. And I wanted to know . . . how strong *is* my sense of self? If it's strong enough, no adventure should be able to shake it." She meets my eyes, sips her drink again. "It was interesting . . . a woman knows a woman's body. She knew where her touch should be light and where to apply just a bit of pressure. She instructed our partner, too, Jason—"

"Joseph."

"Joseph . . . yes, Joseph. We started with me going down on him. I was on my back, my head hanging off the bed, and I took him in my mouth while he stood up. I was totally focused on what I was doing, sliding my hand up and down the base of his erection while my mouth worked on the tip and ridges. . . . I didn't even notice what she was doing until I felt her tongue against my pussy."

I jump slightly, squeeze my legs together a little tighter as if Nidal's here, right now, trying to smooth away my lines in the sand.

"It was a perfect way to begin," Simone says, her voice hushed with memory. "My focus was on him, I didn't even see her, and a woman's tongue feels just like a man's . . . except perhaps more skilled. I started to moan even as my mouth was wrapped around Joseph, I tried to keep my hips still, but couldn't. That's when Joseph asked if he could have a taste, too."

"Simone!" I whisper her name with an urgency that surprises me. I hadn't expected this tale, or its allure.

"Nidal told him how to pleasure me," she continues with a smile. "She stood over him and told him to move his face down to my pussy, she told him to slide his tongue gently around my clit and then back and forth. It started slow but then it was almost too much and I was writhing around on the bed while she watched me and he touched me. She was the teacher and I was the lesson. She told him how to add his fingers to the experience. And in between sentences she would lean down and nibble on my ear, find the sensitive spot there with her tongue; her fingers traced the area around my nipples, making them hard without her ever touching them directly."

I look away as if the scene were right before me rather than in Simone's head. As if I was seeing me on that bed. I could never do that, could I? I could never relinquish so much control, could never challenge so many conventions. I'm not even attracted to women.

But this story caresses me in ways I hadn't anticipated. I cross my arms over my chest so Simone can't see that Nidal has worked her magic on me as well.

"She told me where to touch her. . . . I've never touched another woman's breast before. But I liked the way it felt, firm but so soft. I liked the way Nidal responded to me. Joseph liked it, too."

"Did you actually have sex with them?" I ask. My cheeks are bright red and my question comes out in a whisper.

"Nidal directed that, too. She told him to enter me slowly, she told him how to rotate his hips just right. She asked me to kiss her while he rode me." Simone falls silent, momentarily lost in the memory. "Nidal asked me to face my fears," she finally adds, "and she rewarded me for it."

"With sex?"

Simone hesitates only a moment before replying, "She rewarded me with adventure. And with the most amazing orgasm I've ever had. It ripped through me, Kasie. It almost made me weep. Joseph said he could actually feel the spasms that shot through me. It was . . . it was spectacular. And it's a memory I will hold on to until I die. When I'm eighty I'll be able to look back at that night and remember that I was once daring and bold."

"Yes," I say slowly. For a few moments we let the picture she's painted hang between us, demanding both reverence and wonder. But as it fades I begin to remember what's real and what isn't. I reach for something to pull us both back fully into the present.

"You'll always have the memory," I say slowly, "but . . . you might not remember if you slept with Jason or Joseph."

That makes her giggle and with her laughter the mood shifts to something a little less intense. "Well," she finally says, "that's why we have to stay friends. So you can remind me of these things."

I smile down into my milkshake, relishing the idea of having a lifelong friend. She hesitates only a moment before taking my hand. "It sounds like you have fears you need to face, too," she says kindly. "What's going on, Kasie?"

I take a deep breath and begin to talk. I tell her of the push-pull lovers' game I'm playing with Robert. I tell her I'm being promoted by a man who wants to fire me. I tell her about Asha and Tom and how conflicted I am. "I'm being granted power and influence without respect," I finally say. "I didn't even know that was possible!"

This time Simone's laugh is richer and more boisterous. "Perhaps you haven't noticed but that's the situation with all the dictators in the world and quite a few of our elected officials. We respect the office, we certainly respect the power, but it's fairly rare that we respect the individual who wields that power over us."

I shake my head. "I disagree. When we read our history books, it's the leaders whom we honor and idealize."

"Oh please. The whole point of history books is to bring our attention to the exceptions. There's not enough room on the page to write about those who represent the status quo, the *norm*. My God, how boring would that be?"

I giggle my halfhearted agreement.

"No," she sighs, "*normally* when someone has power over us, we go out of our way to look for that person's flaws. We exaggerate them in our minds and in our gossip. We ridicule our leaders when their backs are turned. We convince ourselves that they're not really deserving. That they're not better than us. Sometimes we're right, sometimes we're wrong. It doesn't really matter because we still respect the *power* and we will still bend to it regardless of how we may feel about the hands that hold it."

I haven't thought of it like that before. "This isn't a direction I've chosen for myself," I say softly. "He's chosen it for me."

"And you're afraid you'll get lost?" Simone asks. She shakes her head, stirs her drink. "You can't retrace your steps, Kasie. What's happened, happened. As long as you're at your firm, people will remember. You can either see this thing through and find out if it takes you to a place you like or you can leave the firm and go somewhere else. Start from scratch."

"Are you kidding?" I exclaim. "I've put six years into that place!

And where would I go? There is no other consulting firm in LA that has their reputation."

"You could work for yourself."

I blink. It's not that the thought has never occurred to me but I've never taken it seriously. The risks involved in being self-employed are too great. The only structure is the one you create. "I'm not cut out for that kind of uncertainty."

"Well then you have a problem." Simone gathers her blond hair into her hands, pulling it up to the nape of her neck. "Everything about your life is pretty uncertain right now. That's not going to change regardless of what you do."

I hang my head, defeated. "I'm lost."

"No, you know where you are, you're just not sure which routes you want to take," Simone notes. "You have to make your own decisions, and you will. But I *will* tell you this, you're not done with Robert Dade. Not by a long shot."

When she says his name, I feel him. Feel his smile, his hands; I feel his lips against my neck. He's never far away. Never out of my mind, always causing ripples. No, I'm not done with Robert Dade. I'm not sure I ever will be.

❁

# CHAPTER 38

THE NEXT MORNING comes too soon. The drum of regret pounds gently at my temples, reminding me of last night's decadence. The moment I arrive at work Barbara tells me in a voice laced with marvel and glee that I'm being moved to Tom's office.

I nod, unable to show enthusiasm. "Did Mr. Dade call?" I ask. He hadn't called the night before. There were no texts on my phone this morning.

Barbara shakes her head, her loose curls holding absurdly still due to an excess of hair spray. "You two didn't have a spat, did you?" She leans forward conspiratorially, "I liked Dave but Mr. Dade is so much hotter."

I bristle at the remark. It's not fair to Dave that he be compared to Robert. They are no longer competing for the same prize. I nod curtly at Barbara and walk into the office I'm about to abandon.

I'll be moving one floor up, a physical symbol of my current trajectory. I don't make a fuss. No one comes to my office to congratulate me or help me in the move. It doesn't take long. Six years and the only things in my office are papers and files. No pictures of kids, no cute little paperweights, no paintings that weren't placed there by the company. There's nothing in here that says, *This is Kasie's office*, except for those files, which, of course, are more than enough. Many a night I have found comfort in the numbers and calculations that are stored so neatly in files and storage disks. Their cold logic is something I can count on. If I could manage to turn my entire life into a math equation, I'm sure I could figure it out.

Still, I've become accustomed to my office, the way the drawers of the file cabinets creak their greetings when I pull them open. I'm fond of my desk with its hardwood dyed black, the subtle curve of its legs that hint at a certain femininity to this utilitarian piece of furniture.

But of course my new office is better. The view shows a little more of the city, the desk is made of a slightly better wood, the chair is a little more comfortable. The only thing that intimidates me is the work that waits for me here. Files stacked on top of one another are filled with information about departments I've never been briefed on. My inbox is flooded with information that needs learning and questions that need answers. I will be organizing teams for projects without knowing the players I'll be picking from. I will be helping those teams address problems I don't understand. Mr. Costin seems to have "forgotten" to give me password access to some files I'll need in order to manage the departments successfully, so I end up spending at least an hour talking to the IT guys—IT guys who, if I didn't know better, were instructed to deliberately try my patience. I might have written it off as the normal inconvenience of tech problems if I didn't see one of them smirk when I wondered aloud why Mr. Costin hadn't given me the authorization he knew I'd need.

And still Robert doesn't call.

I spend the day reading and taking notes. A few of the people who will be working for me stop by to offer congratulations. All the words are right and the bitterness is concealed but I can still detect it. I can see the gleam of resentment in their eyes as they shake my hand, offer their help in the transition, and so on. None of them loved Tom but they all respected his work. Will they feel that way about me? Is that what I want? Respect mingled with animosity? Well, you play the hand you're dealt. I bend my head over yet another file.

And still he doesn't call.

It's a good thing, I tell myself. I need some space from him. I can't have him touching me with his voice, his eyes, his hands every day. He wants to corrupt me. I need space from him so that doesn't happen. It's good that he hasn't called.

I keep reading the file, a low level of anxiety quickening my pulse.

Eventually the night arrives. I don't leave until six thirty. There's no point in staying longer. I can only learn so much in one day.

I'm ill at ease as I enter the garage, step into my car. Mr. Costin did not come to see me and when I tried to call him with questions, my calls were sent to voicemail. He's trying to help me fail.

I pull my car onto the busy city streets. As usual the traffic is an exercise in patience. Most Angelenos can tolerate it as long as we're moving forward. It's when traffic is completely stopped that we become agitated. That's when we have to admit that we chose the wrong route and are not going anywhere at all.

I eye the sign for the 101. South will take me home, north will take me to him.

I need to go south. It's where I live, where I belong. I'm not ready for anything else. I don't want it.

But I need it.

The Los Angeles traffic continues to creep; someone leans on his horn in a useless expression of frustration.

The palms of my hands are moist and slide up and down along the smooth leather of the steering wheel.

*Go south; it's where you belong. You don't want what he wants.*

I'm shaking now. The numbers I reviewed all afternoon have all been left in the office. There is nothing clear or simple for me to hold on to here. I'm closer to the freeway entrance. I see the little arrow pointing the way for me, urging me onto the freeway that will take me home.

But I don't go home. I go north.

And when I pull onto the freeway, I see that the traffic going along this new direction isn't so daunting. The devil has cleared the way.

Soon I get to his exit and in minutes I'm curving up the familiar street.

The gate to his driveway is open; the door, unlocked. I walk in without announcing myself.

He's waiting for me in the living room. A bottle of champagne is chilling in a bucket. Flames dance in the fireplace.

"You're late," he says without animosity.

"I'm not supposed to be here," I say quietly.

He's wearing dark jeans and a T-shirt, his sports coat the only thing that indicates he's not planning on a quiet evening at home. His only response is a smile.

"I haven't heard from you since the meeting," I add.

"So you came to me." He pops the champagne, pours the bubbling gold into two waiting glasses.

I don't answer; I don't like to think of what my being here means.

"Drink, Kasie."

My hand is unsteady as I take the glass. "I'm not supposed to be here," I say again.

He simply wraps his hand over mine, raises the drink to my lips. "You were magnificent in that boardroom," he says quietly.

The bubbles tickle my confidence. I bring the glass down and whisper, "I was. But I'm not ready for this promotion."

His hand caresses my cheek, runs up through my hair before finding its place at the back of my neck. "You're ready for anything."

"If I screw this up, what happens?" I ask. "Will I get another chance? Will you make them indulge my incompetence?"

"You've never been incompetent."

"And what's the price for these favors?"

"Take another drink," he suggests, his eyes smiling. He steps back, watches me, his own glass untouched.

"You were magnificent," he says again. "The only price is that I want you to be magnificent every day. I want people to see it, feel it. And then I want to be inside the power that I've helped grant. I want to make you come, I want to see you command the world and tremble at my touch. I want to fuck you right here, and in my office, in yours; I want you to relish in the pleasure of both authority and submission on a daily basis. It's an intoxicating combination and you are one of the few who can explore both."

"I'm scared."

"If you weren't, you wouldn't be very smart. But"—and with this he slips his hand under my shirt, under my bra, pinches my nipple— "fear can be fun. Like a scary movie or a haunted house. Fear can be its own high."

"How can the man who makes all the rules and takes what he wants without apology, how can *he* be afraid of anything?" I counter. "You're asking me to take pleasure in an emotion you know nothing about."

"Ah, you're wrong there." He steps away from me, walks to the bookshelf, lets his finger slide over the bindings until it stops at one title, John Milton's *Paradise Lost*. "It was my mother's book," he says, pulling it out. "She was the manager of a small office for a large company. My father was a broker working his way up, trading commodities and stocks he himself could barely afford. Buying and selling the promises of companies whose operations he knew little about. Don't get me wrong," he says, turning to me, smiling in the way people do when they relive uncomfortable memories. "He wasn't bad at his job. His firm liked him. He was a team player."

The last words are spoken like a curse. He walks to the fireplace, turns up the gas, making the flames surge. "When they set him up to take the fall for an insider trading charge, he didn't stray from the script. He kept up the party line. Loyalty before survival; that was the way my father lived his life. He believed their promises. He told us they'd take care of him, make sure no felony counts would stick. He wouldn't do a minute of prison time, his career would survive intact. They were such charming promises, dandelions in a field; that's how my mother described them. Weeds, flowers that weren't planned for but were pretty nonetheless."

"They were lies," I say. I've heard this story before. Different actors, same plot. I know how it goes.

"Most promises are," Robert says, his eyes still on the fire giving him an eerie illumination that somehow tantalizes even as it intimidates. "People who are speaking the truth don't have to promise.

When a child promises to never sneak another cookie, or a husband promises to never flirt with another woman, when a criminal promises God he'll be good if he can just get away with one more crime . . . those are always lies. The mother knows it, the wife knows it, God certainly knows it. But not my father, he chose to play the fool, and he paid for it."

"Why are you telling me this?" I ask gently. I am not berating him but this confession doesn't seem to connect to the conversation it was born from.

"Do you know why he couldn't see through the lies?" Robert asks. The question is clearly rhetorical, so I remain silent and wait for him to continue.

"Because disobedience was scary. It's always safer to do what you're told rather than blaze your own path. People find it comforting to follow other people's rules; they'll choose certain destruction over a risk that might lead to possible salvation. They cling to this idea that it could be worse and they're more terrified of that than they are attracted to the idea that it might be better." He sighs, walks back to the bookcase, puts *Paradise* back on the shelf.

"How long was he in jail?" I ask.

"Four years. It turns out there was more to the story and the crimes than my father knew. Securities fraud, false filings with the SEC, and so on. By refusing to explore the unknown he allowed the unknown to devastate him. My mother became a single parent. She put in long hours at her work but was continually passed over for promotion. Too many people she worked for knew about my father and they bought in to the idea of guilt by association. She could have quit, she could have worked a few less hours and spent some of her time sending out résumés to other places. God knows she needed to make more money and she had the intelligence to get ahead in a firm that would give her a chance. But she had been at her company since college. She was addicted to the familiarity."

He comes to me, his arms encircle me, his hands slide to the small of my back. "Their mistakes were common ones. Sometimes we have to step out of our comfort zones. We have to break the rules. And we have to discover the sensuality of fear. We need to face it, challenge it, dance with it."

"Dance . . . with fear?" My voice falters.

He smiles. "Yes. I've always pursued the paths that scare me, not because I want to conquer fear but because I know I have to live with it if I'm going to accomplish anything interesting. I take the risks that will unsettle me, and add an edge to my life because if I can make fear my lover, then she'll serve me." He raises his hands, puts one on either side of my face. "Fear is a lover I want to share, Kasie. I want to share her with you."

I know what he's saying is madness. The rantings of a hurt child whose greatest goal is rebellion. And yet the words entice me. How can they not? Deep down, in the part of me that I've tried so hard to bury, I am like Simone, always desirous of adventure.

He leans in close; his lips rest against my ear. "Come with me, pursue her with me now."

And I let him lead me. We walk out of his home, into his garage, into his car that resembles art and power. It pulls out onto the street too fast; I feel my stomach drop as I'm pressed back in my seat. He takes the turns with the skill of a race-car driver and the reckless-ness of a teenager. I take a breath and realize he's right. The fear is exciting.

I don't ask where we're going as we navigate the back roads of LA, streets that aren't so carefully monitored by the LAPD. We're a little off the grid, playing by Robert's rules.

He finally pulls into a back alley behind a string of small restau-rants and cheap nail salons. Most of these businesses have closed up for the night but I notice that there are still cars parked in a small, dingy lot that Robert slides us into. A light shines down on a white door against a dull brown building. He leads me to it and I see the word "Wishes" in small letters painted in red on the white surface. The color reminds me of blood, and passion and rubies.

He opens the door for me and I see we've arrived at a neighborhood speakeasy. The bar is small, the furniture is composed of sofas and soft chairs, things that would be perfectly at home in a private living room. There are no more than ten people here, but a woman stands at a mic, singing something mournful and beguiling. Next to her a man with wire-rimmed glasses and a golden tan plays the double bass.

Behind the bar is a woman with long red hair, almost as red as the words on the door. She smiles when she sees Robert but her smile gets a little brighter when her eyes land on me.

"Mr. Dade," she says as we approach, "it's been some time."

"Hey, Genevieve. One of your famous margaritas for my friend here," he says as he gestures for me to sit on one of the bar stools.

"I don't drink tequila," I say as I pull myself onto a seat.

"Why? Are you afraid you'll lose control?" he asks. The question is gently teasing and I don't bother to answer or put up further protest.

In a moment I have a margarita on the rocks; a thin layer of salt adorns the rim of the glass. I feel the eyes of the room. When I glance at a man at a corner table he looks away quickly, the woman at the other end of the room keeps her head down as she studies her drink with an intensity that suggests she's actively avoiding some other vision. There are little conversations around the room, drinks are raised and lowered, and yet somehow, in a million different little ways, everyone seems tuned in to us, as if they, too, feel the gravitational pull of the moon, as if they sense the rising tide.

"She's good," Robert says, gesturing to the singer. Her hair is black and falls just past her shoulders; her eyes are closed as she sings about the cruelty of love. She reminds me of Asha.

"She is," Genevieve says, but her eyes stay on me. She puts her finger against the glass in my hand. There's an intimacy there, touching the same glass without touching each other. "Take it slow," she says coyly. "I have a feeling there will be more."

The singer finishes her song. Robert nods at our bartender, who reaches above her head and rings a large, rusty bell that jars the patrons from their conversations and alcoholic musings. "Last call," she cries.

It's nowhere near two and there's some grumbling among the patrons, but no one complains too loudly, accepting this odd twist of fate as the norm rather than an unexpected offense. A few order another drink while they still can but most just get up and leave. The singer and bass player take a seat. Neither packs up. I sip my drink as more and more people file out. "Is this your bar?" I ask Genevieve.

She laughs lightly and pours a drink for herself. "No," she says lightly. "It's his."

I turn to Robert, who smiles secretly. "It's my bar," he agrees. "I set the rules."

And then we're alone. The patrons are gone. It's just me, the musicians, Genevieve, and . . . him.

"I bet you were a good girl in college," Genevieve says lightly as the singer steps up to the microphone again. The song is a little grittier this time, the deep echoing notes of the double bass set the mood. "I bet you never once went to a rave, danced on the bar, made out in public . . . I bet you never even did a body shot."

I shake my head. "I was busy studying. I had goals."

Genevieve's smile broadens. "Don't we all." My drink sits half empty on the bar and she slowly drags it away, out of my reach. "Let me show you how to do a body shot."

The singer raises her voice as the song builds. I send a sharp look at Robert but his eyes are on Genevieve. He's watching her closely, attentively, and I realize that, without saying a word, he's somehow directing this. He's taking me away from the familiar, introducing me to the thrill of unease.

Genevieve places a shot of tequila on the bar before she walks around the counter, a saltshaker in one hand, a wedge of lime in the other. She takes my arm and with a quick look at Robert slides the lime along the inside of my wrist, along that vein that gives away my pulse. She sprinkles the trail with salt before lifting the lime to my mouth. "Bite," she instructs.

My heart is pounding. I look at Robert again. This is beyond unfamiliar. I'm not comfortable with it at all . . . and yet I can't say that part of me isn't eager.

I open my mouth, gently wrap my lips around the lime as she raises my wrist to her mouth. She keeps her eyes on Robert the whole time as she licks the salt off my skin. With languid movements she reaches for the shot, throws it back, and then leans forward for her lime. I feel her tongue slip slightly past the lime and I almost pull back but then I feel Robert's hand, on my knee, sliding up my leg. A familiar delight to ground me. She takes the lime in her teeth and pulls it from me, squeezes the juices into her mouth.

"Your turn."

I start to shake my head as she gets another slice of lime but this time she takes the lime to Robert's neck. He tilts his head, agreeably allowing her to create a trail for the salt. She pours another shot of tequila, places the lime between Robert's teeth. "Go ahead," she says. "Taste him."

I think I hear laughter in the singer's melody but it could be my imagination. I lean forward, let my tongue dip into the salt on his throat. "Get every grain," Genevieve coaxes. "It would be a sin to waste it." She watches and continues to whisper encouragements as I seek out the grains of salt that have fallen behind his collarbone. When I finally lean back, it's Genevieve who reaches for the shot glass. She holds it over his shoulder, urges me on with a raise of her eyebrows. I glance back at the singer and bass player. The music continues with the casual smoothness you would expect from professionals but their eyes are on us. The blush starts in my cheeks and spreads with the speed of a five-alarm blaze. This has been my fantasy, being watched, but I never dreamed I'd have the courage to actually act it out. It's too scary.

But fear can be thrilling and so I stand up, step between Robert's open legs, press my body into his as I reach my chin over his shoulder. Genevieve brings the glass to my lips, tipping it back, letting the alcohol trickle rather than stream into my open mouth. Finally she pulls the drink away as I take the lime from Robert. His hands move down my back, to my ass, through my legs, pressing upward. I take in a sharp breath, murmur his name.

When I pull away I'm shaking. I stare at Robert as he puts the lime down neatly on a cocktail napkin. Genevieve stands behind him, her eyes sparkling with hints of danger as she places her hands on each of Robert's shoulders and leans in to his ear. In a stage whisper she says, "It's your turn, Mr. Dade."

Robert stands up and makes a vague gesture that Genevieve seems to understand. She quickly clears away everything on the bar.

"Lie down, Kasie," he says, his voice quietly authoritative. I stand, a little agitated, a little scared. I glance at the musicians again. They've moved on to a quieter piece; their music offers no distraction from what is happening. Not for me, not for them. I think I see the bass player wink at me but I'm not sure.

"I don't think I—" I begin, but Robert stops me by pressing his finger against my lips.

"You can make the fear your lover."

The words mean nothing, but I'm compelled to acquiesce. I let Robert lift me until I'm sitting on the bar. I pull up my legs, lie back, feeling completely vulnerable to the others in the room. Genevieve is behind the bar; Robert, in front of it. I feel her hands on the hem of my shirt as Robert works to unfasten the buttons on the waist of my skirt.

"What are you doing?" I whisper, but Robert hushes me.

"You've taken the power; now is the time to submit."

Genevieve pulls my shirt from me; I feel my skirt sliding down my legs. The music stops and I hear the whispered voices of the musicians as they discuss what they're seeing.

From the corner of my eye I see Genevieve pour another shot. I feel the cool glass as she drags it along my thigh.

"What's your name?" she asks.

"Kasie," I murmur. "Kasie Fitzgerald."

"Well, Miss Fitzgerald, I need you to spread your legs, just a little, that's right; you're not going to be a good girl tonight."

Robert chuckles softly and I can feel the coldness of the glass through the fabric of my panties. "Hold this in place here, please," Genevieve instructs as Robert smiles down at me.

"Submit," he says again. "For me."

I squeeze my thighs together, holding the glass in place as he caresses me with a lime, along my stomach, to my chest, along the outline of my bra. The lime is then placed between my teeth and I feel the salt as it sprinkles down on me. My skin is so sensitive now, even this light touch is startlingly seductive.

Robert leans down, tastes the salt that lines my bra, reaching inside to pinch my nipples as Genevieve tastes the salt on my stomach; she's moving lower, dangerously lower. I see the musicians moving in closer.

I think of protesting, of spitting out the lime and telling them that this takes more audacity and courage than I have.

But I don't. I'm not pulling away. Genevieve moves even lower, kissing the edge of my panties and then the fabric until she gets to the glass. She laps the tequila up as if she's a kitten tasting milk.

I feel a new shot of coolness as Robert pours a thimble's worth of tequila into my belly button. It spills over, runs down to my panties, which are already wet.

I don't protest this time, not even as he removes my bra from me, runs a lime over my nipples before coating them with salt. Genevieve straightens her posture and watches as he drinks from my belly button, follows the stream down.

Carefully, Genevieve pulls the glass from between my thighs, making sure her fingers touch more than they should as she drags the glass along.

"The tequila must have gotten into her panties," she says, "they're certainly wet."

The singer giggles; the bass player coughs into his hand.

Robert pulls my panties down. He pulls my legs open a little more, then tastes me.

A flash of memory, Mr. Dade touching my clit with a Scotch-drenched ice cube that first night I met him. I close my eyes . . . bite down on the lime. It's the same sensation but so much more powerful under the watchful eyes of these strangers.

My hips instinctually rise to him; my back arches. Again I hear the whispered voice of the singer as I moan.

But he pulls away right before bringing me to the point of climax. My breathing is erratic as I feel his lips move up my hips, along my waist, over my breast and throat until he reaches my mouth and takes the lime. When the juice has been tasted, he hands the lime to Genevieve, who obediently takes it, her eyes running up and down the length of me as Robert leans in again for a kiss. The taste of tequila and sex overwhelm me, making my mouth water. I feel Genevieve's fingers caressing my leg, gently touching my sex.

"I bet she's stunning when she comes," a man's voice says. In my peripheral vision I can see the bass player has moved closer. He's younger than I thought. No more than twenty-three, his wide-eyed innocence gives away his inexperience.

Robert pulls away, smiles again. "May he touch you?"

I don't say a word. Not yes, not no, but in the silence is my consent.

Genevieve steps away as the bass player steps forward; his fingers only touch my inner thigh briefly before rising to my clit.

A jolt of electricity makes me jump. But his solicitations continue as Robert kisses my shoulders, my breasts. I feel this man's fingers moving faster and faster and I moan again. The singer has moved very close now. I see that she stands next to Genevieve, whose hand is around her waist, touching her softly as she watches me.

I can feel that I'm about to come. I cry out softly but again Robert stops me, sharply telling the man to step away. "Only for me," he explains. "She only comes for me." And with that it's his fingers that are touching me, not just playing but entering my body, first one, then two. There's no waiting anymore. The orgasm comes hard and shakes my whole body from the inside out.

In an instant his shirt is off as well, then his pants; he's naked as he climbs on top of me, entering me in front of this small group of employees.

Because in the end, that's what they are, I realize. They're the people Robert hires and fires, the people he would give me similar authority over. The power lies with Robert and me, here on this bar as he enters me again and again. They watch with awe and excitement, privileged to be included in this moment.

I wrap my legs around his waist. The bar is wide but I do wonder if we can maintain this balance. At what point do we go too far, forget ourselves, fall to the floor?

But that doesn't happen. Robert holds us in place. It's as if our will alone keeps us from falling. I hear him groan as my nails run up and down his back. This is no longer submission. The fear has stepped aside, giving us room to revel in the aphrodisiac of power.

"She's magnificent," sighs the singer.

Yes, magnificent. Just like in the boardroom. I feel it. I *know* it. In this moment I'm absolutely sure he's right about everything. I was shy, slow to see the brilliance of my situation. I can do anything. *Anything*. We make the rules. No one else. Just us.

"This is the only price," he breathes into my ear, "to be inside your power."

"Yes," I whisper back and my body starts to shake once more. This orgasm builds slowly, with each thrust. I feel his hands, his mouth, their eyes . . . I feel him grinding inside of me. When I come, he comes with me, no longer able to hold out for another minute. Together we raise our voices and our audience collectively sighs.

I know they want to touch me again. The singer looks as if she wants to touch Robert. But they're not allowed. We've made fear our lover, power our foundation . . .

. . . and we make all the rules.

✿

# CHAPTER 39

I WAKE UP THE next morning next to Robert, in his bed, with another hangover. This one isn't alcohol induced; it's the hangover you're left with when the world changes under your feet, when there's a rewiring of the mind. Everything is different today. I don't fear Fear. I've done things I never thought I would or could and now, if I can do that . . . if I can let myself submit like that, is it so outrageous to think that I can master? Isn't it almost required in order for me to keep the balance? Because if I don't exercise my dominance in other areas of my life, I will feel weak and controlled. I won't let that happen. Not anymore.

I rise from the bed with a new, more primitive energy. Robert watches without saying a word as I make my way to the master bath. I think I smell Genevieve's perfume on my skin, the bass player's cologne . . . a menagerie of lovers. They possessed me but, then again, they themselves are possessed. One word from me could have stopped them. One word from me could destroy them.

I wash them off me under the warm streaming water of Robert's shower. My head is clearing. I know how today needs to begin.

Robert doesn't join me in the shower. Somehow he senses it wouldn't be right. When I return to his bedroom, I see that there are garment bags with new clothes in them for me. Nothing too revealing. A one-hook off-white blazer with matching relaxed trousers. A deep blue camisole makes it pop. It's all perfectly appropriate; the only thing that makes it out of the ordinary is the attitude of the woman who will wear it. I see it when I put the suit on. When

I look in the mirror, the vision I see is one of determination. In my off-white suit and conservatively cut trousers I am anything but conservative.

When I go upstairs, Robert hands me a travel mug of coffee, kisses me gently on the cheek. "My board has decided to contract your firm for further consulting."

It's a misleading statement. The decision was always Robert's. In the end the board will always follow his lead. But I know that in this instance there was no argument or resentment. My ideas were sound; the path I had pointed them toward, a good one.

"Have you had any problems with anyone else at your work?" he asks. "Did getting rid of Tom bring the rest of them in line?"

I think of Mr. Costin. We could destroy him, too. And Asha? Will she be a problem? Regardless, I should tell Robert that everything is fine. I should play fair.

I sip my coffee and smile. "We'll see how it goes today," I say vaguely. "If there's a problem, I'll let you know."

As I gather up my things it occurs to me that I mean it. If necessary, I'll tell him about the people who try to undermine me, let the chips fall where they may.

WHEN I ARRIVE at my firm, I don't go straight to my office. Instead I go to Mr. Costin. His assistant tries to stop me, tells me to wait but she has no power over me. No one does, except Robert Dade.

That thought sits with me funny; it raises my fur, intensifies my need to flex my muscles, flaunt my strength. I throw open the door to Mr. Costin's office, catching him with his teeth half submerged in a jelly donut. His eyes widen with rage as he registers my impertinence.

I slam the door behind me as he drops the donut onto a paper plate.

"You have no right—" he begins, but I have no patience for his admonishments.

"You don't want me here," I say coolly. "Not in your office, not in this building, and certainly not in my new job."

"Tom's job," Mr. Costin growls. "Mr. Love to you."

"No," I say with a shake of my head. "It was his job, now it's mine. And you know what? In the end this firm will be stronger for my rise. You don't have to like it but the innuendo and disrespect will stop."

Mr. Costin leans back in his chair. "Or what?"

"Or you will regret it every day of your life." I walk around the desk, reach forward, and brush some powdered sugar from his lapel. "Please don't misjudge this situation. What happened to Tom wasn't a fluke; it was a warning."

"What are you saying? Are you asking me to fear you?" Mr. Costin asks. He means the words to be challenging but there's a slight crack in his voice that reveals everything I need to know.

"I don't have to ask for what I already have," I say simply. "You're still the boss. I will follow your directives. But remember, the way Tom treated me was unacceptable. I could have sued him for sexual harassment and I'm sure I'm not the only one. There was no lawsuit, only the threat of one. You should be grateful for that. You should be grateful that I haven't brought you down, too. At least not yet."

"You would bring down this whole company just to serve your own interests!"

"Don't be ridiculous." I calmly walk back around the desk and sit opposite him. "As long as I have this job, my best interests and the company's best interests are synonymous. It's you who compromises the company when you deliberately try to undermine my effectiveness. You say your choices were taken away but that's not really true, is it? You could have offered this job to someone else. It would have been a huge risk but you could have done it. You didn't. And now I'm here. You can't erase me. You no longer have that power."

I hesitate for just a split second after the words leave my mouth. My light is brighter now; it's even a bit glaring and harsh, but it's not a supernova. I can maintain this. All these years I've tried to play by others' rules in order to keep myself from being erased like my sister was, but Robert's shown me another way.

His is a scarier path, and I'm not entirely comfortable with it . . . but I can see now that it's much more effective than anything I've tried before. This aggression, this power play? It will keep me visible and in turn it will be my protection against falling to my sister's fate. A possibility that haunts me every day of my life.

"You fucked a client," Mr. Costin says. "There are consequences for that."

"Of course there are." I smile and slowly spread my arms out in an all-encompassing gesture. "You're looking at them, Mr. Costin. Guess the consequences I live with are only the ones I want. Maybe that's what I get for attracting the attention of an earthly god. Your words, not mine."

Mr. Costin stares at me; his mouth is in a thin line, hinting at the hate he knows he must hold back. I smile again. He'll see my smile as patronizing, or perhaps smug. It doesn't matter though. I can smile any way I like. These are my rules.

I get up to leave. I've made my point, but as I start to turn Mr. Costin stops me.

"You aren't the one pulling the strings here. That would be your lover, Mr. Dade."

I turn, lock him in my gaze. "Mr. Dade is my lover," I admit. "To my mind he's the moon and I'm the ocean. You can blame the moon for the high tide but it's the ocean that can flood your village. You'd be wise to respect us both. Oh, and Mr. Costin?" I say as I turn back toward the door. "That's the last reference you will make to my sex life. Ever."

And with that I walk out and go down to my office.

My new office. Where I belong.

THE DAY IS MINE. I call impromptu meetings with each department individually. It's not how it's normally done but things are changing based on my whims. Last night I submitted; today I master. Yin and yang. I can thrive in the extremes if I keep the balance.

It's while I'm having a meeting with my old team that I get the call from the VP of Maned Wolf. As Robert had indicated earlier, they have another project for me, if I want it. They want me involved of course but they understand that I won't be in the thick of it like I was the last time. After all, I have many teams to oversee. My job now is not just to lead but to pick leaders.

Asha looks at me expectantly, understanding everything from my half of the conversation. I look into her dark brown eyes and recall all the other ways she's looked at me. With amusement, cruelty, even superiority. . . . I remember when she stood by my side, touching me without invitation, saying things she knew would demean me and make me feel small and vulnerable to her.

I hang up the phone and tell Dameon that he will be team leader. I see the looks of surprise on the consultants' faces. Before my promotion Asha and I were the two people in this group who had the most seniority and accomplishments. Asha had trained Dameon once upon a time. He continues to pay dues that Asha has long since dispensed with. Asha's brown skin picks up a rosy hue and her mouth turns down into a little grimace as I hand Dameon the scepter. She's always so composed, even this small giveaway is a victory.

"What's wrong, Asha?" I ask, unable to restrain myself.

"Not a thing," she replies. She doesn't want to show her aggrievement in front of her coworkers. That would be a sign of weakness.

But she will show that weakness, she'll hang it out for the entire team to see. She'll do so because I want her to.

I lean back in my chair. "I believe the lady doth protest too much. Do you have a problem with Dameon being your superior?"

I've chosen my words carefully.

Asha registers this and shifts slightly in her seat. "I don't have a problem with Dameon being team leader."

"That's not what I asked," I say, swiveling back and forth in my chair. This chair offers more support than my last. Its design keeps my posture straighter. It suits my mood. "Do you have a problem with Dameon being your superior?"

"No," Asha says. The word is clipped, her anger evident.

"No what?" I ask.

Yes, she's blushing now. I can see it. Who would have thought the malicious could blush.

*You blush all the time.* A little voice says. It's my angel, speaking through the gag I've placed in her mouth. I squirm slightly at her implication but Asha is too caught up in her own humiliation to notice as she answers, "No, I don't have a problem with Dameon being my superior."

Now it's Dameon who sits a little straighter. He smiles at Asha, his eyes impertinent, his gaze a little insulting. Asha turns redder still. I wrinkle my nose. I went too far and now the scent of this revenge is more sour than sweet.

"We're done here," I say quickly. "Dameon, I'll have someone from Maned Wolf call you with more details about the project."

"Of course, Miss Fitzgerald." His voice is deep with respect. I can tell he still wants me but he's also a little afraid of me. He would never make a move unless I told him to.

He doesn't feel that way about Asha. She'll have problems with him. I could help her with that . . . if I felt like it.

I watch as they all file out of my office and wonder how it's possible.

How is it possible that I never fully appreciated the symbiotic relationship between fear and power? Not just the fear of those who have to follow me but my own fear that inspires me to lead?

Fear motivates and encourages me like an admiring lover.

Like Robert Dade.

## CHAPTER 40

I DON'T GO HOME. There's no point, not when I can stay with him, in his home that is bigger than mine, in his bed that offers me pleasures and satisfaction. When I arrive, he's wearing a dark suit and a thick white dress shirt with no tie. Formality and accessibility in one look. A beguiling contrast.

But the rest of his preparations give me pause. His dining room table is covered in white linen. There's a place setting for two and candles in the center of the table. It's clichéd romance more appropriate for love marked with rose petals and midnight walks than one defined by power plays and sexual deviance.

He reads the skepticism in my eyes and laughs it away. "We can have quiet moments of traditionalism on occasion. We can have anything we want."

This makes me laugh, too, as I pull nervously at the sleeve of my blazer. My confidence falters when it's just the two of us.

"Not that it's necessary," he says, "but would you like to change for dinner?"

I look down at my white suit. Images of red wine and olive oil dance through my head. "Yes," I say definitively, "I believe I would."

"I assumed as much," he says, his laughter subsiding to a teasing smile. "I bought you something else today. A dress. It's on my bed waiting for you."

I'm about to say something when I hear someone in the kitchen.

"We're not alone?" Even my question makes me tremble a bit. Memories of being ravished in that bar . . . it had been so intense, frightening, exhilarating. . . . I don't know if I can do that two nights in a row. I don't think I want to.

But if he asked me to, would I? Is that what's needed to maintain the balance? Must I submit every night?

Yet when Robert reaches for my hand his touch is reassuring, not demanding. "It's the chef and his assistant. I hired them for the night. They'll cook for us; that's all."

The relief is stronger than I thought it could be. I grab his shoulders and kiss his lips gently with only a touch of passion. "Thank you."

"Thank me for the dress," he says quietly. "The night's events are set by your moods as much as my ambitions. I'm just better at recognizing them than you are."

I'm not sure I understand his meaning but that's okay. At the moment everything is okay.

Downstairs the dress is red. Red like the words painted on the door of the speakeasy, red as Genevieve's hair, red as a ruby.

The last thought disturbs me. I haven't thought of Dave for a while now. He's fading further and further into my past. How much of what I remember of my relationship with him is real and how much only reflects the reality that works best for me? Memories evolve quickly, more like a virus than an animal. This year's flu bears little resemblance to the flu that killed so many only a few years back. The virus evolves, we've taken our shots, and now it can't hurt us the way it once could . . . back when it looked different, back before we were prepared.

I slide into the dress. It's made of velvet, a fabric I usually think of as tacky and outdated, like something you would see in a 1970s rendition of the *Nutcracker*, although even that wouldn't work since the dancers would sweat too much.

But this dress is different. It's higher quality, the fabric mixed with layers of silk that hang in a cowl neckline and adorn the very low back. The designer is Antonio Berardi. He's redefined the fabric, given it a fierce modern edge, made it sensual and daring.

For a brief moment I wonder if Robert Dade has redesigned me.

I quickly discard the idea and go upstairs.

Robert is already sitting at the table, waiting for me. A bottle of champagne has been opened yet again but this time it's poured by a man in a white chef's jacket. He gives me a deferential nod as Robert rises to pull out my chair.

"You look magnificent."

"There's that word again," I say lightly.

"It suits you." He kisses me on top of my head like a father. It makes me feel safe.

He sits down, raises his glass in toast. "To us."

It's the most common toast in the world. Right up there with "Cheers," and "À ta santé!" But the words seem more loaded coming from Robert's lips. For what does it mean, "us"? We are not Romeo and Juliet. We are Caesar and Cleopatra. We're Henry VIII and Anne Boleyn, Pierre and Marie Curie. Our coupling has consequences, people's lives will be changed. . . .

Like Tom and Dave and Asha and Mr. Costin; for them our romance is as radioactive as anything the Curies cooked up in their lab.

And Cleopatra, Anne, Marie—each one of them was destroyed by the fate they pursued. Each undone by their passions and power. Pierre and Caesar didn't fare much better . . . and then there was Henry.

I study Robert over my champagne glass. Could Robert ever turn on me? I've watched him casually destroy Tom; he's offered to destroy others. What would it take for him to decide to destroy me?

The man in the chef's coat is back. He places a small serving of venison carpaccio in front of each of us. The venison has been seared with a light vinaigrette that smells of rosemary and it's topped with porcini *panna cotta*, a dark red coulis, beetroot, and a sprinkling of shaved Parmesan, culinary adornments that do nothing to detract from the fact that what we're about to eat is raw. A living thing that we kill and consume simply because it suits our tastes. My fork hesitates before piercing the meat. I meet Robert's eyes as he takes his first mouthful.

"Not hungry?" he asks.

I pause for only a moment before admitting the truth. "I'm famished." And I eat what's been served. And I savor it, enjoy it; with each bite I find myself less and less concerned about the symbolism, the moral implications. I like it. That's enough.

"How is the transition going?"

"Mr. Costin was uncomfortable with my promotion at first," I say, my mouth partially full, "but he understands the score now. I'm getting a better sense of all the departments and those who once saw me as a coworker have already come to see me as a boss." I take a sip of the champagne. "I have them all in line."

The last line was delivered as a joke . . . sort of.

"Good. Tell me if Costin gives you any problems. Or Freeland for that matter."

Our plates are cleared; a second small course is served. "It's funny," I say as I pierce the fricassee mushrooms, "I haven't seen Freeland for some time. I mean he hasn't really been a hands-on partner for a while but still, he used to do the occasional walk-through. Stop in to say hello to all the managers, make sure they're still appreciative of his position. But I haven't seen him in weeks."

"Yes," Robert says, "that's strange."

But the way he says it tells me that he doesn't think it's strange at all.

I sit back in my chair. "Do you know something?"

Robert raises his eyebrows. "Yes," he says softly, "I know something."

I imitate his expression, raising my eyebrows and cocking my head mockingly. "Do tell, Mr. Dade."

"I know that your company was in trouble. Tom wasn't a bad businessman from what I've heard but he wasn't innovative or hands-on. None of the managers there are . . . or at least they weren't. You'll do a better job. Tell me, did you call meetings with each of your departments yet?"

"How did you know about that?"

"I know your style," he says simply. "I know that you won't take anything for granted. You'll learn the ins and outs of each department, you'll find ways for your people to differentiate themselves from the other consultants in the industry."

"You're quite confident in me," I say, wondering if it's entirely merited.

"Your recommendations for Maned Wolf were brilliant," he continues. "You said things that others wouldn't dare suggest. People often worry about recommending layoffs or the dismantling or reorganization of entire departments. The corporate world isn't nearly as ruthless as some assume. We carry around deadweight out of sentimentality and attachment to old ideas. We take pride in innovations that were introduced so long ago, they're no longer innovative at all. Polaroid, MySpace, Hostess, BlackBerry, all the same story. But you"—he smiles, takes another bite—"you're like me. You're not sentimental."

I shift slightly in my seat. I've been told that before, never as a compliment. "I can be a little—"

"No. If you were sentimental, you would have asked Dave for a diamond. You would have pictures on your desk. You'd be a different person with different potential and I'd want little to do with you."

The touch of velvet against my skin does little to soften the impact of his words. The things this man likes about me . . . they're not the right things . . . are they?

"You walked into the Maned Wolf boardroom and told us what you believed we should do," he says as the chef clears away his plate once again. "You didn't hold back because you're *not* sentimental and because you knew that your job wasn't in jeopardy. Like a president in his final term, you forged ahead without feeling the need to weigh the political consequences. Now you'll have that same freedom in every aspect of your job. You'll move up quickly there, do what needs to be done. There will be casualties. Jobs will be lost, but in the end that firm will owe us both a debt of thanks."

I push away my champagne. "You make me sound cold," I whisper.

"No," he corrects, "I make you sound strong."

I think back on my day as yet another dish arrives, lamb rib eye, rich decadence delicately served. Mr. Costin had been sentimental about Tom. I'm sure of it. But maybe Robert's right. Maybe that sentimentality provided cover for a weakness. A lack of creativity, an inability to see the full picture. I had always admired Tom's business sense, but did I ever imagine him taking the business world by storm as I dream of doing? No.

We finish our meal slowly, ending it with tastes of bitter chocolate and fruity sorbet.

Each course had been small but so perfect. The chefs clean up as we finish off the bottle of champagne. In the end Robert thanks them, pays them, and sends them on their way. I feel light-headed. I take his hand, bring his palm to my mouth, and place a kiss there.

"It's just the two of us now."

"It always is," he says. "Even when there are others, it's just the two of us."

That's an easy way to look at it, lazy in its inaccuracy but I like the way it sounds. I hold on to his hand, lead him down the stairs to the bedroom. He watches me as I release him, as I walk around to the other side of the bed. I let my own eyes travel the length of him. Even his jacket can't hide his muscular build. His broad shoulders, his powerful arms, the perfect predator. The maned wolf.

"I want you," I say quietly. "Every part of you. Your generosity, your savagery, your romance and your pragmatism, even your ruthless ambition."

"*Even* my ruthless ambition?"

"Especially your ruthless ambition." I laugh. But then my tone grows serious. "I want it all. You say you want to be inside my power?" I reach out to him. "Let me put my arms around yours."

The smile on his lips is almost sad, almost wistful. "Very well," he says. He takes off his jacket, walks to me, but he stops when he's two feet away. "You want it all? Take it."

I step forward, unbutton his shirt, and pull it off him. Then comes his belt. He lets me strip it all away as he stands there, compliant and willing until he's completely naked and open. I press the velvet of my dress against his bare skin. I run my fingers through his short hair, pull him into a kiss as his hands move to the small of my back. I feel him grow hard against me. He's letting me take the lead tonight, letting me flex my newfound strength.

I pull away, cup his cheek in my palm before taking another small step back so I can look at him again, at my leisure. I take his cock in my palm, move my hand up and down until it colors with excitement. "Is that for me?" I whisper.

He smiles again but this time the melancholy is gone. "Always," he answers.

I let go, raise my hands to his shoulders, and then give him a gentle push, which he gives in to, falling back on the bed. "If it's mine, then it's mine to taste."

I get down on the floor, kneel between his legs as I take him in my mouth. I let my tongue outline the head of his penis, teasing the nerve endings until he moans. My tongue then travels down the length of him slowly, one centimeter at a time as his agitation mounts. My fingers gently stroke the delicate flesh at the base as my mouth continues its journey down and then finally back up again at the same torturous pace before steadily increasing my speed. He moans again, though this time the sound is more guttural, animalistic. When he starts to shake I stop and rise to my feet. He immediately sits up and reaches for me, but I stay just out of his grasp.

"This is velvet," I explain. "Such a delicate fabric. You're not allowed to touch it."

"I did pay for that dress," he manages, his breathing uneven, his voice hoarse.

"And you gave it to me," I reply smoothly. "You will never be able to take back what you give, not from me. I won't let you."

Slowly, with a quiet pageantry, I remove the dress, my bra, my panties. I straddle him, my knees pressing against his hips, but I don't lower myself onto his lap. Not yet.

"Show me who you are," I whisper. "Not just the power."

I see a flicker of something in his eyes, something that looks a lot like fear. But it's gone in an instant as he jumps to life; grabs me, turns with me in his arms, pressing my back into the firm mattress and diving inside of me with a fierce, unrestrained energy. And as always I give in to it completely. I wrap my arms around him, feel him as he reaches further into my depths than any other man ever has.

And then something happens; he moves a lock of hair from my face, looks into my eyes as he moves inside of me. Gently, delicately, he traces the line of my mouth with his fingers. And I see another flash—this time it's vulnerability, a need that can't quite be drowned out by this flood of primitive desire. I'm seeing something different here, something I've only had glimpses of before. I put my hand on his chest and feel the beat of his turmoil.

It's only a moment but it's enough. When he drags my leg over his shoulder and thrusts inside of me, even deeper now, the intensity is off the chart. I've seen something I'm sure very few others have seen and the forbidden nature of the reveal has brought our ecstasy to new heights. He bites down on my shoulder as my hips rise to meet him. I smell his sweat, the scent of our mingled desire.

Suddenly he stops and flips me over on my stomach. I spread my legs expectantly but he pulls away. I try to make sense of what's happening as he gets up and stands at the end of the bed. But there's no time. In a moment he's grabbed my thighs in his hands and he's dragging me down the mattress, toward the edge of the bed until he is standing between my legs, which are now supported by nothing but his hands, with my hips and torso still on the bed. And that's when he enters me again. I can't see him, but I can feel every inch of him. With my legs in the air I feel weightless, grounded only by him. His pace is aggressive, as if he can't get enough of me, and with each thrust the world seems to shake. My fingernails scrape the tangled bedsheets as I try to find something to keep me from floating away in a wave of ecstasy as the second orgasm overtakes me.

But we're not done. This time it's my turn to pull away. I turn to him and drag him back down on the bed, climbing on top of him once more. I'm shaky now, still reeling from the heights of passion he's brought me to, but I manage to regain enough control to reset our rhythm. I throw my head back as I ride him, his hands on my waist. Again, I start to tremble but I only move faster. The orgasm has me in its grips but somehow I keep moving as the fire inside me rages, warming me, making me ache with a unique satisfaction, a special triumph as he joins me in this climax, coming inside me in a tender explosion.

And as I collapse on top of him, my breathing erratic and gasping like a runner who has just finished a sprint, I wonder, what is the true nature of the prize I've claimed?

I wonder if I'll ever know.

CHAPTER 41

❀

T HE DAYS BEGIN to take on a certain pulse. I'm getting better and better at my job. Even Mr. Costin's forced display of
respect has taken on a genuine quality. Asha no longer challenges
me, at least not with her words, although when I see her, in the
hall, in a meeting, driving past me in the garage, I always feel her
almond-shaped eyes on me, studying me, calculating, looking for
the weak spot where she can sink the blade. I don't blame her. I had
my chance at revenge and I took it. I made her pay. Why should she
be different? The only thing that separates us now is opportunity.

Today's Friday and I'm going over the new accounts coming in,
strategizing on how to reach businesses that have yet to reach out to
us. The impossible is beginning to feel normal. I don't stop and stare
every time I pass a mirror anymore. I don't fret over my increasingly frequent little displays of aggression and ruthlessness. It's all
part of the game and the game is part of who I am now.

I've been practically living with Robert. Each night he surprises
me. Last night he greeted me with a glass of expensive Scotch, a
reminder of our beginnings. He had prepared a milk bath, like the
ones Cleopatra had once indulged in. I had stepped inside, naked,
watching as the cream enveloped me, feeling the way it lapped
against my skin, between my legs, as Robert had carefully moved
a bath mitt over my back, kissed my shoulders, fed me grapes that
were such a dark shade of purple they were almost black. I had
closed my eyes when he moved to wash my stomach. His hand had
moved down my thighs, then up again, back and forth, until he fi-

nally, gently, touched my sex, building the ecstasy until the creamy sensuality of the milk and the burst of the grape became perfect analogies to the juices and explosions of my own body.

Last night he blindfolded me, tied me to the bed, made it so I was unable to experience anything other than the feeling of him, the touch of his fingers, the sound of his breathing, the smell of his aftershave, even the tickle of his five-o'clock shadow. Helpless, yearning, aching . . . and all for him. In that moment he was my world.

I stay at my place only when I have Simone over. I don't know why but bringing her to Robert's is an idea I've yet to become comfortable with. That part of my life is too private for me to share with my best friend, I suppose . . . or maybe I'm not ready for her to see what I'm like when I'm with him. Simone's not the sort to judge, but this change in me . . . she'll at least have an opinion on it, and I'm not sure I'm ready to hear what that opinion is.

I still haven't told my parents about Dave. In fact, I haven't even called them since the breakup and that was . . . well, a lifetime ago. They've called me a few times but I either don't pick up or I come up with an excuse that requires me to cut the call short. So we've been communicating through e-mails and we've exchanged a text or two, but I've revealed nothing. I haven't even told them about my new job and I'm certainly not prepared to tell them how I got it—as far as they're concerned I'm still their perfect daughter doing all the things they have always wanted me to do. They don't know about the change. They don't know that the woman they know as their daughter is almost unrecognizable. It's almost as if she's gone.

Almost.

My hand shakes, just slightly, as these thoughts move through my mind but I quickly discard the contemplations and open another file. My security blanket is still made up of decimals and dollar signs and I find myself immediately soothed as I lose myself in their concrete comfort.

Yes, everything is fine.

• • •

I KNOW ROBERT is going to be working late tonight. He's meeting with his engineers and marketers, who are preparing for the launch of a new and improved security system for individuals' financial accounts, something to protect us when the retailers we shop with have their systems hacked by cyber-criminals. If it works, it will change the world . . . for those who can afford the change.

I decide to go out to dinner by myself. I haven't done that for some time. I can go anywhere. I can eat at Urasawa, arguably the most expensive restaurant in LA and possibly the country, or Mélisse, a restaurant even the French admire for its quality of cuisine and ambiance. Getting a table at these places is normally impossible but if I call Robert, he'll ensure they have a table waiting for me. He's already given me power and wealth, what's a dinner reservation?

But I don't take advantage of his influence. Not tonight, not for dinner. Instead I go to Chipotle. I don't know why—other than that its middle-class appeal and bare-bones décor offer a certain comfort of their own. There's no pretense here, no airs; just decent, reasonably healthy food at basement prices. It's a simple formula that has all the elements for corporate success and, well, corporate success makes me happy.

So I order an Izze and a burrito bowl with a side of guac and find a clean table in the corner where I can enjoy my meal undisturbed.

I'm only halfway through my bowl when Dave walks in.

Dave. My former fiancé, the man who almost broke me before I turned and broke his heart, the man who wanted to control me, mold me into the perfect Martha's Vineyard–style wife, the man who values image and refinement above all else . . .

. . . the man who normally wouldn't be caught dead in a Chipotle.

I study him from my corner as he gets in line. He doesn't look good. There are dark circles under his eyes. He hasn't shaved in a day, maybe even two. And he's wearing jeans, not a suit. Dave lives in suits during the week. It's barely six o'clock. There's simply no way he went home and changed just so he could drive back into the city to go to Chipotle.

And yet he's here.

He shuffles his feet a little as he moves through the line. I wait until it's his turn to order before I get up, move closer without his noticing as he struggles to explain himself to the eighteen-year-old in the black shirt and white apron.

"I want a wrap . . . or, I guess you call them burritos here? Can I get one with meat that isn't spicy; are they all spicy?"

"Get the pork."

He turns, startled by the sound of my voice. His face colors once he registers that yes, I'm really here, seeing him like this.

"The pork isn't spicy," I explain. When he doesn't answer, I look to his server. "He'll have the carnitas burrito with brown rice and black beans."

The employee nods and complies. I walk Dave through Chipotle's version of a burrito assembly line, instructing them to put in the mild salsa, light on the guacamole, no cheese, no cream. Dave lets me lead him through this foreign ritual without comment, moving like a man who is only partially awake. He doesn't protest when I pay or lead him back to my table.

We sit across from each other in silence for a full minute.

"You've changed," he finally says.

The observation seems comically ironic. His face seems to have aged ten years in four weeks. I have loved this man and I have hated him but right now the only emotion I can muster is concern . . . and curiosity.

"Did you come here from the office?" I ask. Obviously he didn't but the question feels like a safe place to start.

He shakes his head, wraps his mouth around the burrito, and chews.

"So you didn't work today?" I press.

He stares at me, his blue eyes are dulled with exhaustion. "You know the answer to that."

"How could I possibly—"

"I was fired."

"Oh, Dave, I'm so sor—"

"Spare me! You're the one who got me fired. You and your new lover."

The air changes quality; the voices of the patrons around us diminish to an unintelligible hum.

"I didn't know," I whisper.

"No one else will hire me. He's seen to that. I've been blackballed."

"Why are you so sure Robert had anything to do with this?"

His eyes flash with something I've seen before.

"You think I got myself fired? You think it's my fault?"

"Dave—"

Patrons are beginning to look over in our direction. "You think that the moment I lost you I became incompetent?" he shouts. "That I'm unable to live without you even now that I know you're a whore?"

I sigh audibly, my sympathy sliding to the floor like a forgotten paper napkin. This is the version of Dave I know. This is the man I hated. But I don't hate him anymore. Now he just bores me.

I stand up, no longer hungry. "Enjoy your dinner," I say. "Next time your treat."

He keeps his head bowed; I can't see his face but I can visualize the scowl. I've seen it before, no need to retrace my steps on this muddy road. He mutters something that I think is meant for me but I can't quite make it out.

"What was that?" I ask impatiently.

He looks up with bloodshot eyes; the scowl I expected isn't there. What is there is much more disturbing.

"Help me," he whispers. "Please, Kasie. He's taken everything."

I feel a tightening in my chest; slowly I lower myself back to my seat.

"They're saying I embezzled money. That's why they made me leave. They accused me of being a thief."

"You would never—"

"You're right, I wouldn't. I wouldn't risk it. It's not who I am."

Somewhere in the restaurant there is a baby crying, screaming the way babies do when they need to communicate their pain without words. "Are they pressing charges?" I ask.

"No, they said if I left voluntarily, they wouldn't. But they promised me they could prove it, they showed me evidence . . . it's fake but even to me it looked real. These people, they know me, they trained me, promised me a future. They know I'm being set up . . . and they don't care. The club I used to belong to? They revoked my membership. They won't tell me why. These were my friends . . . I thought they were my friends." He looks down at his hands folded in his lap, the carnitas burrito mangled and unappealing on a paper plate. "Help me," he whispers again.

I shake my head. I feel dizzy. Robert couldn't be responsible for this. Would he even have that power?

Of course he did. It's like Mr. Costin said, Robert sits on the boards of many of the city's major businesses and is a major stockholder in the rest. He was able to get women from several of the companies that contract with my firm to make false accusations against Tom. Why couldn't he do the same thing to Dave? It fit the pattern.

And for the first time I realize that this is probably a pattern that started when he saw similar things done to his father.

But *would* he do it? What would be the point? Even if he didn't share in my compassion for this man, there are still other things that would stop him, right? After all, Robert knows I don't want Dave talking to my parents and although Dylan Freeland must know something about what went down by now I really don't need Dave filling in the details. If Robert had stripped Dave of everything he cared about, it would leave me vulnerable to his attacks . . .

. . . which leads me to another realization.

"You didn't tell," I breathe. "You had every reason to betray me and you didn't."

He laughs; it's an ugly sound, heavy with misery and derision. "Don't mistake me for something I'm not. I haven't learned benevolence in the time we've been apart. I went to Dylan."

"But that's not possible; Mr. Freeland would have—"

"Dylan Freeland has always been like a father to me," Dave says in a frightening monotone. "He's always been there for me. I love him, Kasie."

His voice shakes at this last part. I almost reach for him but stop myself, unsure if our history makes such intimacies prohibited. So instead I just nod sympathetically. "I know," I say.

"He's broken. I don't know what your Mr. Dade has on him—"

"Wait, you're saying it's more than just the threat of losing business—"

"Does he enjoy it?" he asks, cutting me off. "Diminishing Dylan like that? Making him feel so weak that he can't even make decisions for his own company? So weak that instead of helping his godson he tells him to keep quiet. He basically told me that if I know what's good for me, I'll tuck my tail between my legs and slink off before more of Robert Dade's wrath is brought down. So does Mr. Dade get off on the dominance?" He hesitates only a moment before adding, "Do you?"

I keep very still, unwilling to react to what might be a lie. And it could be; Dave has always been a liar. Still . . . there's something to this story. . . .

Why hasn't Mr. Freeland been at the firm for a while? Tom being fired, my promotion . . . Mr. Costin had scolded me for it, he was willing to take that risk, but not Mr. Freeland. I cheated on his godson and he hadn't so much as sent me an angry e-mail.

Why?

*Dave is telling you why,* my angel says, *you just don't want to hear.*

My throat tightens. "Have you told my parents? I understand if you did. I—"

Again there's the humorless laugh that prickles my heart. "I won't tell your parents. Believe it or not, I value my life, what little is left of it."

Again the baby screams. "Your *life*? Are you trying to tell me that your safety has been threatened?" I whisper.

Again Dave bows his head. I think I see a tear. "What if they push the embezzlement charge?"

"You just said they wouldn't if you left."

"But they *could*. Don't you get it? I'm completely at their mercy and they're following his directives. I know it, Kasie. I don't know if he's bribed people or threatened them or what, but they're letting him decide my fate. And he wants to destroy me, Kasie."

"He would never take it that far."

Dave looks up at me, bewildered. I don't blame him; it was a stupid thing to say. I don't *think* Robert would take it that far, but then again I didn't think he'd do this, either. Any of it. It never even occurred to me.

I've let Robert Dade change my entire life . . . and I don't even know who he is.

"Do you think I would survive in prison, Kasie?" he asks. "Do you see me getting through a single day in jail?"

No, I don't. Dave is too soft, too vulnerable. Even the tattooed skateboarders on the road along Venice Beach make him nervous. He wouldn't be able to cope with living among drug dealers and pimps.

Another tear slips down Dave's cheek and I wonder if any painter has ever been able to capture the essence of desperation the way Dave's expression does now.

"Help me," he says.

❖

# CHAPTER 42

THIS TIME IT'S me who waits for Robert. I sit in his leather armchair. In my glass there is only water, nothing to soften my edge or dull my intellect. I don't light candles; there is no fire in the fireplace, no velvet dresses or leather ties. Tonight I reject the fantasy. Tonight I want the truth.

When he returns home, he senses it. It takes less than two seconds for him to register that the mood is one of confrontation and not romance, two more seconds for him to adjust.

How does he do that? Make these sharp emotional turns with the agility of a sports car? How can any human being do that?

But then Robert has always been a little more than human. A little more and, oddly, a little less.

"You didn't have to hurt Dave. He wasn't hurting us."

He studies me for a moment as if extracting from my words and the hard line of my mouth the extent of what I know. "He hurt you before," he finally says, calm, unperturbed. "Eventually he would have done it again. All I did was launch a necessary preemptive strike."

"No," I say, shaking my head. "Not everything can be measured in terms of war. We're not fighting a battle."

He smiles ruefully, takes off his coat. "Don't kid yourself. Everybody's always fighting one battle or another. The battlefield changes—the enemies, the allies, even the weapons—but the war wages on."

"I'm not going to live that way."

"You don't have a choice." He sits down on the ottoman, takes my hand. "None of us do. Your only choice is to decide whether you're going to be a victor or a casualty. A foot solider or a commander. These are the choices. I've made mine; I thought you made yours, too."

"Very well, have it your way. Dave and I had a cease-fire, a peace treaty even. We didn't need to be allies. We just needed to leave each other alone. Why did you have to mess with that?" Each one of my words comes out a little faster, a little louder; I feel that I'm close to being hysterical but I suppress it. I have to stay calm.

"Don't tell me you're sentimental about Dave," he says, his tone dangerously close to patronizing.

Robert has never been patronizing. I don't stop to think about what this shift means. All I know is that it pisses me off.

"Sentimentality will get you nowhere in this world," Robert reminds me.

"Right," I say, dragging the word out so my sarcasm shapes it into a different meaning. "You don't like sentimentality. We shouldn't be sentimental about anything. We should just all be vehicles of our own ambitions. We should never lay down our arms, never compromise, never look back."

"It's not a bad way to live," he says softly. "You know that. You've been living by those rules for the last—"

"*Paradise Lost.*"

And there it is. That glimpse of emotion that Robert doesn't like to show. It flies by so fast, I can't read exactly what the emotion is but it was there, and it was something other than ambition.

"I don't understand you," he says slowly. "What does a book have to do with any of this?"

"Not just a book," I correct. "Your mother's book. It's there, on your bookshelf. Why do you have it?"

His jaw tightens; he drops my hand. "I see no reason to throw it out."

"Really?" I stand up, pull the book off the shelf. "It's just a book,

Robert. No need to be sentimental about it." I walk to the fireplace. "Shall we burn it?"

Another flash of emotion, but this one I recognize. It doesn't take long to identify anger. "I don't burn books."

"Paper and cardboard. That's all it is. And it's not like we're burning every copy. Just this one, your mother's copy. Come now, Robert. Be a fighter. We're at war after all. In war there is fire, things are destroyed, books burn." I hold the book inside the grate, over a heap of ash.

"Give me the damn book."

"Your mother was a casualty. She and your father, they lost to more capable opponents. They lost to men like you. You learned so much from those men, those men who set fire to the life your parents had built for themselves, a life they built for *you*. And your takeaway from all of it was to learn to justify evil."

His movements are so quick I barely see him before he's by my side, pulling me away from the fireplace, throwing the book across the room, pulling me to him roughly, his grip so tight it's suffocating. With one hand still around my back he grabs the collar of my blouse, stretching it toward him; the top button pops off, flies across the room.

For the first time ever he reminds me of Dave.

"It's all right," I say. "I understand. This is war. In war women get raped."

Immediately he lets go of me, takes three steps back. "You think I would do that? You think I would hurt you?"

"Oh, Robert, you've done so much more than hurt me. You've destroyed Kasie Fitzgerald. My parents' daughter, she's gone."

"Don't be ridiculous. I helped you discover your true nature!"

I shake my head. "My whole *life* I've been afraid of the kind of rejection that makes a person become invisible. I thought you were protecting me from that," I say, my voice faltering ever so slightly. "But now when I look in the mirror I don't see a woman at all. I see something powerful, merciless, dangerous; something whose moods and actions are determined by the winds, the vibrations of the earth, and the pull of the moon. I see something that has no mind of its own! So I guess . . . I guess there's more than one way to be erased."

"No, these choices you've made, they've been *your* choices. No one forced you to make them."

"My choice was to be obedient. My choice was to be led. But now?" I take another step back from him. "I'm making another choice."

"Kasie . . ." But his voice trails off. For once he doesn't know what to say.

I've already packed up the few things I had here. They wait for me in the trunk of my car. All that's left is for me to gather my purse and coat, both waiting for me on the sofa. I put on the coat, taking my time with each button. I know that if I do it slowly, I'll do it right, I won't fumble. He won't be able to see how shaken I am. If I keep my focus, I might be able to keep the pain behind the mask.

"You have a choice to make, too," I say mildly. "You can take me down the way you took down Tom and Dave. It would be easy to do. You wouldn't even have to lie this time. All you'd have to do is shine a light on the footsteps I've left behind, let them know that the demon who led me no longer offers his protection. Throw me to the wolves. Make me a casualty."

"I would never do that, Kasie."

"No?" The tremor in my voice grows more pronounced. I approach him, stand with less than a foot separating us. I raise my hand, let it graze his cheek. "You've always known how to move me," I whisper. "But I know you now, Robert. I know your nature. It's the nature of a predator."

And then I turn and leave. Nothing else needs to be said. I can't be here. I no longer want to make up the rules as we go. I don't want my waves to crash over my enemies. I want to make another choice.

I want to live like a woman, not an ocean.

✿

# CHAPTER 43

I GET THROUGH THE night, back at my house, alone . . . but, God, it's hard. I want to help Dave. I even want to help Tom now. But I don't know if I can. I certainly can't do it tonight. But I suppose that if Robert has taught me one thing, it's that, when all else fails, help yourself. It's just that now I think that helping myself means making myself better, not through wealth or power, but through the effort of rediscovering my own humanity.

And then the pain . . . in my gut, in my heart, it's overwhelming and keeps me up until dawn. I lost something extraordinary, something that I've come to think of as essential. I lost the moon.

And now it's morning and I'm at work trying to see my coworkers with new eyes. I notice that Barbara is more deferential than she has been in years past, more so than even a month ago. She no longer tries to gossip with me, no longer rolls her eyes when one of the other employees says something silly, not in front of me anyway. I always thought Barbara was a little too familiar anyway but now I find that I miss her casual demeanor. Maybe she respects me more now . . . or maybe she's just scared.

Other people in the office behave similarly. Everyone is polite; many of them go out of their way for me. I've asked for reports from various people and they've all been delivered a day early. Robert would be so proud. I've learned to make fear work for me.

*It's fairly rare that we respect the individual who wields that power over us.*

Simone's words. But if I believe them, if I actually buy in to her whole philosophy on this topic, then I have to accept that I represent the status quo, the norm. I have to accept that despite Robert's influence I'm not exceptional at all.

I sit at my desk, sift through my e-mails. One of the consultants writes to inform me of the three new companies they'll be approaching this month; another reports on the retention rate of the clients we have. The e-mails are so neat and clean. What's being said in the rooms where those e-mails are being written? What are they saying about the woman they address in these messages as Miss Fitzgerald?

*. . . when someone has power over us, we go out of our way to look for that person's flaws. We exaggerate them in our minds and in our gossip.*

Well really, how much exaggeration would be necessary? *She picked him up in Vegas, while playing blackjack, while sipping Scotch, while wearing a dress that revealed all her secrets. She went to his room, where he dabbled the Scotch on her skin, where he tasted her. She called him Mr. Dade.*

*All this while her lover of six years waited for her at home. While he trusted her, while he boasted of her modesty.*

No, no elaboration was needed. Any details they might imagine could not be more salacious than the truth. Barbara buzzes my office, tells me in a polite, clipped voice that a package has arrived. Unreported profits and losses of a client who wouldn't dare risk sending an electronic file out into the wild, robber-ridden west that is our cyberworld.

*We convince ourselves that they're not really deserving. That they're not better than us.*

But I'm not deserving. I'm not better than any of them. Maybe I have the talent and intelligence necessary for the job but I haven't paid the dues. I'm here because I slept with the right men. Everyone knows that.

More e-mails light up my inbox. More reports, more requests for permission to pursue one account or another. All addressed to Miss Fitzgerald, all written with practiced caution.

*We still respect the* power *and we will still bend to it regardless of how we may feel about the hands that hold it.*

I look down at my hands, remember how they feel when they're against Robert's naked skin. I remember the pleasure and the excitement.

I remember how it felt when I first wrapped my hand around his erection, how the ridges rubbed against my palm as I moved my hand up and down.

And I remember how it felt to slip that same hand into Dave's grasp less than a week later when he gently led me to the jeweler where we could shop for a ring.

I close my hand into a fist, turn my head away in disgust. I know how people feel about the hands that hold my power. They're the hands of a slut.

But then again that's not really true, is it? Because it's Robert who holds my power. That's common knowledge. All this time I've fooled myself into believing that people fear and respect the ocean but in the tradition of all the great ancient societies, it's the moon they worship. It's the moon they respect and pay homage to, pray to. The ocean? That's nothing more than a consequence of the greater gods.

This fear I'm banking on, it's fear Robert has loaned me. Once they all find out that Robert is no longer part of my life, what holds it all together?

And how do I live knowing that I will no longer be able to lay my hands on him? How can I breathe without the promise of that sin?

The thought makes me feel slightly ill. I try to focus on other things—the reports, the files, the balance sheets—but in the end my thoughts keep going back to him. I need his guidance, the comfort of his voice.

I look down at the file open in front of me before slamming it closed. Numbers can be comforting but right now I need the distraction of antagonism.

I go down to Asha's office. I don't call ahead first although I should. Her assistant doesn't stop me as I walk to her door, open it without knocking. She's sitting at her desk, poring over a file. Draped over her chair is a fox-fur-trimmed coat, the kind of coat you could never justify a need for here in LA. She looks up at me with her eyes without moving her head, her dark hair hanging loosely over her shoulders. Her lips curl into a slow, sinister smile.

Ah, Asha, I can always count on you to reject fear in favor of hate. I step inside, close the door behind me.

Leisurely, she straightens her posture. "Have you come up with some fresh torture for me today?"

"I could have you fired," I say blandly. "Doesn't that bother you?"

"We've had this conversation, right here in this office. Why retread old ground?" When I don't answer, she presses further. "Why are you here, Kasie?"

I sigh, let my eyes run over her white walls, her dark wood desk. Like me she doesn't have any photos of loved ones and I remark on it.

"I don't take my personal life into work with me," she says simply.

"Do you have a personal life?"

Again she smiles. "Ask me during my personal time."

I nod, although I doubt that she'll ever answer a question she doesn't want to answer regardless of what time it is. "I'm sorry I didn't let you lead the Maned Wolf project," I say, gesturing to the file. "Dameon didn't earn the privilege."

"Don't apologize; it won't do you any good."

The comment takes me by surprise. "You act like you're the one with the upper hand here."

Asha leans back in her chair, swivels back and forth, half thoughtful, half bored. "As you've pointed out a few times, you could have me fired and for a little while there I thought you would. When you gave Dameon the authority that should be mine, I thought you had plans to bring me down slowly, painfully; at least that's what I thought for a second."

"For a second?"

"You know, when you asked me to acknowledge him as my superior. That was quite a move on your part, way up there on the evil scale. Except as soon as you got me to say what you wanted me to say, as soon as I had humiliated myself in front of my coworkers, you got this look on your face—"

"What look?"

"The look of guilt of course." She laughs. "You really want to be bad, you just can't quite carry it off." She stands up, walks around her desk, and props herself on top of it. "I think that's why you're with Mr. Dade. I used to think you were using him to get ahead. But now? Now I think you like him because he gives you permission to be bad, and when you don't take him up on it, he's bad *for* you. He does all your dirty work, pulls you into doing what you want to do but don't dare to initiate. That way you can avoid the guilt . . . or at least that's the theory."

"Your theory?"

"No, no, it's *yours*. My theory is that your theory isn't working out for you. You let him take control, do the things he tells you to do, let him touch you in ways and places you think you should be ashamed of all in the hope that you'll be able to enjoy it without the guilt. But your guilt is a little more tenacious than that. It enslaves you, like it always does."

"*I'm* a slave to my guilt?" I snap. Somehow this accusation more than all the others pisses me off. "Tom is gone. I haven't campaigned for him to get his job back. I haven't let Mr. Costin shame me. I haven't apologized to anyone—"

"You just apologized to me."

I stand there with my mouth slightly open. She's got me there.

And she knows it. She stands up, crosses to me, takes her hands and pulls my hair back off my shoulders. "Why the fascination with me? Is it because you want to be me?"

"Don't be ridiculous."

"Because I live without guilt. I know what I want, and I don't agonize over it. Sometimes I don't get it right away, sometimes it takes a while, but I can be patient and when I need to be, I can be ruthless while smiling." She drops my hair, steps back, and lets her eyes move up and down my body until I cross my arms over my chest protectively. "If I had been in your position during our last meeting, I would have made you call Dameon your superior, too. But I wouldn't have felt bad about it. Then I would have found a way to arrange yet another meeting, just the three of us."

"Why would you want to do that?"

"Because I'd want Dameon to see what I could do to you." She reaches out again, lets her fingers rest against my throat, slide down to the curve of my breast. I step back.

I step back . . . but not away. I'm not shouting at her or threatening her. I simply step back. If fear is my lover, then here in Asha's office it masters me, makes my heart race, keeps me there with its dark allure.

"Can you imagine it?" Asha asks. "If Dameon was sitting right there"—she looks back at her desk and seems to make eye contact with eyes that aren't there—"imagine how he'd react if he saw you jump when I do this." Her hand moves forward again, between my legs; again I jump and step back.

"Imagine if he saw that," she says again. "He'd never leave you alone, not your superior, Dameon. He'd be calling you into his own office every day, just to test you, touching you in a different place each time. Sometimes he'd brush his hand against your breast, seemingly by accident. That's probably where he'd start. Then he'd give you a pat on the butt on the way out, maybe even give it a little squeeze. The next meeting would be worse. He'd see your nipples get hard under your blouse as you anticipate his next move, just as they're growing hard now as you imagine it."

"They're not—"

"And he'd ask you to take off your blazer, you know, just to make yourself comfortable. He'd insist . . . as your superior. He'd walk around the chair, massage your shoulders until his hands slipped a little lower, still massaging but now the top of your breasts, then his hands would slip inside your blouse, play with those hard nipples while his other hand slipped between your legs. You'd start to pro-

test and he'd stop you, tell you to call him sir. And you would because this is what you want, isn't it, Kasie? To be led to debauchery?
To be fondled in public places without the guilt? And really, what
could you do? He's your superior. You would have already fessed up
to that much, in front of me, in front of everyone you work with.
I bet just thinking about it is making you wet. I bet he'd slide his
hand into your panties, feel the wetness before slipping a finger or
two into your pussy while his thumb played with your clit. I bet he'd
make you come right in that chair as you squirmed and called him
sir."

"Why are you saying these things? I could—"

"Fire me. Yeah, yeah, I know. But you're not." This last part she
sings. "You're not going to fire me because you need to study me.
I'm the woman you want to be. Or perhaps more important, I'm
the woman Mr. Dade wants you to be, the woman he's training you
to be. If he only knew there was a premade version right here in
this office . . . well what *would* he do, Kasie? Would he toss you
aside? The missionary's path is hard and riddled with rejection and
setbacks. Why not take the easy route and preach to believers?"
She leans in, whispers in my ear, "Like me. I'm a believer. I walk the
walk, I've embraced this gospel. I'm the real thing, and you?" She
laughs lightly, shakes her head before walking to her desk.

"You never will be."

There's some truth to what she's saying, but what bothers me is
not that I'll never be like Asha; it's that I ever wanted to be. What
bothers me is that if I stay at this firm, my future will be riddled
with these kinds of conversations. I do have options, just not here.

Later that day I go into Mr. Costin's office and hand in my notice.

❦

# CHAPTER 44

THE REST OF the day has a surreal quality. Mr. Costin had been flustered as he wavered between glee and terror. Was Mr. Dade upset about something? Was I?

No, I had answered. Everything was fine. But the office didn't suit me; no, not the room, but the position, the firm, the life. . . . I had reassured him again after that, stumbling over my words as he fumbled his platitudes. There are logistics to think of, too. In a very short period of time I have taken to my job. Things are getting done; new approaches are being explored. It would be such a shame to throw all that away, and Mr. Costin knows it.

But he also knows that my leaving is a gift. It's a gift to him and to many others who work here, people who don't want to structure their lives and careers around the ocean's tide. Understandably they'd rather live where they're safe from the impending tsunami.

So we arranged for me to stay the next three weeks, to help with the transition. Having so much turnover in such a short period of time never looks good but we'll make things as smooth as possible.

My only requirement is that Mr. Costin not give my job to Asha. I forced him to agree to that stipulation. It's the last time I'll flex my muscles here, in this office in this building. Surely this last abuse of power will add another chink in the delicate remains of my cracked morality.

It's worth it.

I don't go home when the day is done, and I certainly don't go to him. Instead I drive around the city, let the lights of the night lead me in random directions, toward this shopping mall, this restaurant, this event that shines its spotlights into the air as if calling for Batman.

I don't park, never stop for anything other than a traffic signal. I just keep driving until I get to a vaguely familiar alley, away from the lights and glaring marketing campaigns. I stop for a speakeasy called Wishes.

I'm hesitant when I get to the door. It's just as white as I remember it; the letters of the name are still just as red. As if wishes were made of blood.

I open the door. A man stands behind the bar, cleaning a glass with a cloth. Men and women talk among themselves; the music in the background comes from speakers, not live musicians. As I approach the bar the bartender makes eye contact with me, offers me an appraising smile. "What can I do you for?"

"What do you have in the means of Scotch?" I ask as I prop myself up on a bar stool; my eyes only briefly flicker to the small plastic cube behind the bar, the one that overflows with precut slices of lime.

"I got a few," he says, naming off a few brands, nothing as grand as what Robert and I indulged in while we were in Vegas. I shake my head and opt for a vodka tonic instead.

He places the drink in front of me in short order, a wedge of lemon in my glass, not lime. I pick it up, look at the little ring of wetness it leaves on the bar. I lay on that bar not long ago; salt had tickled my skin.

"Is Genevieve working tonight?" I'm not sure why I'm asking, not even sure why I'm here. Perhaps it's because I want to understand. What happened to me? Was my night here really the turning point or a manifestation of a bigger decision that I had made even before Robert had led me through that door? A decision to embrace excess and abandon the conventions of society that I was taught to cherish?

Or maybe I was here for a more basic reason. Maybe I wanted to know what Robert and Genevieve had going on. Maybe I wanted to know how many women had been laid down on this bar, how many lovers they had shared. Had there ever been a time when it was just the two of them? Was it just the two of them now that I had walked away?

I smile up at the bartender, who is too busy counting out change to hear my question. I ask again and he looks up in confusion.

"Genevieve? No one by that name works here."

"No?" I put my glass down, suddenly feeling a bit off balance. "The woman with the red hair—what's her name?"

"We don't have anyone here with red hair. We got a Janey; she's Asian. Oh and there's Andrew . . . guess you could call him a strawberry blond, although most just describe him as balding. And there's Henry and me, oh and Elsie . . . she's Haitian. She's something to look at. Black as the night with cheekbones so sharp you could cut yourself on them. When she starts speaking French, the tips start rolling in."

"But no Genevieve?" I ask meekly.

"Only Genevieve I know of lives in Camelot," he says with a smile before stepping away to address the woman waving her credit card in the air.

He doesn't hear me when I reply quietly, "You're thinking of Guinevere and Camelot . . . it doesn't exist."

I glance around the room, study the patrons more carefully. They look normal enough. There are a few hipsters, a few women and men who have worked a little too hard to emulate the visual perfection of Hollywood's stars. But mostly they're everyday folks, people who probably live around here and just wanted to go to their neighborhood spot, a place with little pretense, a place that seems more dedicated to comfort than image. Last time I was here Robert and I were the center of attention. Everyone seemed to be somehow tuned in to us, hyperaware of our presence even before . . . things happened.

Tonight I get a few looks but only the kind you would expect. Glances of hopeful men and competitive women. The energy's different.

And the music comes from a stereo.

When the bartender looks my way again, I crook my finger, beckoning.

"Need another?" he asks, eyeing my drink that I've barely touched.

"No, I was just wondering if you'll be having live music tonight . . . you know, later."

Again he gives me a funny look. "We don't have live music here. We did a karaoke night once, for a holiday weekend . . . think it was Memorial Day . . . maybe Columbus. Anyway, that was a few years ago. It didn't really catch on."

I shake my head, now impatient and a little frightened. "I was here. I heard the music. A woman and a bass player. He played, she sang. I heard it!"

Another quizzical look, and then finally the dawning of comprehension. "You must have been at that private party the owner had a little while back. Yeah, I heard a little somethin' about that. Mr. Dade hired talent, used his own people to tend bar. I was kinda pissed because, you know, I can't afford to just lose a whole night worth of tips, but Mr. Dade, he made it like a paid vacation for all of us, so you know, no complaints."

I suck in a sharp breath, feeling once again unsteady on my stool. The bartender is watching me more closely, a new twinkle of interest in his eyes. "Did he pay you?" he asks.

"Excuse me?" The response is too quick, too visceral. I can't keep the note of offense from my voice.

"Hey, hey, it's okay. One of my friends told me all about it. He got paid, too."

"Your friend . . ." My voice trails off as a new, horrible thought occurs to me. "Your friend the bass player?"

"Nah, I don't know anything about the musicians. My friend was one of the patrons. Mr. Dade doesn't have a clue that I know him and he was sworn to secrecy and everything . . . even had to sign some confidentiality agreement, but like I said, we're friends. You break those kinds of rules for friends."

"We have rules for a reason," I whisper. "There's something to be said for following the rules."

"Yeah, whatever." The bartender laughs, mistaking my statement for lighthearted teasing. "He says he got paid three hundred bucks just to show up. He just had to sit here and look like a regular ol' barfly and then, when the bartender rang the bell for last call, well he had a choice, he could spend some of that money on getting one last drink here or he could head out. But if he got the drink, he couldn't dawdle. And if he didn't, he couldn't just run out the door, he had to get up all leisurely like. Like a real barfly."

"Why?" I ask. There's still emotion in my voice, not offense this time, something weaker that speaks to a deeper pain. But once again the music and the hum of the bar drowns out the nuance and the bartender continues.

"Beats the hell outta me," he says. "But my friend? He says that when Mr. Dade arrived, he came with this really hot chick . . . not like a hooker or anything. He said she was dressed in expensive brands and holding a designer purse. Sounds like one of those uptight Rodeo Drive types looking for a little downtown adventure, you ask me. You know what I think . . ." He falters and then looks away, suddenly awkward.

"What?" I ask.

"Nah, what I think probably shouldn't be said in mixed company." He laughs.

I hesitate before goading him on, trying for my best lecherous leer. "Come on, I'm dying here! Tell me the dirty details. What do you think happened?"

"You really wanna know?"

"Fuck yeah!"

This is not a part that I know how to play well but the bartender isn't very smart so he continues without picking up on that.

"I bet you anything Mr. Dade and this lady were acting out one of those kinky rich-man's fantasies," he says, leaning forward. "I bet once all those fake guests got outta here he fucked her, I bet he fucked her right here on this bar. I bet that bartender . . . whatcha call her, Genevieve? I bet she got in on it, too. And those musicians . . . my friend said they got to stay. Maybe they were part of the little orgy or maybe they got to watch." He shakes his head, no longer here. Instead he's lost in his own little fantasy, a fantasy that is so much more than a fantasy for me. I feel my cheeks heat up; anxiety accelerates my heart.

"Can you imagine it?" he asks dreamily. "Two hot girls going down on each other in front of an audience right here on my bar. Man, what I would have given to have seen that. Man, he wouldn't have even had to pay me. I would have bartended for free and I would have recorded the whole damn thing for him, too! You must have seen the girl though, right? You really were there? Was she hot?"

My cheeks are flaming now; I'm clutching my drink like it's life support. The bartender gives me a strange look and then a slow grin spreads over his face. "You *were* here. It was you, wasn't it?" he asked. "You had sex here, on my bar, by a chick while he watched! Oh man, my friend said the girl was hot but I never dreamed she was as hot as you."

"It wasn't like that," I spat.

"No, tell me, what was it like? Did that bartender, that Camelot girl, did you two strip each other down in front of everyone? And the musicians, did they get a turn with you, too? Or was it just you and Mr. Dade? You know, I've always wanted to have sex in front of other people . . . but hey, you know, I like to watch, too. If you ever—"

I get up abruptly, almost tripping as my feet hit the floor, and then I bolt for the door. My movements are so tactless, it attracts the attention of the patrons, who had been ignoring me. I feel their eyes on me as I leave, but mostly I feel the eyes of that bartender.

People in that bar, they'll ask him what that was about. And *that* bartender? He'll tell them. He'll tell them in demeaning detail, making up the parts that he doesn't know . . . which is all of it. But his imaginings are so close to the truth, I can't say that my reputation is being unfairly sullied.

My hands are shaking so much, I can't get my keys out of my purse. I lean against my car, try to steady myself, try to catch my breath and get rid of this feeling of humiliation.

*You could get him fired.*

It's the voice of my devil. I'm so very familiar with it now.

*One call to your Mr. Dade and that bartender won't ever work here again. He won't work anywhere! Mr. Dade will discredit him to the point that no one will believe anything he says! You have that power, Kasie! Just dial the numbers and ask for the moon.*

And my devil has a point. That's why Robert's ways work. He's able to live without consequences. The only truth that touches him is the truth that he's fond of. People who deviate from his preapproved version of reality pay the price, and so in the end you are left with only followers. I can use that power now. If I stay with him, my mistakes and indiscretions will never come back to haunt me. No one will ever dare to shame me again!

*And more lives will be ruined. People will be punished for being outside our circle of two.*

This from the increasingly unfamiliar voice of my angel. Tom and Dave . . . they both stepped over the line with me. It wouldn't be so outrageous to say that I had the right to retaliate.

Stalin, Mao, Mary Tudor, Napoleon, Caligula . . . how many times did they tell themselves the same thing before they began to retaliate against people who hadn't done anything at all? These were men and women who ruled by fear. For years, sometimes decades, they got exactly what they wanted. No one was allowed to speak of their mistakes or failings; those were erased from the pages of the newspapers, banned from public discourse.

But behind her back Mary Tudor was called Bloody Mary. You can stop the speeches but you can't stop the whispers. That's the cost of ruling by fear.

Can I afford to pay that price? Do I want to spend my life justifying the destruction of others?

"No," I say out loud, to myself, to the night. "It's better to live with the humiliations. It's better to live with consequences."

I get in my car and drive, my cheeks still burning with shame. Even when I'm miles away, I'm sure I can hear the whispered words of the bartender, I can hear his crude laughter as he tells those strangers my most intimate secrets.

But this time I don't have to feel ashamed of how I responded.

This time I'm strong enough to live with the insult.

❀

# CHAPTER 45

T HE NEXT MORNING I'm prepared. I know Mr. Costin won't make a big formal announcement that I'm leaving, not yet, but these things spread quickly. After all, this isn't just gossip. It's the tale of the downfall of a feared rival. Doesn't matter that I chose to quit, the story will be spun as stories always are. Drama will be added; the ending will be rewritten to deliver more satisfaction. *She was pushed out, she couldn't cut it; Mr. Dade tired of her, threw her to the wolves.* Maybe they'll even say I cheated on Robert with Mr. Costin. They might say that when I went into his office, I had not been speaking but had been on his lap, spread out on his desk, my legs open, inviting. Maybe they'd have me on my knees. *She thought she could just keep sleeping her way up the ladder but this time she betrayed the wrong man.*

I smile to myself as I tie my hair back up in a twist. The story has a certain circular narrative that works well. I look in the mirror. I'm not wearing any makeup. It's the way Robert likes me, but he also likes it when I wear my hair down. Dave was the opposite. He wanted my hair neat and tidy but he appreciated the effects of a little bronzer.

But to wear my hair up, with no makeup . . . it's like I have no mask and no shield. This is just me on my own terms. I'm vulnerable but I want to be strong enough to admit that. I want to be touched by the consequences of my actions. I want to reinvent myself once again, this time using only my own definition as a guide.

I want to, but it scares the hell out of me. I never really did manage to make fear my lover; the best I can do is face it.

I walk into the firm, prepared for the fallout, the derision, the whispers that won't be so soft anymore. But the atmosphere remains the same. Everyone is deferential. The whispers remain behind closed doors, too quiet to hear.

When I get to my office, Barbara looks tense. "He's here," she says.

I don't have to ask who he is. I glance at my closed door. "In there? Waiting for me?"

She nods, blinks, straightens her posture. "Would you like me to bring you anything? Coffee?"

"Did you bring him coffee?"

"I brought him espresso."

I can't help but smile. Yes, people will always worship the moon. I decline the offer of coffee or anything else and suggest that she take a little break. Fifteen minutes . . . maybe a half hour; take your time. She gets the message and takes off while I stare at my closed door.

It's my office. I shouldn't be nervous about walking in no matter who's in there.

But it won't be my office for long and this isn't just somebody. It's Him. I felt so strong when I woke up this morning. I felt strong last night when I refused to seek punishment for the bartender. I felt strong when I handed in my notice.

But I so rarely feel strong in the face of Robert's opposition. It's so hard to say no to him, to resist our connection.

"It's only the moon," I whisper to myself. I lay my hand on the doorknob, take a deep breath, and step inside.

He's sitting in front of my desk, facing it, staring out the wall of glass. He doesn't turn as I walk in but I know he feels me, senses me. . . .

I close the door behind me.

"You quit."

Carefully I step forward until I'm only a foot behind him. Still he doesn't turn.

"I handed in my notice."

"Let's dispense with the euphemisms. You've never used them gracefully. You gave up, on the job, on us, on absolutely everything that could ever matter."

I laugh at that. I can't help it. I switch positions again, stand in front of him, lean back on the front of my desk. "There are a lot of things that matter in this world, Robert."

"You should sit," he says, his eyes still on the window, "in your chair."

"Why?"

"Because it's your chair!" He doesn't yell but there's ferocity to his voice that makes me jump. He jerks his eyes from the window and stares directly into mine. "This is your office. This is where you belong until you belong somewhere else, on an even higher floor, with a new throne and a wider empire! You belong here and you belong with me!"

I don't answer; I can't find my voice.

He stands up, slowly; there is less than four inches of space between us now. He takes my face in his hands, lifts it up to his gaze. "You belong with me," he says, his anger suddenly gone, replaced with what seems like exhaustion.

"I thought so, too," I say quietly, "until you showed me your world."

"You don't like what you see?" He shakes his head. "That has not been my observation."

"Oh, it's an enticing world. You make fantasy reality. That bar, Wishes." I smile slightly and repeat the word. "Wishes. It's like a *Pan's Labyrinth*–type fairy tale—"

"Which is a hell of a lot more interesting than the G-rated Disney fairy tales Dave wanted you to live in." He lifts my arm, kisses the inside of my wrist.

"Yes," I say, struggling to keep my focus, "except in this fairy tale good and evil have no meaning. You just make wishes and they come true. Those who don't play along are kicked out of the game.

*Of course* that's appealing when you're the one making the wishes. But it's your world, Robert, not mine."

He releases my arm; his face hardens. Anger, passion, frustration, and yes, love, I can see it all there, smashing together, tearing him apart. "It could be our world. That's what I want, Kasie. I want us to rule side by side. I want the wishes that are granted to be *our* wishes. It could happen, just give me some time—"

"Oh, Robert, you can rewrite history but you can't rewrite the present. I'm leaving you and this job not because of the power that I don't have yet but because I don't want to rule. Not like this."

"So you want to play somebody else's game?" he seethes. "You want to let them trample you? Take everything away from you?"

I reach out, let my fingers rest on his chest, right above his heart. "I used to wonder what it was that connected us. I couldn't figure out why we were so intensely drawn to each other. I've been telling myself that you are the moon and I'm the ocean, that you raise my tides with your gravity."

He smiles for the first time. "The moon and the ocean, I like that."

"It's a pretty metaphor," I acknowledge, "but maybe a bit too simple. I think I sensed in you a kindred spirit, a fellow runaway."

His brow creases; he moves out of my reach. "I'm not running away from anything, Kasie. I never have."

"Robert, you've been running your entire life. So have I. The only difference is that I've been running from my sister's mistakes and you've been running from the mistakes of your parents. We've worked so hard not to be them that we've forgotten how to be ourselves."

"No," he says, almost childlike now. "I saved you from that! It was Dave who wanted to remake you. He was the one who wanted to turn you into a little Stepford wife! I set you free!"

"No, Robert. You just got me running in a different direction."

His hand goes to his stomach; he clutches the fabric of his shirt, and for a moment I see the little boy, the one who was forced to stand and watch as his father was dragged off to jail for a crime he didn't commit. The boy who watched his mother count out how many apples she could afford to put in their shopping cart. I see that boy's confusion. I see that he's lost.

Again I step forward, again I reach for him, and again he pulls away . . . but not by much. When I reach for him again, he stays still, lets me run my hand over his cheek, smooth from his last shave. He closes his eyes and there it is, the thing I didn't think was possible. . . .

The moon sheds a tear.

I kiss it away, then the next one as it falls down his face. And then a soft sob as I pull him to me, take him in my arms, kissing each salty tear as it falls in increasingly rapid succession. I want to soothe the little boy inside. I want to wrap my arms around him and tell him it's okay, he can relax. He can stop running.

He finds my mouth, kisses me fiercely; his arms circle me, pull me closer, his need so intense, it takes my breath away.

"Let's stop running," I whisper, and in a second we're on our knees, both of us clinging to the other. He's pulling off my jacket. His skin is still salty as I kiss his cheeks, his jaw, his mouth.

Gently, he lowers me to the floor and when I whisper his name, a little cry escapes him and I can hear the release of the breath he's been holding for all these years.

Our shirts are off; it's skin against skin. I can feel it but can't see it. Our eyes stay locked, closing only long enough for the kisses that we keep indulging in.

It's never been this way before. It's never been so . . . equal. The only power I feel is the power of our unspoken love. It fills the room, slides up the walls as surely as his hands slide up my thighs. Everything seems to take on a golden hue—soft, rich, nostalgic, and new all at the same time.

My skirt is around my waist; I feel the tight twist of my hair loosen. I grasp his sculpted arms, press my breasts against his hard chest. He's so strong, this man-child of mine. He's built like an athlete. Like a runner.

We roll over the hard floor and I pull desperately at his belt. Nothing can separate us. I want to be connected to him in every way. I need to take him inside of me, inside where he can feel safe.

His pants come off. He's ready for me, needing me. I feel his erection pressed against my hip as his mouth continues to explore mine as if he's never kissed me before, as if each kiss is fulfilling a dream.

And when he enters me I'm the one who cries out. I didn't realize how much I wanted this. How much I've been wanting to make love to *this* man, Robert, the man Mr. Dade never lets anyone see.

I feel his lips on my neck now; his touch is so warm, his heartbeat so strong, as strong as mine. The rhythm pounds together in an enthralling and discordant beat.

And then he stops; still inside me he puts his hand gently against my face and looks down into my eyes, his own hazel eyes wide in wonderment, like he can't believe he's here, with me, making love to me without his mask, without my shield.

And the love I feel pouring out of him . . . it makes me cry and then laugh as he imitates my earlier actions, kissing away my tears.

And he moves again, moving his hips in circular motions, hitting every spot as he holds me. We're so quiet now. No one standing outside the door would be able to hear. This moment is private, special, and so earth-shatteringly beautiful.

I squeeze my thighs together so that I can tighten myself around him, feel every ridge, savor the friction. He turns us on our sides and I intertwine my legs with his. Our bodies are clasped together like two pieces of a puzzle, a perfect fit. He presses inside me, grinding against me, our arms are wrapped around each other. Lightly, I run my nails down his back and he kisses my cheek, my forehead, my hair.

My head is buried in his neck as the orgasm comes, rolling through me like a slow wave. Yes, I'm the ocean again but this is not a hurricane. This is the wave that beckons. I arch my back, shuddering as I give in to it.

In that moment, as he comes inside of me, whispering my name, showering me with loving kisses, I feel the culmination of our devotion pounding through me. I feel him collapse against me, his passion finally spent.

And in that moment I wonder, is this yet another beginning?

The thought should scare me but it doesn't. Nothing could scare me right now. Not now as I hold Robert in my arms, feeling his warm, uneven breathing against my skin. No, there's nothing to be afraid of here. Here, in this moment, there is nothing to run from.

And we stay like that for what seems like forever but is probably only minutes. Just the two of us, holding each other in tender silence.

It's not until I hear Barbara return, hear her drop something on her desk, hear her chair screech across the floor unceremoniously, that the moment begins to fade. The golden hue dissipates. The hard floor begins to feel uncomfortable against my back.

And something in Robert changes, too. He stiffens and without his moving a muscle I feel it. I feel him pulling away.

I don't say anything when he gets up. I don't speak as he pulls on his clothes, tosses mine to me.

He won't meet my eyes.

"You should tell Mr. Costin you're not quitting after all," he says. "He won't give you a hard time about it. I'll see to that."

His words are mechanical but that's not what bothers me. What bothers me is that the things he's saying . . . it's as if the whole conversation that led up to us naked on the floor, making love, it's as if he's erased that whole conversation from his mind. Or perhaps more accurately, it's that he's letting me know he will never acknowledge it again. He's telling me that any moments of truth, any glimpses I may get of the man underneath the ambition, will never be more than that: moments and glimpses. They will never last. They will never influence the greater narrative.

I pull on my shirt. I'm so tired, so incredibly sad. "I'm leaving this job, Robert." I'm still sitting on the floor. I look up at him. He stands above me, once again taking on the posture of a king. "I'm taking a new path," I remind him. And then I add, with just a spark of hope, a dose of pleading, "Will you come with me?"

He looks down at me but he doesn't meet my eyes. It's so odd because just minutes ago he looked so young and now he looks so very old. "Do what you need to do," he says, his voice heavy, despondent. "You'll land on your feet, you always do. You are one of the few who can take any path and still lead the race. But me? I'm not so versatile."

"Robert—"

He leans down, kisses me on the forehead, breathes in my perfume before saying, "I'm sorry."

And then he gets up and leaves, making sure the door opens only a crack as he walks out, making sure that no one sees me with my clothes rumpled, my hair a mess. No one sees me on the floor, crying for the man who I have only now truly come to understand.

All these years he's been running, from his past, from pain. . . .

And now he's running from me.

# CHAPTER 46

❀

L ESS THAN AN hour after Robert left my office Mr. Costin
came to see me, in my office, further contaminating a place
that was only an hour earlier a place of passion and love. He told me
that Mr. Dade had come to see him. He assured Mr. Costin that he
wouldn't be taking business away from the firm just because of my
departure. Mr. Dade told him that this was due to me and my altru-
ism and that if I so much as hinted that I was unhappy with how I
was being treated during my final days on the job, all bets were off.

Mr. Costin then spent about twenty minutes showering me with
praise, kissing my ass, and making sure I was happy.

I can't wait to get out of this place.

DAYS PASS AND I don't hear from Robert. I don't expect to. It's the
way it needs to be.

It breaks my heart.

But there are plenty of distractions. None of them pleasant. Over
the weekend I go to see my parents. I go to tell them the truth about
everything. I sit in their living room, my hands clasped in my lap,
my head bent, the picture of contrition.

I tell them I cheated on Dave, that we're through. I tell them that
I've been hiding this breakup from them for well over a month now.

I sit on their rose-patterned couch, inside their cream-colored
walls, and I wait for the comparisons. The comparisons to Melody.

They come quickly from my father. I'm a disgrace, a disappointment . . . a slut. Just like *her*.

My mother doesn't speak but her quiet tears say it all.

And then something odd happens as my father continues to grill me. Something ugly. It occurs as he questions me about the man who I betrayed Dave with, "this Robert Dade fellow." As it becomes clear that Robert is rich, a power player, a man who had much more than a passing interest in me, it's then that my father's tone softens. Can I make it work with Robert? Will he marry me?

And all of a sudden my father thinks that Dave wasn't such a great guy after all. He never thought he was right for me. I shouldn't sell myself short, aim high; that's what he always says. If this Mr. Dade can make an honest woman out of me—

"Stop," I say. I don't shout the word but it comes out with enough force to bring my father to silence. My mother is by my side, the tears drying on her cheeks. She looks at me curiously.

"It doesn't matter if Robert Dade puts a ring on my finger or not," I say quietly. "The man who helped me deceive another can never make me honest."

"All right, but what I'm saying—" my father begins, his brown eyes still glittering with hope and ambition.

But again I interrupt. "What you're saying is that it's okay to cheat and deceive as long as I get something good out of it. Something that will last. I wanted to believe that, too, but I don't."

My mother puts a hand on my knee, gives it a comforting squeeze. "Kasie, don't be so hard on yourself."

I stare at her, at her hand wrinkled but soft due to an excess of lotion. My father's hands aren't much bigger. Neither of them have a single callus.

I used to think these were hands of virtue, that like the scales of justice they could weigh the weight of another's guilt and come up with a fitting sentence. My sister had deserved to be rejected, hated, cut off. She deserved it because my parents said so. If I took that path I'd deserve it, too.

But now, sitting here on this couch, confessing my sins, an idea is dawning. It's an idea that changes everything.

"She needed help." I say the words slowly, tasting them.

"Who?" my father asks.

I look at him with new eyes. I note the way his stomach hangs a little over his pants, his receding hairline, the gray carefully coated with light brown dye. I look down at his shoes. My mother and I are barefoot, to protect the carpet. But not once has my mother ever asked my father to take off his shoes upon entering the house even as she asked the rest of us to.

I never thought about why that was before. I suppose I just assumed he was the king of the castle and was therefore granted certain privileges.

But now that I think about it, perhaps he wears shoes because when he's the only one who isn't barefoot, it gives him the illusion of height.

"Melody," I finally answer. "My sister. When you caught my sister with that boy in her room, having sex, doing drugs . . . she needed help."

My mother's hand quickly pulls away; my father reddens with anger. "Do not mention that person's name in this house."

"That person?" I ask incredulously. "That person was your daughter. She was my sister and she needed help."

"Kasie, please," my mother breathes. The tears are fresh again. "Let's not relive this. You are not your sister."

"No, I'm not. I used to worry I'd become her. I worried that I'd make a horrible mistake and you'd cut me off, exile me from the family just like you did with her. I think I worried about it as recently as yesterday," I say with a bitter laugh. "I know my role. I know I'm supposed to help you live the illusion. I'm the accomplished, well-behaved daughter who will marry well. You can point to me and prove to the world that anything that happened with Melody was a fluke. None of it was our fault. Her death wasn't the consequence of our rejection. It wasn't because we refused to acknowledge that she was sick, that she needed psychiatric help!"

"She was a dirty whore," my father says, his eyes now glued to his elevating shoes. "She rejected discipline, had no moral center . . . I swear sometimes I wonder how a woman like that could share my genes!" He raises his eyes to my mother, flashes her an accusing glare. "You know she didn't look anything like me—"

"Oh for God's sake, she was yours!" I snap, raising myself to my feet. "You don't get to just invent new ways to deny her! She was your flesh and blood, your responsibility, she was more than you were ready to handle, and you fucked up."

"Kasie!" my mother cries as my father mutters something about my language.

"You fucked up!" I say again. "We all did. We didn't know anything about mental illness or addiction. We were confused, disoriented, and most of all we were afraid. So we made a whole slew of mistakes and now she's dead."

"Kasie!" This again from my mother. "You can't blame your father for her death!"

I give her a withering look. "This isn't about blame, but if it was, I wouldn't *just* be blaming him."

"Kasie!" This time from my father.

"This is about living with consequences. We made mistakes with Melody. Maybe if we can accept that, we can work through it. Maybe we can stop denying that she existed! I came here because I accept my mistakes, the mistake of accepting Dave's ring, the mistake of getting involved with someone else before ending it with him . . . oh, and I've made so many mistakes in the way I've handled myself with Robert Dade. I fucked up and it's affected every aspect of my life. I quit my job because of all the mistakes I've made."

"Wait a minute," my father says, his anger quickly switching to concern. "That's the top consulting firm in the country! Unless they're demanding your resignation—"

"They're not but I can't stay. Everyone there knows what I've done; they don't trust me, don't respect me, and don't want to work with me. That's the consequence of my actions. And maybe it's not fair but that's life. I want to live life, Dad," I say, my voice breaking ever so slightly. "I want to live life the way it actually is. I'm so, so tired of illusions."

My mother reaches for me again. "Sweetie, you're overwrought. If this Mr. Dade fellow is as successful as you make him sound, and if he does care for you, well maybe you could make a go of it. No one needs to know how it all began. And you wouldn't even have to work! You could get involved in a charity! You could say it was a choice you made because . . ."

She keeps speaking but I can't hear her anymore. She's just painting another pretty picture, a portrait of me that skips over my flaws . . . my strengths, too, for that matter. I stare at the mantel above the fireplace. There are pictures of me, of them, of my grand-parents. . . .

There will never be a picture of Melody there. No one in this room is equipped to teach me how to face up to reality. I look at my mother as she speaks, my father as he stews . . . there's no point in being angry. It won't get me anywhere.

I let go of my mother's hand and take a deep, cleansing breath to help me regain my composure before I kiss my father on the cheek. "Thank you for letting me talk," I say quietly, resignedly. I lean down and give my mother a kiss as well. "I love you," I say to both of them.

I gather up my purse, head to the foyer where my shoes wait for me. My mother makes a little cry of confusion, but it's only my father who follows me.

I sit down on their quilted leather armchair and fasten the buckles of my heels.

"It wasn't our fault, you know," he says, his voice soft but deter-mined. "She simply refused to listen. A psychiatrist couldn't have helped us with that. I tell you, there's nothing we could have done differently. Not a damn thing that would have helped. If there was . . . I would have known. I wouldn't just . . . I would have known. Noth-ing to be done." Each word is a little meeker, a bit more desperate.

I stand up, give him a hug that's a bit too hard and lasts a mo-ment too long.

"Of course not," I say. "You did everything you could." And then I kiss him again and say good-bye.

Because I can't change him. And because this is an illusion he wears as a life vest and I don't have it in me to take it away just to see him drown.

❀

# CHAPTER 47

A ND THE DAYS continue to pass. I go into work, do my job.
Mr. Costin keeps the whispers behind closed doors. Even
Asha's stares don't shake me now. That's what happens when you
face the truth, when you choose to live with the pain for a while. It's
so hard to hurt someone who's already in agony.

But I can't get too lost in my depression. There are things to be
done. I just quit my job and though I can get by for a while, I will
need to get another one. I know that I can go to pretty much any
consulting firm I want. Mr. Costin wouldn't dare give me anything
short of a glowing reference, and let's face it, after my current position anything else would be a step down. As my father said, this is
the best global consulting firm in the country. Unless I become an
expatriate I'm going to have to settle for something less.

It's all right though. I rather like the idea of being a big fish in a
small pond.

But boy, how I miss *him*. That's the loss that has me opening up a
new bottle of wine every night. I've heard people say that when they
lose someone they love, they keep thinking that they see him. Like
when a stranger walks by, they'll have to do a quick double take to
make sure it's not him. They'll hear his voice in a café only to realize
that what they heard was the sound of some baritone DJ on the radio.

But I don't have these hallucinations. Robert's voice, his look, his
everything . . . it's too unique. I would never mistake someone else
for him. And since he was driving an Alfa Romeo it's not like I can
mistake other people's cars for his.

He's just gone.

The realization hits me when I'm at home, alone, halfway through a bottle of 1996 Cab. Too good of a wine to get drunk on and yet I'm tempted. This breakup, it doesn't feel temporary anymore and the emptiness of the room fills my heart with a similar feeling of vacancy.

*Even when I'm nowhere near you I'm inside of you. I can touch you with a thought.*

He had told me that once and I close my eyes, try to believe in it again. I lean back into the cushions of my sofa, put my hand against my breast, pretend that it's him.

*Are you thinking of me, Robert?*

And suddenly I'm enveloped with such a strong sense of sadness, I literally cry out, crumple over under the heaviness of it. I don't know if the sadness is wholly mine or if I'm sensing his wretchedness from afar, mingling it with my own and giving it new strength. Either way it's more than I can handle alone. My hand reaches for the phone and I dial Simone.

It doesn't take long for her to arrive. She's become accustomed to these last-minute calls for help. She doesn't show up with a bottle of sin this time. "You're in the middle of a breakup," she explains, taking the Cabernet out of my hand and closing it with a stopper. "Alcohol's great for anxiety but it sucks for depression."

"I'm not depressed," I say sullenly; she laughs, sits cross-legged on the couch, and beckons me to take a seat beside her. "What happened, Kas, did you get lost?"

I nod, my eyes welling up with tears.

"Has he called since it happened?"

To this I shake my head.

She sighs, closes her eyes as if in meditation. "He misses you," she says sagely. "He's just scared."

"How do you know he's scared?" I ask, surprised.

She smiles, her eyes still closed. "Because men always are. They'll sing about bravery, tell you they'll keep you safe, but at the first sign of emotional conflict, they run for the hills like a bunch of frightened rabbits."

I sigh, lean my head against my knees. "Robert isn't a rabbit."

"All men are rabbits," she retorts, her eyes flying open. "They sniff around, fuck whatever's available, and then they run off. Fucking rabbits. And we're Elmer Fudd, inadvertently blowing up our own lives while obsessively trying to hunt one down."

I giggle. It's the first time I've even come close to laughing in a long time. It's a small victory for Simone, one she acknowledges with a gentle sigh.

"Are you sure it's over?" she asks.

I don't answer. I'm not ready to say the words aloud but my tears answer for me as she wraps her arm around my shoulders.

"I think maybe I didn't advise you well, that night with the vodka-laced milkshakes."

"Oh?"

"I told you about my ménage à trois, I suggested that you could indulge in those kinds of things if you had a strong sense of self. But what I didn't point out is that you don't."

I wince at the insult.

"Oh don't get me wrong, you *will* and soon. But right now you're in the self-discovery phase." She pauses before asking in a slow, measured voice, "How's work?"

"I quit."

"Thank God."

I roll my eyes. "You told me that I should stay! You said that I should see things through, accept power without respect! That was you!"

"No, what I said is that you could either see it through or you could leave and go somewhere else. I suggested you work for yourself."

I shake my head, stare at my wineglass, now drained except for a few drops of red liquid at the bottom. "I'm not equipped for that," I say. "And my firm has a habit of punishing those who try that route, particularly if they suspect you might be poaching their clients or posing new competition for them. They'll bury me before I get off the ground."

"Um, yeah, they're not gonna do that." Simone laughs.

"Simone, I've seen them do it to other . . ." But my voice trails off. Of course they're not going to do that. Like his cologne that lingers on my skin after we make love, the scent of his protection is still there. People can smell it. They know what it means.

"How would that be different?" I venture. "If they're afraid to attack me because of him—"

"Kasie, we all have our advantages and disadvantages in life. A kid living in the projects uses his athletic ability to get out of there. The woman with bad teeth uses her family's money to go to an orthodontist. The politician with a weakness for redheads uses his influence to cover up the scandal."

I give her a sideways look and she laughs again. "Okay, maybe the last is taking it too far. But you've had your fair share of disadvantages."

"Like what?"

"Like wounds that will never heal," she says quietly.

We both fall silent. Outside the wind makes the branches of the trees scrape against my window. For a second I imagine them scratching out the word "Melody" into the glass.

"He can't build your business for you," she says. "Considering the circumstances I doubt he would even try. But your past relationship with him can protect you from unfair attacks. Your firm doesn't have the right to undermine your new endeavors. Don't invite them to do so."

I look down at the hard floor beneath us, only partially covered by the Persian rug. "We made love in my office."

"You and offices." Simone laughs, thinking back to the last time I told her about having sex with Robert on his desk.

"This was different." I reach my foot forward, feel the softness of the rug. "This wasn't brutal or playful or choreographed as it sometimes is with us. This was just me and him, touching something inside each other, those wounds, the ones that won't heal. . . . It was so raw and tender and . . ."

I don't finish my sentence. I feel the memory more than see it. I feel the warmth of his mouth against mine, his hands against my bare skin. I feel my face nuzzled into the crook of his neck, the salty taste of his tears still on my tongue. Wrapped up in his powerful arms I was the protected and the protector and for just a brief moment it felt like the whole world was falling into place. Things made sense, I knew who I was, what I needed to do, what my purpose was in life.

And I knew where I was meant to be. Right there, on the floor of my office, in his arms, making everything just . . . right.

Simone's watching me. I don't even have to look at her to sense the concern. "It's another wound," I say quietly. "And it hurts. It hurts so bad, I can barely stand up, barely breathe."

"But you are breathing, Kasie," Simone says. She rubs her hand up and down my arm in an act of comfort. "You're breathing through the pain."

I nod and then collapse again in tears. But this time I have Simone there to hold me.

Simone. My sister.

❦

# CHAPTER 48

D AYS PASS INTO weeks, weeks into months. I don't hear
from him. The wound stays where it is, carved into my lungs
so I feel it with every sigh.

But I don't sigh quite as much anymore.

Initially I thought Simone's suggestion that I start my own business was silly, even stupid. Isn't that why Robert and I had broken up? Because he wanted me to play by my own rules and I had
wanted to play by rules that were already set in stone by others?

It took me a few weeks of unemployment to realize that no, that
wasn't it at all. Robert had wanted me to play by *his* rules. Dave had
wanted me to play by rules that were set in a different time, in a different place, in a world that only truly exists in those men's clubs he
can't get into anymore.

I don't want that, either. And that's when I realize that for once in
my life I don't have to live in the extremes. I don't have to make fear
my lover but I don't have to run from it, either. If I can just face it, a
little at a time, find that elusive middle ground . . . that place where
you set some of the rules but not others . . . then maybe I'll be okay.

So I take the leap, decide to work for myself. I start small, a little office leased out of a big building. I seek out clients whose profits are still
modest, businesses with untapped potential, fledgling entrepreneurs
whose ideas can be spun into gold. I give them my ideas and they give
me their money. And little by little the success grows, slowly, like drip-
brewed coffee. It takes a while but the unhurried process just makes
the coffee a little richer, better, and a hell of a lot more satisfying.

Simone and I have gotten into the habit of hanging out once a week. Sometimes we have dinner. Other times we wear our tightest dresses and go to the most exclusive lounges in LA. I let the men look, enjoy their attention, but it stops there. I have boundaries again, but they're *my* boundaries. The only expectations I'm trying to live up to are the ones I've set for myself. It's a completely new experience for me and at times it's unnerving. I still occasionally doubt myself and wonder if I'm doing something wrong. But the men at the lounges admire me, my friendship with Simone has strengthened, and my new clients respect me. The mistakes I've made have not led to the ultimate rejection. I have not been erased . . . not even by my parents.

Yes, they still call me daughter. We speak every few weeks, never more often than that. They don't understand me but they're afraid to question the change. Afraid I'll mention Melody again. So in that way perhaps fear is still working for me, finding dark ways to keep my parents' disapproval at bay.

I get through my days just fine. It's the nights, when all the lights are out and I lie alone in my bed, it's only then that I find myself sighing. That's when the pain seeps in through the crack under the door.

Sometimes I talk to him. I tiptoe out to my tiny backyard still dressed in my nightgown. I curl up on my patio chair and stare up at the moon. I ask him what mysteries he's seen since we last spoke. I ask if he's angry. If he's hurt. When I'm feeling bitter, I ask if that rock he calls a heart still beats for me. I ask if he ever tires of all the worshipers, if anyone or anything could ever understand him as well as the ocean. All those witches and tribes of men who dance for him, give him offerings and songs, do any of those gifts compare to the tidal waves I gave him?

And then I close my eyes and feel my tides rise. I imagine him standing behind me, his hands in my hair, then my shoulders, finally sliding to my breasts, toying with my nipples until they're as hard as his heart.

I hear his whisper in the sounds of the wind. "One more hurricane, just for us."

And there, in my backyard, he comes to me, illuminated in the darkness. I slip my hand between my legs, the nightgown gathering around my thighs, and I feel his mouth work its way down my spine, across my hips. I feel his hands caressing my stomach, holding my waist, strong hands with a tender touch.

My legs fall open, inviting him to dip into my waters. I'm wet, ready for him, eager and available. When I run my fingers along my sex, it's his tongue I feel, toying with my clit before sliding inside of me, tasting me, making me tremble.

And then he raises himself up, makes a trail of kisses along my hairline, my jaw, my cheek. He bites down gently on my lower lip. Yes, this is where we belong, right here, wrapped up in the cool breeze of early autumn. I look up and all I can see is the deep purple midnight sky. With few stars, the light of the moon drowns them out, all but Mars with its red glow.

Mars. The god of war.

I feel his breath in my hair; it's the wind, and I feel his arms wrap around me.

In those moments all my senses are heightened. The scent of the grass is his cologne; the drops of dew are his sweat as he labors on top of me, taking me, right here in my backyard.

I slide down in my chair and when I press my fingers inside, the moon seems to shine a little brighter—its gravitational pull just as strong and overwhelming as it ever was. The waters rise as my hips move to this imagined rhythm. I can't say either of us is controlling it. This rhythm—passionate, at times frenzied, unpredictable in its periodic change of tempo—this is just who we are. We're lost in it. When I kiss him, the wind moves through the trees; when I arch my back, they bend.

"That's how strong our passion is," he says, and I cry out in the kind of agony that can only be brought on by love.

His hands are everywhere now. On my breasts, my waist, my ass;

I run my thumb to touch myself in just the right spot as I continue to plunge my fingers inside . . . but it's his thumb I feel, his erection thrusting inside my walls.

The ecstasy is almost unbearable. It shakes me, heats me from within, and I'm reminded that the ocean has volcanoes, too.

"Explode inside of me," I whisper. "Make us complete."

And he does, and the waters crash over the shores. Power, beauty, destruction . . . life. It's all there as we cling to each other. I can still feel him throbbing inside of me, each twitch adding ripples to my calming tide.

It's only then that finally the orgasm is complete.

On those nights it takes me a few seconds to catch my breath, a few moments before the fantasy fades, only minutes before the melancholy sets in.

When I walk back to my bedroom, there is no one there to kiss away the tears.

But the sadness doesn't last, either. It weakens as the sun rises and continues to dissipate as I get on with my day, my work, my life. And it's in this process that I find myself. It's while signing another client to another contract, it's when I'm able to hire my first employee, when my file cabinets are filled with documents covered in beautiful, soothing numbers, that I realize, I'm never again going to be lost. I may have some steep climbs ahead of me, some jagged rocks I need to navigate, but I've got my compass.

There are days when I barely think about my past; I'm too wrapped up in my present, my future, my life.

And then there are days like this.

It started off fine. I take a call from a potential client, typing notes into my computer. The woman on the other end of the line is the owner of three successful restaurants, all located in LA County. She's looking to expand outside the area but could use a little guidance in regard to executing her plan. It's the kind of project I was put on in my early days at the firm, back when I was getting my feet wet, the kind of project that's so small no one at the firm really cared if it got messed up or not. But now that it's my business, these types of accounts have become the fuel that keeps the acceleration steady and consistent. So I get her details, set up a time for us to meet face-to-face in the coming days, and ask her how she heard about me.

"I was referred," she says mildly. "By my tax attorney actually. Dave Beasley."

My fingers hover over my keyboard. "Dave," I repeat.

"Yes, that's right."

I type the name into the appropriate line. *Referred by Dave Beasley*. Even when I stare at the words on the screen, I still can't quite comprehend them.

"When was this?" I ask.

"Oh just a few days ago . . . actually it might have been a week. Time's been getting away from me."

Which is what I thought Dave wanted to do, get away from me. But he had to know this woman would mention his name. He had to know I would seek him out. "Can you give me the name of the firm he works for?" I ask casually, as if this is another question for my form.

She gives me the name of a firm I know well. A direct competitor to the firm he was apparently fired from. It's a lateral move, but considering the state he was in when I last saw him . . .

I wrap up my conversation with the woman on the phone, lock up my office, and go to see Dave.

## CHAPTER 49

✿

IT TAKES ME just over a half hour to get to the nondescript building housing this law firm in Culver City. Not knowing if he would have agreed to speak to me, I didn't call first. But unless he's had a complete personality transplant, he'll see me if I show up in person, if only to prevent a scene at his work.

I announce myself to the receptionist out front; I want to keep my voice light and professional but a layer of nervousness colors my tone. Not that it matters. Most people sound nervous when they go to see a tax attorney.

In less than two minutes he comes out. The man I saw at Chipotle has been replaced by a guy who bears a much greater resemblance to my former fiancé.

He graces me with a practiced smile, shakes my hand as if I'm a client, and leads me to his private office. As soon as the door closes his smile drops and his eyes become wary, which is as much as I expected. What I didn't expect . . . or at least was uncertain of, was the sophistication of the office itself. It's nice, maybe even a little nicer than the one Dave had before. And it's so very him. The walls are white, the desk is neat, not a single paper left out. The file cabinets gleam as if they've just been polished. There are no plants. No pictures. A Jack Nicklaus–autographed golf ball sits in a case. Dave isn't a really big golf fan but he thinks he should be. It's a little lie to enhance the bigger ones that he surrounds himself with.

"I guess you got a job," I say while examining the autograph. If it wasn't for the certificate framed directly above it, I would never know what this signature said. Writing on a golf ball with a felt-tip pen can't be easy.

He doesn't answer right away. Instead he takes his time as he walks to the chair behind his desk, ensuring that he's in his place of authority. "A quick glance at the company website would have answered that question," he points out.

"Yes," I agree. I turn, face him. "But it wouldn't have explained why you referred one of your clients to me."

He gives a slight nod. Clearly he had anticipated the question. "So Lynn Johns called you?" He smiles, a little maliciously. "It's a small account but I figured you'd take what you could get. Tell me, Kasie, how does it feel to be playing in the minors again?"

I study his face. "No, you didn't refer her just to see if I'd take a smaller account, to see if I'm desperate. So what was it? Is there a trap here I'm not seeing?"

He holds my gaze, but only for about five seconds before abruptly turning away. "She needed a consultant. Referring her to you seemed prudent."

"Prudent?"

"Look around you," he snaps. "I'm back where I was, different scenery, same position, same prestige. The rumors about my embezzlement disappeared within a week of our last conversation. You whispered a request into that man's ear and suddenly my career has risen from the sewer, freshly scrubbed and smelling of lilacs." He adjusts his position, his cheeks red with anger and embarrassment. "Guess that makes him my hero, too, huh?" he sneers. "Mr. Dade, the man who fucked my fiancée, has now, in his infinite mercy, decided not to destroy the rest of my life. I suppose you're here to ask me to thank him? To humiliate me just a little more?"

I let the words sink in and consider what they mean about Robert and my feelings about him. "No," I say. "I would never ask you to thank a man for not making your destruction his goal. You don't have to thank me, either. Not with words, not with clients."

"Yeah, well I prefer to play it safe if it's all the same to you."

He's still not looking at me. It's kind of funny. Here we are in his office that is so much nicer than mine. The view spans across the city to the hills. He has the power of a well-established firm of lawyers behind him. And yet he's the one afraid of *me*. I haven't been in this position for some time now and like an ex-smoker sucking up the secondhand smoke of others, I will always take a guilty pleasure in the scent of power.

But I won't pick up the cigarette. "You can do what you like, I'm just telling you your future doesn't depend on your support of me."

"I don't support you, Kasie," he retorts. "All I'll ever do is send you a client or two. Try not to sleep with them, will you?"

I smile at the insult; he's earned the right to hurl it. And I've earned the right to walk away. So I do, leaving Dave to his success and anger.

I'M NOT IN the mood to go home. Instead I go to a small hotel, not far from Dave's office. I find the bar, a quiet place with dark corners. I've only been in my seat for a minute before the cocktail waitress approaches. "What can I get you?" she says in a voice a little too high, a tone a little too bright.

I glance at the drink specials: açaí mojitos, peach Bellinis, gingered pear martinis . . . alcoholic sins hidden within antioxidant blessings. I don't want to kid myself today.

"I'd like a Scotch, please," I say quietly.

"Any particular kind?"

I shake my head. "Something expensive," I say with a ghost of a smile.

Her face lights up, a little more eager now as she notes my request on her pad and goes off to consult the bartender.

I close my eyes, remember the moment. Robert and I, sitting in that bar with glass walls. He had offered me champagne. I had wanted something stronger. . . .

The waitress comes back with my drink. I don't ask how much it is and she doesn't offer the price. If I have to mortgage my house for the memory, it'll be worth it.

I clink the ice cubes together. He had taken a Scotch-drenched ice cube, dragged it slowly along the neckline of my Herve Leger, up my thigh, between my legs. . . .

And then he had tasted the Scotch.

I lift the glass, stare into the golden brown liquid. What should the toast be today? Cheers? I'm not that happy. *Salut?* But how healthy can I be when my heart is still in fragments?

I raise my glass a little higher. "To memories," I say quietly to myself before bringing the drink to my lips.

The taste is smoky and luxurious and, yes, it makes me think of him. It makes me think of sex.

It would have been better if Dave had told me that things had changed for him a week ago, a day ago, an hour ago. But it happened months ago; Robert had rectified things for Dave within days of our breakup. Back when he cared, before he had moved on. And now? Who knows what he feels now? Maybe he's with someone else.

I close my eyes against the thought.

Another sip, another memory, another tear.

"This looks like a good table."

I keep my eyes closed, unsure if the voice I heard was from my memory or from a man standing beside me. And not just any man. . . .

My grip around my glass tightens; my breathing gets just a little bit quicker.

I hear the sound of something being dropped on the table.

Keeping my eyes low I look. A deck of cards. A spade on the cover of the open box, a lone queen of hearts pulled halfway out, as if she's trying to escape. I don't look up but I can see his legs, see his strong hands hanging at his sides, as if waiting for something to hold.

"Care to make it interesting?"

It's only then that I will myself to meet his eyes. Were they always that stormy? So hopeful? I want to reach for him but instead I reach for the cards.

"I thought that's what we were doing," I say as I pull the deck out, shuffle it with moderate skill. He sits opposite me, watches the cards dance.

"More interesting," he says softly. "If I have the better hand, we'll leave the table and you'll have a drink with me."

"And if I have the upper hand?" I ask. The words are hard to get out, the emotions too close to the surface for me to keep my voice steady.

He puts his hand over mine, over the cards, stilling them. "Then I'll have a drink with you."

The calluses on his palms seem a little rougher than I remember, the tension between us a little thicker.

I gently pull away. "I'll have the drink, but I'm not ready to leave the table." I continue to shuffle and then very carefully deal the cards. "Not yet."

He watches my motions; there's a flicker of confusion as he asks what we're playing.

"Heads-up poker," I say, the words a little clipped.

"Not blackjack?"

"No." I pick up my hand. "It's a different place, different time, different game." I lift my eyes to his, hold his gaze. "And like all games this one has rules. Are you ready to play by the rules, Mr. Dade?"

His mouth curves up at one corner. Slowly he picks up his cards. "Shall we gamble with coins?"

"With secrets," I say, "and with answers."

"Really?" he asks. A couple enters the bar, their voices are too bright for this mood-lit room. Out of the corner of my eye I see her metal-tipped heels tapping against the floor.

"It sounds like you're making up the rules as you go along, Kasie," he says.

"And changing them at a whim," I say. "But the basic structure of the game, that stays pure. Understand? We can be creative with how and what we risk but the game is poker. The rules are what they are."

He nods, looks down at his cards. "I'm not sure I know how to gamble away a secret."

"I'll teach you," I say, my focus on the cards. I put my hand on the surface of the table as if touching something invisible there. "I'm in for one secret."

He smiles. "I'll see your secret and raise you an answer."

It's odd that we can be so playful when there is so much time, pain, and ambiguity between us. But I sense this is the best way to proceed. *Stay with the cards, Kasie,* my angel whispers. *The numbers will give you something solid to hold on to.*

My angel is learning. She is beginning to understand this version of me.

And so the game goes on and as it does, the stakes are raised again; another answer is offered. His face is blank as a poker player's should be. But his hands shake, only a little, but I see it. And I know it has nothing to do with cards.

I win this hand, beating his flush with four of a kind. The woman with the metal heels is doing shots while her date swears into his phone.

Robert leans back in his seat. "I believe I have a debt to pay."

"Yes, I'd like your answers first." Slowly, I gather his cards and mine, form them into a neat pile. "How did you find me here, Robert? Have you been following me?"

"Yes."

I suck in a long breath, start to shuffle the cards. "Just today?"

"No. I've followed you twice before."

I keep my head down, my heart skipping along with the shuffling cards. What he's describing is the behavior of a stalker.

But the thing about stalkers is that they care. As Simone once explained to me, stalkers know how to commit.

Then again, commitment has never been our problem.

"I still owe you my secret."

My hands still. I raise my eyes, waiting.

"I need you," he says, his voice so quiet I have to lean forward to hear. "That's my secret. I need you more than you have ever needed me."

"That's not true."

He rests his fingers on top of the still deck; the woman at the bar orders another round. "I've been thinking about your metaphor. The ocean and the moon. The thing is, it's not the tides that make the ocean so important. There's so much more to it than that. But the moon? Without the ocean what's its purpose? It's just a barren rock. A mere reflection of the sun's light."

"Are you trying to tell me your life has no purpose without me?" I ask dryly.

"No, I'm telling you that you're the only thing on this earth that has made me feel connected to what's here. When I'm with you, I know what's real. I can feel it, touch it. When I'm with you, I'm something more than . . . other. When I'm not with you, my head's in the stars."

"But that's how you like it," I remind him. "It's why we broke up. You wanted to live your dreams without leaving a footprint, without the cumbersome terrestrial rules the rest of us live by. The rules that *I* live by."

"We broke up because I was afraid."

Those last words come out quickly, impulsively.

For the first time since I've known him I see Robert blush.

Slowly he pulls his hands away.

"That's two secrets," he says. "I overpaid."

I pause to consider before picking up the cards again. "No," I say. "In my opinion you haven't paid nearly enough."

I catch his fleeting smile as I deal out another hand. This game moves faster. I find I have to bluff, a specialty of mine. But he still wins with a full house against my two pair.

I reach for my Scotch. "I need your questions before I can give you my answers."

"If I try to play by the rules," he says slowly, "if I try to live with consequences, will you forgive me? Can we try again?"

"That's two questions."

"You owe me the answers to three."

I put down my drink, reach for the cards. "Those don't sound like real questions."

"What—"

"Are you honestly suggesting that you can change?" I interrupt. The emotion in my voice is taut and rich, my volume loud enough to garner a glance from the garish couple at the bar.

"You have spent your life cultivating power plays and dominance. Your name might not be as well known as Koch or Gates but behind closed doors everyone knows that it's you who can't be crossed. You who can and will ruin a man for an insult. That's who you *are*, Robert!"

"That's the man that they know," he corrects softly. "I'm asking, what if I can be the man that you've seen? You have seen me, haven't you, Kasie? You've peeked behind the curtain. You know the truth about Oz."

I clench my teeth but my jaw still trembles. The cards fall from my hands and splay across the table in a wave of hearts and clubs.

The bartender turns on the stereo. Simon & Garfunkel sing of silence. Robert shows me his hands, palms up as if to prove that he hides nothing.

"The other day Dameon led a presentation at Maned Wolf. It didn't go well. He didn't understand the nuance of our needs the way you did. We won't be using that firm again."

"So?"

"Asha stayed behind. I saw her as I was pulling out of the garage. She said her car broke down. It was threatening to rain so I offered her a ride."

I freeze; my stomach does a little nauseating flip. *I'm the woman Mr. Dade wants you to be.*

"Her car didn't break down," I say quietly.

"I know that."

"You know that *now*."

"And I knew it then." He sighs, casts a wistful glance at my Scotch. "I wanted to understand what you see in them. Dave, Tom, Asha—

they all treated you like you were a prostitute. A whore paid to put up with their leers and abuse. A slut who didn't deserve their respect let alone their civility. And yet you asked me to spare them all. I wanted to understand why."

*He's Robert Dade and I'd be a willing and eager player in his bedroom games. Not because I want his assistance but because I'd like to see if I could break him.*

I reach for the Scotch, then push it in his direction, urging him to take a sip. "Did she . . . help you understand?"

Robert takes the drink but doesn't raise it to his mouth. "In a way."

I close my eyes against the images those words bring up. Robert with Asha in his arms, she underneath him, wrapping her legs around him the way I used to do. Digging her nails into his skin. Asha turning sex into a knife.

"She's a sociopath," he says.

The words jar me. Cautiously I open my eyes.

"She's only interested in herself," he continues, "has no consideration for others, enjoys revenge more than she enjoys love. And you don't want to be her. You asked me to spare her, Tom, and Dave because you're better than all of them. You're better than me, too."

"Robert, did you—"

"Sleep with her?" He shakes his head. "No. It's obviously what she wanted. She left her coat in my car in hopes of giving me an excuse to return it to her."

"Which coat?" I ask. It doesn't really matter but I'm trying to visualize this.

"It has a fox-fur trim."

I nod. I remember it. "Did you return it?"

He shakes his head. "It didn't seem right that I see her again. Not because I'd be tempted to sleep with her but because I know how she treated you and seeing her would tempt me to destroy her the way I almost destroyed your fiancé. I'm trying to be decent, Kasie. To be better." He pauses, takes a drink. "So I decided I'd tone it down a bit and instead of ruining her career I just took the coat to Goodwill."

I break out laughing. It's easily a $700 coat. Not small change for someone in Asha's position. The idea of some unemployed club-going teenager wearing it fills me with a certain kind of glee.

I look down at the cards covering the table. "Thank you, for letting up on Dave."

He nods, his mood serious again. "Tom Love isn't being black-balled anymore, either. He deserves to be, but I let him off the hook."

I look up, take the Scotch back from him. "Why?" I ask.

He shrugs, suddenly seeming almost shy. "Like I said, I'm trying to be better. I think maybe . . . maybe it's time to stop running."

I meet his eyes, take a drink. "I'm building a life for myself," I say quietly. "One that I can be proud of. If I just jump back in where we left off . . . I'm just not sure that's a good idea, Robert. I don't know that I really want it."

I see the hurt but this time he doesn't pull away or grow cold. "What do you want, Kasie?"

"I want to stand on my own two feet. I want to know what independence is. I want to . . . to pace myself. I only get one life, I want to savor it and make it count for something."

"So we can't pick up where we left off," he says in a whisper, "because then your life wouldn't count for something?"

"No, because we started it all wrong. If Dave and I tried to build a relationship based on conformity, you and I . . . we built a romance based on betrayal."

He nods, twirls a card around on the table. "I thought you might say something like that. So I was thinking . . . what if we try for a do over?"

"Excuse me?"

"You know." He smiles; it's a boyish grin and endears him to me immediately. "We could do it right this time. Last time I met you I was in disguise in a way. I was hiding away everything that hinted at my . . . my sentimentality."

I raise my eyebrow at that but don't interrupt.

"I was hiding anything that could be seen as being warm or vulnerable. I was . . ."

"You were a stranger," I finish for him.

He nods. "Yes. A stranger to you . . . and you were a stranger to yourself."

I sigh as I relive the memory. "I let a stranger pick me up at a blackjack table."

"Yes," he says cautiously. "And now I'm asking if you'll let a friend pick you up at a bar."

I laugh. I can't help it.

He meets my eyes and the way he looks at me . . . it just brings back all those old feelings. The excitement, the longing, the arousal, everything.

"You're still my ocean," he whispers.

I shake my head. "No," I say.

His face falls, but again he doesn't get angry. "All right then. I won't try to pressure you—"

"I'm not your ocean," I say. "But if tonight goes well, I might consider being your girlfriend."

He stops.

And then his smile, bigger than the last one, it brightens up the whole room.

It brightens my heart.

Never taking his eyes off mine he waves the cocktail waitress over. "This Scotch you just served us," he says to her. "I'd like to buy a bottle to take up to a room."

"Oh, we can't do that."

He takes out his wallet, puts $400 on the table. "I think maybe you can."

The waitress hesitates only half a second before scooping up the money and then after a minute more, returning with a paper bag concealing a bottle of Scotch.

We leave the bar quickly, head straight down a large hallway that leads to the lobby.

"I can't believe—" I begin, but before I can finish, he pulls me to him. His arms are around me and he kisses me. His hands move gently through my hair, then up and down my back. My hands stay on his shoulders, squeezing hard, almost afraid to let go.

A couple of teenagers pass us. "Get a room!" one yells.

Robert pulls back slightly.

"That boy's wise beyond his years."

I giggle as he leads me the rest of the way to the front desk and hang back almost shyly as he checks us in, gets a key for a suite.

As I watch him give his information to the check-in clerk I have a moment's pause. This is reckless . . . more reckless than that night in Vegas because now I know what I'm getting myself into. What if it all goes wrong again?

But when I turn my head, I catch my reflection in a mirror hanging on the wall. I recognize the reflection. I know who I am now.

I can't be controlled anymore. I have the courage necessary to be my own person. The very fact that I'm even aware of this, can contemplate it and turn it over in my mind . . . it means something. It means that this time I'm not going to get lost.

And so when he turns, offers me his hand, I take it without hesitation, without trembling, and instead of letting him lead me I walk by his side. In minutes we're in our room. This one is less grandiose than the one at the Venetian but it's also warmer, its colors and lines are softer and compelling. He lifts me up into his arms like a princess in a fairy tale and then lays me down on the king-size bed so gently it makes me sigh.

Carefully he takes his place beside me, touches my cheek. "Kasie," he says.

"Yes?"

"Promise me you won't let any more strangers take you up to a hotel room, okay?"

I grab the pillow and hit him over the head with it. In a moment we're rolling on the bed, laughing, our clothes tangling together as I kiss him again and again and again.

Finally he pins me down, pressing my arms into the mattress and smiling into my eyes before lowering himself to kiss my neck. "No perfume today."

"Is that a problem?" I laugh.

"Not at all," he says, his voice softer now. "I like the scent of you. Still . . ."

His voice fades and he rolls off me. He rises and goes to the dresser where we placed the bottle of Scotch and brings it back to the bed.

My eyes cloud over with the memory of the first time he had poured me a glass of Scotch . . . back when he was still a stranger.

*"You're not joining me?"* I had asked.

*And he had smiled, his eyes filled with mystery and mischief. "Oh, I'll be joining you."*

But now there is no glass. He simply sits on the edge of the bed, opens the bottle and dips his finger into it. When he draws it out it's slick with the liquid. Carefully, he runs a cool finger against the tender flesh behind my ear; I lie perfectly still, knowing what's coming, vibrating with anticipation.

He lowers his face into my hair and then I feel his tongue tickling my skin as he licks off the Scotch, then nibbles on my earlobe, then tastes and teases until my breathing grows uneven and I reach for him.

But he pulls away. He's not done marking me with this strange perfume.

"Take off your shirt," he says quietly.

And I do.

There's nothing stopping me this time. No guilt, no betrayal, no fear. I know what I want. I arch my back, allowing him to remove my bra. My nipples harden as he dabs them with Scotch, and I groan as he flicks his tongue over them and grazes them with his teeth, his hands exploring my contours all the while.

He dips into the Scotch once more, but this time he slides his finger into my mouth so I can taste the smooth, smoky liquor tinged with the salt of his skin. He draws his finger in and out as I gently suck and lick up the drops. His free hand moves between my legs, pressing up against my sex as I grab the fabric of his shirt. I writhe against the soft comforter beneath me as he strokes me.

He pulls back long enough to yank off his shirt and again I reach for him. This time he acquiesces and I pull him down. I guide him onto his back before climbing on top of him.

"My turn," I whisper.

I pull off his belt, my eyes never leaving his. He fondles my breasts as I work on the buttons of his pants before pulling them off him, then come the boxer briefs. I make my hand into a cup and pour in a small pool of Scotch; as it drips between my fingers I coat his erection with the cooling liquid before enveloping him with the warmth of my mouth.

This is the taste I want.

He groans, slides his fingers into my hair as I devour him, sliding my lips up and down, my own hands roaming his body. I relish the feeling of my breasts pressing against his muscular thighs.

Robert once tried to make us like gods. But like the ancient Greeks, it's the human form that I worship. He's my Olympian and I cannot wait to possess him.

I release him, get up, and slowly remove the rest of my clothes while he watches, his desire radiating across the distance that separates us. Just the intensity of his stare sends shivers of pleasure through my body. One look from this man, that's all it takes to excite me. Is that normal? Really, will we *ever* be normal?

Maybe, maybe not. But maybe we don't have to be. Now that we know how to do it, we can just be us.

I stand by the side of the bed, now naked and oh so ready. Sitting up, again he presses his hand up between my legs, feels how wet I am. Standing, he leans forward and kisses me ever so gently before grabbing me roughly and throwing me back down on the bed. I like this, the enticing mix of tender romance and brutal passion. It's *us*.

He lies on top of me, brings his face to mine, and kisses me again. I wrap my arms around him, press myself into him. His body is so familiar . . . it's home.

Gently he turns me on my stomach and I stretch my arms over my head and open my legs for him, but only a little. I don't say please this time, I don't order him to perform. Instead I savor the kisses that are tracing a path across my shoulders, each one a little different, each one fueling my mounting fervor.

And when he finally does press inside of me, I gasp. No memory could ever compare to this feeling. I cross my ankles together, squeezing my walls tighter around his erection so I can feel every ridge, every pulse as we rock together, creating our own quiet love song. I feel his tongue toying with my ear as his hands move back to my breasts, stroking them, making my nipples ever harder.

When he whispers my name, the world erupts.

But I want to see him; I want to see the real Robert Dade. The man so very few people have been allowed to see.

As if sensing that, he sits back on his knees, turns me on my side so I can look up at him. I've never seen him this open before. The way he's looking at me . . . he loves me.

He loves me.

With one leg still extended along the bed I raise the other up in the air and rest it against his shoulder. I lift my arm and let my fingers gently touch his chest, coaxing him forward.

And there, kneeling before me on the bed, he enters me.

Looking into his eyes as he thrusts inside me, I feel dizzy with the overwhelming sensations shooting through my body. But even as the room spins I hold his gaze.

He caresses my thighs and as he continues, my happiness builds to indescribable ecstasy. I cry out as he brings me over the edge. My muscles contract around him and my body trembles as he growls his approval. This feeling is so much better than any fantasy. This orgasm isn't just intense . . .

. . . it's beautiful.

I whisper his name as he calls out mine, coming inside me with intimate force. I feel him fill me, know that in this moment I'm connected to Robert in a way that I've never really been before. He throbs inside me as I slowly lower my leg.

As if unable to support himself a moment longer he collapses by my side, quiet, one arm wrapped around my waist.

For a few minutes we don't say anything.

"If we're starting over," he says, quietly, "is it too early to say I love you?"

"Maybe," I say, with an exhausted smile. "But I love you, too."

Of course we're moving too fast. Only this afternoon I thought Robert was my past. This is the first time I've seen him in months. It's chaotic to say the least.

But maybe just a *little* bit of chaos is okay. It's all about balance after all. And it's not like I could have helped it. I got pulled into his gravity.

He's no longer a stranger. He's my moon.

# ACKNOWLEDGMENTS

T HERE ARE A lot of people who helped me with this project. There's my amazing editor, Adam Wilson, whom I can always count on to champion my work as well as help me refine it and make it sparkle. There's also the teams at Pocket Star and Gallery Books, who have been fabulously supportive and done an amazing job with their promotional efforts. And then there's *Cosmopolitan* and its "Sex Position of the Day" articles. Thank you, *Cosmopolitan*, for helping me figure out what's the best way to make love on a table. I strongly believe you should be every steamy romance writer's number one reference magazine.

# ABOUT THE AUTHOR

---

**Kyra Davis** is the author of the critically acclaimed Sophie Katz mystery series and the novel *So Much for My Happy Ending*. Now a full-time author and television writer, Kyra lives in the Los Angeles area with her son and their lovable leopard gecko, Alisa.

Visit her online at KyraDavis.com and on Twitter @_KyraDavis.